This Time Next Year

To Tamsin,

Hope you enjoy!

Love

Liz x

LIZ HINDS

To my family who lived with me
and this novel for too many years,
who've put up with the excitement and the despair,
and who've always had faith in me.
Special thanks to George and Harvey who together
were the inspiration for Charlie.
And despite what anyone says, Alison is not me.

Chapter 1

14th April

11.15 pm

'Done him in, have you?'

'Aaahaa!'

The voice from beyond the fence made me jump and I lost my precariously-crouched balance; I sat down on wet grass.

'You've finished him off, haven't you?' my next-door neighbour continued. 'And now you're burying the evidence.'

I peered up. By the moonlight, which was bouncing off Mr Price's glasses, I could see him nodding. 'Don't worry, I won't tell anyone. I'd have done the same thing if my missus had left me for a bit of crumpet.'

Slowly my brain registered what he was getting at. 'Oh no, I haven't murdered Brian. I was just ... um,' I stuttered, 'burying ... er ... the gerbil. Yes,' I hesitated. 'The gerbil died.'

'And you're burying it in your nightie?'

'No, in a plastic bag. Why would I want to use ... ' I glanced down and saw that the torch, which I had dropped when spoken to, was spotlighting my fallen-open dressing-gown and exposed bosom. I clutched the two sides of my dressing-gown together and tried to get up without revealing any more of my anatomy.

Mr Price was scratching his chin. 'I didn't know you had a gerbil.'

'Um, oh, yes, had it for years, since the children were small.'

He shook his head. 'Who'd have thought it, a little thing like a gerbil living that long. And you couldn't wait until morning to bury it?'

'No, Adam was very upset. I thought it better to do it straightaway.'

'I wouldn't have blamed you, mind, if you had done him in. Must have been off his head leaving a fine body of a woman like you.'

'Well, I think I'd better go in now.'

'That's right, you do that,' he leaned forward and winked. 'And this'll be our little secret.'

∞

I must remember to tell Adam that, should Mr Price make any comment, he is to say that he was devastated by the loss of his beloved gerbil. It may come as a surprise to him as we haven't had a gerbil for ten years but, no doubt, he will put it down to Mum's increasing eccentricity.

Why didn't I just tell Mr Price the truth? Lots of people write letters to themselves, although most probably don't bury them in the garden in the middle of the night. But, as tonight is my last night as a forty-something, burying a letter setting myself goals for the year seemed to be a sensible thing to do.

At least it seemed a good idea when I thought of it. Which was an hour ago. After a glass of wine.

But I'm impressed with the ease with which I was able to concoct such a convincing lie on the spur of the moment; with skills like that I could have been a politician. Indeed, if I'd thought of that before, I could have added 'get involved in local politics,' to my list of 'things I want to do before I'm fifty-one'.

But I'm not sure if it were that convincing; I suspect Mr Price now thinks that I'm guilty of murdering my husband.

I'd like to say that the thought has never entered my head — but I'd be lying. At least it would have added something to my highlights of last year, which currently stand at:

having to call plumber to unblock the toilet (and being told off for putting 'feminine items of hygiene' down it);

being egged on Halloween for asking a witch where her manners were;

eating too much on Christmas Day and burping during the Queen's Speech (although from the fuss Mum made, you'd have thought HM herself was in the room);

having to call the plumber to unblock the toilet again (and being told off that time for using too much toilet paper);

husband leaving me for a bimbo.

I don't want another year like that. I will get a new plumber.

In fact that's number one on my list. Just before 'lose weight' and 'find new man'. No, I remember, I crossed off new man and put 'acquire a new skill' instead. Far more worthwhile. I've wasted enough of my life on useless men who only let you down. And what are they good for? When it comes down to it who needs men anyway? Not me. I am happy to be a woman alone. I am independent. I do not need a man.

11.55 pm

In five minutes I will no longer be able to say that I am in my forties. I will be fifty. Fifty! That is so old. How am I ever to find a new man when I am old and past it? Not that I want a new man. I really only want my old man. But he's chosen a twenty-eight-year-old bimbo in preference to me and I've accepted that. Although how you can have a meaningful relationship with someone who doesn't know the complete words to YMCA is a mystery to me.

Being fifty will be fine. How much different can it be to being forty-nine?

12 midnight

Waaaaaaaaah. I'm not sure if I want to wake up in the morning. I wonder what my obituary would say.

Alison Turner, aged 50 — I would forever be recorded as being fifty when I died without having lived to enjoy it — if you can enjoy fifty. That would be very unfair. Not only to me but to my children. And my mother.

It's probably best for everybody if I do wake up in the morning. I don't want to be responsible for an error in perpetuity.

15th April, my 50th birthday

7.50 am

Cards received (6) from:

Mum and Dad (flowery); daughter (with ancient native American quotation); Pippa (arty); Bev (rude); brother and sister-in-law (cute, her choice without a doubt); and Great Aunt Millie (to five year old nephew).

Cards missing (2) from:
son (predictable); and husband (admittedly ex but did think he might send one anyway as it is a special birthday and I am the mother of his children, with whom he spent twenty three years. And they can't all have been bad surely.)

Other letters received (3):
two offers of a loan in return for a small percentage (probably of my soul); and one letter from the solicitor enclosing my Decree Absolute.

The solicitor had said it wouldn't take long but I thought - hoped - it would take longer than this. But I'm not going to let this bring me down, especially not on my birthday.

It used to be breakfast in bed with a daffodil in a milk bottle on the tray, followed by birthday bed romp. The last time I got a cup of tea and a perfunctory peck on my forehead. Should I have read the signs? No, I will not think maudlin thoughts, not on my birthday.

I'll switch on the radio. Chris Evans always cheers me up.

According to the news three thousand people have been killed in an earthquake in Outer Mongolia. This should be a sign that I am actually very fortunate and blessed - in spite of husband trading me in for a twenty-eight year old bimbo.

Later

I was about to leave for work when there was a knock on the door. I opened it to find a delivery boy almost hidden by a huge bunch of roses. My heart leapt: my husband has had a change of heart, and realised that a mature woman is far preferable to a flighty young thing, and he decided flowers would say this better than a card. My shaking hand made it difficult to open the envelope attached to the bouquet. My heart sank as I discovered it was from my daughter and son. Instantly I felt very unworthy of the title 'best mum in the world'.

After yanking my heart back up to its correct position I rushed for the door, leaving the flowers in the sink with last night's dishes.

It took ages to find a parking space making me very late for work. When I arrived wheezing impressively, Young Mr Davies and Muriel were already in the office.

'Sorry I'm late,' I panted.

'Well, you're here now,' Muriel smiled sweetly.

'I had a lot of extra post to open this morning,' I hinted.

'Never mind,' smiled Young Mr Davies. 'But perhaps you could answer the phone that's ringing?'

'Oh, yes, of course,' I grabbed the receiver. 'Good morning, Davies and Davies, Financial Advisers, how may I help you?'

'I'd like to speak to Mr Davies, please.'

'Would that be Mr Davies Senior or Young Mr Davies?'

'I don't know I'm afraid. The gentleman I have been dealing with must be in his fifties so I don't think he can be Young Mr Davies.'

'Oh, no, that is our Young Mr Davies. One moment and I'll put you through. Who shall I say is calling?'

'Mr Davies.'

'Yes, I'm putting you through to Mr Davies but who shall I say is calling?'

'Davies Davies.' Young Mr Davies went into his office, closing the door loudly, just as my caller spoke.

'Davies Davies?' I thought I might have misheard but as he replied again Muriel dropped a heavy file on the floor.

'Davies Davies.'

I didn't think it was very likely, even in Wales where we have some strange customs, that a man would be given what was obviously a surname as a Christian name so I said, very slowly and clearly, 'I am putting you through to Mr Davies but what is your name?'

'My name is Davies. David Davies and I would be thrilled to speak to Young Mr Davies or anyone who has more than a grain of sand where their brain should be.'

I was about to come back with a witty retort but I was aware of Muriel's eyes on me. And I couldn't think of a witty retort.

But I shouldn't have to put up with unpleasantness on my birthday. Not that anyone happening to walk into the office right now would realise it was my birthday as there is no card to show it. I don't understand: Muriel always sends me a card and I'm sure I might have mentioned once or twice that this was a special birthday.

I tried to raise the subject while talking to a waiting client this morning.

'Good morning, Mrs Matthews, please take a seat, Mr Davies won't be long. I have to look up your record on the computer – would you mind telling me your date of birth?'

'Twenty-third of March, 1932.'

'Oh, you haven't long had your birthday then?'

'Pssh, I'm too old for birthdays, I've given them up. When you get to our age, you don't want reminding that you're not long for this mortal coil, do you?'

I was rather pleased when Mr Davies called her into his office.

Now I am all alone in reception drinking my coffee and I'm finding that coffee tastes very bitter when nobody loves you.

11.15 am, very late end to coffee break

They do love me after all! Muriel, Mr Davies Senior and Young Mr Davies all came in singing 'Happy birthday', followed by 'For she's a jolly good fellow'. Mr Davies Senior started on 'She'll be coming round the mountains when she comes' but had to give up halfway as he couldn't remember the words.

Muriel was carrying a Marg Simpson cake with fifty candles. It took me four attempts to blow them all out. They gave me a card they'd signed: 'Many happy returns, Richard'; 'Happy 50th birthday, Alison, and many more, love from Muriel'; and 'Best wishes, Barbara (crossed out), Hilary (crossed out), Alison (in Muriel's writing), from AP Davies.' I was very touched, also, by their gift of thermal underwear.

I'm not sure what the choice of a Marg Simpson cake says about their opinion of me, but I think she's a good role model. On the whole. Although I'd have preferred Wonderwoman.

Tea-time

Adam returned from a hard day at college. I met him just inside the front door.

'Had a good day, love?'

'Urh.'

'Many lectures today?'

'Urh, one, what's for tea?'

'There's a pizza for you in the fridge. I'm going out for a meal, remember?'

He wandered into the kitchen and opened the fridge door. 'Big Spicy Meat, good.' At least, I think that's what he said. It was hard to tell with his head buried in the fridge. Then he headed for the lounge where my cards were displayed. I followed. He looked round, his brow furrowing. He's remembered, I thought.

'Where's the remote?'

I sighed. 'In the drawer, I expect. I bought you a pizza as I'm going out for a meal. If you remember, Adam, I told you Pippa and Bev were taking me out to celebrate my birthday.'

He stopped rummaging in the drawer. I could hear the penny turning the cogs, 'Oh, yeah, happy birthday, mum.'

'Thank you, darling.' I held out my arms for a hug. He leaned forward far enough to allow me to grasp him for a moment before he pulled away. 'Won't be a minute,' he said.

Two minutes later his voice called down the stairs, 'Mu-um.'

'There's wrapping paper on my bed along with the sellotape, scissors and a pen.'

'Thanks, mum.'

I'm nothing if not prepared for my son.

He returned five minutes later and handed me a parcel. It amazes me that two children can have the same genes, be brought up in the same environment and one could wrap for Britain while the other has not yet worked out that the sellotape is to be attached to the paper not the present inside.

Still, the present inside was lovely – a collection of my favourite Body Shop goodies. I was surprised that he knew what I liked until he told me that Chloe had told him what to get.

My delight was only slightly spoiled by Adam asking if he could 'borrow' ten quid as he had no money left to go to the pub with his mates. This makes total owed to me = £423.75. I'll be rich when he pays me back. If he pays me back.

A little later

At one minute past six the phone rang.

'Hello, Alison, is that you?'

'Yes, hello, mum.'

'It's your mother here.'

'Hello, mum.'

'Just called to say happy birthday. Did you get our card? I told your father he should have posted it earlier but you know what he's like. I told him Marjorie – you know Marjorie from next door? – I told him she had sent a cheque to her grandson in Aberystwyth and it never got there. Are you having a nice day?'

'Yes, thank you. And thanks for the voucher.'

'That's all right. I never know what to get you, you've got so much, and you can use a voucher to get what you want. A Marks and Spencer voucher is always useful. They've got their new summer range in – have you seen it? It's very orange. Not my colour but it might suit your skin. I told your father we'll have to get down there and get him a new jacket. His old one is only fit for gardening. Still, mustn't grumble, he's had it thirty years. That's the thing about Marks, their clothes are made to last. A new jacket now will outlast your father. Adam will be able to have it when he's gone.'

'Don't talk like that, mum. Dad's all right, isn't he?'

'Yes, he's fine, always under my feet, but you never know. Look at Marjorie's husband. Out playing golf one day, dead the next.'

'But he did get knocked down by the captain of the golf club's car, mum.'

'That's not the point. I'm just saying you don't what's around the corner. You have to be prepared. Did I tell you our wills are at the bank?'

'Yes, mum.'

'So are you having a nice day? What are you doing this evening? Have you had a card from Brian?'

I ignored the last question. Mum has never been able to accept that Brian, perfect, polite, handy, son-in-law-in-a-million Brian had 'played away from home' as she put it.

'Pippa and Bev are taking me to Marco's this evening.'

'Oh, that'll be nice. It'll be good for you to get out for a change. And have you thought any more about coming to Tenby with us? We've booked the caravan for the first week in June. I do wish you'd come. You know how your father gets under my feet when he's got nothing to do. You'd be company for him. And it would do you good. You won't be going away otherwise, will you?'

'I told you, Mum, I think Muriel's away then. I'll have to cover for her. Look, I'll have to go now and get ready. The girls will be picking me up soon. I'll see you at the weekend.'

'Why, what's happening then?'

'We're going for a family meal, remember? Dad suggested it. Chloe's coming home for it.'

'Oh, yes, of course, that'll be nice. Well, have a good time and don't do anything I wouldn't do.'

I thought that didn't leave me much scope but I didn't say that to mum.

Later again

I did a twirl in front of the long mirror in Chloe's bedroom. Not bad for a fifty year old, even if I say it myself.

Benjamin Bear was stretched out on Chloe's pillow. I thought she'd taken him to university with her but I guess there's not enough room in the bed for Chloe, Benjamin and Tryboy. I must try and remember what his real name is without having to ask Chloe again. That was the nickname Brian gave him when he scored a try in the game he went to watch. But I mustn't think of Brian now, not on my birthday. I must think of other things.

Oh-oh, but not Chloe in bed with Tryboy. I definitely must not think about that. Our roles have been reversed: Chloe is an adult having sex; I am a naughty child who forgets her manners in public.

When I was her age sex was barely on the agenda. Will it ever be again?

Very very very late

'Snot fair, not my birthday any more. I love birthdays. I love Pippa and Bev. Love Adam and Chloe. Love Brian. NO, no, don't love Brian. Brian is lying cheating ratbag. Don't love Brian. Brian has dimples when he smiles. Doesn't smile at me any more. Only at bimbo. Brian left me for a bimbo. Bimbo, bimbo, bimbo. Don't love Brian. Love me. Am new woman. No, Pippa and Bev are making me new woman. That can't be right. Don't want new woman, want Brian.

16th April

I am a fifty year old divorcee with a hangover. I might as well go the whole hog, bleach my hair, buy a black leather mini skirt and hang round dimly-lit bars.

John Morris, my favourite client, an old gent with old-fashioned manners, who always pays me a compliment, came in this morning. He looked me up and down and said, 'You look different this morning, my dear. I hope you're not going down with something.'

I was tempted to tell him that it's too late, I have already succumbed. I am old and unloved.

I once would have thought that forty-nine was ancient. Now I would give anything to be forty-nine again. I mustn't be so silly; I'm just feeling bad because of this long-lasting headache – which almost certainly isn't a brain tumour. I am very fortunate. I have my health (so far), family, home, and a job. I should be grateful. There are worse things in life than being fifty and divorced. I will pull myself together.

Lunchtime

It appears that undesirability has rendered me invisible. I was in Eatz, waiting to place our sandwich order, when a young executive-type came in. Jeff looked up from behind the counter, where he was buttering bread, and said, 'Good afternoon, sir, what can I do for you?' I was so amazed that neither had acknowledged or even noticed my presence that I said nothing until Moira came out and served me.

I crept into the loo to check my appearance when I returned to the office. I was definitely older-looking and less attractive than I remember. I wonder how long I've been in decline. Probably ten years at least. The only wonder is that Brian stuck it out so long.

Early evening

Pippa phoned. 'Just a quick call as we have the Residents' Association meeting here tonight but I wanted to make sure you're okay for Saturday?'

'Saturday?'

'For our trip to Cardiff. I need to know if I have to swap turns on the rota for the Oxfam shop.'

'Cardiff?'

'Have you been eating parrot-seed, Alison?'

'Parrot-seed?'

'For goodness sake, stop repeating everything I say.'

'I'm sorry, Pippa, but I don't have a clue what you're talking about.'

'No, well, I suppose that's our fault. We did tell you just before you grabbed Marco.'

'I grabbed Marco?'

'And made him tango with you.'

'I can't do the tango.'

'That was obvious. Still, the rose between the teeth looked authentic.'

'You are joking, aren't you?'

'No, oh, there's the doorbell, I've got to dash. I'll speak to you again.'

Of course Pippa wasn't joking. Pippa never jokes. At least that explains my sore tongue.

I phoned Bev for clarification. She greeted me cheerily, 'Hi, Aliss, or should I say "Ole!"'

'Oh, no, I was hoping you could tell me it wasn't true.'

'Why? You had a great time. Let your hair down a bit, it was just what you needed.'

'But I'm going to Marco's again on Saturday with my family.'

'Ah. Oh, well, never mind, he'll probably have forgotten by then. Now are you are okay for Saturday?'

'Pippa just asked me that and I didn't know what she was talking about.'

'It's our birthday present to you.'

They'd already given me a voucher to use for a head massage in Heaven Scents but Bev explained that was just part of their present.

'You've had a rough time recently what with Brian having an affair with a twenty-eight year old and then the divorce and then turning fifty on top of all that.'

'Thank you for reminding me, and, by the way, you're only four years off fifty yourself.'

'Huh, four years is a lifetime. Now listen, we thought the best thing we could give you was your confidence back. Make a new woman of you. Help you make a fresh start. And find a man.'

'And how are you going to do that?'

'You've seen that programme on telly, *Looking Bad, Looking Good*?'

'No.'

'You must have done. You know the one where the two presenters help women change their style of dressing?'

'You know I don't watch fashion programmes.'

'Well, it's on television tonight at nine so watch it and I'll speak to you again afterwards.'

9.40 pm

I've just watched *Looking Bad, Looking Good.* The show involves a victim having her entire wardrobe rubbished by two bitchy presenters, Tracey and Sal. I was reminded of a programme that used to show clips from Japanese endurance shows. Everyone asked, 'why on earth do they put themselves through that?' A similar question came to mind after watching *LBLG.* The only good that comes from it, as far as I can see, is that, having endured the humiliation, the victim is rewarded with a free wardrobe of clothes.

A major source of concern to me here is that the victim was volunteered by her best friends. I'm very anxious now. They wouldn't have done that to me, would they? I can't see any hidden cameras but I suppose I wouldn't. I'll phone Bev now; I want reassurance.

I wasn't totally reassured by the conversation with Bev. She has promised that I am not going to be filmed, from the rear, in my baggy sweatpants and holey jumper. She said their present was much better than that.

'We're going to be your own personal Tracey and Sal!'

'But they're horrible.'

'They have to be cruel to be kind. We're going to take you to Cardiff and help you choose the right clothes to wear – Pippa's bought their book so we know what we're talking about. There, what do you think of that?'

I think – but I didn't say – that there are many other birthday gifts I would have preferred. But I do need some new clothes and they do mean well. And they are my friends and won't be as nasty as Sal and Tracey. And a day in Cardiff will be fun. So I said I was delighted and would look forward to it.

But what if it's all a ruse? I've seen other make-over type programmes before and it inevitably involves the victim being told numerous lies in order to get her co-operation. Perhaps Bev telling me that they're taking me to Cardiff is all part of the plan.

Hidden cameras would, of course, have to be well hidden. I didn't have a very thorough look. I'd better look again.

Right, I've checked everywhere and I'm sure there are definitely no cameras. There would have to be some sign if there were and there isn't. So that's all right. The only places I didn't check were Adam's bedroom and the toilet. They know I never go in A's room and I'm confident that not even Channel Five would sink to filming in lavatories.

Nearly midnight

I couldn't sleep so I got up and checked the toilet: camera-free.

Chapter 2

19th April

The alarm went off as usual and I'd crawled out of bed and was halfway to the shower before remembering it was Saturday and I didn't have to get up. I hurried back to bed, cursing myself for forgetting to switch off the alarm previous night. I snuggled down and tried to get back into the pleasant dream I'd been having of Brian and marshmallows but something was naggling at my brain. I tried to ignore it but it wouldn't go away. Then it came back to me: today was *Looking Bad, Looking Good Day*. I groaned and climbed back out of bed.

I showered, put on my best bra - the one I'd bought for my cousin's wedding two years ago - and best knickers - the ones with elastic. Now I can face the changing rooms with confidence. As long as they're not communal or full of young girls.

After a day in Cardiff

Our first stop was a Costa coffee shop. I'd just sat down with coffee and a muffin, ready for a good natter when Pippa said, 'Right, Alison, go and stand over there.'

'What?'

'Go and stand over there, in that gap, so we can appraise you.'

'This is a Costa coffee shop, Pippa, I can't just go and stand in the middle of it for you to look at me.'

'Don't be daft, Aliss,' Bev said. 'Nobody's going to watch, they're all too busy chatting.'

I sighed. I could see I wasn't going to be able to enjoy my muffin until I'd done as they wanted so I crept out into gap. 'Just hurry up then,' I hissed.

'It would help if you stood up properly, Alison.'

'Yeah, and hold in your tummy and your bum.'

'No, Bev, she mustn't do that. We want to see her as she normally is, when she's relaxed.'

'Of course, yes. Ignore that last comment, Aliss. Just slouch as you normally would'

By now every eye in the room was fixed on my belly and bum. 'Get on with it, will you?'

'Well, big boobs for starters, that's obvious.'

'Yeah, and a short waist.'

'No, Bev, I don't think she has a short waist.' Pippa got up, came over and stood behind me. Then she scooped up my boobs, 'See, her waist only appears short because of the dangling boobs.'

'Pippa!!!'

'Oh, don't fuss, Tracey always does it.'

'Surely not in the middle of Costa!'

'Yes, you're right, Pippa. Flabby tummy though. Give us a twirl, Aliss.'

'And large drooping bum. Okay you can sit down now, Alison.'

'No, wait! What about her ankles?'

'What about them?'

'They're thick, aren't they?'

'Pull your trousers up, Alison. No, see, they're all right. You're thinking of when she was pregnant. Ankles like an elephant's then.'

I've often thought there's a lot to be said for the burqa worn by Muslim women. I'd also been under the impression that Pippa and Bev were my friends and I said as much to them.

'But we have to identify the problem areas first so we can work out what will best conceal them,' Pippa said.

'It'll be worth it, you won't be able to move for men falling at your feet when we've done,' Bev added.

'That may be true, Bev, but we're not doing this primarily to help Alison find a man.'

'Aren't we?' Bev was surprised.

'Aren't you?' I was disappointed.

'No, we're doing this to help Alison find herself. When she is comfortable in who she is, she will be ready to start another relationship but if she enters into a relationship without first establishing herself, it will be bound to fail.'

I lost the thread somewhere between comfortable and fail, but gathered that I have to be me first. I asked if, as well as hiding my bad points, clothes should be chosen to make the most of my good points. Assuming I have any. There was a long silence.

At last Pippa said, 'I suppose big boobs could be considered an asset.'

'Definitely,' said Bev. 'If you've got it, flaunt it, that's what my granny used to say.'

'Did she really?' said Pippa.

'No.'

Pippa announced that the next stop was Madame Fifi's. Bev and I both looked at her. 'I didn't know a massage parlour was on the agenda for today.'

'Don't be silly, Alison, Madame Fifi's is an old established lingerie specialist.'

It was also the kind of place neither Bev nor I would have ventured into on our own. It turned out that Pippa was a regular customer there. She introduced us to Marilyn, a busty platinum blonde. 'I think we were right in our first guess at what this place was,' Bev whispered to me. Marilyn ordered me into a cubicle and told me she'd come in with the tape when I was ready. I decided if she brought a whip as well I was off.

I pulled the curtain behind me and took off my jacket. I wasn't sure of etiquette for bra measuring so was dithering over whether to remove my blouse when Marilyn appeared. 'I can't measure you through your blouse, madam,' she sighed.

'Sorry.' I took it off as she hovered.

Marilyn wielded her tape expertly. 'What size bra are you wearing at the moment?'

'I'm not exactly sure.'

'You're not sure?'

'No, it's my best one and I haven't worn it for a while. I think it's 36 or, maybe, 38 B.'

'When will women ever learn?' she sighed again. 'The way they treat their most precious assets is nothing short of scandalous.'

She disappeared and returned a few moments later with a cream lace contraption with more metal supports than the Severn bridge.

'Try this one on.'

I expected her to leave the cubicle but she stood behind me as I removed my bra and revealed dangling blotchy mammaries. I wouldn't have been surprised if her drawn-on eyebrows had flown off her forehead. I tried to reassure myself that she had probably seen worse, although probably only on very aged matrons. I turned the new bra inside out and back to front to do up around my waist.

'What are you doing?!' Marilyn screeched.

'I'm sorry,' I said, quickly undoing the bra and giving it back to her. 'I thought I was meant to put it on. I'm very sorry.'

'That's not the way to put on a bra. Really, do mothers teach their daughters nothing these days? Lean forward.'

I did so.

'Now let your breasts fall into the cups.'

No problem there, falling breasts I could do. I waited for the next instruction. At last the words, 'Are you going to put your arms through?' were exhaled through smoking nostrils.

'I'm sorry.'

I was beginning to sweat. She grabbed the back of the bra, yanking me up to a standing position, and fastened it.

I began to breathe again, then, 'Eek!'

Marilyn had thrust her hand inside the right cup and was fiddling with my boob.

'You have to get it into the right position,' she said, before repeating the procedure with the left one. All I could think was that my breasts hadn't had this much attention for many a year.

'There,' she said, when she was satisfied, 'see what a difference it makes.'

She ran her hand up from my ribcage to my nipple, 'See how it lifts,' and from nipple to cleavage to nipple, 'and separates.'

Pippa and Bev stuck their heads round the curtain. 'Wow,' Bev said, 'go get 'em, girl.'

Pippa was nodding, 'It looks fantastic, Alison.'

Marilyn repeated her feely routine to demonstrate the separation and cleavage. I was beginning to suspect that this woman enjoyed her job too much.

'She'll take it,' Pippa said.

'And the matching panties?' Marilyn asked.

Pippa's 'yes, please' drowned out my 'no, thank you'.

Marilyn made to walk away then stopped, 'Or perhaps the support pants would suit madam better?'

'That's a good idea,' then, seeing my face, Pippa added quickly, 'Sal swears by them. She'll try them on, please, Marilyn.'

I was still snarling when Marilyn returned with flesh-coloured pants. I waited until she'd gone before whispering to Pippa, 'She's brought the wrong size; these are extra small.'

'No, you idiot, they're meant to be like that. They stretch, look.' She stretched them to make a pair of pants to fit an anorexic model. 'Now put them on while I go and look at the matching panties.'

By pulling and twisting and breathing in and swearing, I managed to get them, rolled up, halfway up my bum. I stopped, exhausted, and took a deep breath. Then Marilyn re-appeared. I swear she possessed a sixth sense. She assessed the situation in an instant. Gripping the roll-top with both hands, she lifted me off the floor and shook until the roll-top had unrolled and was vaguely where it was supposed to be, around my stomach.

'There, how's that? Hm, not right yet, is it?'

My tummy was more millennium dome-shaped than the big top it is normally, but I had ballooned up over my midriff. I looked like Michelin Man with wind. Marilyn continued to tug and poke and squeeze until I was less concertina-ed. 'There, that's better. Would you like to come and have a look now?' Marilyn invited my so-called friends to view my torture.

'That's a great improvement,' Pippa said. 'How does it feel?'

I moaned. 'I can barely breathe.'

'You don't have to wear it all the time; you can keep it for special occasions.'

'Yeah, like if you're hoping to pull,' Bev grinned.

I didn't want to disappoint her but the possibility of making any sort of movement, let alone pulling, seemed unlikely.

Pippa meanwhile had had another good idea – that I should keep my new bra and pants on as I was going to be trying on more clothes. 'And, by the way, Alison, do you want panties or a thong?"

'A thong!'

'Don't say it like that. They're very good for getting rid of VPL.'

'VPL?'

'Visible panty line.'

I thought Pippa was joking and tried to laugh. The support pants prevented me doing so.

Anyway Pippa wasn't joking. 'Well, Alison, what's it to be? Pants or thong? Hurry up, Marilyn's waiting.'

'Pants, please,' I squeaked.

I had dressed and was just stuffing my old bra and pants into my handbag when Marilyn appeared. 'May I take those, Madam?'

'What are you going to do with them?' I eyed her suspiciously.

'Put them in a bag for you,' she sighed.

'Oh, all right then.'

I handed then to her, resisting the urge to kiss them goodbye. She took them between the thumb and first finger of her outstretched hand and dropped them into a bright pink carrier bag with Madame Fifi written on both sides.

I couldn't wait to pay and escape this hellhole of radical women thinkers for ever. I moved as quickly as was possible (a speed that wouldn't have over-stretched a snail) to the counter

'If madam would just sign here.'

I was about to sign when I noticed the amount: ninety four pounds.

New underwear made long sentences impossible so I grunted as best I could. 'Ur?'

'What?' said Pippa.

I pointed at the amount.

'Yes, what? Ninety four pounds, that's right, isn't it, Marilyn?'

'It most definitely is. Bra £37, matching panties £25, support pants £32. I think you'll find that adds up to £94, Madam.'

I could see I was fighting against the odds. It was my turn to sigh.

I finally exited the shop a good five seconds behind my newly-pinioned bosom.

Over lunch I told the girls that my new bra size is 34F. Bev said that's bigger than Barbara Windsor. She'd heard a programme on the radio about her. A discussion followed about how someone as short as Ms Windsor, with boobs that size, manages to walk without gravity causing her to topple forwards all the time. We came to the giggly conclusion that there is a lab somewhere in which geeky scientists are researching this very phenomenon. We bemoaned my lost opportunity of stardom.

'You could have been a starlet in a Carry On film!' Bev was enthusiastic.

'But she can't act,' Pippa pointed out.

'With boobs like that you don't need to act,' Bev retorted.

'But with my luck,' I said, 'I'd have ended up with crumple-faced Sid James, as opposed to boyish-faced Jim Dale.'

Over the coffee, I explained that I usually bought the 'four for a fiver' variety of pants from Poundstretcher ('That's obvious,' Pippa sniffed), and I queried my need for both matching pants and support pants. Pippa started to speak but Bev interrupted.

'You need the support pants to make you slim and attractive so you can pull, then when he invites you back to his place, you make an excuse to pop to the loo where you change into your sexy panties.'

'Which I just happen to have in my handbag?'

'Of course, you have to go prepared. Look what happened to Bridget Jones and Hugh Grant. You don't want to be caught in that situation, do you?'

I hated to admit it but Bev had a point.

'But that's not real life, Bev; it's only fiction.,' Pippa said.

'You can call it fiction if you like; I call it the stuff of nightmares,' Bev shivered.

Pippa looked at her and rolled her eyes. 'Anyway, Alison, as I said earlier, it's not just about 'pulling' as Bev so charmingly puts it.'

'What is it about then?' Bev sounded disbelieving.

'It's about Alison taking control of her own destiny, finding fulfilment and contentment in whatever form that may come.'

They both looked at me. I was slowly sucking the free mint chocolate that came with the coffee.

The rest of the day was spent less painfully finding new trousers and top to go with my seductive new underwear. There was a slight dilemma over the trousers as, according to the book, I need them high at the front (to hold in tummy) but low at the back (to give impression of less bum). Such a pair has not yet been designed. We compromised by buying me an extra-long top. This does make it appear that I have a midget's legs but I can't have everything. I'm going to wear my new outfit (but without the support pants – I must be able to eat) this evening for my belated birthday celebration with Mum, Dad, Adam, Chloe and Tryboy.

Bedtime

His name is Hyn. It's an unusual name but he is from the deepest Welsh valleys so it must be traditional. In fact, is probably spelled Hwn, considering the well-known lack of vowels in the Welsh vocabulary. Which reminds me: I really should find out about Welsh classes. I was relieved to be able to address him properly at last. I said, 'Good night, Hyn, it's been lovely seeing you again.' I could see the relief in Chloe's eyes.

∞

I hid behind Mum on entering Marco's restaurant but it was no use - Marco spotted me. He came over, grabbed my arms and kissed me on both cheeks. 'I have the red roses ready ... for later,' he winked. I giggled nervously and pushed Mum over to our table.

'That waiter was being rather forward, wasn't he? And what did he mean about red roses for later?'

'I've no idea, Mum. You know what these Italians are like. Now, sit down, let me take your coat, what would you like to drink? Are you comfortable there?'

'All right, all right, give me a chance, don't rush me.'

Over starters, Mum told the kids she was trying to persuade me to go to Tenby with them.

'You should go, Mum,' Chloe said. 'It'll be a nice break for you and it's not as if you'll get to go anywhere else, is it?'

'Huh,' I said. 'That's what everyone keeps saying. Maybe I'll surprise you all, find myself a toyboy and go back-packing to Nepal.'

Everyone laughed at that, even Tryboy. I don't know if it was the idea of me having a toyboy or me back-packing anywhere.

I suggested that the kids and I might get a cheap package week to Majorca. Then the bombshell was dropped. It turned out that Brian has already offered to pay for them to go and spend two weeks in a villa in Ibiza with him and the bimbo.

'We won't go, of course, Mum,' Chloe said.

I flashed a grateful smile at her then remembered the marriage counsellor's advice: a divorce is between husband and wife, and should never affect the children. I bit my tongue.

'Oh, ouch!'

'Are you okay, mum?'

'Yes, fine. I just bit my tongue. No, of course you must go,' I said. 'It will be a great treat. And it will give you a chance to get know the ... your father's girlfriend.'

'Her name's Gina, Mum,' Adam said helpfully.

'Hush, Adam,' his sister hissed. 'Are you sure you don't mind, Mum? Only it would save me money and I'll need all I've earned to keep me going after I graduate.'

'You go and enjoy yourselves. You'd like it, wouldn't you, Adam?'

'Whatever.'

He doesn't fool me. I know he can already see himself, drinking, on the beach, drinking, in the clubs, drinking.

Chloe asked if I'd started reading her present "I am Woman; I am Me." Apparently it is the latest thing; everyone in university has read it.

'It's all about affirming our womanhood, and rediscovering Me. It's really inspirational, Mum. It's the new bible of post-modern ironic feminism.'

I'd heard the phrase 'post-modern' before and I didn't want to appear a complete idiot so I said, 'Ironic feminism?'

'Yes, you know, when a woman chooses to wear a bra, she's making a point.'

'Two points actually.'

'Oh, ha ha, very funny, Adam. We might have known we could rely on you to be immature and childish.'

I quickly straightened my own face and said, 'Yes, Adam, don't interrupt your sister. It sounds fascinating, Chloe. Have you read it?'

'No, not yet. Thought I'd borrow your copy when you've finished.'

I was tempted to say she could take it straight away but feared that would sound ungrateful.

∞

I'm not lying awake because I'm worried about the holiday revelation. If Brian thinks he can buy the children's affection, he is welcome to try. They're not that easily bought. Well, perhaps Adam is, but not Chloe. Although offering to pay for Tryboy, I mean Hyn, was a crafty move. That must have been the bimbo's idea. Brian's not devious. Correction, was not devious. Until he met her.

I often find it hard to sleep after a big meal in the evening. I'm not at all concerned about children going on holiday with my ex-husband and his lover.

I'll begin "I am Woman; I am Me." I think I need to affirm Me-ness.

It's written by an American with long blonde hair, a flawless complexion, and perfect teeth peeping out between immaculate red lips. I'd worked that out by the time I'd read the first two paragraphs and a quick check inside the back cover confirmed my theory. It's no good; I can't read a book intended for people like me, written by people like her. I affirmed my Me-ness by chucking the book on floor where it belongs. I'll curl up instead with Trollope (Joanna not Anthony.)

The middle of the night after a sudden awakening

Ohmigosh! His name is not Hyn. No-one was ever called Hyn except maybe Attila. Hyn is short for Honey, as in a term of endearment often used by young women for their beloveds. Or by Chloe for what-is-his-name. It wasn't relief I saw in Chloe's eyes but shock. Or horror.

I wish I had taken Miss Lloyd's advice. I still recall with pain that day in class when she asked a question and I put up my hand to answer it, almost bursting in my eagerness. She looked at me and spoke slowly, 'Now, Alison, I want you to think very carefully – are you absolutely sure you know the right answer to my question?' I nodded and gave my answer. Everyone in the class burst out laughing. Even Tommy Johnson and he was the stupidest boy in school – although Mum tells me he's now a headmaster. Miss Lloyd shook her head sadly, 'Oh, Alison, Alison, when will you ever learn to think before you speak?'

The answer appears to be 'never'.

I'll have to ask Adam what Tryboy's name is. He will know surely.

I've been made to look a fool and it's all Brian's fault. I'm not sure why at this point, but I'm convinced his hand in it somewhere. My life is ruined and it's all his fault.

22nd April

Muriel tells me that, if she recalls correctly but it was six years ago so she may be wrong, there are twenty ways to say 'yes' in Welsh. Learning to say 'no' would be more useful. My tea went cold last Thursday because I couldn't get rid of the lady on the phone trying to sell me a conservatory. I don't want to learn more options for 'yes' so I won't begin a crash course in Welsh just yet. I might enquire about assertiveness course at the Women's Education Centre though.

Later

I've been booked onto the next assertiveness course starting in July. I'd only intended to make an enquiry, but the lady on phone misunderstood and sounded so pleased that I was 'taking this first step' that I didn't like to disappoint her. I'm sure it will do me good though.

23rd April

Muriel read me an article out of her Daily Mail about a teenage boy's drug-fuelled frenzy and the reaction of his bewildered parents. '"We never even suspected he was taking drugs; he's always been such a good boy," said Mr & Mrs Robinson.' Muriel tutted into her tea. 'I don't know, it's dreadful, isn't it, what the youth of today get up to?'

'Mm. Could I have a look at the paper after you, please?'

Mr & Mrs Robinson looked like a normal middle class couple with a normal suburban home. I scoured the rest of the paper, convinced there would be a 'list of things to look for that indicate that your child is taking drugs,' but, for once, the Daily Mail let me down. (Why am I surprised to be let down by anything 'male', ha ha.)

'Where do you suppose you would get hold of drugs, do you think, Muriel?'

'From what I hear, they're all too easy to get hold of in this town. If you know where to go.'

Does Adam know where to go? It would explain the money-borrowing. Would I know if he were taking drugs? Or would I be as unsuspecting as frenzy-boy's parents? I must do some surreptitious probing this evening.

Later

Over dinner with Adam, I raised the subject of drugs. 'Where would one go if one wanted to get hold of some, say, Ecstasy?'

'Ecstasy?'

'Yes.'

'What do you want to know that for?'

'I'm just curious.'

'There are always dealers in the clubs. It's easy to get hold of.'

'And they would be able to supply other kinds of drugs as well, I suppose?'

'Yeah, sure.'

I was about to take my courage in my hands and ask Adam if he had ever used any when the phone rang and he disappeared to take the call in his room.

I'm reassured by his lack of a guilty air when he replied to my questions. I'm sure if there were something amiss, he would have been less open. I don't have to worry about him — he is sensible, well brought-up lad.

But Frenzy-boy's parents would probably say their son was a sensible, well brought-up lad too. I'll look on the Internet later, after Adam has gone out, for signs of drug-taking.

Bedtime

The internet was not wonderfully helpful. It seems to me that most signs of drug-taking could equally be signs of being normal surly teenager.

I'm sure there's nothing to worry about but I left the website, including details of hideous deaths following drug overdoses, open on Adam's computer, where he can't fail to spot it.

24th April

I had a most peculiar telephone conversation with Chloe this evening. She called, said she'd been talking to Adam and they were worried about me. 'You wouldn't do anything stupid, would you, Mum?'

'I do stupid things most days; just ask Young Mr Davies or Muriel, they'll tell you.'

'No, I don't mean that.'

'What do you mean then?'

'Well, we know you've been unhappy since Dad left, but we thought you'd improved a bit lately.'

'I have, sweetheart. I feel much better now.'

'Are you sure?'

'Yes, of course.'

'You know, you could go back to the counsellor or you can talk to me if you want. I'm a good listener. You don't have to, well, resort to ... anything else.'

'I don't need to talk to anyone, Chloe, I'm fine, really I am.'

'Cries for help come in many different forms, Mum. I've experienced it helping at the Women's Refuge.'

'I'm sure you're right.'

'And lots of the women there are in denial.'

'Really?'

'But no-one has to suffer their emotions alone.'

'That's good.'

'So you won't forget what I've said, will you?'

I promised I wouldn't but couldn't bring myself to admit to not having a clue what she was getting at. I was so confused by the conversation that I forgot to ask her about Adam and drugs.

Chapter 3

1st May

I'm surprised I haven't yet received an invitation to Luke's 18th birthday party. I'm only assuming, of course, that Pippa and Rog are throwing a party for him but they gave Helen a fabulous 'do' on her 18th and Pippa is always careful to treat her children the same. I expect the invite is on its way.

7th May

Mum rang mid-morning, very distressed. Great Aunt Millie has been asked to leave the Lady Mary Home for Gentlefolk after an incident with a custard slice. Apparently Matron was reluctant to give details over the phone, but is insistent that Auntie Millie leaves as soon as possible. I tried to calm Mum down but she kept saying things like, 'I should have known she would go this way, it's Albert all over again.' I don't remember Great Uncle Albert very well, but I do know that he was only ever spoken of in hushed voices.

Mum has arranged an appointment with Matron tomorrow morning to discuss the situation. I've said that I will go with her. Young Mr Davies was most understanding when I asked him for time off. He said, 'These old people are a trial, aren't they?' I thought there was a wistfulness in his voice as he spoke.

Later

Mum has called four times this evening. First to check that she had told me the time of the appointment tomorrow (9.30 am), then to ask how we are getting there (I'm driving), then for my opinion on whether she should wear her blue suit or her green dress (green dress), before spending three quarters of an hour repeating what Matron had said and trying to work out what it might have meant. I find it impossible to imagine anything Auntie Millie could have done with a custard slice that would warrant expulsion but Mum kept repeating, 'Ah, well, you didn't know Uncle Albert.' She would not be drawn, though, on what he did.

Adam's A-level exams begin at the end of the month. His idea of revision is to sit in the lounge, television blaring, books on floor, a can of lager next to him. However, if I ask him to wash dishes, he says, 'Can't you see I'm revising, Mum? Do you want me to fail my exams? Oh, and, Mum – could you bring me another can, please?'

He manages to drag himself away long enough to run up my phone bill by calling several different friends at least three times an evening though. 'I'm just checking things, Mum. You don't want me to fail my exams, do you?'

What can I say? I'm defeated by his reasoning.

∞

Chloe called this evening. I told her about Great Aunt Millie. She was horrified and indignant. She said I have to make sure we don't let the old crow of a matron get away with it. We must stand up for Auntie Millie's rights: she fought in the war and shouldn't be treated like this. I was touched if not a little surprised at Chloe's vehemence. I'd forgotten she is very 'into' rights.

She also informed me that she has decided that she will work, or rather, volunteer, full time in the Women's Refuge after graduation. My suggestion she could continue to do it in her spare time while earning a living was greeted with, 'Mum, you just do not understand. You live a comfortable life; you can't possibly know what it's like for these women. They need people like me.'

'Unemployed poor people, you mean?'

'Oh, Mum!'

'Well, what will you live on?'

'I'll get benefits, and Dad has said he will help me out. Gina thinks it is a very selfless gesture on my part.'

'Oh.'

I wonder if the Lady Mary Home would take me in as it is soon to have a vacancy. I'm obviously not suited for, or am too old to understand, the life my children lead.

I'll have to take a short lunch hour tomorrow to make up for going in late. I won't have time to go out and buy sandwiches so I must remember to make them in the morning. Prawns would be nice. There are some in the freezer I can defrost. That reminds me that I'm hungry now. I'll just have bowl of corn flakes – that's not too unhealthy.

Lying in bed

I shouldn't have eaten those chocolate biscuits. Corn flakes and banana would have been quite enough. I'm turning into a little piggy. No wonder all my clothes are feeling tight. I shall diet but, first, I must weigh myself. No point dieting until I know what my starting weight is although I'm not sure I can trust the scales in bathroom: they seemed to have weighed heavy ever since I bought them.

8th May, Thursday

Lunchtime

I'm eating cheese sandwiches at my desk. They'd be tastier if the bread were fresher, or if I'd remembered to defrost the prawns. Still, I consider it an achievement that I managed to make them at all, in between phone calls from Mum, first reminding me that we were going to see the matron this morning, then checking what time I planned to pick her up, then asking if I had considered the rush hour traffic. 'It's very bad at this time of day, should we leave earlier, do you think? We don't want to be late, do we?'

I finally managed to convince her that three quarters of an hour was plenty of time, even with busy roads, for a journey that normally takes twenty minutes.

Mum looked very nice in her blue suit when I collected her and she was in a good mood. Chloe had called her and told her what to say.

'Aunt Millie has rights, after all, Alison. We mustn't forget that.'

'No, Mum.'

'It's thanks to her generation that we are a free people today.'

'Yes, Mum.'

'Did Chloe tell you she is going to work in the Home for Fallen Women?'

'The Women's Refuge. Yes, Mum.'

'It's wonderful, isn't it? She's such a generous child.'

I couldn't argue with that. I have two very generous children, especially when it's someone else's money they're being generous with.

The interview with Matron was unsuccessful. She will not allow Great Aunt Millie to stay. 'What she did was quite unacceptable and there is no question of her remaining in this home for genteel folk.' She stressed the word 'genteel'. Mum went strangely quiet during the interview, leaving it to me to argue. I tried to put forward a considered response based on Chloe's suggestions. I floundered around a bit as I realised how ridiculous it sounded and I ended up saying I thought Auntie Millie's action showed great creativity and resourcefulness to which Matron replied, 'That's one way of putting it.'

'It's the only way of putting it,' I said. 'We shall be delighted to take Aunt Millie away from a place where her natural spirit is obviously being stifled by tight-lipped mean-faced old bags.'

I possibly shouldn't have said that as Matron might have been on the point of wavering.

We left quite soon after that. We have to go back at weekend to pick up Auntie Millie and her bags. Mum is torn between loyalty, and agreeing with my sentiments, and dread at the thought of having Auntie Millie to live with her for any length of time. She is phoning around other homes urgently.

I would like to think that, when I am old, I will show Auntie Millie's spirit. I suspect I may have no choice in the matter if it's in the genes. I should start planning now, saving for a good home. I'll tell the children to put me there and not feel guilty. They may visit from time to time but, when the time comes that I do not recognise them, they are free to stop coming and forget about me. I can see myself telling them this. They will hug me and say, 'Don't be silly, Mum, we could never forget you. We'll come every week and take you out for rides in the car to the seaside and wrap a blanket over your knees and buy you an ice cream and let you sit and look at the sea — and then we'll wipe the dribbles off your chin (if we can find it under your beard) and change your incontinence pads.' Oh, dear. I've depressed myself now. Is this what happens when you hit fifty? I knew it wouldn't be good but hadn't realised that the rate of decay would increase quite so rapidly.

The phone won't stop ringing and is putting me off my sandwiches. Muriel is out at lunch so I suppose I had better answer it.

Honestly, the cheek of some people. The man had the nerve to complain that I had taken a long time to answer the phone. 'I am a busy man and I don't have time to hang around waiting for phones to be answered.'

'Well, I'm sorry but I'll have you know that I am actually on my lunch break. I only answered the phone out of the kindness of my heart.'

'In that case, I am deeply touched by your commitment to your job. Now, could I speak to your Young Mr Davies, please?'

'I'm sorry, he's at lunch. Would you like him to call you back when he comes in?'

'Thank you, yes. It's David Davies. He has my number.'

I knew it was him. Who else would phone during what is nationally accepted as the lunch hour? Intolerable man. And I very much doubt the sincerity of his comment re my commitment to the job too. Bet he is hell to work for. Even if he does have a gloriously seductive Burtonesque voice.

Later

There is a vacancy in Fairyhill Home for the Expectancy Challenged and they have agreed to take Great Aunt Millie on a trial basis. Mum is very relieved as am I. I don't think I could have coped with the constant phone calls that Mum would be sure to have made to tell me what Auntie Millie had done now. We are picking her up from Lady Mary on Saturday morning and taking her straight to Fairyhill.

When I told Adam the good news he said, 'Auntie Millie should be well at home there then.'

'What do you mean?'

'She's been away with the fairies for ages.'

I tutted at him, and told him not to be so cheeky. He will be old himself one day. However, I couldn't help chuckling and wondering if the proprietors have given due thought to the name.

10th May, Saturday

Auntie Millie is settled in Fairyhill. She has a room of her own with a view of the woods (lots of trees) and they all seem very nice there. The doctor in charge wanted to do an assessment when she arrived. He had received a letter from the matron of Lady Mary saying, amongst other things, that Great Aunt Millie's periods of lucidity were getting few and far between and he wanted to check it out for himself.

Apparently one common test is to ask the patient the name of the current Prime Minister. Auntie Millie answered, 'David bloody Cameron.' Doctor was impressed both with Auntie Millie's lucidity and her perceptiveness. He thinks she will settle in quickly.

∞

I saw Adam briefly when I got in after taking Mum home. He was on his way out but stopped long enough to tell me Pippa had called while I was out. Which reminded me that it's nearly Luke's birthday. I asked Adam what he thought Luke might like for a present. I might as well have asked Auntie Millie for all the use he was. I mentioned that I was surprised Luke wasn't having a party. Adam was already outside door when I said that but I'm fairly sure he said in reply, 'Yeah he is. See you in the morning.'

I must have misheard him. Pippa would not be having a party and not inviting me. Unless it's a teenager only party. But we all went to Helen's, grandparents, cousins, everyone. Pippa's mother led us in the birdy dance. Perhaps that's why Pippa's decided to make it teenagers only.

I don't think Adam should be staying out so late this close to exams. I'll have to have serious talk with him and I'll mention it to Brian when next I speak to him as well. A fatherly talk is what's needed. He does not seem to appreciate the fact that his future depends on these exams.

11th May

Pippa has just left. I cannot believe she said what she said: they've invited Brian to Luke's party.

'Luke has always got on well with Brian, ever since he and Adam were little and Brian used to take them to football on Saturday mornings. You do understand, don't you?'

Of course, I understand, I thought. You'd rather have a lying cheating ratbag at your party than one of your best, and most misused, friends. I took a deep breath.

'I understand completely, and there's no need to worry. I won't cause a fuss. Now you've warned me, I'll be prepared. Brian and I have to learn to get on for the sake of the children. I haven't seen him for a while — not since the incident with the saucepan, in fact — but I'm much more accepting these days. So don't worry, when I see Brian at the party, I will be perfectly polite. Of course, if you were inviting the bimbo that would be a different story.'

'Um, well, actually, Alison.'

'You haven't?!'

'We couldn't very well not, it would have seemed rude.'

'Seemed rude! Did she think about whether it might seem rude to steal my husband? Did she consult her book of etiquette, and say, "Oh, no, Brian, I mustn't, you're a married man"?'

'I'm sure she didn't plan it like that. Gina is very pleasant when you get to know her...' Pippa's voice trailed off.

'You've met her then?'

'They called in to say thank you for the invitation.'

'So they're definitely going to be at the party?'

'Yes. Look, Alison, I know it will be difficult for you. If you'd rather not come then we will understand.'

'You're afraid I might create a scene, is that it?'

'No, not at all, I'm just thinking of you, and how you might feel, seeing them together, enjoying themselves. Together.'

Pippa left soon after that.

I can't think clearly, I feel so let down. I think I'll go and do some gardening. I'm sure there were some little daisy-type flowers in that bed at the side before weeds took over. The bush Brian planted in the corner needs pruning too.

Later

What a shame. I fear may have overdone bush pruning.

I couldn't find the daisies but I have a tidy flower-bed now. I've never before appreciated the beauty of simple soil. God's good earth. Maybe I could start a new fashion for soil-beds. Garden design based on shapes and purity, greens and browns. When I find myself wondering if Capability was Mr Brown's real name I realise I am trying to avoid thinking about the party. I've told Pippa I will let her know if I intend to go. I am a mature woman who has moved on; I can deal with this.

Later again

I've decided: I will not go to the party.

Even later

But why shouldn't I? I won't be stopped by Brian and the bimbo.

And later still

No, I cannot face them together. I'll tell Pippa no.

Getting ridiculously late

I am woman, I am me. I will go.

Way past my bedtime

I'm exhausted after all that gardening and I'm not in a fit state to make a decision about the party. I will decide after a good night's sleep.

In bed unable to sleep

Now if I had a man to go with it would be different. I'm sure I remember Bev saying that Simon had a friend who was recently divorced. I'll call and ask her.

Actually it is rather late; they will be asleep, no doubt. It's a good job I only let it ring three or four times, which won't be enough to wake them. I'll ring her again after work.

In bed having been rudely awoken by the phone

I don't think there was any need for Bev to be so cross with me. It was a genuine mistake on my part. And she didn't *have* to ring me back. Her reasoning that I might have been in the process of being attacked doesn't stand up to close examination. I think Bev has been watching too many horror films but I probably shouldn't have said that. She was only concerned for my safety. I'll call her this evening and apologise.

I'm less convinced than ever that being able to find out who has called you is a good thing. Especially not if you're in a bad mood.

12th May

Bev has forgiven me. When I explained the situation she could see why I had been distracted.

'I told Pippa she should have told you sooner. It's not fair springing it on you at the last moment like that.'

'You knew then?'

'Yes, Pippa told me ages ago. She was worried how you'd take it.'

'I'm fine about it, really I am. It just came as a shock, that's all.'

'So you're going to go to the party?'

'That sort of depends on you.'

'Me? How?'

'Didn't you say that Simon had a friend who was recently divorced?'

'A friend? I don't think so.'

'Yes, you did, I'm sure. It's somebody he works with.'

'Oh, Anthony.'

'Yes, that's it. I remember his name now.'

'Anthony's not really a friend of Simon's; he's just a colleague.'

'But does Simon know him well enough to ask if he'd like to go to a party with me?'

'Anthony? Oh, no, Aliss, you wouldn't want to take Anthony to the party with you.'

'Why not?'

'Well, he's ... You just wouldn't, take my word for it.'

'Is the ugly younger brother of the hunchback of Notre Dame?'

'Nnnnooo.'

'Does he smell of rancid cheese or scratch himself in public?'

'Nooo.'

'Well, what's the matter with him then?'

'He's just a bit boring.'

'That doesn't matter. He won't have to speak to anyone. As long as he's half presentable. I just don't want Brian and the bimbo to see me at the party looking like a lonely reject. Please ask Simon to ask him. Unless you have any better suggestions?'

After running through: the milkman (I've never seen him so that could be risky); the postman (who's at least seventy three and surly); and, briefly, the dustbin-man; Bev asked, 'Isn't there anyone you've met through work you could invite?'

For some inexplicable reason, the name David Davies flitted into my mind. I swatted it straight back out and said, 'No!'

'Okay, it was only a suggestion, no need to snap at me.'

'Sorry, but there's this man — I've only ever spoken to him on the phone and he is *obnoxious* — but he has a gorgeous voice.'

'And you fancy him?'

'Don't be ridiculous, I haven't even met him. And, as I said, he is a complete pain.'

'Yeah, yeah, yeah.'

'Oh, shut up. Just ask Simon for me, please.'

13th May, Tuesday

Simon has asked Anthony and he will be delighted to go to the party with me. I've phoned Pippa and told her. I can't think why she sounded surprised when I said I wanted to bring a guest. It is not as if I am totally devoid of charm. Brian found me attractive once upon a time. And I have been chatted up more than once since. Well, once actually, but it was by a man, even if he did look like the Duke of Edinburgh, only with less hair.

The party is a week Saturday. That gives me eleven days to lose weight, have my hair done and buy a sensational outfit. No problem.

I've just looked in the mirror. I have to add to the list of things to do before the party: have face lift and grow nails. Better rule out face lift as it's probably too expensive, not to mention impractical (I suspect scars would not heal in time) so will have to search make-up counters for products to conceal drooping jowls, baggy eyes and furrowed brow.

Meanwhile, I'll start the diet immediately.

Bother – just remembered, I had planned to watch Casablanca video again tonight and can't watch that without chocolate. I'll start the diet tomorrow.

14th May

Lunchtime

Corn Flakes for breakfast, apple and banana for lunch. Diet is going well so far.

I spent half an hour in the chemist's browsing through their make-up. There is an enormous choice of creams to prevent/reverse ageing process. I'm amazed at the selection. Unfortunately I couldn't determine exactly what each promised as I forgot to take my glasses. You'd have thought that manufacturers of these creams would have spotted the link between ageing and poor eyesight and labelled their jars appropriately. Perhaps I should only buy cream that has big writing on the jar as it shows the manufacturers have really thought about, and catered for, their customers.

While browsing I was pounced upon by a representative of one of the companies, a child of about nineteen. What can she possibly know about the ravages of time? I shall refuse to buy their products on principle.

Back in the office I asked Muriel what she uses. 'Ponds Cold Cream. It was good enough for my mother and it's good enough for me.'

Muriel's face is kind and grandmotherly but not sexy and alluring. I'll have to find something better than Ponds.

Evening

I'd planned to cook low-fat chicken for tea but forgot to take it out of freezer this morning. After my lunchtime walk around town I felt too weak and hungry to wait for it to defrost so I sent Adam to the chip shop. I'll definitely start the diet properly tomorrow.

15th May

Lunchtime

There was no fruit in house so I've had a small bag of crisps for lunch. There can't possibly be many calories in something that weighs so little and makes absolutely no impression on a rumbling stomach.

Muriel cut an article on skin care for the over fifties out of yesterday's Mail and brought it in for me. It says I can look forward to thinning, drying skin, increased brown age spots and sprouting hair. My chin already does good impression of designer stubble if neglected for more than two days.

I wonder if life is intended to be lived for longer than fifty years. Surely it passes its sell-by date? Like a bag of potatoes — keep them too long and they shrink and go wrinkly. Only medical science is keeping us alive.

Muriel heard me sigh and forced a bar of chocolate on me to cheer me up. Life never seems so bad when you've got chocolate. I was day-dreaming about becoming a t-shirt designer millionaire when I dropped chocolate on my blouse.

Damn, I should have remembered my mother's mantra: don't rub it, you'll only make it worse.

When Mr Davies Senior came out from his office he asked me if it was raining outside.

'I don't think so but I haven't been out,' I said.

'Oh,' he looked up at the ceiling above my desk. 'Do we have a leak then?'

Muriel, Mr Davies Senior and I were all looking at the ceiling when Young Mr Davies came back from lunch.

'What are you looking at?'

'I was just asking, um, er,' Mr Davies Senior pointed at me, 'if we have a leak.'

'Do we?' Young Mr Davies asked.

'I don't think so,' I said.

'That's all right then,' Mr Davies Senior said, before going back into his office. We all watched him go, and then Young Mr Davies said, 'How is your great aunt settling in the new rest home? Does it seem ... pleasant there?'

Five minutes later

I realise that I have a big wet mark on my blouse where I tried to wash off the chocolate stain, which would explain Mr Davies Senior's comments about a leak. He hasn't lost his marbles completely. I must tell Young Mr Davies before he takes action he may regret.

16th May, Friday

I've had very good diet day today. Adam's went out for a curry with friends so I made myself a mushroom omelette for dinner. I still feel hungry so that must be sign that the diet is working. It's very satisfying to feel in control of one's eating, I'll be down a dress size by next weekend, no problem. I think I may even have a Jane Fonda exercise record somewhere.

Later

Oh dear, I shouldn't have exercised immediately after eating. I'm feeling slightly sick now. I also must remember to empty my bladder before doing star jumps. Having babies does nothing for muscle control. I think I'll have a nice restful bath and curl up in my nightie and watch comedy shows on the television.

Later again

My nose is being assaulted by the smell of curry. Adam called in briefly, on the way between restaurant and club, to drop off the leftovers. It's very good of the restaurant to supply 'doggy bags' and there seem to be a quite a lot of leftovers.

Nearly bedtime

I was going to make myself a cup of tea and have a biscuit, but I don't suppose it would hurt if I had just a spoonful or two of curry. It's probably less fattening than a biscuit, in fact.

In bed

I really didn't intend to eat so much. I'm convinced there's a secret ingredient in curry that makes it irresistible. It was only one plateful anyway. And I did have a very small dinner.

Early hours

I have a terrible pain in my stomach and I can't remember which side the appendix is on. Brian had his removed — think, what side was his scar? Right. No, left. Or was it my left? I'm in too much pain to think straight. I'll have to crawl to the bathroom to see if we have any medicine. But is it dangerous to take medicine if it is appendicitis? I can't remember that either but I can stand this agony no longer: I will have to take a chance. There must be something in the bathroom cabinet.

Back in bed

On my way to the bathroom I bumped into Adam.

'Yo, Mum, all right?'

'Do I look all right?' I groaned.

'Yeah, cool. Night, Mum.'

This confirms my belief that Adam has inherited Brian's sensitivity gene.

I finally found some Milk of Magnesia in the cabinet and, more amazingly, a spoon as well. On my third attempt I managed to unscrew the top and tipped the bottle up. A sprinkling of white dust floated onto the spoon. I checked the sell-by date: January 97. I threw it in the bin.

Rummaging further I found a tin of Andrews Liver Salts that had only passed its sell-by date by a year or so. I forced the lid off and peered in. It looked okay but I thought I'd better take an extra-large dose, in case it had lost some of its potency.

I feel better already.

Almost dawn

I've just made my twenty third trip to the loo. Do not think I will be going ...

Ten minutes later

Will definitely not be going shopping for my party outfit today.

Chapter 4

19th May, Monday

I was wrapped in a towel, ironing my blouse for work this morning, when a strange man walked past the kitchen window. It turned out to be postman with a parcel. He claimed he knocked but could hear the radio so he assumed I was in shower and was bringing it round to the back door to leave in safety. His eyes were on my towel when I opened the door but as they moved up to my face I swear his dropped. I'm sure he must have seen worse sights in the early morning. My mother sleeps in curlers, but, then again, she won't answer the door while wearing them. Or before she has put on her lipstick. Maybe I should start listening to my mother.

Pippa and Bev both phoned this evening. Pippa has made an appointment for me at her hairdresser's for Saturday afternoon and Bev is taking me shopping Saturday morning. They are taking me in hand, they say. Anyone would think I was a teenager going to her first party.

20th May

Honestly, the cheek of some people! I'd only just arrived in work when the phone rang.

'Good morning. Davies and Davies, Financial Advisers.'

'Good morning. This is David Davies. I would like to speak to your Young Mr Davies, please.'

'Certainly, Mr Davies, I'll put you through now.'

I transferred the call, put down the phone and carried on opening the mail. A minute later, the phone rang again.

'Good morning. Davies and D...'

'You cut me off.'

'What?'

'You were supposed to be putting me through to Young Mr Davies and you cut me off.'

'No, I didn't.'

'I assure you, you did.'

'And I assure you I didn't. It must have been your mistake.'

'I cut myself off, you mean?'

'Precisely.'

'Why would I want to do that?'

'I have no idea but you obviously did.'

'I didn't.'

'You did.'

'I ... oh, for heaven's sake, this is turning into a pantomime. What happened to the "customer is always right" ethos?'

I took a deep breath. '... One moment, sir, I'll connect you again.' I emphasised the final word.

Once again I was amazed at the cheek of the man. Anyone would think I didn't know how to operate a telephone. I've never cut anyone off before. Well, not for a long time anyway.

I was still muttering under my breath when Young Mr Davies just came out of his office and said, 'Aliss, could you email the Vivemort Fund information and an application form to David Davies, please, when you've drunk your coffee? I have his email address here. You know the information I mean?'

'Yes, of course, Mr Davies.'

I quickly found the information that was required and attached it to a very polite email; I even included my wishes that he should have a good day. And I resisted the urge to add, 'In spite of spoiling mine – again.'

Ten minutes later I noticed an email from David Davies arriving. Normally I deal with email correspondence twice a day but I was curious to see if there was any sign of an apology in his email. I clicked to open it.

"I am curious, Alison – if I may call you that – as to why you should think I would have a husband at all, let alone a dead one. Regards, David."

I stared at the email. I understood the words but I didn't have a clue what he was talking about. I clicked on the Reply button.

"Mr Davies, are you feeling quite well? I only ask as your email to me was utter gibberish. Yours, Alison Turner."

I clicked the Send button and waited. I didn't have to wait long.

"Mrs Turner, I am in perfect health. However my concern is growing for your state of mind. David Davies."

I was just composing a cutting reply when the phone rang. I snatched it up.

'Davies&Davies,FinancialAdvisers, yes?' I snapped into the mouthpiece.

'You sent me a Widow's form.'

'What?'

'The Vivemort Fund information you sent me: it was for a widow.'

'No, it wasn't.'

'Yes, it was.'

'It can't have been.'

'I have it here in front of me.'

While we were talking I flicked through my Sent folder and checked what it was I had actually emailed to him. I wouldn't have put it past him to make up a complaint. I groaned to myself when I saw that he was right. I bit my lip. I certainly wasn't going to admit that to him.

'Very well, Mr Davies, if you say so. I'll resend the information straightaway.'

'The correct information this time?'

'Of course. Will there be anything else?'

'No, that's all, thank you, Mrs Turner.'

'It's Ms actually.'

'Then, thank you, Ms Turner.'

23rd May, Friday

Success at last! I found a simple black top to wear with my old, but still smart, black trousers and I'll finish off the outfit with the gold chain necklace that Brian bought me for my fortieth birthday. I phoned Bev to tell her there was no need for us to go shopping in the morning but she insisted that she'd have to come round to inspect me.

She brought Pippa and a bottle of wine with her and the two of them settled down on the sofa with their glasses, while I went and changed.

'Ta ra.' I did a twirl for them. 'What do you think?' There was a moment's silence and then Bev said, 'Good grief, Aliss, has someone died?'

'Don't be silly, Bev, it's an ageless classic look. I'm thinking Audrey Hepburn.'

'Pass me the bottle, Pip. I'm going to need another drink.'

I could see I was wasting my time on Bev who has definite leanings towards tarty, so I turned to Pippa.

'What do you think, Pippa? It's stylish, isn't it?'

'It would be if you were going to a funeral.'

'Oh come on, I think I look good. What's wrong with it?'

'How can I put this? Oh, yes, it's drab. And didn't you remember any of the things we said about choosing clothes when we took you out for your birthday?'

'Yes, I remembered black was slimming.'

'Not when it's high up round your neck.'

'Yeah, honestly, Aliss, you look about as sexy as a sack of swedes,' Bev sighed. 'Never mind, I'll take you shopping tomorrow morning and we'll get a real stunner of an outfit for you.'

'But I don't want to look like mutton.'

'For goodness sake, Alison,' Pippa said. 'It's possible for older women to look good ...'

'And sexy,' Bev interjected.

'Without dressing like their teenage daughters.'

24th May, Saturday

I've showered, dressed and am sitting waiting for my lift now. It's not due until 7.15 but I dare not move more than necessary for fearing of falling out of my dress. I'm sure it didn't reveal quite so much bosom in shop. They must have had subtle lighting casting shadows and giving the effect of modesty. I wouldn't have allowed Bev to persuade me to buy it if I had realised it was quite so ... sexy. I can't say I'm entirely displeased with the result though. It might just remind Brian what he's missing. If he's missing them. Huh, probably not with bimbo to distract him.

I'm not looking forward to this evening. I can't avoid speaking to Brian but really I cannot make small talk with the woman who stole my husband. I also hope these shoes wear in quickly. Although, there's so little of them, they're more likely to wear out before wearing in. I should never have allowed Bev to talk me into them. I managed to walk from the bedroom to the living room (with the aid of the wall) but a dance floor might be more difficult. I'll have to keep tight hold on my partner. Just hope Anthony is worth keeping a hold on.

Anthony has offered to drive us all (Bev, Simon and me — Adam is meeting friends in the pub beforehand) to the party as he doesn't drink. I can't decide if his teetotalism is a good or bad thing. Good: he will not do anything to embarrass me in front of Brian and bimbo. Bad: he might not be able to relax as he doesn't know anyone. I always find a little drink helps. But probably good thing on whole that he doesn't drink as he can carry me home afterwards! (That is a Joke although I must remember not to drink champagne as it doesn't agree with me. Last time I recall being very poorly after drinking it.)

I hope Anthony will look presentable. Bev has assured me that he is not unattractive, 'in a Barry Manilow type of way.' Does she mean he has an excessively large nose? Not that a large nose is necessarily unattractive although that might depend on how large.

In bed

Don't know why Bev dragged me out of the car and into the house when I was getting on so well with Anthony. 'Spect she was jealous that I was the one being prospo .. popo ... prospopositioned.

Pippa is cross with me too. But it wasn't my fault. Her mother sat on the floor first. I told Pippa that but she wouldn't listen to me. She was too busy being cross. Pippa is boring old fart. Think me and her should swap mothers. That is good idea, will suggest it.

Bed now. On my own. As usual.

Anthony's nose isn't that big either. Not compared to ... an elephant. Tee hee hee.

25th May, Sunday

Urrgggh. I feel dreadful. It must have been the champagne toast. Obviously I was not born for the high life. I can't remember much about the party; I hope I didn't do anything embarrassing.

I've just read last night's diary entry. Why was I sitting on the floor with Pippa's mum? Did Anthony really proposition me? Oh dear. I'd better phone Bev to check.

I was feeling rough before; I am overcome now. Bev told me that the reason I was sitting on floor was that Pippa's mum was teaching me a dance that is much favoured by drunken holidaymakers in Ibiza. It involves sitting between each other's legs and rowing. This was after we had done the birdy dance, superman dance and Simply the Best. And that was after I had insisted on clearing the dance floor so I could demonstrate the tango with Pippa's dad. Which would have been all right if at least one of us had known how to do it. We got a round of applause apparently but only because Pippa's dad retrieved the rose from my cleavage with his teeth.

Bev went on to tell me that the reason she had dragged me out of Anthony's car was to prevent me dragging him (unwillingly) to my bedroom. When he refused my offer of coming in for coffee saying that I ought to be in bed, I grabbed him and said, 'come on then, gorgeous'.

Bev's fairly sure that Brian and the bimbo had left before I kicked off. I do hope so.

And at least I won't have to see Anthony again.

Should I apologise to Pippa? But it was her mother who taught me the dance after all, and I am the one left scarred by the tango. But maybe I should adopt a slightly repentant tone when I speak to her.

I can remember having a brief conversation with Brian when we arrived at party. I also recall turning sharply and attempting to walk away when the bimbo joined us. Regrettably I'd forgotten I was standing next to the chair Pippa's Uncle Dick was sitting in. I ended up bent over his knees. I put the blame on Bev and my new shoes but Uncle Dick said not to worry, he'd enjoyed the experience. I'm fairly certain the bimbo didn't notice; she was too busy wrapping herself round my husband (ex).

Brian was wearing a new suit. At least, it wasn't one I'd seen before. He looked different. I'd like to say he looked older and sadder but that wouldn't be true: he looked young and happy. I'm glad for him, really I am.

No, I'm not. I wish he were miserable and regretting what he'd done. I don't think I'd want him back but I do want him to want to come back.

I hope Anthony turned me down because he was a gentleman not because he didn't fancy me. I definitely need a new man in my life. I'll have to take the search more seriously. But right now I'll get some paracetamol and a cup of tea, and then will settle down to watch Eastenders to cheer me up.

Lunchtime

Adam finally emerged from bed ten minutes ago. He greeted my surprisingly bright 'good morning' with silence and a look that would have frozen penguins in their tracks.

'What's that for?' I asked.

'I think you know,' he said.

I tried to do a rapid memory recall. Had I washed his favourite dry clean only jumper? Called him sweetie in front of his friends? Recorded *Last of the Summer Wine* over his *Jackass Strikes Back* video? Nothing sprang to mind.

'No, sorry, sweetie, sorry, I mean, Adam, you'll have to give me a clue.'

I could see he was battling with himself. At last he muttered between his teeth, 'Last night.'

'I don't seem to remember the events of last night very well — it was the champagne, I shouldn't drink it, it doesn't agree with me. Was there something in particular that upset you?'

'You mean like my mother getting drunk and humiliating me? Is that particular enough?'

I had a sudden memory of my mother saying almost the same thing to me after a cousin's wedding party when I was seventeen.

I quizzed Adam further but it doesn't appear that I did anything in his presence other than dance badly and I can't see why that should be so embarrassing for my son. I hadn't realised he was such a sensitive flower. Although I probably should have refrained from saying so at that precise moment. But I'm sure he will forgive me. In time.

Later

I plucked up my courage and phoned Pippa. She was cool at first but she can never stay mad for long. She thanked me for Luke's present, and then said, 'It was really generous of you, Alison, giving him £30. Brian gave him twenty and you don't earn half what he must be making. Or even a quarter.' I couldn't help glowing smugly. Fifteen love to Alison - not that I'm trying to outscore Brian in any way.

And I only have one week to survive before pay day. I don't have to pay for my dress, shoes and hair until next month thanks to my lovely little plastic card so I should be able to last as long as I'm careful and don't buy sandwiches for lunch.

By the end of our conversation Pippa and I were laughing hysterically so I think I'm forgiven. But surely my dancing wasn't that funny?

27th May, Tuesday

Bev called. Anthony has asked Simon for my phone number!

'Why?'

'Well, obviously he wants to see you again.'

'Are you sure? Perhaps I just left something in his car.'

'He would have given it to Simon if you had, wouldn't he?"

'I suppose so.'

'So? What shall I do?'

'What do you mean?'

'Do you want him to have your phone number?'

'Didn't Simon give it to him when he asked?'

'Don't be daft. Simon doesn't know anyone's phone number. He told Anthony he'd get it from me. So do you want to see him again?'

'I don't know. What do you think?'

'Personally I wouldn't touch him with rubber gloves but it's not up to me.'

'Oh, bless him, he's not that bad.'

'So he can have your phone number?'

'Yeeees, no, I suppose so, no, no, I don't think so. No, definitely not. But, Bev, what if it's the only offer I ever get?'

'For goodness sake, Aliss, you go out with a man, make a complete fool of yourself and he still wants to see you again. Seems to me that he's the desperate one, not you.'

I think Bev was trying to reassure me but I can't help feeling she could have phrased it better.

1st June

Mum called to remind me that she and Dad are off to Tenby next Saturday. She wants me to call in to their house at least twice, but preferably three times including Sunday, during the week to make sure: a) they haven't been burgled; b) there is no important mail; c) she didn't leave the gas on; and d) she remembered to cancel the milk. She also wants me to water the tomatoes and the houseplants, check that old Mrs Roberts next door is all right, and, if I have time, mow the lawns.

'Oh, and will you go and see Auntie Millie? We always go on a Saturday and she'll miss us if we don't go. She'd love to see you; she always asks how you are.'

'Yes, of course, I've been meaning to go and see her for ages. But, Mum, I don't know if I'll be able to call into your house three times. Couldn't Geoff do it once or twice? He and Trisha do live closer to you.'

'Oh, no, I couldn't ask Geoff, he's much too busy. And Trisha always has so much on her plate what with the Red Cross and reading to the deaf, I wouldn't want to trouble her.'

I sensed my words were also falling on deaf ears and gave up.

3rd June, Tuesday

Mum called to give me her mobile number in case of emergencies. I told her I already have it but she insisted on me writing it down again. She also gave me the telephone numbers of the caravan site reception desk, the plumber and Mrs Roberts's doctor.

4th June, Wednesday

Mum called to remind me that they are leaving Saturday morning and to tell me that they don't have restricted visiting hours at the home but that Auntie Millie doesn't like to be disturbed when the football results are on.

5th June, Thursday

Mum called to say that they wouldn't get back until late the following Saturday but that Auntie Millie was going on an outing to Porthcawl with the residents so I wouldn't have to go and visit her then.

6th June, Friday

Mum called to repeat everything she had already told me and to remind me that their wills are in the bank.

'Mum, don't think of things like that! You're supposed to be going to enjoy yourselves.'

'You never know what's around the corner. It's better to be prepared. And you'll remember that your Dad wants to be cremated and I want to be buried, won't you?'

'Yes, mum,' I sighed.

I am going to tell my children that, if I ever show signs of turning into my mother, they are to shoot first and ask questions later.

Chapter 5

7th June, Saturday

I went to see Great Aunt Millie today. It's not a chore; I'm very fond of Auntie Millie. The nurse, who took me to the lounge where Auntie was sitting, said, 'Ah, Millie, she's a character all right.' It was said with feeling but also, I think, a smile.

The staff are well trained to make sure the patient knows who the visitor is: the nurse said, 'Hello, Millie, look who's come to see you. It's your great-niece, Alison.'

'Hello, Auntie, how are you today?'

Auntie Millie looked around, 'Where's whatisname?'

'Who, Auntie?'

'Your husband.'

'I've told you, Auntie Millie, Brian and I are divorced now.'

'Are you? Never liked him anyway. His lips were too thin. And he smelled. That's the trouble with butchers: you can never get rid of the smell of blood.'

I was about to correct her on several points i.e. thin lips and butchering as Brian's career, but then thought, why bother?

I updated Auntie Millie on the family then asked how she was settling in. 'Do you like it here? Is everyone nice?'

'Yes, very nice. They don't listen to you, mind. I must have told the girl twenty times not to put grass on the potatoes but she doesn't listen. I ought to get rid of her but she's been with me for years. But they've got some right ones in here. You see him over there?'

She pointed to a man standing looking out of the window. He had his thumbs stuck in his waistcoat and was talking to himself.

'He thinks he used to be Prime Minister. Silly old bugger. He won't believe me when I say he wasn't.'

'Really?'

'Mind, in his day, he was a very good Chancellor of the Exchequer.'

I looked again at man in question. I couldn't be sure whether he had or had not ever been Chancellor. My knowledge of politics is sadly lacking.

Then Auntie Millie took me to see her room. While we were there a nurse popped her head round the door. 'Would you like a cup of tea?'

'Yes, please.'

Auntie Millie leaned forward, grabbed my hand and whispered, 'If she offers you a biscuit, take two.'

'But I thought we could have a slice of the cake I brought for you'

'Pssh, I'll save that for later. You've got to get your moneys-worth out of this lot.'

The nurse left us a plate of biscuits. I was about to take one when Auntie Millie swooped in and scooped them all up in her hankie. 'Here, put these in the drawer for me, there's a good girl.' She pointed to her bedside cabinet. I carefully carried the hankie over and opened the drawer; it was full of broken biscuits. I picked out as many of the oldest-looking as I dared and slipped them into my handbag.

Just before I left, Auntie Millie suddenly said, 'You're better off without him, you know.'

'Who, Auntie?'

'Brian. A man who runs after a young woman once will do it again sure as eggs is eggs. You're too good for that.'

I kissed her papery cheek. 'Thank you, Auntie.'

'Mind you, he did make lovely sausages.'

I asked the nurse when she let me out if they had anyone famous staying. She laughed and said, 'Everyone's famous here.'

Later

Adam asked me for a lift into town.

'I'm tired,' I said. 'Can't you get the bus?'

'I can't afford the bus fare — but if you want to give it to me...?'

'All right, give me my purse.'

'Where is it?'

'In my handbag.'

I was just wondering how he was planning to pay for a night out if he couldn't even afford bus fare when he said, 'Mum, why is your handbag full of biscuits?'

I can't decide how I feel after trip to see Auntie Millie. She has deteriorated slightly mentally, but seems happy. She has always been happiest when she has had something to grumble about. And she is ninety-two and has outlived both her brother and sister by a long way. Because her sister, my grandmother, died when my children were babies she's the closest thing they've got to a great-granny, and they love her.

Which reminds me: I thought we, i.e. Adam and me, had agreed that he would not go out clubbing again until his A-levels finished. I'm sure he has some left to do. I must remember to ask him in the morning. Brian tells me I do not take my role of concerned parent seriously enough. Huh, I don't not think walking out on your family in favour of a girl young enough to be your daughter (almost) shows particular concern for parental responsibility, but I didn't say so. Not out loud anyway. Personally I think Adam with his rational mind shows signs of being highly successful. I gave up trying to encourage him to revise when he asked me what good my A-levels had done me.

10th June, Tuesday

Young Mr Davies came over to my desk this afternoon.

'Alison.'

'Yes, Mr Davies?'

'I have David Davies coming in to see me at 11 o'clock tomorrow morning.'

'Oh.'

'Yes, and I was wondering if you could try to be a little more efficient — I know you are very efficient as a rule, very efficient, it just seems that Mr Davies has been unfortunate in his dealings with you before, and I wondered if you could make that special effort to be extra efficient with him when he comes in? If you wouldn't mind?'

Honestly, as if he had to ask me specially. I am always very polite and efficient. I bet Mr Smartarse made him do it. He has probably even suggested that Davies and Davies would be better off without me. 'A more efficient receptionist would project a much better image for the firm.' Yes, I can hear him saying it. In his chocolatey-brown voice.

It's not even as if I have given him anything to complain about. A couple of little mistakes and it's suddenly a big deal. Well, I'll show him.

11th June, Wednesday

At twenty-five to eleven a man, in his late forties, I would think, came in to the office.

'Good morning, sir, can I help you?'

'My name is David Davies. I have an appointment with your Young Mr Davies.'

'Oh. You're a little early, I'm afraid Mr Davies has a client with him.'

'That's quite all right, I know I'm early. It didn't take me as long to find a parking space as I had anticipated.'

'If you'd like to take a seat, Mr Davies won't be long. Would you like a cup of coffee? Or tea? Or hot chocolate?'

'Coffee would be very welcome, thank you.'

'Milk? Sugar?'

'Just milk, please.'

I was going to show him that I wasn't a useless bimbo; I was going to make him eat his complaints. Efficient? I was going to be more efficient than Miss Moneypenny and Bridget Jones combined.

'Excuse me,' the chocolate-brown voice spoke.

'What?'

'I said no sugar.'

'Yes, so?'

'So you've just put in three teaspoonfuls.'

I was stirring the coffee as he spoke. 'Actually, this isn't your coffee,' I stuttered. 'This is ...' I glanced across at Muriel who had a mug in her hand. 'someone else's.'

I picked up the mug, carried it across the room, knocked on Mr Davies Senior's door, breezed in, and said, 'Here's your coffee, Mr Davies. Just as you like it, with three sugars.'

I waited a moment then, 'That's quite all right, Mr Davies. My pleasure.'

I scurried back to reception closing the door before Smartarse could see an empty chair.

Unfortunately, two minutes later, Mr Davies Senior came in through the front door.

'Morning, all,' he said. 'Sorry I'm late ...'

'Late?' I tried to laugh as I stood up. 'You're not late. You've already been in, you just popped out, remember? Through the back door. You had to, um, do something you said. When I brought your coffee in. Which reminds me, it'll be getting cold, you go in and drink it.'

I took his arm and hurried him into his office.

'Oh, thank you, um, er, dear.'

'My goodness,' I said loudly to Muriel, 'he is getting forgetful.'

Smartarse was holding his newspaper in front of his face but I could see his shoulders shaking. It was a relief when Young Mr Davies came out to greet him.

'Has our lovely Alison been looking after you all right?"

'Very well, thank you. I couldn't have asked for a better morning's entertainment.'

Suddenly I realised I hadn't got round to making his coffee. I wished I'd had it in my hand at that moment so I could have thrown it at him.

When he emerged from Young Mr Davies's office, Smartarse said, 'Thank you, Richard, you've been most helpful.'

'That's what I'm here for, David. See you same time on the 25th then.'

'Good bye.'

He nodded at me as he walked to the door. 'See you again.'

Not if I can avoid it.

I happened to mention to Bev when she phoned that Smartarse had unusually blue eyes. Being Bev, she jumped to the wrong conclusion.

'So you fancy him?'

'Don't be silly, I just told you how impossible he is.'

'Yes, for the last half-hour you've been telling me how impossible he is. Admit it – you fancy the pants off him.'

'Of course I don't, he is insufferable. And anyway, fifty-year-old women don't *fancy* people.'

'What do they do then?'

'They see if they might ... like people … as friends.'

'Pshah.'

I don't know why she finds the idea of platonic friendships so hard to comprehend. She is forgetting that I am fifty and have probably had my fair share of sex. Then again perhaps not by today's standards.

14th June, Saturday

9.30 am

Chloe is home for the weekend. Her results are out next Thursday and she has not sat still since she arrived yesterday evening. I have suggested that we go shopping to take her mind off things. I will treat us both: she needs new jeans and I could do with some sandals. I've noticed last year's (four-year-old) sandals are starting to split.

After shopping

I am a fool. I thought jeans were jeans were jeans. How wrong could I be? Each pair I picked out, Chloe turned up her nose. Too dark, too faded, too narrow, too baggy, too last year, wrong designer. Seemed the only thing they couldn't be was too expensive.

'How much?!!!'

'Only seventy-five.'

'Pounds?'

'They're reduced, they're normally a hundred and twenty. Honest, Mum, it's a bargain.'

I found it hard to concentrate on sandals after that but in the fourth shoe shop I found the perfect ones. It was busy and the assistants hadn't got round to putting all the shoes away when I spotted my ideal sandal all by itself on the floor next to my seat. I picked it up and turned it over: it was even the right size. I slipped it on. It was perfect.

'Look, Chloe, what do you think of this?'

'Nice.'

'Yes, see if you can find an assistant to get the other one for me.'

'Excuse me,' a woman interrupted us. 'That's my shoe you're wearing.'

I looked down at her feet. 'Oh, you've got the other one. I was just going to ask an assistant for it.'

'No, they're my sandals.'

'I'm sure they'll have another pair — we don't have to fight,' I laughed.

'No, you don't understand,' she said. 'They really are mine.'

'No, they're not yours,' I said, 'not until you've paid for them. Now let's get an assistant to sort this out.'

'Look, these sandals are mine.'

She went to grab my foot and I was about to remonstrate further when Chloe hissed, 'Mum, the sandals *belong* to this lady, they're *not for sale*.'

We left the shop speedily. I asked Chloe if it would be okay for me to go back in and ask the woman where she'd bought them, but she grabbed my arm and led me down the street.

In Costalotta Coffee, I bemoaned the downturn in my mental capacity to Chloe, 'It was like a switch being switched off, chunk, that's it, you've had your share of brain power and memory. Only so much to go round and there are others who need it now.' I sighed. 'They told me that my flesh would give up its fight with gravity but they didn't say my brain would fly out of the window too.'

'What are you talking about, Mum?'

'It's obvious, isn't it? Since turning fifty, I've become completely dippy.'

'Mum,' she patted my hand, 'you've always been dippy. It's one of your more endearing qualities.'

Why do my children have this impression of me? I've always tried to be the perfect mother, like Marmee in Little Women. Admittedly I can't sew and visiting sick orphans is not high on my list of things to do, but I've tried my best. Now it appears that my mask has been seen through, and my true self revealed. But, at least, it is regarded as an endearing thing. By Chloe anyway. Don't know if Young Mr Davies would agree.

I didn't buy us anything for dinner as I thought Chloe and I could have a girls' night in; we haven't had one for ages. But when I suggested takeaway and video, she said, 'Didn't I tell you, Mum? I'm going out with Dad tonight. He and Gina are taking me to that new posh place by the Town Hall.'

'You didn't mention it.'

'I'm sure I did. You don't mind, do you?'

'No, no, of course not. You go and enjoy yourself.'

It wasn't worth getting a takeaway and video for one so I made myself a cheese sandwich before settling down to watch Casualty.

Later

Now I remember why it is that I never watch *Casualty*. Tonight's episode was about a nine-month-pregnant woman pulled out of car wreckage. The accident happened when she was on her way to the station to collect her husband who had been working abroad for the last three months. Result: baby saved, mother lost; another box of tissues emptied.

19th June, Thursday

Chloe phoned, she got a 2:1. I feel incredibly proud of my beautiful and talented daughter.

When I'd stopped crying, I called Mum to tell her. 'Hi, Mum, just wanted to let you know that Chloe's had her results. She got a 2:1.'

'A two?'

'No, a 2:1.'

'Two one? You mean she got twenty-one?'

'No, Mum, she got a, oh, it just means she passed very well.'

'Well, why didn't you say that to begin with? I knew she would. She's always been a bright little thing, takes after her father.'

I would have argued with her but I suspect it's true. I don't need my own mother to tell me that though; she, at least, should be on my side. Then again she knows me better than anyone.

25th June, Wednesday

1.35 pm

Smartarse was early again. I bet he does it on purpose to catch me out. But I was ready for him this time. I handed him coffee (milk, no sugar) before he'd had time to hang up his coat. I was determined to show him what I'm really like so when the phone rang I answered it in my absolute best telephone manner.

'Good morning. Davies and Davies, Financial Advisers. How may I help you this fine morning?'

'Hello, it's me.'

'Hello.'

'How are you?'

'Fine, thank you. And you?' I didn't recognise the voice but she obviously knew me so I played for time.

'Oh, not too bad. And how's the family?'

'They're well. What about yours?'

'Well, his lordship hasn't been that good, you know.'

'I'm sorry to hear that.' Whoever he is.

'Mustn't grumble really. At our age you can't say much, can you, when bits stop working?'

'Er, no, I suppose not.'

'Now I know I shouldn't phone you at work so I'll be quick. I wanted to invite you round for a meal.'

'A meal?'

'It's been so long since we've seen each other.'

'Remind me, when did we last see each other?'

'It must have been at Ted and Alice's ruby wedding party.'

I paused. 'I don't think I know a Ted and Alice.'

'Don't be silly, we were sitting at the same table.'

'Were we?'

'Yes. What is the matter with you today, Muriel? You don't seem with it at all.'

'Muriel?'

'Really, Muriel, dear, you must pull yourself together.'

'I'm not Muriel.'

'What do you mean, you're not Muriel? Who are you then?'

'I'm Alison.'

'I don't know anyone called Alison.'

'No, I didn't think I knew you. One moment, I'll hand you over to Muriel. I don't suppose the invitation for a meal is still open now, is it?' I trilled.

'Of course not, are you mad?'

Smartarse disappeared behind his newspaper but not before I'd seen what looked suspiciously like a smirk. Doesn't he know it's rude to listen in to other people's conversations? It confirms my opinion of him.

I couldn't help noticing, though, that Smartarse's shirts are very well ironed. This means that either he's married, he has a girlfriend who does his ironing, he's single and good at ironing, or he's single and rich enough to use an ironing service.

So statistically the chances of him being unattached are — I have absolutely no idea. Not that it's important. It would only be important if a female were interested in him as more than an acquaintance and I'm not. Not at all. He is insufferable. The way his hair just crinkles over the top of his collar might be appealing to some women but not to me.

26th June, Thursday

I am good for my age. It's official: I've been told by both dentist and optician. Despite getting long in the tooth I'm pleased to report that my teeth and eyesight are okay. Apart from needing a tiny filling and a slightly stronger pair of glasses. That aside, my teeth and eyesight have 'not deteriorated more than would be expected'.

Thinking about it, I seem to recall that both dentist and optician added 'quite' before the 'good'. Still, that's not a disaster; that is 'quite good'. I can live with that. At least I'm not bad for my age. I would probably be incontinent as well if I were.

The nurse called me in to see the dentist just as I was engrossed in a fascinating article about 'Your best friend'. According to the article, forget dogs, a woman's best friend is her best friend i.e. another woman. 'A woman's best friend is her life support. She lifts you up when you are down, confirms that your ex is a total cad, and in every way, is there for your benefit. In return, all she asks is that you do the same for her.' I was tempted to tear the article out so I could show it to Bev and Pippa. I'm not sure they're living up to the ideal.

28th June, Saturday

It's Mum's birthday next weekend and it's my turn to host the celebrations. Last year we all went round to Geoff & Trisha's for a spectacular dinner party, complete with silver candelabra and white linen tablecloth. Which reminds me: did I ever collect Trisha's tablecloth from the dry cleaners I had to take it to after Adam spilled his red wine? I have a horrible feeling I didn't. That would explain why she was a bit iffy with me last Christmas. No, actually she's always a bit iffy with me.

I can't compete with smoked salmon canapés and tiramisu so perhaps I should take everyone out for a meal. But that will look as though I can't cope without Brian – and would be hideously expensive.

Later

Adam is a genius. He has suggested having a barbecue to celebrate Grandma's birthday. He assures me he is expert at cooking sausages and burgers. When I said I thought our guests would prefer something more sophisticated Adam said that was no problem, 'Burger, steak, no difference.' He shrugged nonchalantly. I suspect there's something dubious about his argument but I can't put my finger on it.

Anyway if he is cooking, he will take the blame if there are problems, and because he is the only and adored grandson, he will be forgiven. This is such a brilliant solution. All I will have to do is marinade the meat and make salads and dessert. I'll check the weather forecast for the weekend and then invite everyone.

A little later

According to the seven day weather forecast the sun will be shining and the temperature hot. Everyone is able to come so there will be eight in all: Mum, Dad, Geoff, Trisha, Chloe, Tryboy, Adam and me. We only have four garden chairs so I must ask Pippa if we can borrow hers. And her umbrella as Mum is sure to want to sit in the shade.

Bedtime

I've spent the evening scouring cookery books to plan the menu for the birthday barbecue. I must put on a good show so we're having: spare ribs in spicy sauce (oven-cooked), Thai fish in foil, steak Creole, chicken wings in Szechuan sauce, pork and leek sausages, green salad, Greek potato salad, Iranian rice salad, garlic bread, French bread, pavlova, and red berry compote. Not even Trisha, the hostess with the mostest, could do better. Not that I resent my sister-in-law. I don't at all, not even the way she manages to look down upon me from all of her 4'6".

29th June, Sunday

I've spent the day in the garden, mowing the lawn, weeding the flower-beds, sweeping the patio and scrubbing the table, which came up remarkably well apart from the bits that have ingrained bird poo. I understand now why Brian used to store the table in the garage over the winter. I also discovered that one of our four chairs is broken, so I need to borrow five.

Adam asked if he can invite Sophie to the barbecue.

'Sophie?'

'Yes.'

'Sophie?'

'Yes, Sophie.'

'Who's Sophie?'

He shrugged, 'She's just this girl.'

'A girlfriend type of girl?'

He shrugged again.

'Yes, of course you can. I'll look forward to meeting her.'

'You won't make a fuss, will you, Mum?'

'Me! Make a fuss? Of course not, what do you think I am?'

Later

I phoned Chloe. She knows all about Sophie. 'Adam's been keen on her for ages but they've only been going out for a couple of weeks.'

'Two weeks? And no-one told me?'

'I expect Adam would have done soon. Anyway, he's bringing her to the barbecue so you'll meet her then.'

'Yes, but...'

'I've got to go now, Mum; I'm on duty at the Women's Shelter tonight. See you Friday, bye.'

'Bye, darling.'

My children's lives are going on without me. They don't need my help any more. It seems only yesterday that I was up to my elbows in baby poo not bird poo.

'You won't say anything like that when Sophie's here, will you, Mum?' Adam was at my shoulder.

'Like what?'

'Anything about baby poo.'

'Did I say that aloud?'

'Yes.'

'Oh.'

'So you won't, will you?'

I looked at him. He was the image of his father.

'I promise you, Adam, I will try my very best not to embarrass you.' But judging by recent experience, it could prove to be a hard promise to keep.

30th June, Monday

1.30 pm

Had just got into work this morning when phone rang. 'Gooth morning, Davith and Davith, Finanthial, oh — yeth?

'Good morning, it's David Davies here. Are you all right?'

'I've been to the denthith.'

'I see, I hope it wasn't too painful.'

'Urrgh.'

'All right, I won't ask you any more. Is your Young Mr Davies available? Just grunt once for yes and twice for no.'

'Yeth.'

'Perhaps you could put me through to him then, and I hope you're back to normal very soon. Or should I say, as close to normal as is normal for you.'

He almost seemed human then. One might even have said that he sounded genuinely concerned. Of course, one would only say that if one didn't know his true personality. And I'm not quite sure what he meant with his last comment. Now I think about it, it sounds rude.

I'm going to forget about rude men and concentrate on looking forward to Mum's birthday. I'm going to give her a party she'll never forget. The sky is beautiful blue with a few wispy white clouds and the forecast for Sunday is excellent. I feel very calm and relaxed about the whole affair. It is going to be a marvellous day, I just know it is.

Chapter 6

2nd July, Wednesday

The sky, which according to last night's forecast should be clear blue, has distinct large white patches. Still, white isn't bad; it's not black, or even grey. And it's only Wednesday. Plenty of time for the clouds to clear before Sunday.

3rd July, Thursday

I am becoming obsessed with the sky. I wonder if the weathermen ever look out of their windows when they dream up their forecasts. There is more cloud than sky visible now. But it's still white. Or whitish, at least. There's very little grey amongst it. And it is warm.

I think I'd better start cleaning tonight. I only need to especially clean the bits that will be seen i.e. kitchen, hall and downstairs toilet. I must remember to remind people that the downstairs toilet door sticks when locked from the inside. I should probably look in Yellow Pages for an odd job man. That is, if they exist these days. They probably call themselves Home maintenance and charge £50 an hour just for coming to look. The door probably just needs oiling anyway; I'll do it myself.

Getting cleaning out of the way is a good idea as it will leave me all Saturday to shop and prepare. Perhaps I should do the upstairs toilet as well, in case of emergencies. And I must remind Adam to keep his bedroom door tightly closed.

Later

I am of the opinion that toilet cleaning should be a compulsory part of the National Curriculum. I'm self-taught and while I'm fairly confident that my ministrations result in a germ-free toilet I would prefer to have fewer bleach-stained clothes. Two jumpers and three pairs of trousers destroyed in twenty three years of marriage. Although that might be a good average; I don't have a standard to compare against. Perhaps I should write a book - *Things Mrs Beeton Didn't Mention.*

And I've squeezed oil into the keyhole of the downstairs toilet door. Most of it seemed to come out the other side, but it must have done some good. I won't test it yet; I'll wait until Adam is here to let me out should it fail to work.

4th July, Independence Day

I wish I were independent of the weather. The sky, which earlier in the week promised so much, is now turbulent grey. Muriel says thunder is on the way. She knows because her cat has gone in the cupboard under the stairs and won't come out. That is a sure sign, she says. Mr Davies Senior came in when we were talking. He agreed. His left calf is twitching and it always does that before a storm. 'Look,' he said. He pulled up his trouser leg and, sure enough, his calf was twitching.

'What are you doing, Father?' Young Mr Davies had snook back in from lunch when we were engrossed in watching the spasmic muscle.

'Just showing the ladies my leg.'

'Oh.'

Young Mr Davies turned and went into his office.

'I worry about him, you know,' Mr Davies Senior said, looking after his son and sighing. 'He can't cope with too much stress.'

I don't think I am built for stress either. In forty-eight hours the barbecue is due to start. If there is going to be a storm it needs to happen tonight, so everything will dry up before Sunday.

Later

Trisha rang. 'Everything all right, Alison? Barbecue still on for Sunday?'

'Yes, everything's fine.'

'You haven't seen the weather forecast then?'

'Not since last week, no. Why?'

'Tonight's forecast for Sunday doesn't seem to be awfully good.'

'Oh, I don't believe weather forecasts, they're always wrong.'

5th July, Saturday

First thing

The storm didn't materialise over-night. Clouds are still hovering round but look as if they might be thinning out. Just a bit. I must stop worrying about weather. I'll make a list of things to do to take my mind off it.

Eating breakfast

I wish I hadn't made a list. It's far too long. Now I have even more to worry about, like how on earth I'm going to fit in all the things on the list. Chloe and Tryboy are here and have said they will help me, and I've asked Adam to get the barbecue out of the shed.

Shower is first on my list followed by a trip to Sainsburys. If I get the shopping out of way I can concentrate on final cleaning touches and food preparation.

Lunchtime

I got back from Sainsburys to find my usual car parking space taken. The closest gap that I would even consider was halfway down the road. I parked, picked up four carrier bags and headed for home. I opened the front door, dumped the bags in the hall and yelled, 'Someone come and help me carry stuff in, please. I'm down the road.'

I went back to car and unloaded all of the shopping onto the pavement. There was no sign of any help coming. I carried another four bags to the house. 'Hello, will someone come and help me carry the shopping in, please?'

I was just coming out of the house when the car that had parked in front of our gate pulled out. I ran down the street, leapt in the car and reversed smartly back to the space, which unfortunately looked a lot smaller when viewed from inside the car. I studied the gap. A car driver (male) tooting behind me, made me jump. I was about to give up and drive away when I remembered the little motto on my sanitary towel wrapping that morning. "During ovulation, a woman's sense of spatial awareness is improved. Parking in small spaces is a doddle." How fortuitous I thought. As if it were meant to be. Inspired by these heartening words, I was determined to persevere.

I finally managed to park, sort of, despite irritable male tooting, at my fourth attempt. I wonder where manufacturers of sanitary products get their information from and whether it's possible to sue on the grounds of misinformation. Still that's what bumpers are for and I don't think Tryboy will notice another tiny bump in his.

By now I was sweating but as I started for the house I remembered the bags of shopping still on the pavement 100 yards away. I looked down the round in time to see a scruffy dog heading for them. 'Go away!' I screamed. 'I'm warning you! Don't you dare pee on my shopping!' I hadn't noticed Mrs Evans and her sister who were in the garden as I ran past. As I returned laden with carrier bags, I heard Mrs Evans say, 'No wonder youngsters today are like they are.'

It took me four trips altogether to bring in the shopping. As I was finally closing the front door behind me, Chloe came downstairs. 'Hi, mum,' she yawned. 'Anything I can do to help?'

I took a deep breath before replying. 'Getting dressed might be a good idea.'

'Oh, yeah, okay, I'll just make some toast for us first.'

I put away the shopping, carefully walking round Chloe in the middle of the kitchen. When she'd finished, if I hadn't known better, I would have sworn that she'd been making breakfast for a troupe of starving body builders. There were piles of dirty plates, knives, mugs and spoons everywhere, not to mention jam jars without lids, a cafetiere full of grinds, an open bag of sliced bread, a toaster still plugged in, and crumbs over everything but especially the margarine. I had just finished clearing it away when Adam wandered in and started rummaging in the fridge.

'What are you looking for?'

'We got any bacon? I fancy a bacon sandwich for breakfast.'

'Have you only just got up?'

'Yeah, it's Saturday.'

'Well, have you got to have a bacon sandwich? I've just cleared up after Chloe and I'm trying to get things ready for the party.'

'That's not till tomorrow.'

'I know, but I have to start preparing now. There's a lot to do.'

I was aware that my voice was getting higher with each word I spoke.

'Okay, calm down, I'll just have cereal.'

Adam + cereal = kitchen littered with dirty bowl, milk bottle (contents spilled generously over work surface), spoon, sugar bowl (grains scattered equally generously over floor), two cereal packets (one now empty, the other dug into to find the free plastic space rocket) and yesterday's sports page from the Guardian, bought by Chloe.

Tomorrow I'll suggest, no, I'll treat, everyone to a big breakfast at Butties cafe.

Damn, damn, damn. I've forgotten all about Mum's present. The Toe Cosy that I ordered from the mail order catalogue was out of stock when I ordered it but I'd been assured it would still arrive in time. I was so busy basking in the unusual situation of having planned ahead and ordered Mum's present in advance that I hadn't given it a second thought.

Could I give Mum the flowers I bought to decorate the house tomorrow and say her present has been held up in the post? No, Trisha will have a wonderfully wrapped and beribboned gift; any excuse from me will sound like what it is. I'm going to have to go to the shops this afternoon and find something else and it's time I really can't afford. I'll have to ask Chloe to clean the living room and Adam to sort out the barbecue. I can make the desserts this evening. That will be fine.

In bed at last

I am knackered. I think everyman and his auntie were in town this afternoon. I queued for half an hour for a parking space, dithered round Marks & Spencer's for three hours, and then queued for half an hour to get out of car park.

When I got back, I found the kitchen full of dirty dishes and Adam eating a sandwich.

'What are you doing?'

'Having a sandwich — don't worry, I used the old ham not the stuff you've bought for the barbecue.'

'But why are you eating?'

'I was hungry.'

'But dinner's soon.'

'Good, I said I'm hungry. What's for dinner?'

'Dinner? Um, er, takeaway. Did you clean the barbecue?'

'Yeah.'

'There's a good boy, thank you. Where's Chloe?'

'In the living room.'

I found Chloe and Tryboy stretched out on the sofa, newspaper spread all over the floor, the television blaring and empty beer cans lying about.

'Chloe! I asked you to clean in here!'

'I have done!'

I decided the mess was superficial and that the weather tomorrow would not necessitate us using the living room anyway. Then I checked the barbecue. I can't believe I put it away last year in such a state. I called Adam.

'Adam, I asked you to clean this!'

'I did!'

Two brillo pads, half a bottle of Jif and a broken knife later, the barbecue looked safe to cook on. Adam watched me do it.

'Don't know why you're fussing, Mum; the heat will kill any germs.'

I sent him to the Bombay Brasserie for curry for four, then checked my to-do list. Bad mistakes are getting to be a habit with me.

At nine, I was still hysterically trying to separate egg yolks from whites for pavlova when Pippa rang. I couldn't help blubbing down the phone to her.

'Don't worry, Alison, I'll make the desserts for you.'

'You will? But you don't have the ingredients.'

'Course I have. I'll have everything I need. Don't worry, I'll bring them round in the morning with the chairs.'

Pippa is an angel in disguise - and she will know what I can do with eight broken eggs.

6th July, Sunday

7.00 am

I couldn't sleep so got up early to make a start on the salads. The sky was downcast, much like me. But I only have to marinade the meat, make the sauces, make the salads, make sure I have enough clean dishes/cutlery/glasses, have a final dust round, shower and wash my hair, and I'll be a perfect hostess.

I've invited everyone for one o'clock so I'll call the children at nine so they can shower and take themselves off to Butties for breakfast. That will give me a clear house to settle myself. Everything is falling into place nicely. I will not panic.

Evening

At half past eleven Pippa arrived with five garden chairs plus a fabulous crispy white pavlova laden with kiwi fruit and cream, and a crystal bowl brim-full of luscious red berries soaked in white wine with another huge dish of crème fraiche. I burst into tears when I saw her.

'Alison, what's the matter?'

'I forgot to get rose water.'

'Rose water? What on earth do you need rose water for?'

'The Iranian rice salad.'

Pippa packed me off to shower while she curried the rice salad, made a dressing for the green salad and rescued the potatoes, which were in danger of boiling dry. By the time I re-appeared, she'd made the sauce for the spare ribs and was putting them in the oven to bake slowly.

'Okay, I've got to now, Alison, as Roger's taking me out for lunch.'

'Thank you so much, Pippa, you're a life-saver.'

'That's what friends are for. Now have a glass of wine, calm down, and enjoy yourself. They're all family after all.'

I couldn't very well tell Pippa that was precisely what was worrying me.

At twenty past twelve there was an ominous noise outside. I couldn't bear to look so I made Adam peer out to check what it was. 'It's all right, mum, it's not thunder. It's only the chair blowing over ...'

'Oh, that's all right then. Stand it up, will you, and make sure it's safe?'

He headed for the front door. 'Adam, what are you doing?' I said. 'I asked you to sort out the chair.'

'That is what I'm doing,' he sighed.

'So why are you going out the front door? The chair's out the back.'

'No, it's not.'

'What do you mean it's not? Where is it then?'

'In Mr Price's garden.'

'What's it doing there?'

'I was trying to tell you, Mum, it blew over the fence.'

This news didn't bode well for eating outdoors, so I decided I'd have to make space in the dining room. I called Chloe. Tryboy came instead. 'Chloe's dyeing her hair,' he said, 'but I can help if you like.'

I was so grateful for his help I didn't give a single rant about Chloe's timing and lack of thought. I gave him a duster, stood to attention and said, 'England – or in this case Wales - expects that every man will do his duty.' He looked at me bemused so I smiled and asked him to push the dust off a few surfaces.

The guests arrived at five minutes to one precisely just as the sun came out. I was so relieved I gave Trisha a welcoming kiss, completely forgetting her dislike of physical contact. She immediately disappeared to the bathroom to repair her make-up. Good job I put clean towels in there.

Mum seemed pleased with my gift of a Marks & Spencer voucher, but was more delighted by an ugly china cat given her by Geoff and Trisha. 'I had to order it especially from an exclusive little boutique in Florence. I was awfully afraid it wouldn't arrive in time, but as soon as I saw it, I thought of you, and I said to myself, "Blow the expense, Trisha, Eunice will love it."'

'Oh, I do, Trisha, it's just gorgeous, isn't it, Alison?'

'Yes, Mum, beautiful.'

I could see Adam was about to say something - probably rude - I so leapt in, 'Right, Adam, would you like to start cooking now?'

Sophie didn't arrive until later as shed been to church first. I hope some of her obvious goodness will rub off on Adam.

Try as I might I couldn't help but compare Sophie and my own daughter. Chloe was happy to be waited on; Sophie was keen to help me. Chloe was on her fifth (to my knowledge) glass of wine; Sophie was sticking to orange juice. Chloe had her tongue in Tryboy's ear; Sophie was keeping a discreet distance between her and Adam. I'd like to be able to blame an absent father for these flaws in my children's characters but he wasn't.

In a moment of forgetful gaiety I told Trisha there were spare glasses in the cupboard in the kitchen and to help herself. Later I heard her whisper to Geoff, 'You should see inside the cupboards – the shelves are filthy. I don't believe she's ever cleaned in there. Make sure you give all your dishes a wipe with your napkin before you use them. I dread to think what we might catch.'

I didn't know I was supposed to clean inside cupboards. Do other people do that? How does the dirt get in? Why wasn't I taught that in school? I am humiliated by Trisha. Again.

During lunch, Chloe asked me if I'd finished reading her birthday present 'I am woman; I am me'. I told her I'd been busy.

'Anna Jorgensen was on Parkinson last week talking about it,' she said.

Mum piped up, 'That's all they talk about these days. Young girls. If they're not doing it, they're talking about it. It wasn't like that in my day.'

'What are you talking about, Mother?' I asked.

'Sex. It's all anyone talks about, isn't it? You can't switch on the television without hearing some tale about a woman who's left her husband to go off with another woman. For heaven's sake, I don't know what the world is coming to.'

'No-one's talking about sex, Mum.'

'Chloe was.'

'No, I wasn't.'

'Yes, you were. You said somebody was on Parkinson talking about it.'

'Not about sex, about a book.'

'A book about sex?'

'No, Mother, nothing to do with sex.'

'There's no need to take that tone with me, young lady.'

'I'm sorry, Mother. What Chloe said was that Anna Jorgensen — you know that blonde presenter who's on lots of quiz shows — was talking about the book Chloe had given me for my birthday.'

'Anna Jorgensen?'

'Yes, you know, granny, she's always in the tabloids, having men trouble.'

'Yes, I know who you mean, dear; I just didn't know that your mother knew her.'

'I don't.'

'But you just said that she was on television talking about your birthday present.'

'No, Mother. She was talking about a book and it happens to be the book that Chloe gave me for my birthday.'

'Well, why didn't you say so?'

'We ... oh, never mind. What did she have to say about the book, Chloe?'

'It has changed her life. She's adopted it as her mantra. Whenever she's feeling low, she says to herself, 'I am woman; I am me,' and straightaway she walks taller and more confidently. She said it should be given to every female child on her eighteenth birthday.'

I suspect adopting a tiger would be useful to me than a mantra, but I kept that thought to myself. Still if it helps a slim, gorgeous, blonde to walk tall, who am I to argue? I'll definitely try reading it again tomorrow. Or maybe the day after.

Mid-afternoon, Geoff said, 'Where's Trisha?'

We all looked around as if expecting her to be hiding behind the bushes.

'I think she went to the toilet,' Mum said.

'Yes, but that was ages ago.'

Chloe and I looked at each other, jumped up and ran inside.

'Trisha, are you in there?' I yelled through the toilet door.

'At last! I've shouted myself hoarse in here.'

'Well, the cavalry's arrived,' I tried to laugh. 'Okay, Trisha, just pass the key out through the window.'

I almost felt sorry for her when we let her out; she was in such a state. 'I couldn't breathe,' she panted. 'I was running out of air.'

'You couldn't have done that; all you had to do was open the window.'

'I couldn't think of things like that, all I could think was that I was locked in this horrid small space.' She started hyperventilating. Chloe took over. 'Don't worry, Mum. Okay, Auntie Trish, just come and sit down outside. It's all over now.'

In the garden Trisha fell into Geoff's arms. 'I was locked in, Geoff! Why didn't you come to look for me? I could have died in there and no-one would have cared.'

Mum looked at her. 'Don't be so silly, Trisha, everyone knows you've got to sing in Alison's toilet. "Some Day My Prince Will Come."' She sang this last bit.

Trisha said, 'Oooaaahhhh,' and Geoff fanned her with the colour supplement. They left soon after.

Still, apart from that, the day went rather well I think.

I wonder if my lack of housewifely skills e.g. interior cupboard cleaning, caused Brian to look elsewhere. I asked Chloe and Adam if he'd suggested anything like it to them.

Chloe said, 'Of course not, Mum, Dad isn't bothered by things like that.'

Adam said, 'Naah, more like it was Gina's neat arse that did it.'

Bedtime

I can't say I've noticed that Gina's arse is particularly 'neat'.

It's difficult to view one's own bottom in a mirror, but I don't believe mine is unattractive. Not for a fifty-year-old. Not when I clench it. Some men prefer a shapely bottom like mine. Perhaps curvy is a better description.

Then again, flabby is more apt. I have a flabby bum and dirty cupboards. No wonder my husband left me.

A little later

What is Adam doing studying Gina's arse? That is no way for him to treat his potential step-mother. I shall have to speak sternly to him.

Step-mother. I don't want my children to have another mother — even step. Especially a twenty-eight-year-old with a neat arse. Step-mothers should be horrible, it should be a law.

I wonder if David Davies has children. I wonder why I wondered that? It's of no concern to me whatsoever.

10th July, Thursday

I was under the desk when I heard the door open and someone walk in. I knew no clients were expected, so I assumed it was the postman with a delivery.

'I'll be with you in a minute,' I shouted.

There was no reply so I shouted again, 'Did you hear me? I'll be with you in a minute, I'm just ...'

'No, don't tell me, I'd rather guess.'

The rich Burtonesque voice came from just behind me.

'Ouch.'

'Careful, watch your head.'

'It's a bit late to say that,' I snapped. I stood up, straightened my skirt and wiped the dust off my blouse and face.

'You missed a bit.' David Davies stretched out his hand and brushed a cobweb off my fringe.

'Thank you.'

We stood and looked at each other for a moment, and then I sat down and busied myself at the computer before saying, 'Did you want something? Young Mr Davies is out this morning, I'm afraid. You didn't have an appointment, did you?'

'No, actually, I was hoping to see you.'

'Me! Why, what have I done now?'

'Nothing, everything's fine, I just wondered if you might like to come out for dinner with me?'

I couldn't think what to say. I seemed to have lost the power of speech. At last I said, 'Okay.'

'Good. What about Saturday?'

'This Saturday? The one coming?'

'Yes, unless that's inconvenient for you?'

'No, that's fine.'

'Good. Shall I pick you up?'

'Thank you, that would be nice.'

I started to move papers around on my desk as a sign that he should go now. But he hovered some more. I looked up again. 'Was there anything else?'

'Your address?'

'My address?'

'Yes, if I'm to pick you up I'll need to have your address.'

'Oh, yes.'

I started to write it down.

'Should you do that?' he asked.

'I thought you wanted my address.'

'No, I meant, should you be writing it on that paper? It looks like an Inland Revenue document.'

'Oh, yes.' I moved paper around trying to find a blank sheet but at last he opened his diary and handed it to me. 'Here use this.'

I scrawled out the address and gave it to him.

'Okay, I'll pick you up at 7.15, is that all right?'

'Yes, thank you.'

'Goodbye then.'

'Goodbye.'

This evening I phoned Bev.

'HiBevIhaveadate.'

'Aiieeeee, that's fab, Aliss. With who?'

'A man I've met through work, I think I might have mentioned him to you.'

'The obnoxious one with gorgeous blue eyes, you mean?'

'Okay, okay.'

'So, where's he taking you?'

'Out for a meal on Saturday.'

'Excellent and what are you wearing?'

'Gosh, I haven't thought about that yet. I'm still getting over being asked.'

'But it's crucial. What you wear on your first date will set the tone for your relationship.'

'Really?'

'Yeah, or affect the course of the evening at least. Let him see what sort of person you are and where you expect the relationship to go. I know — you can wear the dress you wore to Luke's party.'

'So you think dropping my bosom onto his side plate would give him an idea of where the relationship is heading, do you?'

'Look, you might as well be honest: you want a man.'

'Not like that.'

'Every woman wants a man that way, if she's honest.'

'Well, I'm not every woman.'

'Oh, come on, Aliss, don't be so stuffy. Go out, enjoy yourself.'

Then I called Pippa.

'Hello, Pippa, I thought you'd like to know that I have a date.'

'Alison, that's brilliant, I'm so pleased for you. With whom?'

'His name is David Davies; I met him through work.'

'So he has money, good.'

'You don't know that. He could be the window cleaner.'

'Yes, Alison,' she laughed, 'so where's he taking you?'

'For a meal on Saturday.'

'Excellent, and what are you going to wear?'

'I don't know. Bev has suggested that I wear the dress I wore to Luke's party.'

'Oh, no, Alison, that would be quite inappropriate for a dinner engagement. Let's see ... I know, what about the first top you bought for the party?'

'The one you said looked drab? The one Bev said I looked like a sack of swedes in?'

'We only meant it wasn't suitable for a party. It would be perfect for a tête a tête. And if you wear your best bra, it'll show off your figure nicely.'

I'm very confused now. Tart or turnip? Which shall I be?

Chapter 7

12th July, Saturday

I opted for turnip. I was ready and waiting at 6 o'clock when Adam wandered in. He said, 'Hi, Mum, off to a séance, are you?'

'What do you mean?'

'All in black.'

'No, Adam, actually...' I hesitated. I hadn't told him about my date. I wasn't sure how he'd cope with the idea of his mother seeing another man. I feared it could be traumatic for him. At last, I said, 'Actually, Adam, I have a dinner engagement this evening.'

'With Bev and Pippa?'

'No, it's, um, with a man.'

'Woohoo, good on you, Mum! Gonna hang a "do not disturb" sign on your bedroom door tonight, are you?'

'Certainly not! Mr Davies and I are just having a quiet meal together. As friends.'

'Mr Davies?'

'Yes, that's his name.'

'You haven't got onto first names terms yet? Don't take it too slowly, Mum, or you'll be too old to enjoy it.'

More like I will have forgotten what it is I am supposed to be enjoying.

Later

Things I now know about David Davies.

He is 52. He is a childless widower. He is a psychiatrist. He doesn't want to see me again. I don't know that for sure but have a pretty good idea that it's so. Which is fine by me as I wouldn't want to date a man who can say no to treacle pudding. His wife was killed in an accident when they'd only been married two years. 'Were you driving?' I asked.

'No, she was on her own, coming home from work.'

'That's good.'

He looked puzzled.

'I mean not that she was killed but that you weren't driving so you don't feel guilty. You don't feel guilty, do you?'

'Not at all.'

'Good. Not that you should — it wasn't your fault. Not unless you'd put off getting the brakes repaired or something.' I giggled. 'Not that you'd have done that. Not deliberately anyway. But I mean, well, some people would blame themselves even if they weren't to blame. Look at me, I blamed myself when they closed the local corner shop and Mrs Mac had to move into an old people's home. Even though I'd done all I could, signed petitions and, um, things. But it's so much cheaper at the supermarket, although I suppose that's probably because of slave labour and if I really had principles I wouldn't shop there. So, in a way, I was to blame. But she was eighty-three.'

David was looking intently at me. 'Who was?'

'Mrs Mac at the corner shop. And I went to visit her at the home and she was very happy there.'

There was a moment's silence then I said. 'You could be in a book though.'

'I'm sorry?'

'With a tragic story like yours, you could be in a book.'

'I've been thinking the same thing about you.'

'Me? Really? Why?'

'I find it hard to believe that you could be real, you must be a character from a book.'

I smiled sweetly and filed that away to dissect later i.e. now. Was that a compliment? Or was he laughing at me? I would say the latter but he did add, 'Fortunately I enjoy reading.' So that makes it all right. I think.

When I first asked him what he did for a living, he replied, 'I work in the medical profession.'

'A doctor?'

'Sort of.'

'Sort of? You mean you're not very good at it? People keep dying on you?' I flopped back in my chair in an impersonation of a dead body.

'No, actually, I'm a psychiatrist.'

'Really?' I sat up abruptly. 'That's ... interesting. You must meet some fascinating people.'

'I do, and not all through my work.'

'And I can see now why you might be reluctant to say what you do.'

'You do?'

'Yes, I bet it happens all the time — people find out what you do and then start telling you all their problems.'

'I suppose that is part of it.'

'And did you see that Fawlty Towers episode...'

'Yes.'

'The one where there are psychiatrists staying in the hotel...'

'Yes, I saw it.'

'And Basil is neurotic, convinced that they are analysing him and that they put everything he does down to sex.'

Suddenly I realised I was rolling my napkin ring between my fingers. I put it down quickly in case my action was misinterpreted. Then I found it difficult to do or say anything much at all during the rest of the evening.

At least when we were eating we had an excuse not to talk. I'd enjoyed wonderful crispy duck in a tangy fruity sauce when he said, 'Are you having dessert?'

'No, I don't think so; I'm quite full, thank you.'

'The dessert menu looks rather good. I see they have treacle pudding.'

'Treacle pudding? Oooh, my favourite, well, if you're having some...'

'It is tempting.'

'Go on then, let's have some.'

'No, on second thoughts, I don't think I will, but don't let that stop you.'

'Oh, no, I won't if you're not.'

'No, if it's your favourite I insist — waiter!'

I wonder what he made of my choice of treacle pudding, which, incidentally, was the best I've ever had. Do psychiatrists see everything as psychological tests? Will he be studying me? Not that he'll have the opportunity as we won't be seeing each other again. We are obviously not suited to one another.

Sitting in the bar after the meal, I had a brandy. I don't normally drink brandy when I'm out as it makes me chatter like a parrot but the unnatural quiet was getting me down.

Unfortunately as David appeared with the brandy a thought came into my head: the evening is almost over. He will take me home: do I invite him in for coffee? If I do, will he interpret it as an invitation to my bed; if I don't, will he mark me down as prissy and tight-laced? My dilemma was not helped by two familiar-sounding apparitions on my shoulders, whispering in my ears.

'Go for it, Aliss, let whatever happens, happen. It's time you enjoyed yourself.'

'Invite him in for coffee by all means, Alison, but only if you are confident that you can remain in control of any situation that might develop.'

I'd almost reached a decision when, 'Alison, are you okay?'

'What?'

'You were miles away.'

'Sorry, David, I was thinking about ... coffee.'

'Would you like some? I'll call the waiter.'

'No, no, I'm fine, thank you.'

We pulled up outside my house.

'Well, thank you for a lovely evening, David. I have enjoyed myself.'

'I'm glad, I've enjoyed it too.'

'I wonder, um ...'

'There appears to be someone trying to catch your attention.'

'What?' I looked around in time to see the curtain dropping back into place, the front door opening and Adam coming running out. 'Chloe's on the phone, Mum.'

'What's happened? Is she all right? Where is she?'

I was already out of the car and running into the house. This was my punishment for going on a date: my daughter had been fatally injured in a car crash, or given that terrible date rape drug that I keep hearing about and struggling to call for help.

'Chloe, what is it? Are you all right?'

'You've been on a date! You went on a date without telling me — Mum, how could you? Have you had a good time? What's his name? What's he like? Adam said he drives a Mercedes. Is he rich?'

'Chloe, I thought you were in hospital at least!'

'Why ever would you think that?'

'Because I'm your mother.'

'Well, I'm fine so tell me all about this mystery man.'

'His name is David, he's very nice and he's...' I lifted up the curtain and peered out, 'just left.'

'I told him Chloe was all right,' Adam piped up, 'but that you'd probably be on the phone for ages and he said to tell you he'd give you a ring sometime.'

So that's it. 'Sometime' always means never.

In the kitchen as the clock strikes 2

I was finding it difficult to sleep so I've made myself some hot chocolate and I'm waiting for it cool. I can't help wondering if this is all I have to look forward to in the years to come. Bed on my own with just a drink to warm me up. It's not an enticing prospect. I wonder how elderly spinsters manage. With a good book and a cat. That's it, I need a cat. And a bed-jacket. Can you still buy bed-jackets? Probably only from shops for old ladies. I'm not old! Not really. I have many years of life left. On my own.

No, I'm not going to be an old misery. Just because my date with David wasn't a huge success doesn't mean that I am destined for solitary divorcehood.

The hot chocolate must have cooled down now.

I shouldn't have tried to remove my glasses at the same time as picking up my mug. I know that my co-ordination has never been good but I can't help feeling that rate of deterioration has increased since I reached fifty.

And I shouldn't have tried to remove the chocolate stain from the duvet cover. What was a minor splodge is now a major catastrophe.

If I squidge up my eyes, the chocolate splodge looks a bit like Sean Connery, when he was a young and dishy James Bond. He is well over fifty and he enjoys life. I should copy his example of positive living. 'The name's Turner, Alison Turner. Make mine shaken not stirred.' It doesn't sound quite the same when I say it; I'll have to work on the accent.

13th July

I was woken by the phone ringing. It was Bev who wanted all the details. I told her there was nothing to tell, that I had simply enjoyed a pleasant evening out with a friend.

'Yeah, right, Aliss. Come on, give, tell Beverley all about it.'

'Really, Bev, there's nothing to tell.'

'I can see we're going to have to lubricate your mouth to get all the gory info, so Pippa and me'll come round tomorrow night, bring some wine, and you can tell us about it. But no spilling the beans to Pippa before me, right?'

I could see I wasn't going to be allowed to go back to sleep unless I agreed.

14th July

No call today from David. But maybe he's too busy with patients. Maybe he is talking a potential suicide off a roof or helping a victim of abuse come to terms with herself. That is the sort of thing psychiatrists have to do.

Later

Bev & Pippa turned up at seven, Bev with wine and Pippa with little nibbles and dips from M&S. The trouble with little nibbles is their littleness. By 8 o'clock, we were scouring cupboards for suitable dipping items. I found crisps; Pippa peeled and sliced carrots, peppers and celery.

Then I filled them in on the events of Saturday night. It didn't take long.

'Oh,' Bev said, when I'd finished.

'Well,' Pippa said, 'just because he hasn't phoned doesn't mean he's not interested. It's only been two days, and, as you said, Alison, he's probably been busy with patients all day.'

'Huh,' Bev grunted. 'That's a pretty crappy excuse.'

'Well, I did make a bit of a fool of myself, one way and another.'

'But that's you, Alison.'

'Yeah, and from what you've said before, he already knows what you're like, so he should have been prepared.'

The words from magazine article I'd read in the dentist's suddenly come back to me. 'Your best friend always thinks well of you.' I pointed this out to Bev and Pippa.

'Oh, Aliss, we only ever say things because we love you.'

'Yes, Alison, you know it's your interests we have at heart.'

Pippa tried to reassure me by telling me about her first boyfriend. 'He wasn't really a rotter so much as thoughtless. Never thought to tell me that I looked nice or that he'd be late or that he liked being with me. It just didn't occur to him.'

'Huh, one of my boyfriends was a real sonofabitch,' Bev joined in. 'He was seeing three of us at the same time, but we found out and we got our revenge.'

'How?'

'We turned up at his regular pub, debagged him in front of his friends and made belittling comments about his equipment!'

'Bev, that's brilliant,' Pippa said. 'Men are so sensitive about their thing.'

'And goodness knows why! Once you've seen one, you've seen them all.'

They both screeched just as I said, 'Why, how many have you seen?'

'Oh, only...' Pippa stopped and did a mental total, 'three. No, four if you count Ian but that was only once and in the dark so it hardly counted. In more ways than one!'

Bev was still counting and appeared to have run out of fingers.

‘I didn’t realise you were both so experienced,’ I was shocked.

‘I don’t think three, or even four, would be counted as experienced these days,’ Pippa said.

‘Really?’

‘Definitely not, kids today are into the tens before they’ve left uni.’ Seeing my face, Bev added, ‘Course that’s only some of them, not the ones like Chloe who have a steady boyfriend.’

‘Honestly, Alison, there’s no need to look so horrified. Don’t tell us you haven’t seen a few in your time.’

‘Yeah, come on, Aliss, confess, what’s your rating?’

‘One.’

They both stared at me.

‘You’re not serious?’

‘You mean just Brian?’

‘Yes, there’s only ever been Brian.’

‘But, but...’ Bev was stuck for words.

‘I think what Bev’s trying to say, Alison, is that you’re not that much older than us. You grew up in the sixties and seventies. The permissive society had begun. How could you miss it?’

‘I was sixteen when I started going out with Brian, we got engaged before he went to university and then married straight after.’

‘Well,’ Bev said, ‘you’ve got some catching-up to do, girl. Here’s to you!’

By nine thirty, we had agreed that all men are a waste of space (except Roger and Simon) and that I was better off without Smartarse if that was the way he treated women. ‘And, of course,’ Bev added, ‘you only have his word for it that he wasn’t driving when his wife was killed. In fact, you only have his say-so that it was an accident!’ She nodded wisely. It confirmed my belief that Bev is unduly influenced by television.

We spent the rest of evening comparing the relative attributes of George Clooney and Brad Pitt and choosing who to take as a lover. Pippa refused to make a choice as she is a happily married woman, I said either and Bev said she'd have to give both a try before committing herself.

15th July, Tuesday

I received phone call from Women's Education Centre reminding me that I am booked on their assertiveness course starting on Thursday evening. 'We'll see you then,' a deep jolly voice told me.

She caught me out — I wasn't expecting to be reminded. What could I say except, 'Yes, thank you. I'm looking forward to it'?

Still no phone call from Smartarse though. The girls are right: I am definitely well rid of him.

17th July, Thursday

I do not need a man. So what if Smartarse has not called me? I do not need him. I am a strong and courageous woman. I am one with the sisterhood. Together we can defeat the common enemy. Kate says so. Kate has brought up four children alone since her husband ran out on her; she runs her own pottery; she is a local Green Party councillor. Once she was arrested for protesting outside an American base but today she is a school governor. She is vegan and makes all her own clothes. I feel tired just writing about her.

The assertiveness class was cancelled as not enough people turned up. Hermione, she of the deep cheery voice, said it often happens. 'Poor dears, they're just too scared to take charge of their own destiny.' I was about to go home when she grabbed my arm. 'Since you're here, why don't you join Kate's class?'

'What is it?'

'Feminism is a feminine issue.'

I shook my head, but Herms had a tight grip on my arm. 'It's through here, you'll love Kate, she's whizzo fun.'

Kate has salt'n'pepper hair, tied up in a bun. She wears kaftans, no bra and is a stereotypical feminist. Can't you be a feminist and dress well? No, Kate says. That is pandering to the dictates of society. I suspect that Kate is a dinosaur from the days of early feminism. Maybe when she dies she will be mummified and kept in a museum. She should be pleased with that — at least it's not daddification. I am all for 'sisters doing it for themselves' but I won't be going to her class again. I haven't told them that — I just won't go. Or answer my phone for a few days after. Just in case.

19th July, Saturday

David phoned: he has been away at a conference all week! Of course, now I remember him telling me he was going. He apologised for not calling before he left on Sunday but he had last-minute preparations to make.

'That's quite all right; I didn't expect you to phone anyway.'

'I knew you'd understand. Now I know this is short notice but I wondered if you're free this afternoon?'

'Yes.' I bit my tongue. Should I have at least pretended to check my diary?

'Good, because it's such a beautiful day, I was wondering if you might enjoy a picnic?'

'A picnic? That would be lovely.'

'Excellent, I know just the place. Shall I pick you up at one?'

'Marvellous. What would you like me to bring?'

'Just yourself. I have the food planned.'

'Well, let me bring some wine then.'

'No, I have it all under control, I assure you. Just relax and I'll see you at one.'

How lovely. So romantic, to be swept away for a picnic, it's just what happens in books like — I am searching for the right analogy but the best I can come up with is the Famous Five, which isn't quite the image I'm trying to create. I feel I should wear a flowery dress and a large straw sunhat, tied under my chin with ribbon. Unfortunately I have neither but I can wear my light cotton trousers — slacks, yes, I should call them slacks if I'm going on a picnic — and a t-shirt. Oh, it is so long since I've been on a picnic, I can't wait.

Later

I'm feeling slightly woozy, it must have been the afternoon sun that did it. I've had two cups of strong coffee and I'm starting to feel a little better and clear-brained enough now to record the afternoon's events.

David arrived spot on time. I was watching out for him and ran out to join him to save him getting out of the car (or meeting Adam). He drove us a few miles round the coast and then parked at the top of a small lane.

'We have to walk from here, I'm afraid.'

'That's all right, I enjoy nothing more than walking in the sun.'

But as soon as I got out of the car into the dazzling sunshine I was overtaken by a sneezing fit. David looked concerned.

'It's all right,' I said, 'I'm just allergic to sunshine.'

I realised this made me sound like a vampire.

'It's the sun, I mean. Going out in it makes me sneeze.'

Judging by his expression, I was making things worse.

'I mean, only sometimes, unexpectedly. It must be the type of light or height of the sun or something.' I trailed off.

'So why do you cross your legs?'

'What?'

'Each time you sneezed, you crossed your legs.'

'Oh, I see, that's because ...' I stopped.

I could hardly tell a possibly-prospective lover that, thanks to childbirth and not doing follow-up exercises rigorously enough, muscles 'down there' had lost their grip — rather like me — and I was in danger of wetting myself when I sneezed. 'Um, well, oh, yes, it's lucky.'

'Lucky?'

'Or rather it's considered unlucky to sneeze, let's the devil in, and crossing your legs is an, um, antidote type thing.'

'I thought that's why people said, "bless you".'

'Yeeeesss, they do, this is just another old wives' tale. You know, like throwing pepper over your shoulder when you see a cow through glass or ... touching a cat in thunder.'

'I've never heard of either of those sayings.'

'Perhaps they're only said in this locality.'

'I was brought up in this area.'

'Oh.'

'Maybe a picnic isn't the best idea though, if you're — allergic to the sun.'

'I'll be fine, I'll get used to it soon. Honestly, it's not a problem. Tisshhhooo!'

It was a fabulous spot David took me to, sheltered but overlooking the sea, and very quiet. We didn't see another soul on our walk there. The closest thing to a passer-by was a sheep that had lost its flock.

He spread out a large tartan rug that made me wish again that I was wearing a flowery dress. Then, as he started to unpack the picnic basket (a proper wicker one), he said, 'I tried to call you back this morning as I realised I hadn't asked if there was anything in particular that you didn't like to eat.'

'I must have been in the shower, but it's fine, I eat everything. I'm a real piggy,' I laughed.

'Good, I bought some delicious ham from the little delicatessen in the market.'

'Lovely.'

He handed me a plate (china) with a beautiful baguette bursting with ham and lettuce, and two lovely warm tomatoes on the vine.

I took an enormous mouthful of the baguette ... and spluttered.

'What's the matter? Are you all right? Did it go down the wrong way?'

'M-m-m-mustard,' I squeaked. 'It's got mustard on it.'

'Yes, lashings of wholegrain mustard. Oh, no, you don't like it, do you? How stupid of me, I should have thought and brought it separately.'

'No, don't worry, it's fine, I'll just scrape it off.'

I opened the sandwich: everything had a thin covering of mustard on it. 'Well, the tomatoes look lovely,' I said.

I ate both packets of crisps he'd brought as well as most of the fruit and all of the cake. Plus I drank most of the bottle of wine as he was driving.

Apart from the little disaster with the mustard, the afternoon went quite well, I think. I even got away with the sellotape. We were stretched out on the rug when David noticed something. He said, 'You have a piece of sellotape sticking to the bottom of your trousers. Shall I pull it off?'

'No! I mean, thank you but it's fine.' I leaned over and pressed it back into place. I felt some sort of explanation was in order. 'It's holding my hem up.'

'The sellotape is?'

'Yes, I don't like, I mean, I didn't have time to sew it up.'

He nodded. 'That's a good tip; I'll have to remember that.'

The rest of the afternoon passed amicably. I told him about my children, my divorce — I even managed to mention the bimbo without spitting — and my job.

'You probably think I'm awfully inefficient,' I said, 'but I'm not usually. You just seem to have that effect on me.'

'Really? Why would that be?'

I sighed. 'I don't know, I've been trying to work it out. Of course, Bev thinks it's because I fancy you.'

I must have been drunker than I realised. I can remember what I said, but cannot believe I said it.

'And do you?'

'Do I what?'

'Fancy me?'

I giggled. I can distinctly remember giggling. 'I don't know,' I said. 'It's been such a long time since I've been anything but married. I can't tell.'

He leaned forward. 'Would it help if I kissed you?'

'It might do.'

Ooooh, I cannot believe that I did that. Not the kissing — that was okay. More than okay — rather nice. Toe-curlingly nice actually. But how could I be so school-girlish? Although it didn't seem to deter him. He appeared to be enjoying the kissing too. I think. But perhaps he was just being polite. I had better phone Bev and Pippa: this calls for a conference.

Bev and Pippa agree that all the signs are good. He has said he will call me tomorrow to arrange a dinner date, so that must mean that I have not put him off. As long as he does call.

Chapter 8

20th July, Sunday

David phoned this evening. He apologised for not calling earlier but his mother had rung in the morning and asked him to go and sort out her leaky toilet. She pooh-poohed his suggestion that she should call a plumber as it was only a little job and he was perfectly capable of doing it. It took him five hours.

I think his mother would get on well with mine.

We were on the phone for thirty minutes comparing mothers and toilet problems. What a kind man he is. I can't believe I misjudged him so badly. He has a really busy week ahead so he is taking me to Claude's next Saturday evening. The girls were very impressed when I phoned to tell them.

'Claude's?' Pippa said. 'My word, Alison, he knows how to treat a woman. You know it's the only restaurant round here that has Michelin stars, don't you? It costs a fortune just to breathe in there. Roger took me there for our twenty-fifth wedding anniversary.' She sighed. 'It's so romantic, I am pleased for you, Alison.'

'Claude's?' Bev said. 'Aye aye, Aliss, you know what he's after.'

Honestly, Bev doesn't have a romantic bone in her little finger. She is convinced all men only think of one thing.

At least they both agree that I should wear my party dress. Pippa did wonder if I should buy something new but I put my foot down. I can barely afford to eat as I'm still paying off the last credit card bill.

I phoned Pippa again. 'Should I offer to pay my half in the restaurant? Is that what women do these days?'

'You could offer, I suppose, but I'm sure he will be far too much of a gentleman to take you up on it,' Pippa said.

'But what if he did? I can't afford it!'

'I'm sure he won't, he's more likely to be offended at the suggestion.'

'Offended?'

‘Oh, relax, Alison, you’ll have a wonderful time, don’t worry about it.’

Bev was more adamant. ‘Of course you don’t pay. And don’t offer, that’s stupid. He’s a psychiatrist, he can afford it.’

26th July, Saturday

David arrived early. I came downstairs to find him and Adam watching Blind Date and chatting like old friends. I hope Adam was circumspect in what he said, but I doubt it.

The restaurant was stylishly understated with quietly attentive staff. We had a delicious meal, thoroughly deserving of its stars, although, perhaps, less of it than I would have liked. When we were ready to leave, David took my jacket from the waiter and held it out for me. I stood and turned to put it on. Suddenly he grabbed my shoulders, pushed me to one side, scanned the nearby tables, grabbed a jug of water from the nearest and threw the contents over our table. As I turned to look the last flame was disappearing. I was still spluttering, 'What...?' when the other diners started clapping. David took a bow, smiling graciously.

The owner, Claude himself no less, came hurrying over. ‘Are you all right, sir?’

'I'm awfully sorry, I'm afraid my friend was rather careless and didn’t look where she was tossing her napkin. Please allow me to pay for any damage.'

The owner took him by the hand, ‘Good heavens, sir, no, it was thanks to your quick thinking that we don’t have a more serious fire on our hands. There's no question of charging you for anything. On the contrary, please accept my thanks.' He leaned closer into David, ‘I understand women. My wife is also of that certain age. A difficult time for them. We men have to make allowances.'

David laughed, ‘Actually Alison is rather prone to these little mishaps; I don't think she can blame it all on her age.’

Embarrassment kept me quiet until we were outside the restaurant, but then, ‘Just who do you think you are?'

'I beg your pardon?'

'Who do you think you are to talk about me in such a patronising way?'

'I wasn't intending to be patronising, I was just explaining...'

'That your friend was rather careless, I know, I heard you.'

'Well, you have to admit it was rather foolish to throw your napkin on the candle.'

'I didn't throw my napkin on the candle. I threw it on the table. It was just unfortunate that it landed on the candle.'

'Which you could have avoided it if you'd given it any thought.'

'For goodness' sake, if a restaurant has candles on its tables, what can it expect? It should be prepared for fires now and then.'

'So it's the restaurant's fault now, is it?'

'Well, yes, since you mention it. I'm surprised that there aren't regulations to stop restaurants from having exposed candles altogether. In fact, there probably are. There must be no end of fire alarms set off by fires caused by candles.'

'Okay, okay, I'm sorry; shall we just leave it at that?'

'No, I haven't finished yet.'

'Why doesn't that surprise me?'

'Indeed, I would have thought it was all you could expect from a woman of my age.'

'I didn't say anything about your age.'

'No, that's true. You blamed it on me being me.'

'I was trying to placate the owner, who, I think, was being very understanding, considering.'

'Considering? There you go again, blaming me.'

'Well you did throw the napkin on the candle.'

'I didn't throw it on the candle!'

'All right, let's calm down, shall we?'

'Why should I be calm? I am a woman of a certain age. I am expected to be irrational and stroppy.'

'Well, fine, I'll just take you home and we'll forget all about it.'

'No need, I'll get a taxi.'

'Don't be silly, I'll take you.'

'I'd rather get a taxi.'

'Fine, suit yourself!'

And he went. And left me on my own in town in the middle of the night. Although I'm not at all surprised at his behaviour. It's just what I would have expected from him.

Adam was watching a film when I arrived home so I sat with him and shared his popcorn. It reminded me of when he was little boy and we watched Disney cartoons together. Except this film was about man whose son had committed suicide after being dumped by his girlfriend. The man was taking revenge on single women out alone at night by posing as a taxi driver and killing them at random. I was struck by the fact it could have been me.

27th July, Sunday

Lunchtime

David phoned to make sure I had got home safely.

'It's a bit late to be worrying about that, isn't it?'

'I beg your pardon?'

'I could have been raped, murdered and tossed in the canal by now.'

'And which canal would that be?'

'Don't pick hairs, you know what I mean.'

'I didn't phone before because I didn't think that phoning you last night would be a good idea.'

'What do you mean?'

'I suspected that you would still be in full flow. I hoped that you would have calmed down by now.'

'Calmed down!' I was aware that my voice was getting rather high-pitched so I made an extra effort to speak normally. 'I am perfectly calm, thank you.'

'Good, then perhaps I could take you for lunch and we can talk about ...' he hesitated.

'About what? My underlying problems maybe? Is that what you'd like? It must be wonderful being a psychiatrist and being so good at understanding people. And knowing how to deal with them in all situations. By simply walking off and leaving them at the mercy of ... any crazed taxi driver.'

'I can see we're not going to get anywhere today.'

'Not today, not ever.'

'You're probably right. I apologise for, oh, whatever it is you want me to apologise for and I won't bother you again.'

'Thank you!'

I slammed down the phone. I'm better off without him, without a shadow of a doubt. Clever thinks-he-knows-it-all smartarse who doesn't actually know anything. Didn't even know what it was he was supposed to be apologising for and thought a blanket apology would make it all right indeed. And him a psychiatrist of all things. It doesn't offer much hope for his patients. I wonder if I should stick a sign on his door warning them: This man knows nothing. Nothing at all.

I wonder if Bev is in. I'll call her. She will understand.

I phoned Bev thinking she'd be understanding when I told her about the fire in Claude's but it was hard to tell as she couldn't speak for laughing. Every time she tried to say something, she started cackling and had to stop. In the end she said, 'I'll have to call you back, Aliss, I'm peeing my pants here.'

So then I called Pippa who didn't laugh but wasn't much consolation, suggesting that I had over-reacted and that, maybe, I should call David back and invite him to lunch.

'Honestly, Pippa, have you listened to a word I've been saying? The man is a perfect jerk.'

'Well, you have to admit that he did have a point: you do seem to have been a bit excessive in your reaction.'

Excessive in my reaction, my foot. I can do without friends like these.

A little later

Stupid lawn-mower. I'd decided to cut the grass as mowing was a calm repetitive occupation that I could do without getting stressed but the mower broke down in the middle. Now I have half a mowed lawn and a broken mower.

I called to ask if Dad could come and repair my mower but he's playing golf all day. And I wish I hadn't phoned. I had to listen to a long saga involving Mrs Rees down the road, the WI and allegations of cheating in the jam competition. And this was after Mum had told me, in some detail, about the sad demise of Kathleen, who is the sister of 'Auntie' Jean who works in Billie's but only on Wednesday afternoons now and I must remember her because she's the one who used to make me woolly hats when I was a child. I don't remember 'Auntie' Jean but I do remember woolly hats. They were responsible for some of my worst experiences in infant school.

I've opened a bottle of wine. I'm going to sit for a moment to collect myself before starting weeding.

Later again

I have been stung by a wasp! I was minding my own business, enjoying a glass of wine, when the stupid thing attacked me viciously after I tried to carefully flick it away from my glass.

I'm not having a good day and I feel very sorry for myself. I'm going to forget the weeding idea and instead will stretch out and read — while nursing my throbbing arm.

In bed

I love Pippa and Bev; they are the best friends a girl could have. They turned up just after seven, bearing chocolate and wine. And they did not even mention strange sunburns marks on my face, the result of me falling asleep with sunglasses on.

I had a lovely evening with them, infinitely better than the previous night's experience. All are agreed that: a) I am far better off without smartarse; and b) restaurants should not be allowed to have exposed candles on display. Only thing we didn't agree on was how likely it was that one of our local taxi drivers could be a psychopathic killer. Pippa thought it unlikely as they have to go through very rigorous checks (as if that would stop a psychopathic killer!) while Bev thought it was highly likely, especially if the one who pulled out right in front of her on the big roundabout just by Sainsburys last week was anything to go by.

28th July, Monday

Official financial forms were returned in the post from David, Mr Davies, that is. I was surprised to see how attractive his handwriting is. Quite unlike a doctor's, more like an artist's. It's unusual for a man to have stylish writing. It's rather girly, in fact, now I think about it more clearly.

And, no matter what young Mr D thinks, I was not sniffing the forms when he walked in. I had just happened to notice a rather strong, over-powering even, scent of after shave being given off by them.

29th July

Just woken up. I've had such a vivid peculiar dream I feel I should record it.

In it I was the Queen's illegitimate half-sister. She announced this to a packed house in the Albert Hall (the one in London, that is, not the bingo club in town) and told me – I was sitting in the circle – to come on down and take my rightful place at her side. I woke up then but not before I had been mortified by the creases in my dress.

I wonder what it means?

Perhaps I am adopted and I have known it all along in my subconscious. People often remark how un-alike Geoff and I are and he is the image of Dad. Perhaps Mum and Dad tried unsuccessfully for a baby, gave up, adopted me and then mum fell pregnant with Geoff. That often happens, I believe.

But I was born ten months after they married. Surely they would have had to be trying for longer than that before they could adopt. Unless they lied about my birthdate and actually I am younger than I am. Or would that be older?

Lunchtime

A picture of the Queen on the front of Muriel's newspaper reminded me of my dream. I asked Muriel what she thought it might mean – after all, she is a Daily Mail reader and knows about these things.

She listened carefully, had a think then said she thought it suggested a deep sense of insecurity and longing, adding that the creased dress was, in her opinion, very significant. She nodded wisely but wasn't prepared to delve any deeper. 'It can be dangerous for the untrained, you know,' she said.

Mr Davies Senior had come in when we were talking. 'I once went to a garden party at Buckingham Palace,' he said. 'The Queen was in one of those see-through things.'

I shuddered at the vision of the Queen's New Clothes but he held his arm out and waved it up and down like a flag. 'You know,' he said, 'keeps the rain off.'

'I had an umbrella like that,' Muriel said. 'I bought it on the Isle of Wight. Only ninety-nine pence. It had yachts on it.'

'Don't think there were yachts on hers. Could have been though, she's fond of the sea, isn't she?'

'No, that's the Duke, he's the sailor. Were they corgis maybe?'

Just then the phone rang. I answered it with relief; I was feeling out of my depth in the conversation.

'Good morning, Davies and Davies, financial advisers.'

'Good morning, it's David here.'

'Oh. Hello. How may I help you?'

Mr Davies Senior suddenly chortled behind me.

'I hope I'm not calling at an inconvenient time.'

'Not at all, we were just discussing the Queen's plastic umbrella.'

'I see. Er, and how are you, Alison?'

'I'm fine, thank you.'

'Have you...' he hesitated and I could hear him smirking down the phone.

'Have I what? Set any more restaurants on fire? Thank you for reminding me but, strangely enough, it's not the sort of thing I make a habit of doing. But you couldn't resist bringing it up, could you? Couldn't miss the opportunity to point out what an idiot I am. Well, let me tell you...' I paused, desperately trying to think of a stunning put-down, '...Mr David flipping Davies, what were your parents thinking of giving you the same Christian name as surname?!'

I was suddenly aware that the office had gone quiet and that Muriel and Mr D Senior were looking at me with amazement. And worse, Young Mr D had come into reception from his office.

'As I was going to say,' David's voice sounded distinctly cooler, 'before my secretary asked me something and you assumed that you were the only thing I could possibly have on my mind – have you received the forms I completed and returned?'

'The forms? The forms - ah, yes, we did receive them, thank you. I passed them on to Young Mr Davies. He's here now; do you want to speak to him?'

'Yes, please, if he's available and it's all right with you.'

'Yes, of course, one moment, Young Mr Davies is just returning to his office, I'll put you through to him.'

I put down the phone and flopped across my desk.

'Dear me, oh, dear me, um, er,' Mr D Senior said, 'why don't you go and make us all a nice cup of tea? Nothing like a cup of tea when you're feeling a bit, um, off weather. Hetty wouldn't drink anything else.'

Then he disappeared back into his office. As soon as he'd gone I said to Muriel, 'I thought his wife was called Barbara. Don't tell me he's forgotten her name as well!'

'Don't be silly, Alison, Hetty is his spaniel.'

I knew that. He has a photo of her on his desk next to the photo of him with Jimmy Tarbuck at a golf match. My brain was just addled by the confrontation – again – with DD. I wish the stupid man would take his business elsewhere instead of bothering me. Actually, come to think of it, that's what he might be doing now. Telling Young Mr D that, unless I am sacked, he will take his custom elsewhere. That would be typical abuse of power by a man.

A little later

They have been talking for a long time.

Maybe Young Mr D is refusing to sack me, smartarse is trying to convince him he should, and Mr D is standing firm. 'We consider Alison to be a great asset to our firm. The clients all love her.' Way to go, Mr D, you tell him. Wonder if I should go in and put my side of the story?

Then again maybe he is agreeing and listing all the mistakes I've made. The ones he knows about anyway. Maybe it's better to wait in a dignified silence to hear my fate. I will be able to walk out with my head held high.

Then again again, why should I take all the blame? Smartarse is the one who phoned me during office hours and raised the subject of the fire. Oh, no, he didn't — that was me.

But still I am sure there must be some legislation to prevent someone from being sacked because of the pettiness of a client. I will go to my union and ask them ... damn, I'm not in a union. I will join one. Any union worth its name would be glad to take on a fight. They don't get much opportunity these days. I wonder what the office workers union is called.

Muriel thinks it might be Jackdaw. Or that might be the name of the nice young snooker player she was watching on the television last night, she can't be sure.

I can hear Young Mr D laughing loudly. I bet he's being told about my little mishap at Claude's. I don't trust myself to speak. .

Later still

It was nearly lunchtime when Young Mr D came out of his office again. He didn't say anything about firing me but asked if I was going to Eatz would I get him a tuna and mayo baguette. I don't think he would have asked me that if he was planning on sacking me.

Although he might have wanted me out of the way so he could discuss the situation with his father but I'm sure Mr D Senior will be on my side. If he can remember who I am.

Young Mr D didn't say anything when I took his sandwich in (except 'thank you') so perhaps my job is safe. Unless he can't face me and is sending me a letter. I'll have to pay particular notice to the mail I am asked to post. Although, I don't suppose he would ask me to post my own notice. So that means I have to wait until tomorrow's post (or the day after if he uses a second class stamp) to see if I am 'surplus to requirements' – I think that's how they say it.

Evening

By 3.30 I could stand the suspense no longer and I marched into Young Mr D's office and said, 'I'd rather know now, if it's all the same to you.'

'Know what?'

'I don't want to go home and be put through one or two, or even more if the post is delayed, sleepless nights. I would rather you told me to my face. I think I am owed that courtesy at least.'

'What are you talking about, Alison?'

'I think you know.'

'No, I'm afraid you've lost me.'

'I know it's difficult and he put you under enormous pressure, and I understand that you're having to take this action for the good of the firm but I would prefer ...'

'Take what action?'

'Sacking me, of course.'

'Sacking you? Why would I want to do that?'

'You don't have to cover for him; I know what he's like: he can be very persuasive. And I realise that his account is worth a lot to the firm and that you have your good reputation to consider...'

'Alison, please, stop! Let me assure you that I have no intention of sacking you. I am very pleased with what you bring to the firm, and if you think that Mr Davies – I assume it's Mr Davies you're speaking about – has asked me to sack you, again, let me assure you that you are quite wrong,'

He went on to say that I am irreplaceable. 'There's no-one quite like you, Alison.'

Chapter 9

1st August, Friday

Reasons for getting a man about the house:

sex;

a man is bigger than a hot water bottle;

men tend to be good at stripping chicken carcasses, and don't mind getting their fingers greasy;

spiders - Adam is off to university soon;

there's always a bit on your back you can't reach to scratch yourself;

fuses. Before he left Brian showed me where the fusebox was. I'm not sure why but he seemed to think it was important that I knew;

you can talk about him to your friends.

Reasons for not getting a man about the house:

sex;

they fart and burp;

they insist on wearing matching socks (although perhaps that was just Brian) and grumble if there are no boxers in their pants drawer (ditto remark about Brian).

So, discounting sex, that comes out as six to two in favour of a man about the house. The 'ayes' have it. I must take the search more seriously, especially with Adam's pending departure.

5th August, Tuesday

I didn't have the best of days in work today. It all began with the key.

Young Mr Davies came bustling out of his office.

'Aliss, where's the key?'

My computer had just accused me of performing an illegal action and was threatening to close me down when Young Mr D asked me this so I was slightly distracted.

'What key?'

'The key to the filing cabinet.'

'Which filing cabinet?'

'There's only one that's ever kept locked.'

'Oh, that one.'

'Well?'

'Well what?' Computer screen had gone blank now.

'Where's the key?' Young Mr D yelled.

'Ummm, I don't know,' I jumped at his tone.

'I'd better go and tell Mr Davies that I'll phone him back when you've found the key. Please look for it now!' He stamped back into his office and slammed the door. I should have guessed it would be Smartarse on the phone making poor Young Mr D so nervous. He's normally very mild-tempered and never gets red in the face. At least not in work.

Once he'd gone it didn't take me long to locate the key it's just that I can't think when I have someone breathing down my neck. I knew the key had to be somewhere safe — I'm not the sort of idiot who leaves keys lying around just anywhere — it was simply that the actual location that escaped me at that precise moment.

Once I'd remembered when I'd last used the key it was a simple matter of retracing my footsteps.

And, when you think about it, a fridge is a good place to keep a key. What person in their right mind is going to look in there for a key?

It turned out to be a good thing that I happened to look in the fridge as I noticed we'd run out of milk. I was surprised as I had taken a two-pint carton in the day before and we can't have used all that. Unless Mr Davies Senior has started feeding the seagulls again.

Then it was the stapler that took it into its head to throw a staple in the works. I've been using the same stapler in the office for five years so I've no idea why, today, I put staples in upside down causing it to stop working completely, making the urgent collating and stapling job impossible.

It did nothing to improve my standing with Young Mr Davies.

The one bright spot in my day was the arrival of the window cleaner. He looks as though he works out, but maybe it's the window-cleaning that gives him his rather stunning physique. Perhaps if I cleaned my windows more often it would improve my shape. Or I could just get him to come and do it while I sit in the garden and relax. I could wear that rather flattering t-shirt with the v-neck, and could offer him a long drink to cool him down. He'd probably be wearing the same vest he was wearing today, with his shoulders bulging out, all shiny. He has very strong shoulders. Not obscenely strong and bulging, like those misshapen weight-lifters, just nicely so. It must be carrying his buckets that does it.

I noticed he wasn't wearing a wedding ring and I'm convinced his smile was saying a bit more than 'thank you', when I paid him. He's not that much younger than me and it's not unknown for women to date younger men.

Later

I've just re-read the previous paragraph. It would only take a dirty mac to complete my transformation into lecherous old woman. On reflection it's probably wiser if I clean my own windows.

7th August

I went to the pub with Pippa and Bev. The sole topic of conversation for the evening was 'How to find a new man for Aliss'.

Bev was grinning ecstatically and could hardly wait for us to get our bottle of wine and settle in the corner before bursting out with, 'I have a plan.'

Pippa and I looked at each other nervously. Bev's great plans usually involve something illicit, illegal or fattening.

'Okay, Bev,' Pippa said cautiously, 'tell us more.'

Bev leaned forward, said, 'Internet dating,' and then sat back, folding her arms across her chest, waiting for the plaudits. 'What do you think of that? Great idea, yeah?'

'Hmm,' Pippa said. She thought for a moment and then carried on, 'You might have something here, Bev.'

Bev looked as pleased as a dog with a wet nose. 'See? What did I tell you? This will be the answer to all Aliss's problems.'

I suspect I have rather more problems than she realises but I decided to keep quiet until Pippa had pronounced fuller judgement. 'I don't know about all Alison's problems, but it certainly could be a way for her to meet a new man.'

'And she doesn't have to restrict herself to one. That's the beauty of it, she can flirt with dozens, choose which ones to meet up with and the rest need never know.'

'Hmm,' Pippa seemed surprisingly taken with the idea.

'Hang on a minute,' I said, 'you seem to have forgotten something important.'

They both looked puzzled. I pointed out that me not having a computer might be a flaw in this great plan. But Bev had anticipated this. 'Adam has one, doesn't he?'

'Yes, but that would involve me going into his bedroom.'

'So?'

'I don't go there if I can avoid it, burrrh.'

'You must go in sometimes to clean,' Pippa said.

I didn't want to tell her that I don't so smiled enigmatically.

'You don't, do you? Urgh, Alison, how can you live knowing the germs that are festering in that room?'

'I like to work on the Turner Principle,' I said.

'The what?'

'The Turner Principle, as discovered by Alison Turner, Doctor of Creative Houseworking. The principle that says that mould that grows on dirty plates must surely contain enough penicillin to kill 99% of household bugs.'

They looked at me for a moment then Bev laughed and Pippa tutted.

'Anyway,' I said, 'Adam will be off to uni soon and will be taking his computer with him.'

'That's all right,' Bev said. 'Don't worry, Pippa, I expected some negativity from our victim and I have a back-up plan.' She paused to let the impact of her words sink in.

'A back-up plan?' Pippa said.

'Your victim?' I said.

'I didn't mean victim, it just slipped out. I meant, oh, you know what I meant. Anyway, to my back-up plan: there's always the library.'

'The last time I went to the library,' I said, 'it was full of old men reading The Sun and greasy-haired students catching up on sleep. I don't think either of these groups is likely to proffer much hope in way of a new man.'

'No, you idiot, I mean they have internet access there. And it's free.'

I'm to be taken to the library on Saturday and taught to surf. I just hope it's easier than skating; I broke my ankle doing that.

8th August

Young Mr D pointed out that my leave year ends on 31st August, and that, as I took so little leave in the previous year, I am ending this year with more leave left than I should have started it with.

'Don't you think it is time you took a holiday, Aliss?'

I was about to say, 'no-one to go with', but thought better of it. I don't want to appear like Alison No-Mates. I could go on my own, I suppose, but the idea doesn't particularly appeal. I suppose I will just take time off and spend it in garden, if the weather's nice, or in the house, if not. There's plenty to do in both; I've been promising myself that I will redecorate the bedroom ever since Brian left.

I told Young Mr D I would take the last two weeks in August. Adam gets his results on the 14th so there will be lots to do after that getting him ready for university. And it will be good to spend some quality time with him before he goes. Maybe we could take some day trips together to Bath or Weston-super-mare. I've never been to Weston but it has a certain old-fashioned seasidey sort of sound about it.

Later

It turns out that Adam is going camping in Newquay with his friends straight after he gets his results.

'What about preparing for university?'

'What about it? What's to do?'

'Well, you'll need ... stuff.'

'You'll be sorting that out, won't you?'

'I thought we could do it together.'

'I've already said I'll go to Newquay. There's a crowd of us going, a final holiday together before we all go our separate ways.'

'That's nice.'

'We're only going for a couple of weeks anyway. I can sort out my stuff when I get back in September.'

That's fine. It's good for him to go away with his friends. It's nice that he has friends he can go away with. I might as well look on Teletext, see what last minute bargains I can find.

I found plenty of bargain flights to Boston, family deals in Majorca, and weekend breaks in Prague, but nothing saying, 'Miserable? Depressed? Lonely? Come to us for the holiday of a lifetime with other sad lonely people.'

After a phone call

It's settled: I'm going to Tenby with Mum and Dad for a week. Mum phoned and when she asked if I were busy I foolishly said, no, I was only looking for a holiday. I'd forgotten that they always go to their caravan for the last week of August.

Still, I haven't been to Tenby for many years and it will be a break. In fact, it will be nice to be looked after for a change.

9th August, Saturday

Bev accompanied me to the library first thing. She got me installed on a computer, showed me what to do, but then had to rush off and leave me. It was a relief when she went; I was able to have a good look round. I haven't been in the library for a long time and how things have changed. It's all done by magic machines now, with not a date-stamp in sight.

I always fancied being a librarian. As a child, I spent hours thumping my books, practising the wrist action. Then as I got older, the books I read always featured librarians who were encouraged by the handsome hero, who librarian thought was in love with glamorous but bitchy rich girl, to let down their hair and take off their glasses, and 'My word, Miss Jones, but you're beautiful.'

I was thinking this when a hair-bunned, bespectacled lady peered over my shoulder.

'Everything all right?'

'Yes, thank you, fine,' I said, trying to lean forward to conceal the screen. The librarian looked around furtively, crouched down and whispered, 'I find "Dating-4-Pros" a good site. All professional people, like ourselves.' She managed to resist winking before she slunk off.

So I tried Dating-4-Pros. Like most of the others it required me to register before letting me beyond its golden portals. I'm rather anxious about taking such a step. If I give them my details, will they ever leave me alone again? Or will they send me letters by post with Dating-4-Pros on the outside for the postman to see and laugh at?

I decided not to commit myself but, so that the visit to library wasn't a complete waste of time, I took out two books from the Highly Recommended stand: one called 'Zing Into Your Life'; the other called 'Meditation for Beginners.' I feel they are far more likely to be of use to me than internet dating.

Tea time

When Bev phoned to find out how I'd got on I told her I had decided against it. I expected her to object strenuously but she just said, 'We'll see.'

I've already flipped through 'Zing'. It includes lots of handy exercises to 'build your self-esteem, restore your confidence, and make you the person you know you ought to be.' This will be far more useful than spending time on the computer trying to find a man. I think I'll do an exercise now.

Later

No wonder my marriage collapsed: I am no use to anyone. It's true; I am a failure. I can see it all clearly now having done the exercise in book. I had to go through a list of statements and tick the ones that applied to me. They all said things like, 'I am capable', and 'I am well-organised.' Not one said, 'Well, I tried hard'. Trying obviously is not enough. Perhaps I should have it on my gravestone.

Here lies Alison Turner.
She tried her best.
Unfortunately it wasn't good enough.

I shall return this book to the library on Monday and ask the librarian if they have a list of non-recommended books. For now I'll see what the other book is like. I'm sure that relaxation and meditation will do me more good anyway.

Much later

The relaxation technique described in the book is very effective: I've only just woken up and it's nearly midnight. I didn't manage to do any meditating but I'm sure that will come - if I can stay awake long enough.

After midnight

That's the problem with dozing in the evening: it makes it impossible to sleep properly afterwards. I'll use the time sensibly and try meditating.

Finding it hard to concentrate on emptying my mind. Odd as normally it comes quite naturally to me. Thoughts keep crowding in like: how tired I am, wonder what's on television now; what's that creaky noise; wonder if Adam's eaten all the crisps as well as all the biscuits; why do they call them 'Nice' biscuits; and how am I supposed to concentrate when I'm so hungry?

Still awake at 1 am

Definitely can't sleep now, not with crisp crumbs under me. Will move over to Brian's side.

Everything looks different from over here. Crisp bits have followed me though. How is it possible for one small packet of crisps to make such a mess? I'll have to get up and shake the duvet and wipe the sheet. I'm never going to get any sleep tonight.

10th August, Sunday

Bev and Pippa were here all afternoon. Both appear to have gone deaf. Either that or they are ignoring me when I say I am not going to join a dating site.

They insist I need a photo of me to register and they're ignoring my concerns: 'I'm not sure I want my face to be seen by millions, or tens, of men on a dating site. There could be perverts out there.'

'Don't be stupid, Aliss, it'll be fine as long as you're careful,' Bev said.

'Yes,' Pippa said, 'and we'll be backing you up all the way.'

Out of gratitude to them for their friendship, I dug some photos out of the memory chest.

'Oh my gosh, Aliss, don't you look young there?'

'Were you really that slim?'

'I suppose curly perms were fashionable then.'

'Where did you get that skirt?'

When I could take no more, we all sat back and heaved a collective sigh.

'I think this is best,' I said, holding up my favourite photo.

'They do have laws about false misrepresentation even on the internet, you know, Aliss.'

'What do you mean false representation? It is me.'

'Yes, twenty years ago. It's hardly a true likeness now.'

'I think it's quite nice.'

'Precisely.'

'Don't worry, Alison,' Pippa intervened, 'we anticipated this.'

'Yeah, I've brought Simon's digital camera with me. These cameras are brilliant: we should be able to get a really flattering shot of you.'

After two hours of turning this way and that, smiling, pouting, ('pout I said not snarl') and posing to their satisfaction, I was finally shown the result of their labour. I can put aside my concerns about my safety: there can't be too many serial killers out there with a Dot Cotton fetish.

'I look terrible!'

'I think it's rather good.'

'Me too. At least it hides your double chin.'

'And your wrinkles.'

I'm seriously considering finding myself some new friends. These are definitely past their use-by date.

13th August, Wednesday

Adam's results are out tomorrow. I offered to go into work late so I could take him in to school to pick them up, but he said it was okay, he and Sophie were going in together in her car.

He needs 2Bs and a C for Exeter, his first choice. He is perfectly capable of getting that but I wish he had shown slightly more earnestness in his revision.

14th August, Thursday

10.00 am

Phoned home. Couldn't get a reply. I assume Adam is still in school, probably comparing results with friends, and congratulating/commiserating as appropriate.

11.00 am

Phoned home again. Still no reply. I thought he would have phoned me by now. It is taking him a long time. Maybe there has been a delay in posting the results.

11.30 am

I don't have his mobile number else I could have called that. I hope he hasn't done disastrously and is sitting in a corner somewhere, very depressed. His insurance choice was 1B and 2Cs. I'm sure he would have managed that. And even if he didn't there's still clearing. He does not have to give up his ambitions because of a little hiccup.

I hope he knows that we will love him whatever results he gets. I should have reminded him of that before. I hope he isn't feeling that he's let us down. The strain of exams is very hard, even the brightest crack and fail under pressure sometimes.

I'm getting very worried about his welfare now. I wonder if I should phone the school?

11.45 am

I don't think it was necessary for the secretary to be so abrupt. I know she is busy, I know she has lots of people to see to, but that doesn't mean she has to be rude. I am a parent, after all. If I didn't send my son to her school, then she wouldn't have a job. At least she wouldn't, if no-one sent their children to her school, which would serve her right. There was no need for her to imply that I was being an over-pushy parent. I'm simply concerned about my son's well-being, which she should be too. After all, it will not look good for the school if he has thrown himself off a cliff because of high expectations.

I'll give it thirty more minutes before I ... do anything.

11.55 am

I phoned home again. Adam answered this time.

'Well?' I asked.

'Well what?' he yawned

'How did you get on?'

'Eh?'

'Your results - how did you get on?'

'Oh, I haven't got my results yet. Give us a chance, Mum, I only just got up.'

'You haven't been to school yet?'

'That's what I just said. Soph's picking me up at one. We decided to wait until the crowds had gone.'

'I sighed. 'Please phone me as soon as you get them then, okay?'

'Yeah, whatever.'

1.30 pm

No phone call yet.

1.45 pm

If Sophie picked him up at 1, they would reach school for quarter past, get their results by half past and he should have phoned me BY NOW!!!!

2.05 pm

He got 3Bs!! I always knew my son was cleverer than he appears. I'm so pleased for him. I phoned Pippa. Luke got 2As and a B (she hid her disappointment over the B well). What clever children we have!

Muriel was as pleased as could be - she has always had a soft spot for Adam. Young Mr D said to give Adam his congratulations and now did I think there was any chance of me being able to concentrate enough to reprint the letter I did this morning.

'Mr Banstead is an amiable old gentleman,' he said, 'but, unfortunately the same can't be said for his wife. She has been known to write to the ombudsman for less serious mistakes.'

I had addressed the letter to Mr & Mrs Bumstead

16th August, Saturday

I'm now a fully registered member of Dating-4-Pros, People-like-u, Meeting-me-meeting-u, and Here4U. I was about to sign up with Boys2Men when Bev came back with the coffee and pointed out that it was a gay site. Which was a shame as they were by far the most attractive bunch.

We flicked through the options. There are an awful lot of available men out there. Awful being the appropriate word. We started by agreeing to avoid all those without photos. (And we couldn't help wondering whether some of those with photos had made a wise decision.)

Then we sorted them into those who lived less than thirty miles away, and were between forty-five and fifty-five.

'Forty-five? Are you sure, Bev? Isn't that a bit young?'

'At your age, five years is neither here nor there, it's a mere pinprick.' She sniggered, 'Although I hope it won't be!'

Then we got rid of those with unkempt beards, and those who were bald on top but long-haired at the back, smokers, those who listed climbing and orienteering as hobbies, those who called themselves strict fundamentalists (of any religion), Elton John fans and one man who said he was looking for a woman who could make apple pie like his mam.

Not that the ones who were left were much better. I'd like to borrow the mirror that some of them, who described themselves as attractive, must be using. Add to that the fact that most of them were either overweight or looked as though they might have criminal tendencies, and it wasn't an appetising choice.

'You can see why they don't have a woman,' I said.

'Honestly, Aliss, you are so hard to please.'

'It's okay for you; you've got a nice-looking kind man to go home to.'

Bev screwed up her nose. 'Have you seen Simon recently? He might have been good-looking once upon a time but he's gone downhill now.'

'Well, haven't we all?'

'Huh, speak for yourself. Now what's wrong with Christopher here?'

I looked at his profile.

Christopher, 52, single, 3+ children.

'How can you have three plus children? Surely you know how many you have? Unless he's lost count. Probably a drunk. Or a serial lecher. No, not interested in him.'

'Okay,' Bev sighed, 'what about Malcolm? Fifty-one, single, one child.'

'Does he mean single or does he mean divorced or widowed? He will have a lot of baggage if he's one of the latter, and if he's actually single, why is he? How has he got to this age and never married? What's wrong with him?'

And the worst ones were the ones who used those silly little face things to show how you're meant to respond to the information they're giving you. 'I've been alone now for a while (sad face) but I'm ready (eager face) to start having fun (smiley face) with the right lady (coy face).' Bah!

I think Bev was getting a bit fed-up with me. I spotted her talking to the librarian who was nodding, and then they both looked over at me and shook their heads.

By 12.30 I was ready to give up and go home, or better still, to Costa Coffee: I felt I deserved a blueberry muffin after my morning.

'A stud muffin is what you *need* though,' Bev said.

'You really shouldn't give up so easily,' agreed Daphne (I wonder if her parents knew she was going to be a librarian when they named her). 'Honestly, there are some lovely men out there, you just have to persevere.'

'You've met Mr Right through a website, have you?' I asked.

'Well, no, not yet, I have been rather unfortunate in my choices. The last one was only interested in one thing.'

'Tut, typical,' Bev said.

'Well, not really, there can't be that many men who have a passion for rhubarb.'

Bev said she wasn't letting me go anywhere until I had made email contact with at least one man. 'Daphne has keys. She will lock us in if she has to.'

Daphne nodded.

I could see they were serious.

'Okay, come on, let's look again.'

We finally narrowed it down to Richard (solicitor, 55) and Barry (teacher, 47). Daphne thought I should go for Richard while Bev favoured Barry. 'He's a PE teacher – bound to be a bit fit, you know what I mean?' I've tried to get it into Bev's head that I am not looking for a quickie (as she calls it) but a lasting relationship with a good, honest, reliable, fun, kind, intelligent, romantic, compassionate man. When I said that, she and Daphne looked at each other and shook their heads, again, sadly this time. 'You're gonna be disappointed, girl.'

'I have come to the conclusion that you can have all of these qualities in men,' Daphne said, 'but no more than one, or two at the very most, in any individual man.'

'Brian had most of those qualities.'

'Oh, yeah, remind me — was this the Brian who cheated on you with a twenty-eight-year-old?'

I'm not sure that I want to rejoin such a cynical world. I was happy with my life, my marriage, my little island of contentment. I was about to stand up for my ideals when my stomach rumbled loudly and Daphne suggested we toss a coin.

Barry won. Bev and Daphne wrote him a very nice email from me and now all I have to do is wait for his response.

'It's a bummer you not having a computer,' Bev said. 'It means we'll have to wait until next Saturday for his reply.'

'I can't come in then, I'll be on my way to Tenby.'

'Oh, shoot. Oh, but you're on holiday now, aren't you? That's brilliant; you can come in each day and check progress. Daphne, you'll be able to help Aliss if she gets stuck, won't you?' Bev shared a raised eyebrows look of exasperation with Daphne.

'Oh, yes, I'll be thrilled to help; it's so exciting, isn't it?'

I'm glad someone is excited.

Chapter 10

19th August, Tuesday

In the garden, on sunlounger

This is the way life should be— stretched out in the warm sunshine with my book and a drink, mmm. I can almost forget the real world, and especially the world of internet dating.

Barry seems keen, rather too keen, in my opinion. Daphne says that's a good thing but I am not convinced. I suspect he has not had a woman for a long time. He is very eager to meet up, he says. He believes you cannot get to know a person, not really know them, by email. You need face to face contact for that. And as we live so close it seems more logical as well. I wrote back saying I thought email was fine for starters.

Later

Daphne is a traitor! She told Bev that Barry wanted to meet me and that I refused. Bev is very cross with me. I am very cross with Daphne.

Later still

Now I am very cross with everyone. Bev told Pippa about Barry and Pippa phoned me to say I must be brave and that I will never get a man if I am a wimp. It is not wimpish to not want to rush into a relationship with a man who uses a computer to meet people. It can't be entirely normal.

Pippa and Bev are taking it in turns to harangue me but I will not be forced into doing something I do not want to do.

20th August, Wednesday

I'm going to town to buy the essentials Adam will need for university. I must remember to get: extra boxers (5 pairs enough?), socks (7 pairs?), duvet cover and sheet. Think that is all he needs.

After shopping

I've bought: boxers (21 pairs to keep him going as I fear trips to the launderette might be few and far between), socks (ditto), new duvet, 2 duvet covers (so he will have no excuse for not changing it), 2 sheets and pillowcases (ditto), 2 bath towels, 2 hand towels, slippers (he never wears them at home but will be different in lodgings), pyjamas (ditto), new toothbrush, bottle opener, tin opener, and recipe book (Cheap'n'Tasty - meals for hungry students). I can get the rest like food, toothpaste and washing-up liquid closer to date. Or I might suggest that Brian provides some of it; Adam is his son too after all.

21st August

Pippa took me to the library today. She wanted to see Barry's photo.

'He has a nice face,' she said. 'Trustworthy. Hmm, yes, he'll do to practise on.'

'Practise on?'

'You've got to kiss a lot of frogs, you know.'

Daphne nodded knowingly.

'Do I have to? Couldn't I just wait for my prince?'

'You could be waiting for ever,' Daphne sighed.

'But he's so keen,' I said. 'He must be desperate.'

'But that's good,' Pippa said. 'It means he won't be too fussy.'

Between the three of us, we composed an email agreeing that I would meet up with him when I got back from holiday. Pippa suggested the name of a pub, which Barry knew, so it's all set up. A week in Tenby followed by a date. Who said I should get a life?

25th August, Bank Holiday Monday

Mum & Dad's caravan in Tenby

Already the days are blurring into each other.

Dad has never been able to get out of the habit of getting up at 7 o'clock. I hear him whispering every morning. 'Eunice, are you awake? Do you want a cup of tea?'

'Of course I'm awake. I've been awake for hours; you know I can’t sleep these days.'

'You were snoring five minutes ago.'

'Honestly, Bill, if you can't tell the difference between snoring and breathing deeply, I hope I never have to rely on you in a crisis. Now stop rabbiting and go and put the kettle on.'

After breakfast, Dad reads the newspaper, Mum watches television and I shower. Then we all get in the car ('Bill, is that door shut properly? Did you lock the caravan? Have you got the key? Alison, put your seat belt on.')

While they’re staying at the caravan, Mum and Dad normally spend their time sitting in the sun, or more often, in the caravan in the rain (this is west Wales after all) but they feel obliged to take me down memory lane. Today we ended up in one of the parks.

'Aaaah,' Mum said, smiling sentimentally as we walked round it, 'that's where you dropped Geoffrey on his head.'

'Are you sure, Mum?'

'Oh, yes, this bit of town hasn't changed at all in forty years.'

'No, I meant, are you sure it wasn't the other way round? Geoffrey dropping me? Only it seems he's the one who's made a success of his life and I'm the failure.'

They both looked at me.

'Oh, Aliss, love,' Dad said, 'how could you ever think you're a failure? Your Mum and I are very proud of you. Isn't that right, Eunice?'

'Of course it is. Honestly, Alison, what nonsense you do talk. You're getting as bad as your father. Now look, there's that thingummy - you used to love to go on that, do you remember?'

Later, when Mum was getting tea and Dad and I were sitting in deck-chairs outside the caravan, he said, 'Why do you think you're a failure, love?'

'Oh, don't worry, Dad, I was just being silly.'

'No, come on, tell your old Dad. I might not be your mother - although maybe that's a good thing - but I'd like to think you can still talk to me.'

‘Okay, I'm fifty, divorced and working in a silly little office job, not really much of an achievement, is it?'

'What about Adam and Chloe? Don't you think raising two fine caring intelligent children is an achievement? You should be proud of them.'

'Oh, I am, Dad.'

'Seems to me that regarding yourself as a failure is putting them down too. They are who they are because of you and Brian.'

I must have flinched because Dad said, 'You can't deny the part he's played, but a Dad's role is never as influencing as a mother's. I know that. And I don't mind, that's the way it should be. If men were solely responsible for bringing up children, the world would be in an even sorrier state. And then there's your Mum and Great Aunt Millie. Your Mum relies on you more than she realises, you know. You're never too busy to find time to help them.'

'But too busy to clean my cupboards.'

'I'd be ashamed to call you my daughter if cupboards were your highest priority.'

I laughed, 'Have you looked inside Trisha's cupboards? I bet they're sparkling.'

'Trisha has a tidy house and an empty mind that she fills with bleach and polish.'

'That's very perceptive of you, Dad.'

'You'd be surprised what goes on in this old head of mine.'

'It's not that old. You've got plenty of thinking to do yet.'

Just then Mum called out, 'Come on in, tea's on the table, and you'll both need to wash your hands. And, Bill, you can open this wine. It's from the site shop, it was all they had but I thought you'd like it, Alison. It's Italian, they didn't have any Australian, but it's all the same, isn't it? It's red, I thought it would go down well with ham and salad. Or should I have got white, but you prefer red, don't you, Alison? Although it's all the same to me I'm sure. Hurry up both of you, before your tea goes cold.'

I got up and kissed Dad. He took my hand and said, 'And do you know something else, Aliss? Even if you'd never had the children, if you'd spent your life doing nothing but housework and just being you, your Mum and I would still love you and still be proud of you. You're a grand girl and I wouldn't want anyone else for a daughter.'

I had sudden urge to climb on his lap, as I did as a child, and be cuddled.

Later on we went down to the clubhouse where Matt Dimple and the Dimplettes were playing. Watching Mum and Dad quickstep round the dance floor just like they always did, I got quite sentimental for the old days, when the most difficult decision I had to make was whether to have strawberry or pineapple Mivvi.

When they came back to our table, and Dad had got his second wind, he said, 'Come on, Aliss, your turn.'

'Oh, no, Dad, you can't have forgotten that I can't dance?'

'We'll do what we used to do when you were little then, do you remember?'

Of course I remembered.

'Don't be silly, Bill, Alison will break your feet if she stands on them.'

'Thanks, Mum.'

'Oh you know what I mean.'

I did. I weighed slightly more — probably double at least — than I did when I used to stand on Dad's feet to be carried round the dance floor.

'Well, if you don't want to dance with an old man I'll understand,' he shrugged and went to sit down.

I laughed, 'Okay, but on your own feet be it, mind!'

We got to the end of the song and I had only stood on his toes four, or maybe six, times. It was a waltz and I knew the basics at least. The odd seconds when I allowed myself to go with the music and be led by Dad were wonderful. I felt like Ginger Rogers being accompanied by Fred Astaire.

Back in the caravan Mum got out the playing cards. 'Right, who's for rummy?' It was just like the old days, except this time Dad didn't let me win.

26th August, Tuesday

Another day doing the rounds of our old holiday haunts, Mum with a tale to relate about each one, then the evening in the site clubhouse.

We'd been there a while when Dad stood up. 'Right, I'll get us another drink, shall I?'

'No, let Alison get them,' Mum tugged at his sleeve.

'Yes, I'll get them, Dad.'

'Don't be silly, love, I'll get them. Another red wine, is it?'

'No, Bill, Alison will get them.' Mum spoke firmly.

'I don't know what your mother's playing at, love, but I recognise a "significant look" when I see one, so I'll have a half, please.'

'Okay, Dad,' I laughed, 'and you, Mum, another snowball?'

I got the drinks and took them back to the table.

'That was quick,' Mum sounded disappointed.

'There was no-one else at the bar.'

'Precisely.'

We looked at Mum. 'I thought you would have taken the opportunity to chat with Karl,' she said.

'Karl?'

'The barman.'

Dad and I turned to look at Karl, a 6' 3" tanned god with sun-streaked blonde hair.

'I think he'd have better things to do than chat to me,' I said.

'He's Australian, you know, working over here for the summer. He's off to Ireland in September. Wants to travel all over Europe before he goes back to Australia and settles down.'

Dad's glass was half-way to his lips. 'You seem to know a lot about him.'

'He was by the pool yesterday and we were chatting. I told him about you, Alison. He's single, you know.'

All became clear. Dad and I burst out laughing.

'Mum, he's half my age - I could be his mother. It would be like going out with one of Adam's friends.'

'Don't be silly, he's twenty-seven. And, anyway, I'm not asking you to marry him. I just thought you could, well, practise on him.'

'Practise what, Mum?'

'Your, um,' Mum coughed, 'chat-up skills.'

'I'm sure, Eunice, that when the time is right, Alison will have no difficulty with her chat-up skills, as you put it. In fact, she won't need them as she'll be the one being chatted up.'

'I'm only trying to be helpful. She hasn't had a lot of practice and it's been a while now since Brian and there's been no-one else on the scene.'

I'd kept quiet up till now about David but I felt my reputation needed some boosting.

'Actually, Mum, there has.'

'Ooh, Alison, you never said. What's his name? What does he do? When are we going to meet him? You could bring him round for dinner one night, I'll do my roast, men like that. And my sherry trifle. Why didn't you tell us? What about the weekend after we get home? No, Deirdre and Jack are coming round then, but it doesn't have to be a weekend, what about Wednesday? That'll give your father time to get a haircut.'

'Mum, slow down,' I sighed. This was precisely why I hadn't mentioned David to her before. I took a deep breath. 'There was a man but he didn't last long.'

'Why not? What did you do?'

'Why do you assume it was my fault?'

'Your Mum didn't mean it like that, did you, Eunice? It just came out wrong. But you'd better tell her all about it now or we'll never hear the end of it.'

Mum huh-ed.

'I realised I would be better off without him, that's all.'

'Why?'

'Well, he wasn't very understanding when I set fire to the tablecloth in Claude's.'

'In Claude's! You set fire to a tablecloth in Claude's?! Oh, Alison, how could you? That is just like you.'

'I'm sure she didn't do it deliberately, did you, Aliss?'

'No, of course not, it was an accident.'

'Accident or not, you're never going to keep a man if you do that sort of thing. And in Claude's of all places.'

Mum put her head between her hands as another thought hit her. 'What will the girls say?'

'Pippa and Bev were very supportive of me, as it happens, Mum.'

'I don't mean them.' Mum brushed them away with her hand. 'I mean, Audrey and Madge, oh, and Julia, dear Julia, she's ladies' president, you know. At the golf club. You know your father's standing for the committee this year...'

'No, I'm not.'

'He'll never get elected if they know we have a daughter who sets fire to restaurants. In fact, Audrey was rather short with me last time I saw her now I come to think of it - don't tell me they all know? Why do I have to be the last to know everything?'

'I can't imagine how they would have found out and, anyway, it was back in July. If they haven't heard about it by now, then it's not likely that they ever will. But thank you for your support, Mum.'

'Now, you know she means well, love, it's just her way of saying it.'

'We just want to see you happy again, Alison.'

'I am happy, Mum, perfectly happy. I'm enjoying my independence and freedom. I don't want to rush into anything and I certainly don't need a man.'

When Mum had calmed down a bit, I told her, because she plied me with questions, about David.

'Oh, he's sounds ideal, Alison.'

I could see she was imagining what a coup it would be for her to introduce her son-in-law, the psychiatrist, down at the golf club.

'That's as maybe, Mum, but it's over.' I stressed the last word and I was surprised to feel a strange pain in my chest as I did so.

But it's true, what I told my parents: I am enjoying my independence. First time I have had to do things for myself since, well, since forever, really. I had my parents and then Brian taking charge. It's a challenge to look for strengths that I didn't know I had. And I'm sure I'll find some soon.

Although I don't think that I want to be alone for ever.

I'm sure that I don't.

Karl is rather a dish. And he did give me a very special — intimate even — smile when I went to the bar. Perhaps he prefers older women. I could be Mrs Robinson to his Dustin Hoffman, giving him lessons in love. Then again, with my experience – or lack of – perhaps he could give me lessons. Although don't think I can face him again now I know that Mum has told him my story. In fact, thinking about it, the smile he gave me was knowing rather than intimate. A sort of 'Poor you, having a life like yours and a mother like that.'

I can hear her now. 'That's my daughter, Alison, over there. She looks quite young for her age, don't you think? Well, she does in a good light, In fact, she looks better in the dark, now I come to think of it. But she's divorced, you know. Husband left her for a younger woman. She let herself go, you know, but she's not bad for a woman of her age. She's been on her own ever since he left. That's why Bill and I brought her here with us, get her away from things, meet some new people, make some new friends. Have you got a girlfriend, Karl?'

27th August, Wednesday

Sitting on the sea front alone

I do love Mum and Dad but it is good to get away on my own for a bit. This morning when Mum said, 'Right, where shall we go today?' I heard Dad sigh quietly.

'Actually, Mum,' I said, 'I'd quite like to go for a walk into town, post some cards, buy some souvenirs for the children. There's no need for you to come with me. You stay here and put your feet up.'

'Don't be silly, we can't let you go on your own. We'll come with you. Dad will drive us, won't you, Bill, and we'll all do some shopping.'

'Honestly, Mum, I am perfectly happy going on my own. You and Dad have been great running me round everywhere but this is supposed to be a holiday for you too.'

'But you don't know the way. Anything could happen, No, it's better if we come with you. Just wait while I get changed.'

'Eunice, we're not going. Stay where you are.'

'Bill, what are you talking about? Of course, we're going; we can't let Alison go into town on her own.'

'She's a big girl now, and used to going places on her own. And you've been working hard all week - and we both appreciate that, don't we, Aliss?' I nodded frantically and Dad continued, 'but we all need a bit of space now, so let Aliss go into town and we'll just stay here and put our feet up, as Aliss suggests.'

I wasn't used to Dad being so masterful and I expected Mum to argue some more but she acquiesced quietly.

I bought postcards (sunset over Caldey Island for Pippa and one of the saucy sort that I thought had been banned for being too sexist, fattist and wife-ist for Bev) and souvenirs. I bought Adam a t-shirt with a drawing of a sheep in a leather jacket and an Elvis quif and the words 'Ewe're looking good'. I don't suppose he will wear it but it was a choice between that and a beer glass with the words 'A gift from Tenby' on the side.

But I nearly couldn't buy anything as I was almost in the shops when I realised I'd left my purse back in the caravan and had to go back for it.

The caravan was very quiet when I got there so I assumed Mum and Dad were having a snooze. I tried to be quiet but couldn't help yelping slightly after banging my toe on the side of bed. I heard noises then from their bedroom so shouted out, 'It's only me, I forgot my purse.'

I decided I might as well go to the loo as I was there and was just coming out of the bathroom when Dad appeared from their bedroom.

'Ah, Aliss,' he said, 'what a surprise, we weren't expecting you back so soon. We're just having a bit of a lie-down, your Mum and me. We were, er, a bit, er, tired.'

'Well, don't let me disturb you,' I said. 'I'm off again, you just go back to whatever you were doing.'

It was very odd but I could have sworn that Dad blushed. But there's nothing to be embarrassed about, older people need their rest. I'm not averse to an afternoon nap myself.

Later

Ohmigosh, they were having sex! No, they can't have been, not Mum and Dad, they're - well, no, they just can't have been. But it would explain why Dad looked so embarrassed and, indeed, flushed when I came out of the bathroom. But they're not teenagers, they're old, they need their sleep.

My parents - at their age - having sex - in the middle of the afternoon.

I don't know what disturbs me most.

But why am I so appalled? I should be glad that they have a healthy sex life after all these years. Really I am. I hope I'll be as active when I am their age.

Of course, a happy sex life will require the participation of a man. Or a partner of some sort. I can't see myself with a woman; it will have to be a man. I need a man! If only David hadn't been so obnoxious. Still there will be others ... I'm sure.

I might have to wait a bit but I have plenty of time.

Unless I die young (is fifty considered young to die? Well, youngish anyway.) Hope I don't die just yet; I wouldn't want to die a lonely divorcée.

I wonder if Brian would come to my funeral. Or David. He would probably be unable to resist the opportunity to make a comment about me and flames. I hope he doesn't come, I don't want my mother to be reminded of what she will have missed i.e. psychiatrist for a son-in-law.

28th August, Thursday

Note to self

Stop writing in diary late at night. I've noticed a tendency to become maudlin.

Mum and Dad went out to lunch today with Bernard and Joan, who also own a caravan here. They wanted me to go too but I said I'd like to explore a bit. Dad let me take the car in spite of Mum. 'Are you sure she'll be able to manage it, Bill? It's bigger than she's used to and these lanes are very narrow. Make sure you wear your seatbelt, Alison, and don't be late getting back. Shall I make you some sandwiches?'

I told her I'd make my own.

'Well, there's a nice bit of ham in the fridge, use that. There are some tomatoes too you can take. I think there are some crisps as well and don't forget to make yourself a thermos of tea. I'll do it for you, shall I?'

I finally managed to convince Mum that I could get my own lunch, went through the obligatory 'How are you, dear? Your Mum told us all about the d-i-v-o-r-c-e' quizzing from Joan and waved them off in Bernard's car. They'd gone about 100 yards when the car stopped, and Bernard reversed back to the caravan. Mum stuck her head out of the window, 'Davies the baker on the corner of the street where that shop is that I bought the picture in the hall — you know the one — daisies or is it poppies in a field — they sell beautiful pasties and cakes. They're as good as home-made. If you don't feel like making sandwiches, you could do worse than go there.'

I waited until I was sure they'd definitely gone then grabbed a towel and set off to explore. I've eaten so much over the last few days I didn't want any lunch. After driving for a while I found a place to park the car and followed a track down to a deserted beach.

I spread out my towel, took off my sweatshirt and stretched out. After a few minutes, I decided the heat and dangers of skin cancer justified the effort involved in sitting up and putting on sun cream. As I did so, an old man in an enormous sunhat walked by. 'Afternoon,' he said, raising his hat. 'Wonderful day, isn't it?'

'Yes.'

'You're wise to make the most of it, forecast for tomorrow says rain's moving in overnight.'

'Oh.'

'On holiday here, are you?'

'Yes.'

'Well, enjoy your stay,' he said, doffing his hat again and continuing on his way. I tried to look away but my eyes kept returning to his bottom - as naked as a baby's but hanging in brown flat leathery-looking folds.

When I told Mum and Dad about the naked man on beach neither seemed surprised. 'Your father should have warned you not to go to any lonely places,' Mum said.

'Yes,' Dad said, 'although there are no officially designated beaches, there are plenty of quiet spots where it doesn't upset anyone.'

'Silly old fools,' Mum said.

'They're not hurting anyone, Eunice.'

'Huh!'

As I'm taking us all out for dinner tomorrow, Mum made her traditional last-night-of-the-hols supper of hot dogs tonight. She's done it ever since Geoff and I were children and Dad says she does it even when it's just the two of them. Dad was just about to take a bite of his thick juicy hot dog when he stopped and said, 'I've always thought naturism must be rather liberating.'

'What?' Mum said. 'With all those bugs?'

I thought she'd got naturism confused with naturalism and said, 'Not bugs, Mum, nudity.'

'Precisely, all those bugs, flies and those little things that hop around in the sand...'

'Sand hoppers,' Dad and I said together.

'Yes, those, all those little - things, crawling over you and biting your private parts. Uckifee.'

I put down my hot dog but Dad was undeterred.

'Apart from that, you've got to admit there must be a great feeling of freedom. Look how many ordinary people do it these days; there must be something in it.'

'But have you seen the ones who do it?' Mum said. 'They're always the ones who shouldn't. Who wants to see an old man's dangly bits wobbling around. Enough to put you off for life.'

I could see Mum's point but thought I sensed a certain longing in Dad's voice. I can't imagine my retired bank manager father playing volleyball in the nude. And I really should not have conjured up that image. I shouldn't even have allowed the thought brain-space. I feel quite discombobulated.

Chapter 11

29th August, Friday

I took Mum and Dad to one of Tenby's finest hotels for our last night meal. I was engrossed in the menu when Mum began whispering at us, 'Look! Look who's over there.'

Dad and I both turned to peer over our shoulders.

'No, don't look!'

'Who are we not looking at, Eunice?'

'Whatsername, you know the one who had the affair with thingummy, you know who I mean.'

Dad and I both shrugged.

'Oh, you do know, oh, what is her name? It'll come to me in a minute.'

I tried to surreptitiously peep over my shoulder. I hadn't realised the waitress was standing right behind me. I jumped.

'Are you ready to order, madam?'

'I don't think we're quite ready yet, thank you,' I said.

'Could you come here and explain something please?' Mum was making wide eyes and calling gestures with her head.

When the waitress reached her side, Mum signalled her down to ear level. 'That lady over there, the one dining alone,' she whispered, 'I am right, aren't I? It is whatsername, isn't it?'

'I'm afraid I have no idea who she is, madam.'

'Come on, you can tell me. I know you have to respect confidentiality but I won't tell a soul, I promise you.'

'Honestly, madam, I don't know who she is.'

Mum sighed and waved her away. 'It'll come to me; you wait and see if it doesn't.'

She turned her attention to the menu.

'I think I'll have the mussels followed by the lamb with lightly curried risotto,' I said.

'Curry! Mum exclaimed loudly. We looked at her, as did everyone else in the restaurant including the lady diner. Mum started patting the air with her hands and mouthing, 'Your secret's safe with me' at the lady diner, who was looking slightly bemused.

'Edwina Currie! That's who it is' Mum whispered loudly across the table to us. Dad and I both glanced around again at the woman who was reading a book while eating her meal.

'Are you sure, Eunice, love?'

'Definitely. Her photo's on the back of the book Geoff and Trisha gave me for Christmas. It's definitely her. I've got the book with me, I'll show you when we get back to the caravan.'

'But what would she be doing in a hotel in Tenby?'

'Waiting for someone, I expect,' Mum said nodding her head sagely. I almost expected a nudge nudge, wink wink to follow. 'You've seen the book I'm reading, Alison, you know I'm right, don't you?'

'Mum, I could be sitting at the same table as her and I wouldn't know who she was unless she introduced herself to me.'

Mum tutted, 'Such a shame I don't have it on me. Bill, you wouldn't be a dear and nip back...'

'No, I wouldn't. I'm not nipping anywhere. We'll believe it's Edwina Currie if you'll decide what you want so we can order. Some of us are getting hungry.'

We were having pudding when the lady diner left. 'She smiled at me!' Mum exclaimed. 'Did you see that? What did I tell you: it was her. She knew I knew and was showing me that she appreciated the fact that I hadn't bothered her. There's a lady for you.'

'I don't recall you calling her that when she kissed and told of her affair,' Dad said.

'No, well, she was obviously being taken advantage of by a man of power.'

Even I snorted then but Mum carried on, 'She's had a difficult life but has come shining through to the other end.'

As soon as we got back to the caravan Mum rushed into the bedroom and brought out her book. She waved it triumphantly in our faces. 'See? What did I tell you? Joanna Trollope.'

Dad and I exchanged glances but said nothing.

Being with Mum this week has given me a brief glimpse of my future. And it is scary. I must eat more fish; it's good for the brain. Mum says so.

2nd September, Tuesday

Young Mr Davies came into reception this morning, walked up to Muriel, slapped himself on forehead, and said, 'What did I come out here for?'

'I do that all the time,' I said, 'forgetting things. It drives me mad.'

'I used to,' Muriel said, 'but now I take these marvellous tablets from the health food shop. They've worked wonders for my memory.'

'Perhaps we'd better take them too, then, eh, Alison? What are they called, Muriel?'

'They're called ...now what are they called? Don't worry, it'll come to me in a minute.'

This incident reminded me of my plan to eat more fish for brain improvement. I mentioned it to Muriel. 'Oh, no, you mustn't do that' she said. 'Haven't you seen the report in the paper?' She flicked through her Mail. 'Here it is: American scientists say British fish is full of toxins.' She handed me the paper, 'You can read it for yourself.'

Apparently the Americans have discovered that British fish is bad for you. I didn't read the whole of the article as I was too busy wondering how they determine which fish are British and which not. I assume the sea is marked into areas - of course, Fastnet and Dogger, and all those other mysterious names that they use on the Shipping Forecast - that must be it. Though why should only British fish be affected? What happens if a fish strays out of its designated area? Are there border shark patrols? I'm not convinced by this report.

Still, when Muriel remembers the name of the tablets she is taking perhaps I should start taking them too, along with cod liver oil for my joints, evening primrose for women-type things, vitamin C for colds, the stuff that makes vitamin C work properly, and the ones you need to make you go to the toilet because of constipation caused by too many pills. Or maybe I should just stop reading free health magazines full of adverts.

Alternatively eating a balanced diet could be the answer. A Mars bar and apple for lunch is probably reasonably balanced. Carbohydrate, fibre, vitamins, little bit of fat. That's quite good really.

I managed to pin Adam down for five minutes so I could ask him, 'Adam, what day do you want to travel to university? I'll need to book a day's leave.'

'Oh, are you coming too?'

'Of course I'm coming. Why are you so surprised?'

'Didn't think you'd want to be in the car with Dad for that long.'

'With your dad?'

'Yeah. You weren't planning on bringing your car as well were you?'

'As well? Do you mean to tell me your Dad's taking you?'

'Yeah, didn't I tell you? We arranged it ages ago.'

'Oh.'

'You can come as well if you want.'

'No, no, that's fine, as long as it's all arranged.'

'Yeah.'

'Um, is Gina going too?'

'Shouldn't think so. Why would she want to come?'

'Just wondered.'

It's good of Brian to take such an active role in his children's lives. But he's always been a good father. Being a cheating scumbag has not altered that. Although, it would have been nice to have been informed sooner of the plans.

Chloe has said that she and Tryboy are coming down this weekend. She wants to spend some quality time with her little brother before he leaves. I'm not quite sure when that quality time will be as Adam is going out on Friday night and Chloe wants us to go shopping on Saturday. She wants my opinion of a coat she's thinking of buying.

5th September

Chloe hadn't been home for ten minutes before she marched into the kitchen waving a handful of envelopes.

'What are all these, Mum?'

'Hmm?' I was trying to put back together the sponge cake I'd made that had fallen apart when I'd taken it out of the tin.

'These letters, Mum? I found them on the shelf in the hall.'

'Oh, those. Just boring letters.'

'They haven't been opened so how do you know they are boring?'

'They looked it.'

'So you didn't bother opening them?!'

'Well, no-one interesting ever writes to me.'

'You can't just not open letters.'

'Why not?'

'They could be important.'

'No, I doubt it.' I could see she was concerned. 'It's all right, I make sure I open any which look like a gas bill or electricity — we're not going to get cut off, don't worry.'

'But you just left them on the shelf!'

'I didn't like to throw them out without opening them so I thought I'd save them until I had nothing better to do.'

'But some of them have postmarks weeks old!'

'Do they really? Time flies, doesn't it?'

'Honestly, Mum, I don't know what you were thinking of. Come on, open them now.'

'I was just going to make a cup of tea and watch Eastenders.'

'Now, Mum.'

As I suspected they were all boring, all except one that is. That was a letter from Breast Test Wales that said, 'It is our policy to invite all women of fifty and over for regular mammograms ... blah blah blah ... Your appointment is on Wednesday 10th September at 2.30 pm.'

'That's next Wednesday, Mum. It's a good job I made you open this letter now.'

I thought that's a matter of opinion, but I made myself smile and said, 'You were right, Chloe. I'll call on Monday and cancel it.'

'You can't do that!'

'Why not?'

'Firstly, it's too short notice to cancel — they wouldn't be able to find someone else to take it and it would be a waste of valuable resources — and secondly, why would you want to cancel it anyway? It's important for a woman of your age. You read what it said; you're in the highest risk bracket.'

'But I'm in work on Wednesday.'

'I'm sure Mr Davies will be pleased to allow you time off when he realises how important it is.'

'I can't tell him what it's for!'

'Don't be stupid, Mum, of course you must.'

'But I don't know who'd be most embarrassed.'

'Better be embarrassed than dead.'

'Well, if you put it like that. But all the same, it's not just that, it's ...'

'What?'

'Chloe, I'm fifty.'

'Yeees.'

'And I've fed two babies.'

'Your point is?'

'I've got floppy boobs.'

Chloe burst out laughing, 'Oh, Mum, don't be daft. The doctor will have seen much worse, I'm sure.'

I'm not convinced. When not encased in Madame Fifi's support system, my boobs almost reach my waist.

I knew there was very good reason for not opening mail and it also confirms my suspicions that being fifty was all that I feared it would be.

6th September, Saturday

Shopping with Chloe turned into a day-long expedition. Tryboy stayed here and spent quality time with Adam playing on the Playstation.

The coat Chloe sought my opinion on turned out to be just perfect but 'rather outside my budget, Mum.' I'm well aware that my opinion is only ever sought when my plastic card is needed, but I don't mind. It's what mums are for.

Sometimes.

When I got home I took Adam into the kitchen.

'Now, Adam, you're off to university and there are some things you need to know.'

'It's all right, Mum,' he smiled reassuringly, 'I know about contraception.'

I was so shocked I was momentarily speechless. I hadn't even thought that I should be telling him about that. I wonder what else I've forgotten about.

I pulled myself together. 'I wasn't thinking about contraception actually. There are other things in life apart from sex, you know.'

There was a chortling behind me. Chloe had followed us into the kitchen. I gave her a look.

'Life is about far more than that. There are some basic things you need to know, like,' I held up the shirt I was carrying, 'how to do your own washing.'

He laughed and started to walk away.

'No, Adam, I'm serious, you need to know this. I had to give your sister this very same talk before she left for uni too. So just listen for a few minutes, will you?'

He shrugged and gave an 'anything-to-keep-Mum-quiet' nod.

'Right, the first thing to do is look at the label on each item of clothing. You see, like this one.' I pointed it out for him. 'It tells you what temperature the item has to be washed at. Some like it warm and some prefer it cooler. So first you sort your clothes out depending on temperature. Then the next thing to do, within each of these piles, is to sort them out according to colour. Dark clothes have to be washed separately from light clothes. Chloe, what are you doing?'

She'd jumped down off the work surface she was sitting on and had taken the shirt from me.

'Okay, Adam, listen to me, I'll tell you the reality about washing your clothes. First of all you wait until people are starting to complain about the smell whenever you go near them. Then you gather up all your clothes — all of them because they're all dirty or you wouldn't be doing this — from wherever they are — down the side of the desk, under the bed, anywhere else you can think of - and put them all in a big black bag. Take the bag to the nearest laundrette, tip the clothes in the washing machine, add whatever powder they have there, close the lid and press start. When that's finished, if you're feeling really really rich, you can put them in the tumble dryer, but more likely you'll take them home and drape them over every available radiator. A good tip is to make sure no-one else is doing their washing on the same day, otherwise you can end up with very crowded radiators and a sauna while you're watching telly. And that's washing clothes student-style.'

She bowed. Adam clapped. I sighed.

'Okay,' I said, 'well, what about ironing?'

'Ironing!' Chloe hugged me. 'Mum, you're priceless.'

∞

My big date with Barry is next Saturday. Daphne has been carrying on email communication with him in my absence (but using my name). I assume he now has rather erroneous view of me i.e. as someone intelligent and witty. I fear it will come as a great disappointment for him to meet the real thing.

9th September, Tuesday

Adam was sitting on the edge of his chair this evening, unable to get comfortable. I assumed he was nervous at the prospect of going to university and realised this was an ideal opportunity for the mother/son chat I'd promised myself.

I was about to begin on a reassuring talk when I realised that I'm not best person to talk about life on one's own. I was forty-nine before I had to undergo it and it has not been an entirely enjoyable experience. Then I realised further that, strictly speaking, I could still not consider myself as living alone as I have Adam with me. Not until he leaves, the day after tomorrow, will I be entirely on my own. I'm not sure that I'm looking forward to this, but had to put on a brave face for Adam.

'Well, Adam,' I said as heartily as I could, 'Nearly time for you to be off into the big world on your own. How are you feeling about that? Bit nervous, I expect.'

'Nah, can't wait.'

I could see he was trying hard to hide his real feelings.

'You know, Adam, I'm in the same boat as you. When you go, it'll be the first time I'll have been alone. And I'm not looking forward to it, I can tell you.'

His expression changed from one of pretended jollity to one of seriousness.

'I hadn't thought of that, Mum.'

'No, well, I didn't want to make a fuss, but all I'm saying is that you don't have to suffer alone. You can come home for a weekend any time you like, I'll pay for your train ticket. Or phone me, day or night, it doesn't matter. You don't have to be alone when I'm on the other end of the phone. And I can come and visit you, take you out for a meal. We could go for a curry together; you'd like that, wouldn't you?'

He nodded slowly.

'So it won't be that bad, will it?' I patted his hand. 'I'm glad we've had this chat, Adam.' I grabbed him to hug him to me.

'Ouch.'

'What's the matter?'

'Er, nothing, Mum.'

'What do you mean nothing? Does something hurt? Do you need to see a doctor before you go away?'

'No, Mum, it's fine, it's just, well, when you pulled me out of my chair, I caught my, um, arm on the side.'

'That shouldn't have hurt enough to make you yelp.' He had a slightly shamefaced look about him. 'Is there something you're not telling me, Adam?'

He sighed. 'I've got a tattoo.'

'A what?' I screamed.

'See, I knew you'd freak, that's why I didn't tell you.'

I took a deep breath.

'I'm not freaking,' I said as calmly as I could manage. 'I'm just surprised. Where exactly is this tattoo?'

He turned round, lowered the back of his jeans and revealed a fire-breathing dragon on the top of his right buttock.

For a moment I was unable to speak. I wanted to scream again but I felt that wouldn't be a wise move. Eventually I squeaked, 'Did it hurt? Having it done, I mean?'

Adam seemed relieved that I was taking it so calmly.

'Not that much actually, not as much as I expected.'

'Oh, good.'

I felt that, as he had shared his tattoo with me, I should respond in adult fashion and not clip him around the back of his head, while saying, 'how does this hurt then?' as felt inclined to do. I tried to say, 'It's a very nice dragon,' but the words came out as, 'What about Aids?'

Adam laughed. 'I'm not stupid, Mum, I went to a proper tattooist where everything's sterilised and clean and done properly.'

'Well, what about skin cancer then?'

'What?'

'I read it in Muriel's Mail: tattoos cause cancer when they're exposed to the sun.'

'Don't worry, Mum, I'm not planning on exposing my arse to the sun that often.'

I couldn't help wondering what was the point of a tattoo if no-one sees it although, on the whole, I'm grateful that no-one will see it.

'It will only be flashed, in the pub, when Wales beat England at rugby.'

That's all right then.

'I'm a Welsh boy, Mum, going to university in England. I wanted something to remind me of home.'

If he'd said that before I would have bought him a fluffy sheep.

10th September, Wednesday

In waiting room of Breast Test Wales clinic

There are two other ladies here. One looks about twenty-six and has no boobs to speak of; the other, who has just 'been done' and is waiting for her lift home, is nearer ninety-six and flat as a young boy. I'm sitting huddled over to make my own mammaries look less obvious.

I'm not reassured by the poster on wall. It has two cartoons: one shows a smiling boob being inserted into a thumbscrew-like device; the other shows the same boob frowning and puffing as all life is squeezed out of it. I would feel happier if there were a third cartoon showing boob returned to normal. Full and dangling is infinitely preferable to flat and dangling. Perhaps the old lady was as well-endowed as me before she went beyond that door. I feel strangely affectionate towards my bosom; I don't want to lose it now. I am patting them gently when the nurse comes to call me in.

Later

Mammogram machines were invented by a man. I don't know that for a fact but I'm sure they must have been.

Still I'm glad I went. It will be good to be reassured over the health of my breasts. Assuming I am given the all clear.

But I'm not thinking about that now. I have to make sure Adam is all packed and ready for the morning. Brian is picking him up at 9.30.

Much later, in bed

I can't believe my baby is off to university tomorrow. It only feels like yesterday that he was screaming and spilling food on the sofa. Ah, no, wait, that was Tuesday during the big match.

I will miss him. Miss the empty beer cans and crisp packets all over the place, the empty fridge that could never stay full — the empty house. He's done well and I am proud of him. He is good in all the right ways. We must not have been such bad parents. I hope he will be happy.

I suppose this is the beginning of the end really. I don't imagine he will come back here to live after college. It'll just be the holidays and then, like Chloe, he'll be finding his own place — and wife and family.

Adam heard me sighing and came in to see if I was all right. He is a good boy.

And anyway, according to the leaflet they gave me at Breast Test Wales, if I am recalled it does not mean I have cancer. It could be any number of reasons and if it turns out to be the worst, then early detection gives me a much better chance of survival.

I wouldn't make a good hero; I'm a terrible coward who cannot stand pain.

I wish I hadn't thought of this at this time of night. I have to be up early to make sandwiches for Adam ... and Brian, I suppose.

11th September, Thursday

I forgot to set the alarm and overslept. As a result I didn't have time to shower, dress and make sandwiches before Brian arrived so I decided making sandwiches should be my first priority. I was about to hand over these hastily-prepared sandwiches when Brian said, 'We'll stop at the services just before Reading and get some lunch, okay, Adam?'

I quickly returned the sandwiches to the fridge. Then I was so busy packing everything into the car and trying to remember what it was that Adam was likely to forget that I didn't have time to think about Brian being in the house again.

When everything was loaded, Brian said, 'Okay, Adam, think that's it?'

'Yeah, I guess.'

'Let's go then. Bye, Alison, I'll phone you if you like when I get back to tell you what his accommodation is like.'

'That would be nice, thank you.'

Brian took his seat behind the wheel. Adam and I stood and looked at each other for a moment, then I hugged him and said, 'You phone me now, do you hear?'

'Yeah, Mum.'

'At least once a week. And take care. And work hard — you're not there just to get drunk.'

'No, Mum,' he laughed.

'And ... oh, just remember all the things we've taught you over the years.'

'Yes, Mum.'

'And, Adam — enjoy yourself.'

'I will.'

He leaned over and kissed me. 'Love you, Mum.'

'You too.' I bit my lip. 'Go on now, your Dad is waiting.'

I waved until the car turned the corner then noticed that Mr Price next door had come out to watch.

'That's that then,' I smiled weakly at him, 'another big step along the way.'

Mr Price looked me up and down and said, 'Is that your nightie you're wearing?'

∞

Muriel had the kettle on ready when I got into work. She told me to sit quietly for a while until I felt like working. I was just enjoying my tea when the phone rang. I wondered if Muriel would answer it but she was busy typing and didn't look up.

I sighed and lifted the receiver. 'Davies and Davies, Financial Advisers, how may I help you?'

'Good morning, Alison, it's David.'

'Oh.'

Suddenly felt enormous lump in my throat moving up to my eyes rapidly. I sniffed quickly.

'Are you all right, Alison?'

'Adam's just left for university,' I stuttered down the phone.

'Oh, I see. Well, that's good, isn't it? You must be pleased for him.'

'Oh, yes, I am, very,' I sniffed again.

'Look, perhaps I could ...'

At that moment Young Mr Davies came hurrying into the office. 'Sorry, I'm late, folks. I'm expecting a call, Alison, from ... oh, you're on the phone, that's not Mr Davies, is it?'

I nodded.

'Excellent. I'll take the call in my office, put him through, will you, please?'

'Young Mr Davies has just arrived, I'll put you through to him now — shall I?'

'Er, yes, yes, please. Thank you.'

I wonder what David was going to suggest he could do. Not that I'm interested anyway. I have my hot date with Barry on Saturday. That will take my mind off things. As long as he's not a psycho or a stalker.

Later

Brian phoned. Said they had got to Reading safely and that Adam was in a flat with three girls and one boy. He'd met them and they all seemed thoroughly respectable and the other boy was cooking tea for them all. He said Adam's room was fine. I would have liked a bit more information but I assume it is like Chloe's room in Halls was, and probably like every other room in student accommodation.

'You know, Alison, he'll be fine.'

'Yes, I know.'

And I do know, it's just that, well, he's gone and I'm going to miss him.

Chloe phoned to ask if Adam had got off okay. I told her what her dad had said and we laughed at the fact that Adam seems to have fallen on his feet already being in a flat with three girls and a keen cook. Then Chloe said, 'You know, Mum, if you're ever lonely, you can phone me.'

'Yes, of course, love, but I'm not lonely.'

'Not at the moment maybe, but now Adam's gone, it's bound to be strange, especially at first.'

'I know but I'll have to get used to it. And anyway, I have lots to keep me busy.'

'You don't have to be brave, you know, Mum. You don't have to put up a show for me.'

'No, dear.'

'Adam told me what you said.'

'Did he? About what?'

'Him going and you being alone. I just wanted to reassure you that, even if you're alone, it doesn't mean you have to be lonely. I'm always here for you.'

I thought that was my line. I had been feeling quite brave but I'm not so sure now.

Chapter 12

13th September, Saturday

This is the plan. I am meeting Barry at the Rock & River at 8.00 pm. Pippa and Bev will arrive at the pub before that and find a table from which they will have a clear view of the entire lounge bar. I will arrive just after 8 — to give him plenty of time to get there — and will join Barry. If at any point during the evening I am uncomfortable and wish to escape, I will signal to the girls, they will ring me on my mobile and I will say that my mother has been taken ill and I have to go. The signal is me scratching the middle of my back. I suspect that if I start scratching myself, it will be Barry who will be looking for an excuse to leave, but it will serve its purpose, and it was the best we could come up with.

After my date

I arrived at the pub at 8.15 pm — I didn't want to take any chances. I quickly spotted Pippa, Bev and Daphne — I didn't know she was coming — at a corner table. I looked around the lounge but couldn't see anyone resembling Barry's photo. I was about to give up and join the girls when a short (-er than me) and well-built (podgy) man stood up and came towards me, holding out his hand, 'Alison, you made it. You look just like your photo.'

I laughed weakly, 'That's a shame.'

'Nonsense, it's very flattering. I'm afraid my photo is a bit old,' he went on. 'Couldn't find a newer one.'

Yeah, right, I thought, and I bet you didn't look too hard. It's not that his face was unpleasant, it was just that there was so much of it. However I told myself that a man is more than he looks. Which was rather profound of me especially as, at the time, my hand was being squeezed between his sticky chubby ones.

He led me over to a table, got me seated then asked what I'd like to drink. I told him red wine. Then he asked if I'd like some peanuts. 'Or crisps, maybe? Or scratchings?'

'No, thank you.'

'Can't resist them myself. Won't be a tick.'

I glanced round at the girls. Pippa and Daphne gave me a thumbs-up while Bev shrugged non-committally.

Barry came back with my wine, a pint (an empty pint glass was already on the table) and the biggest packet of peanuts I have ever seen. He tore them open and offered me some.

'No, thanks.'

'Don't know what you're missing.'

He munched through the peanuts while I desperately tried to think of something to say. It's strange how your mind can empty itself when faced with an anthropological throwback. At last, I managed, 'So, Barry, you're a PE teacher. That must keep you fit.'

'Bah, you're joking. I can't be doing with any of that fitness nonsense. I just tell the boys what to do and leave them to it. Mind you, I help the girls when I can, you know what I mean. But, no, you wouldn't get me in a gym of my own free will. All those ponces prancing around, pah.'

I scratched my back.

'You're not into that keep fit rubbish, are you? Not that you look as though you need it. I must say, you've got a lovely figure. Especially for a woman of your age. I like a woman with a bit of shape, a bit of something up top, if you know what I mean.'

I scratched my back again.

'These skinny girls today, they do nothing for me.'

I rummaged in my bag to check that the phone was switched on.

'Expecting a call, are you?'

'No, it's just that, my mother isn't very well and I'm a bit concerned about her.'

I was shocked at how easily the lie came out.

'Wouldn't it be better if you switched it off? You're supposed to be out enjoying yourself. I'm sure your mum wouldn't want to trouble you when you're out on the town. My mother fell down and broke her hip but she wouldn't let anyone phone me until the rugby on the telly was over. That's mothers for you.'

He went to take it from me. 'I'll switch it off for you, shall I?'

'No,' I grabbed it back. 'No, really, you mustn't do that.'

I scratched my back violently.

'It's infuriating, isn't it,' Barry said, 'when you get one of those itches that you just can't reach? Would you like me to scratch it for you?' He started to stand up.

'No! Really, I'm fine. Please sit down. But, um, I think I need to, er, spend a penny. I'll just nip to the Ladies.'

'Don't be long; I'll be waiting for you.'

I smiled, 'Huueer.'

I started to head for the girls' table when Barry called out, 'It's the other way, you're going the wrong way. The Ladies is over there.'

I made frantic eye gestures to the girls then turned and smiled again at Barry. 'Silly me.'

I was relieved when Pippa and Bev followed me in through the loo door.

'I've been signalling! Didn't you see? Why haven't you phoned me?'

'Alison, you've only been with him ten minutes — how can you possibly judge on such a short acquaintance. Give him a chance.'

'A chance? Did you see him eating peanuts? Handfuls at a time. And with his mouth open! I bet he chews gum as well. In fact he's bound to, his sort always do.'

'That's hardly a criminal offence, Alison. Give him a bit longer, make small talk, get to know him better.'

'I know he likes busty ladies and thinks that the gym is for ponces. How much more do I need to know?'

'Well, you should still give him a bit longer. He's probably nervous, don't you think, Bev?'

Bev shook her head. 'I'm with Aliss on this.'

'Oh, Bev! That is very shallow. I am surprised at you both.' Pippa looked at Bev again. 'Well, I'm surprised at you, Alison.'

'I'd have phoned you, Aliss, but she wouldn't let me.'

'Thanks, Bev. But you'll do it when I go back, Pippa?'

'If you insist, but I still think you're making a mistake.'

I'd been sitting at table for five minutes before the phone rang. It took me another five to work out how to answer it. 'You're not very good with this modern technology, are you, Alison? I like that in a woman.'

'Huueer. Hello. Yes, hello, mum. No, you're not disturbing me, it's fine. Have you? Oh, dear, no, that's all right, I'll come straight away. Don't worry, I'll be with you in a jiffy. Byyeee.'

Barry looked disappointed. 'Said you should have turned it off, didn't I?'

'Well, she is ninety-three, and ... I fear she could go at any time. I would never forgive myself if I wasn't there. You do understand, don't you?'

'Course, I do, what do you think I am? Anyway there'll be plenty of time for us to get to know each other next time. I'll give you a ring, shall I? Oh, wait, I don't have your phone number.'

'You can email me, that's fine.'

'But you said you can't access your emails that often.'

'Oh, often enough, don't worry.'

I fled from the pub and waited in the car until Pippa and Bev came out.

'What you looking for, Aliss?'

I was huddled down over the front seat. 'Nothing,' I hissed. 'I'm hiding. Has he gone?'

'When we left he was just going up to the bar and ordering another drink.'

'Oh, charming.' I sat up. 'He wasn't overly distressed by his experience then?'

We spent the rest of the evening at the nearby Plough & Partridge where Bev told us of her latest plan.

'What you said that Barry said made me think of it: Aliss can join a gym.'

'Whaaat?'

'There are always tasty men at gyms and getting fit would do you good too.'

'I agree that getting fit would do Alison good but have you ever seen her after exercising?'

Bev put her head to one side and thought. 'No, you know, I don't think I ever have.'

'Well, I have,' Pippa said.

'When?' I asked.

'When we joined that aerobics class, remember?'

'Oh, yes. That was hard work. That — what was her name who ran it?'

'Julie.'

'Yes, her. She was evil.'

'It was quite a gentle class, actually, Alison.'

'Yeah, right.'

'Anyway, Alison when she is hot and sweaty is not a pretty picture.'

'Charming.'

'You've got to admit a bright red shiny face and sweat marks all over your t-shirt is not a man-puller.'

'I wasn't sweating, I was ... glowing.'

After some discussion, we came to the conclusion that watching Brad Pitt — or anybody really — working out would be rather more appealing than doing it ourselves. But Pippa and Bev (especially Bev) are still determined to find me a man. I have refused point blank to go back on the internet. Bev said I will never find a man with this attitude but I would prefer to die a lonely old woman than live with someone who chews with his mouth open.

14th September, Sunday

Daphne phoned. She wanted to tell me that she had got chatting to Barry after the rest of us had left last night and that she was going out with him, on a proper date, next Saturday, and did I mind? I said I was delighted for her and that I thought Barry probably had very many good qualities that I hadn't seen. I was so relieved I embellished a little saying that Barry had commented on how unlike the me he had got to know, and really like, from my emails, I was. She seemed pleased with that. I feel it will all have been worthwhile if two people come out of this happy. Although I am rather disappointed that one of them is not me.

Just re-read last night's entry. I don't really want to die a lonely old woman. Being alone is one thing; being lonely is quite another. But I don't have to worry as have I children and good friends.

16th September

I'm having to pluck hairs from my chin with frightening regularity. The beautician on television this evening said you can get quite a good pair of tweezers for £12; I would expect an electric razor for that. Come to think of it, that might be what I will need in a year or so.

Tonight I plucked a black hair a full inch long from halfway up my neck. I hope I am not mutating into a werewolf. I feel rather like a turkey, the one no-one wanted at Christmas. Jowls are developing in much the same way as those dangly red bits on a turkey too.

I wonder if I was being unnecessarily harsh on Barry. Is it so bad to chew with your mouth open? He seemed to have a good relationship with his mother. Men who are kind to their mothers cannot be all bad. But I've missed the opportunity now. And have no-one to blame but myself. Mum always said I wouldn't recognise a gift horse if it kicked me.

17th September

I put clothes in the washing machine before I left for work this morning; I came home to flooded kitchen. And clothes not washed.

I'm reluctant to call the plumber I used last year as I suspect his opinion of me is low enough as it is so I'm trying to find an alternative. I've phoned five plumbers so far. Got three answering machines, one wife who doesn't know where her husband is but if I find out would I please tell her as he owes her maintenance, and one plumber who is busy from now until Christmas. There are only four more in the book, including last year's chauvinist.

Plumber six could probably fit me in if I can wait three weeks, although if it's really urgent, he might be able to make that two.

Plumber seven 'is not home at the moment but if you'd like to leave a message he'll get back to you within a fortnight.'

Plumber eight can come on Friday. He will be with me at 8.15 am. I can last that long without clean clothes but next time I must remember not to leave washing until I am desperate.

But how is it that he is free to call on Friday? Is he no good? Not that not being good would necessarily make him available as no-one would know he was not any good until he had been to them so he would be busy anyway.

I wonder if there is a quality control mark for plumbers. It seems I have uncovered yet another gap in my catalogue of household wisdom. It's Brian's fault, he always took care of everything. Perhaps — no, that is a stupid thought: I cannot phone Brian. Just because we managed to converse without insults when he took Adam to university doesn't mean that he would want to talk to me about plumbers. And, anyway, if I phoned would probably get Gina and definitely do not want to speak to her.

I'm sure the plumber will be fine for the purpose. It can't be that hard to mend a washing machine.

19th September

The plumber was due at 8.15. At 9.00 I called him. He couldn't get his van out as his road was blocked by workmen, 'I will be along as soon as they've finished.'

I called him at 10.00 — his wife was having trouble with her car, 'I'll just get it going for her and I'll be along.'

I called him at 11.00 — he'd realised he needed some parts, 'I'm just going to the wholesaler's then I'll be with you.'

I called him at 12 — he'd had an emergency call, 'Old lady up to her ankles in water, couldn't say no, could I?'

I called him at 1 — still with old lady, 'Could be some time, what about if we say Monday at 8.15?'

I felt like saying, 'what about tonight at 8.15, or better still, forget it!' but he is my best hope of getting the machine fixed within the next month, so I expressed my displeasure only mildly and said I'd look forward to Monday.

20th September

I took my washing to Mum's and used her machine. Dad was playing golf and as Mum was going to see Great Aunt Millie I said I'd go with her.

Auntie Millie is the undisputed Queen of Fairyhill. When we arrived she was in her room, but she decided that we'd be better off in the communal lounge. She took Mum's arm and we walked the short distance very slowly. As we entered the lounge, we heard a sharp intake of breath from Auntie Millie. She marched, rather unsteadily but very determinedly, over to a chair by the window and stood next to it, glowering. The old lady sitting in it glanced up, then looked down again quickly. She seemed to shrink in her seat. Auntie Millie began tapping her fingers on the back of the chair. The old lady shrank further. Auntie Millie's finger-tapping became louder and faster. The old lady gave up and crept out of the chair. Auntie Millie sat down and said, 'Honestly, it never ceases to amaze me.'

'What does, Auntie?'

'The cheek of some people. No respect. She's only been here five minutes and she thinks she can have the best seat. Huh! You've got to earn these privileges, you know. Now, have you brought me any sausages?'

'Not this week, Auntie, I thought you might like some grapes.'

'Have they got pips?'

'No, they're seedless.'

'That's all right then. Now, Ruby, we need to get this sorted: are you coming to me for Christmas as usual this year?'

Ruby?

'We thought it would be nice if you came to us this year for a change, Auntie.' Mum was smiling kindly.

Great Aunt Millie always goes to Mum's for Christmas. I was confused by this conversation but especially by Mum's reaction i.e. this is all perfectly normal.

Auntie Millie tutted, 'I'm not coming if you've still got that animal.'

I know for sure that Mum has not had pets since Geoff and I left home so waited eagerly for her response.

'No, Auntie, we had him put down last year.'

'Brrr, nasty brute of an animal. I suppose he's still with you though.' Auntie Millie curled her lip as she emphasised 'he'.

'Yes, Auntie.'

'Huh, thought he'd be dead by now,'

'No, he's still alive and kicking.'

'Who is?' I whispered to Mum.

'Your father,' she hissed back.

I was surprised at this as Dad and Auntie Millie have always got on famously, sharing, as they do, a common love of wrestling.

'You should never have let him have that shed. Once a man's got a shed, there's no telling what he'll be up to in it.'

'No, Auntie Millie.'

'I knew a man who had a shed. Police never found his wife's body.' She fixed me with her cloudy grey eyes. 'Has your husband got a shed?'

'No, Auntie, I'm divorced.'

She nodded, 'Better that than let him have a shed.'

Just then one of the nurses came over with a tray of tea and biscuits. As she was laying it out for us, she said, 'How are you today, Millie? Enjoying your visitors?'

'Mrs Rees to you, my girl.'

'Oh oh, one of those days is it?' The nurse looked at Mum and me and smiled, 'Good luck.'

When she'd gone, Auntie Millie said, 'Tut, they think they can control every part of your life, these nurses and doctors with their white coats. Do you know what they're trying to make me to do? Use a contraception! Never heard the like of it. What's it to do with them?'

Even Mum was startled at this news and stared at me, speechless.

'Are you sure, Auntie?' I asked.

'I told them to mind their own business, and if I want a contraception, I will use one, but not on their say so.'

'Oh.'

'They told Fred he ought to use one too.'

'Fred?' Mum squeaked.

'He told them to bugger off.'

'Good for him,' I said.

I looked at mum. She had gone very pale. 'Have a drink of your tea, Mum.'

'Yes, I think I will.'

The nurse who'd brought us tea was on reception when we left. 'Okay?' she smiled at us.

'Actually we're rather concerned,' I said, 'about something Auntie Millie said.'

I told her and she spluttered, 'Contraceptives!'

'That's what she said. And she said you were trying to make Fred use them as well.'

The nurse was as surprised as we were and said it didn't sound very likely. 'She's probably just confused, she has her good and her bad days, you know.' But she could see we were worried so she'd make some enquiries and get back to us.

'Thank you, dear,' Mum said. 'That would put our minds at rest.'

On the way home in the car Mum was very quiet. Guessed she was thinking about Auntie Millie's obviously vibrant sex life. I'm rather shocked myself, not about the sex — for heaven's sake, my parents have sex! — but by the fact that Auntie Millie is indulging in it outside of marriage. She has always been a very active member of the local Methodist church.

I thought I should try to cheer up Mum. 'Are you all right, Mum? You've gone a bit quiet.'

'I was just wondering ...'

'Yes?'

'Why your father's never wanted a shed.'

Later

Mum phoned to tell me that the nurse had rung her. Mum was very relieved. Auntie Millie's 'contraception' is a zimmer frame.

She also mentioned that Dad knows the man, with the shed, whose wife's body was never found. Word at the Golf Club is that she ran away with the undertaker who buried her mother. I can empathise with that. To a vulnerable woman a kind word can be a great aphrodisiac. Although I would have thought carefully before choosing to swap a man with a shed for a man who handles dead bodies on a daily basis.

22nd September, Monday

The plumber arrived at 9.20. I took him into the kitchen and explained the problem. 'Hmm,' he said. 'Hmm.'

He stood and looked at the machine for a while.

'Had it long, have you?' he asked at last.

'About five years.'

'Ah, well then...'

I waited eagerly for the rest of the sentence that I thought must be coming. Eventually he said, 'Probably need a new one.'

'Oh, no, surely not.'

'Not made to last, you know.'

'But surely they're meant to last longer than five years?'

'Built-in redundancy, that's what they call it.'

'But I haven't had any problems with it up till now.'

'There you are then.'

'But you'll have a look at it, won't you?'

'Tshewww, hardly worth the effort.'

I was beginning to understand why his timetable was so empty.

'Oh, please, go on, as you're here.'

'Well, as I'm here, then. Mind you, I don't do washing machines as a rule.'

'But you're a plumber ... aren't you?'

'Yeah, yeah, but what you need is a washing machine repair man.'

'I told you it was a washing machine when I phoned you.'

'You sounded so desperate and I wasn't busy so I thought I could take a look anyway.'

He pulled the washing machine out from its slot under the work surface and started to unscrew the back.

'Should you do that?' I said.

'What that's then?'

'Should you take the back off while it's still plugged in and switched on?'

'Probably all right, but if you want me to, I'll unplug it. Do you want me to then?'

Secretly I suspected that a quick shock would do him the power of good but I didn't think my home insurance would cover it so I said, 'I think it would be best. I don't want a dead body on my floor. Not first thing on a Monday morning.'

He looked at me, nodding thoughtfully. I unplugged the machine while he thought.

He lifted the top off and looked inside.

'Looks all right, don't it?'

'I don't know, does it?'

'Well, nothing obvious there. No, you know, nothing obvious.'

He stepped back and scratched his head, 'See, that's these new machines for you. They can look all right and still go wrong.'

'I thought you said it was an old machine.'

'Well, aye, it is. You'd be better off with a new one.'

He stepped back and studied the front. 'Nasty scratch you got there.'

He checked the sides. 'Hmm.

He leaned over to look at the back. 'Aah, that's the problem see?'

'What?'

I tried to peer over but he took up most of the space.

'You've come undone.'

'What?'

'Your pipes. They've come apart. And see, look, that's why.'

He rummaged around a bit and then held up a sock. 'You got a sock stuck, see, and the pressure, likely, pushed the pipes apart. And then you get a flood. See I knew it wouldn't be anything serious.'

He screwed the two pipes back together. 'That's the beauty of these old machines, nothing much to go wrong on them.'

He collected his tools back together, and then said, 'I won't push it back for you now, you'll want to clean behind it.'

I could think of no earthly reason why he should think this. I was tempted to ask, 'why?' but didn't trust my mouth to speak, so I nodded while grinding my teeth.

'Right, that's call-out £35 plus parts, let's call that £10, that takes us to then, let's say, a nice round fifty.'

I nodded mutely and went to get my handbag. 'A cheque all right?'

'I'd rather not, if you don't mind. Cash would suit me better. Won't have to go into the bank then.'

'I don't have fifty in cash on me, I'm afraid.'

'What you got then?'

'About thirty-five, I think.'

'That'll do. You give me that and we'll call it quits.'

Call it quits! Call it quits, my arse! I pay thirty-five pounds for a charlatan to come — late — and de-sock my pipes and he calls it quits. I call it daylight robbery. I'm going to check out evening classes; there must be some on home maintenance – and they might even be run by an attractively-handy man thus killing two birds with one stone for me. Not that I need a man; I am quite capable of doing anything a man can do. Except perhaps peeing out of train windows and opening pickle jars.

I felt obliged to clean under the washing machine and I am amazed at what can get into such a small gap. As well as seven grapes, I found £1.53 (I'm surprised plumber didn't notice it and suggest adding it to his fee as a tip), 2 francs, three pens, something that looked like a shrivelled-up mouse (but I'm sure it is nothing of the kind) and a Lego brick (in spite of the fact that Lego has not been played with in this house for at least ten years).

But if it had been a mouse I would have found droppings surely. Most probably it was a piece of cheese gone mouldy and hairy.

Perhaps I should get a cat. A cat would not only catch mice but also would be good company especially now I am alone. It would curl up on my lap in the winter, and greet me with a friendly meow when I got home from work. It would be much nicer than coming into an empty house and it might help slow down the onset of insanity. I noticed that Mr Price next door gave me a strange look when he heard me saying, 'hello, house,' when I came home tonight. And if Mr Price thinks I am strange I must be in serious trouble indeed.

Chapter 13

24th September, Wednesday

Bev phoned. Before I had even managed to say hello, she was off, 'Have you see the Evening Mail today?'

'No, I don't take...'

'Right, get the bottle opened, I'll be round in twenty minutes.'

Bev came in waving her copy of the Evening Mail. 'Look at this. It's just what you need, Aliss.'

I scanned the page it was open at but the only thing that stood out was an advert for motability scooters. I feared Bev's latest idea was going to involve deception on my part.

'No, I don't think that's a good idea,' I said firmly.

'Why not? It's perfect. Oh, Aliss, you are such a downer on everything.'

Pippa, who'd come with Bev, had taken the paper and was reading it and nodding. 'Well, it's a possibility,' she agreed.

'Just a minute,' I said. 'I don't want men just because they feel sorry for me.'

'Well, you'd all be in the same boat, why would anyone feel sorry for you? It's nothing to feel ashamed about.'

'Nothing to be ashamed about? Taking advantage of people's good natures, making them think I'm something I'm not. I'd be ashamed. And what would happen afterwards? How long would I have to keep up the pretence? And what do you mean, we'd all be in the same boat?'

'Alison,' Pippa said, 'what do you think Bev is suggesting?'

'Pretending to be disabled, of course.'

'What?!' Bev yelped. 'Where, what, what on earth gave you that idea?'

'The motability scooters. That's what you were pointing at, wasn't it?'

Bev and Pippa both burst out laughing. 'Oh, Alison, you a star.'

'Try again, Aliss, and this time, read the bit just next to the advert for the scooters.'

I read aloud, ' "Walco's to start Singles Night." What's that mean?'

Bev sighed. 'You are hard work sometimes, Aliss. One evening a week Walco's is going to be aiming its marketing at single shoppers.'

'Oh, I see. Oh, that's good. Does that mean there'll be lots of special offers for one?

Like 'buy one get it half price', instead of the 'buy three, get the fourth free,' that they usually do. I mean, it was fine when Adam was here — we could eat four packets of chocolate biccies in no time between us, but when it's just me, I do struggle a bit. So how will they do it, I wonder. Will they...'

'Yes, yes, special offers will be part of it, but that's not all. They're going to be offering free glasses of wine...'

'Oooh, nice.'

'and playing smoochy music...'

'Smoochy music? Why would anyone want smoochy music when they're shopping? It would put me off. What I need when I'm shopping is something bright and lively and ...'

'Oh, Aliss, you are so thick sometimes. The idea is to that Walco's becomes a sort of dating agency.'

'A dating agency?'

'Yeah, it says in the article that they've piloted it in some of their stores and it's been a great success. They've even had their first wedding in Milton Keynes. It says the groom pushed his bride down the aisle in a shopping trolley.'

'Oh.'

'So they're introducing it all over the country including here. It's going to be on Tuesdays, starting next week, so you'll have to go.'

'Oh, I can't go on Tuesday. "Upping Sticks" is on television on Tuesday.'

Bev looked at Pippa. 'I think we're just in time, Pip.'

'I hate to say it, Bev, but you could be right.'

'No, honestly, it's reached a really exciting bit: the old couple who gave up everything and moved to France are facing disaster, and...'

Suddenly I could hear myself. I ended lamely, 'But I don't shop at Walco's.'

'That doesn't matter, for goodness sake, you can still go.'

'But I don't like their frozen veg. It's not half as good as ...'

'Aliss, you're not going shopping for food; you're shopping for a man.'

'Oh.'

Bev sighed again. 'You talk to her, Pippa. I'll open another bottle of wine.'

'I think it's worth a try, Alison. I mean, where else can you meet single men in a safe, non-threatening environment? There's just nowhere.'

'I don't know, it still sounds a bit scary.'

'Don't worry, I'll come with you,' Bev said.

I didn't like to say that made it even scarier so I just said, 'Doesn't that defeat the object of it being Singles?'

'We won't walk together; I'll be a few steps behind you, then if you get approached by someone gross, I can leap in and rescue you.'

'How?'

'I don't know, I haven't thought that far. It was only in the paper tonight, for goodness sake.' She shrugged. 'We can pretend we're gay or something.'

I am very fond of Bev but not that fond.

Bev threatened to fetch her Leonard Cohen tapes from the car and play them all night unless I agreed to give it a try. I was defeated. What with dead mice and brain-dead plumbers I've had enough misery for one week. I said I'd go with her next Tuesday.

But I can't believe I gave in. I've never heard such a ridiculous idea. Who goes to a supermarket to get a date? Can I have a pound of sausages and a Harrison Ford — preferably from his Hans Solo days — lookalike please?

But it could be quite fun, I suppose. Although knowing my luck, I'd probably get the Darth Vader lookalike. Although I've often thought that the heavy breathing he does is quite sexy.

(Good grief! I'm finding Darth Vader attractive! I need to take drastic action. At least shoppers in Walco's are likely to be human or close to it.)

30th September, Tuesday

There were hundreds of people going into Walco's tonight. The entrance hall was decorated with pink and blue balloons and banners welcoming 'everyone whether you're looking for love or loo rolls!'

A girl in a short skirt was handing out glasses of wine. I hoped she wasn't intending to hang around all evening. I could already see men dribbling.

I took a sip of my wine; Bev downed hers. 'Right, you go first, I'll be close behind if you need me. If you pull, I'll make myself scarce. Otherwise I'll meet you back here at...' she looked at her watch, '8.30, okay?'

'But it's only ten past six. It won't take me that long to do my shopping.'

Bev sighed. 'Concentrate, Aliss. Why are you here?'

It was my turn to sigh. 'To meet a man.'

'Right, so take your time, have a good look round and don't rush. Okay?'

I nodded.

'Then let's get to work! And, ay, what's that I see? Potential at three o'clock.'

I felt like a fighter pilot going out to shoot down baddies. I turned to my left to see if I could spot 'potential.'

'Not there, you idiot, over to your right!' Bev hissed.

I missed potential because by the time I had given Bev a dirty look and turned to my right, there was no-one in sight.

It's been a while since I shopped in Walco's and I was pleasantly surprised by the variety and apparent quality of goods on display. It's definitely gone upmarket.

I was just sniffing strawberries when a voice behind me said, 'Does that tell you something?'

I turned round to face David Davies.

'Um, yes, no, what?'

'Does sniffing the strawberries help you judge the quality?'

'Not that I know of.'

'Do you mind if I ask why you were doing it then?'

'I like the smell.'

'Ah, of course. Eminently sensible.'

I thought I could see just the hint of a smirk appearing.

'How are you, Alison?'

I'm never at my best when taken by surprise. I wish I were a quick thinker who could come up with witty comments, instead of, 'Very well, thank you. And you?'

'I'm very well.'

There was a moment's silence then we both spoke at once.

'After you,' David said.

'Do you come here often?' I sparkled.

'I often pop in on the way home from work. It's close to my consulting rooms so it's handy.'

'I'm a Sainsburys girl usually myself.'

'It's never usually this busy at this time of day though.'

'No, well, it's the first one. I expect the interest will wane after a few weeks.'

'First what?'

'Singles Night.'

'Singles Night?'

'You know, Walco's attempt at a dating agency.'

The look on his face told me everything. He peered around. James Brown's 'You're my first, my last, my everything' was belting out of the loudspeakers, and everywhere you looked there were men and women behaving like they were in a night-club not a supermarket.

'You didn't know, did you?' I had to ask the obvious.

He shook his head, appalled. Then he looked at me and said slowly, 'You said you don't usually come here. You mean you've come for the ... Singles Night?'

I wished I could think of a convincing lie.

I nodded, biting my lip, then I spotted Bev viewing David with interest. 'It was Bev's idea, yes, that's it, I'm here with her. She wanted to come. Her husband left her, oh, ages ago, and she is looking for a new man. So, because she's desperate, I agreed to come with her. I wouldn't have come otherwise.'

Part of it was true anyway.

David replaced the punnet of strawberries he had put in his basket. 'I think I'll leave my shopping for now, there's nothing I need urgently. I'll see you around, Alison.'

And he hurried out of the shop.

Bev marched over. 'Oh, Aliss, what on earth did you say to him to make him rush off like that? He was a bit gorgeous. You should have kept a grip on him, girl.'

'That was David.'

'David?'

'Hm-mm.'

'You don't mean David of the fire in Claude's? Oh, Aliss, what a waste. Ah, well, he's gone. Better get back to the basics, and some of these specimens are pretty basic from what I've seen, but there are sure to be some good ones around too. Come on, are you buying those strawberries or not?'

I tried to push David out of my mind but the look of horror on his face when he'd realised what he'd walked into (and what I was involved in) kept coming back to me. As a result I was churlish to a school-teacher, who said he was researching e-colours, in Soft Drinks, irritable to an eco-friend, who was after his orgasmic oats in Cereals, and downright rude to a dirty mac in Cleaning. Not that he didn't deserve it.

He squeezed my arm, just as I was trying to remember how much toilet cleaner I had left, and cackled, 'Do you know where they keep the Viagra? Not that I'd need it with you, darling.'

I took his trolley, gave it a hefty push and sent it zooming to the other end of the aisle. 'It's a Zimmer frame you need, not Viagra,' I said, before stalking off. I did feel a bit guilty when I saw him hanging onto the shelves as he made his way very slowly down the aisle — but not enough to go back and help him, the pervert.

I couldn't spot Bev anywhere so decided to pay for my shopping and have a coffee in the cafe while I was waiting for her.

That was a bad mistake.

I had to put bags of shopping on each chair to stop men joining me. That and scowling at them if they spoke did the job so I wasn't in the best of moods when Bev finally appeared.

'Well that was good, wasn't it?' she said. 'How many phone numbers have you got?'

'None,' I snapped.

'None?' She tutted. 'Have some of mine then.' She opened her bag and took out a sheet of paper covered in numbers.

'Bev! You're a happily married woman!'

'So? It doesn't hurt to play a little sometimes. Anyway they won't remember who they were talking to. You can phone them and they won't know any difference. Men are thick; a woman is a woman to them.'

'Beeevv!'

'Look, you see I used a code. Each name has its telephone number plus an extra number at the end. That's my rating. I judged them on looks and personality. Ten is super-brillo, and one is forget it.'

I looked at the list. There was one eight as well as two sevens, three fives and a two. 'I'm surprised you even bothered talking to a two,' I said.

'I'm not completely shallow, no matter what Pippa thinks. I gave him the benefit of the doubt but it turned out that not only did he look like a pot-bellied pig, he had the conversation skills of one as well.' She sniffed. 'The eight would be worth a call though. In fact, I might keep him for myself.'

'Bev!'

'Just joking.'

'Just a minute,' I said. A sudden horrible thought had crept into my brain. 'If you exchanged telephone numbers with all these men, whose number did you give them? You can't have given them yours. Please tell me you haven't given them mine?'

'No, of course I haven't. What do you think I am? I made up a number.'

On way out of Walco's was stopped by very pleasant young girl who said she was from Evening Mail and could she ask us a few questions. Bev pushed me forward and said, 'She'll talk to you. I can't. I'm not here.'

As the girl was so friendly and interested in everything I said, I felt I couldn't be too harsh. Instead I said I thought it was a good idea of Walco's to try to bring people together in this way, and that if more people made the effort to get on there would be fewer wars. Even managed to bring in a rather astute comment about the prime minister taking a lead from Walco's. I also said it was good to see the single person being catered for and getting the service they deserved. I wasn't keen to have my photo taken but the reporter insisted it would be tiny and they would only use it if nothing better came up, 'And it's sure to.'

Bev was waiting for me in the car. I had a question to ask her.

'What did you mean, Bev,' I said, 'when you said, "'I'm not here"?'

'Hmm?'

'Does Simon know you've come with me?'

'He knows I'm with you but you know what he's like, Aliss, very touchy. It was simpler to let him think we were having a girls' night in at your place.'

I can foresee trouble. I don't know what or how but I feel it in my water.

Later

Have just re-read last entry. Obviously I mean 'organic' oats. I must remember to destroy my diary if death appears to be imminent as I would hate it to fall in the wrong hands i.e. anyone's but mine. I cannot imagine what kind of picture it would paint of me for anyone else reading it. My children would never look at me in the same way again.

Although I would be dead by then so perhaps it wouldn't matter. It might even be a good thing for them to get an honest insight into their mother's life. I will give this more thought. Possibly I could mention it in my will – which I must consult Young Mr D about. He is a financial expert and should know.

However, I definitely do not want anyone to read it before my death. Brrr.

Find it hard to believe that, even if he only called in on chance, David could have failed to notice all the decorations and signs in the entrance, to say nothing of the wine and smoochy music. And I only have his word for it that he was an innocent dropper-in to begin with.

Although the look of horror on his face when he discovered the truth was very convincing.

1st October, Wednesday

Mum phoned. 'How could you, Alison? When you know your Dad's standing for the committee at the Golf Club?'

I couldn't follow much of what she was saying as it was too garbled but gathered that whatever it was I had done had brought shame on the entire family.

Bev called. 'Aliss, how could you? Simon is furious — yes, all right, Si, I'm coming now — I'll have to call you back later, Aliss.'

I phoned Pippa. 'Hi, Pippa, it's me.'

'Oh, hello, Ms Walker.'

'What? Has everyone gone insane?'

'Go and buy a copy of tonight's Evening Mail.'

'What?'

I am a Page One Girl. I'm surprised, considering the size of my boobs, that they didn't put me on page three but no: there's a large photo of me on the front of the Evening Mail next to a headline saying, SINGLES BEING SERVICED. The report goes on to say that "Lonely divorcée, Alison Walker, was amongst hundreds who crowded into Walco's city centre store for their first Singles Night. Alison, 60, said she was delighted with the service."

The newsagent looked me up and down when I went in to get the paper. 'Hmm,' he said. 'Wouldn't have said you were a day over fifty-five. Not bad for your age, are you?'

I'm just relieved that they got my name wrong. With a bit of luck not many people will realise it is me.

2nd October

Muriel and Young Mr Davies were looking at last night's paper when I arrived this morning. Muriel tried to push it into her drawer quickly but only succeeded in making Young Mr D yelp when the drawer corner caught him on his knee.

'Can I just make it clear,' I said, 'that I didn't say that? About being serviced, I mean. And I am not lonely, nor am I sixty. But, yes, I did go to the Singles Night and I have got what I deserve for being so foolish. My mother has already told me that.'

Young Mr Davies looked again at the paper. 'Oh dear, oh, dear,' he said. 'I thought it said "served". "Serviced" does have unfortunate connotations, doesn't it?'

'Why?' Muriel asked.

He coughed. 'I have to go to my office now. Alison will explain.'

Ten clients phoned this morning, seven of them simply to confirm that 'it was you, wasn't it?' and one of them suggesting he didn't like to see a lady lonely and would I care to go out with him next week. I told him I never mix business with pleasure. Not any more anyway.

It's strange how everyone studies the local rag so thoroughly these days. No-one — not even my parents — noticed my picture in the paper when I won a colouring competition when I was ten.

3rd October, Friday

It's Chloe's birthday today. I thought she might have come home for the weekend but she's working in the Refuge, and 'their need is much greater than mine, Mum'. Course it is. Very noble. I hope Tryboy will spoil her when she isn't in work.

I can't get used to not celebrating my children's birthdays with them but I suppose I must. I'd planned to make special cake too. Never mind, it's Dad's birthday soon: I'll make a cake for him.

Mum usually buys him one from Marks. He would appreciate home-made I am sure.

7th October

I was asking Young Mr D about will-making (a subject on which, it turns out, he has no knowledge unless I am talking about inheritance tax and then he could put me in touch with a man who does know — as if I am going to be affected by inheritance tax!) when he casually mentioned that David Davies is coming in tomorrow morning at 11 o'clock. He took the phone call while I was at Eatz fetching our lunch.

I am pleased that I was not here and did not have to speak to David after the fiasco of Singles Night. Although meeting him will be unavoidable tomorrow unless I can time a trip to the loo to coincide with his arrival. And his departure. But he is always early. I can't stay in the loo for half an hour or more. I will just have to talk to him. Well, not talk so much as be polite. That's all I have to do. I can be polite; that's not a problem.

8th October

'Damn you stupid thing! Will you do as you're told? Come on, please — look, I am warning you: I can do without this today of all days.'

I was so engrossed in haranguing the computer that I failed to notice the window-cleaner coming in to be paid until he said, 'Would you like me to have a look?'

Normally the arrival of the window cleaner brightens my day no end but I wasn't in the mood for flirty banter. I wasn't in the mood for anything much except possibly computicide.

'Oh, right,' I snapped, 'so this would be "Me man therefore good with computers, while you woman, thus inept with anything inanimate", would it?'

'Actually it would be me, computer science graduate, offering to help you, very nice lady, with problem computer.'

'Oh.' I crumpled. 'I am so sorry, it's just ... well, it won't do anything I say and now it's just not doing anything.'

'Don't worry,' he grinned, 'I can see you're stressed out. Would you like me to have a look?'

'Oh yes please, I would love it.'

He walked round and joined me behind my desk. I moved slightly to allow him access but he still had to lean over me to reach the keyboard. He had a very strong masculine smell.

I thought I should make small talk. 'So how does a computer science graduate come to be cleaning windows?'

'Couldn't get a job when I graduated, started doing windows to earn some money, found it was a simple stress-free life so carried on.'

'That's nice.'

He started doing something with the keyboard.

Noticed his nails were clean and neat-edged, obviously cared for but not excessively so. And his hands were very capable: no doubt he knows how to use them in all sorts of ways.

He turned his face and looked at me expectantly. I blushed. He said, 'Has it?'

'Has it what?'

'Has it tried to reset itself?'

'Oh. I have no idea. It might have done.'

He turned back to the screen.

Resisting the temptation to stroke his shoulders, I asked, 'Do you work out?'

'Hmm?'

'Only I was thinking of joining a gym and I wondered if you could recommend one. The one you go to, maybe?'

'Hmm, I don't know, this doesn't look good. Have you checked the connections?'

'The what?'

'Don't worry, I'll do it.'

He got down on his knees and squeezed under the desk between my leg and the computer. I could feel the muscles in his arms move.

Then I felt his fingers walk up my calf before stopping in the bend of my knee as though waiting for a sign from me. His breath was warm against my leg. I leaned back in my chair and closed my eyes.

Chapter 14

'Alison — are you all right, Alison?'

'What?!'

I'd been so carried away with my reverie I'd failed to register the sound of the front door opening. I was so appalled to be caught mid-fantasy, and by David of all people, I leapt to my feet, kneeing the window-cleaner's head against the metal box of the computer. He ouch-ed, I squeaked and David peered over the desk.

'My computer's not working,' I said hurriedly.

'I see and this is the computer repair man, I take it?'

'No, he's the window-cleaner.'

David stared at me, his expression getting colder by the moment. 'I did hope we could be civil to each other, but if that's not the way you want it, so be it.'

'No, honestly...' I began just as Young Mr Davies came out of his office.

'Ah, David,' he said, smiling, 'perfect timing. Come on in. Alison, could you make us some coffee, please?'

'Not for me thank you. I wouldn't want to disturb Alison.'

And he marched into young Mr D's office, leaving Young Mr D looking confusedly from one of us to the other, before following him in.

'Is he always such a grumpy sod, or is he just having a bad day?' the window-cleaner asked as he stood up.

'He's a grumpy sod.' I sighed. 'So, any joy?'

'I'm afraid it looks like your computer's knackered.'

'I know how it feels.'

'I think it might be the disc drive. Hope you've got all your data backed up.'

'Oh, yes, I am very careful about backing up.'

I am highly efficient; I do it every week. Unfortunately I was due to do it today. I screamed quietly under my breath.

The man at the computer shop said it would be tomorrow at the earliest before he could even look at it.

'And how soon after that will you be able to tell me if I have lost my data?'

He shook his head, 'That depends.'

I wonder if psychiatrists can tell from the look on your face what is going on in your head. Possibly some could, but I'm sure I don't have to worry about DD. He is far too insensitive to notice a woman's mood unless she were waving an axe in his direction. Even then he'd probably put it down to her being of a funny age.

∞

I wonder if I am fanciable. How do you tell? Security of life with Brian made me complacent — and look what happened: I became less fanciable. But only less fanciable than a twenty-eight-year-old and that's something to be proud of really.

I suppose David must have been attracted to me for at least a brief moment. And Internet Barry was interested (although I suspect he would have been interested in anything available with boobs).

But I've definitely lost the art of flirting; I must put in some practice.

9th October

We were having terrible weather today, so bad that Mr Davies Senior held open the door for five minutes so we could all 'look at that rain!' To be fair to him, I suppose he wasn't aware of the draught that blows through the office when the front door is open or that I had emptied the filing cabinet onto the floor. His comment that it 'was a bit of a silly thing to do,' was uncalled for though. Still it's only A to G, and I'm sure I'll be able to get it all resorted by the end of the afternoon.

And at least my Pending tray is clear! That was my first job this morning. I was delighted to find that most of the items in it could be thrown away. Either they were out of date or I had forgotten what it was I was supposed to be doing with them. It's a very handy hint, I think. "If you're not sure what to do with something, leave it alone and it will probably go away of its own accord."

Later

I was late home from work as I didn't finish re-filing A to G until well past normal home time. I was going to leave it until tomorrow but Young Mr Davies' comment as he was going, albeit said in a light-hearted manner, made me determined to get it done. I don't think that the filing fiasco is at all typical of me and I am not in the habit of making more work for myself. If anything, it was his father's fault but I'm much too nice to point that out.

Anyway, it's done now including one or two folders that had been filed incorrectly originally. Muriel must have done it. There is no way I would file Jacobson under G or Serys Computers under C. Although computer does begin with C, so that, at least, is a rational mistake to make.

Thanks to the filing incident, as I prefer to call it, I didn't have time to go to Eatz and practise my flirting technique on Jeff behind the counter, and the only male client to call in today was eighty-three and fragile. I did try looking through my lashes at him, but the expression on his face suggested a heart attack was imminent so I didn't prolong the exercise. I would hate to have him on my conscience.

13th October

What a good job I decided to make Dad's cake tonight. I forgot to set the timer and my first attempt was burned around the edges - only slightly, it's still edible (and very tasty) but crispy edges wouldn't impress Mum.

The second one sank a little as I took it out a fraction too early (as I was fearful that it would burn) but I can stick extra cream in the middle to make it stay up.

14th October

I finished work early to give me time to ice the cake and take it to Dad before he and Mum go out for the evening with their friends.

I've had to put the icing in the fridge to see if that helps solidify it a little. I don't think it's meant to drip off the cake.

Later

Chilling didn't help but more icing sugar did. Sadly I'm having to reconsider my plan of writing Happy Birthday Dad in icing is it's now too thick to squeeze out of the nozzle. Maybe a little extra water would help.

Later again

Mum phoned just as I was adding water so I now have a runny liquid icing. I hope I didn't sound too irritable when I told Mum I will be there when I get there and I will be there sooner if she does not keep interrupting me to ask how it is going and when I will be there.

I've run out of icing sugar so have abandoned writing idea; instead I'm going to cover the cake with Smarties.

Much later

Dad was thrilled with the cake, said it made him feel like a kid again. It took him a while to get his breath back after trying to blow out the candles but he didn't mind. Mum was a bit concerned though as she didn't want him to pop his clogs on his birthday.

18th October, Saturday

I met Pippa and Bev for lunch today. Bev had that pleased-with-herself look that I am coming to dread. It means she has thought of another way to find a man for me.

Today's effort: when we sat down and were waiting for our baguettes to arrive, Bev produced a rather crumpled flyer from her bag.

'Sorry,' she said, straightening it out. 'It's been in my bag for days.'

When it was just about legible she held it out to me. 'What about this then?'

I read it aloud, '"Love to dance but don't have a partner? Look no further. Join Franco's Lessons... for ballroom and love." Oh, purleese, you can't be serious!'

'Why not? You said when you came back from Tenby that you wished you could dance, and this way you get to meet men as well. Sounds ideal to me.'

'Everything sounds ideal to you, Bev. Internet dating sounded ideal to you; Singles Night sounded ideal to you. But I'm the one who ends up looking a prat.'

'The photo in the paper wasn't that bad.'

'I wasn't talking about the photo! I meant generally.'

'I'm just trying to help. If you don't want me to, you only have to say. There's no need to get all uppity on me. Huh.'

'Now, come on, you two,' Pippa intervened. 'Let's look at this sensibly. You did say you wished you could dance, Alison.'

'Don't you start, Pippa. Obviously these classes are for sad losers who can't find a partner any other way.'

They both just looked at me, Bev with her eyebrows raised halfway up her forehead.

I downed what remained of my wine. 'Okay, I'll give it a go.'

Bev insisted on coming home with me from the pub and making me phone Franco's Dance School. Franco must have been teaching at the time as man who answered the phone was distinctly Welsh.

'I'd like to enrol for the Tuesday ballroom class, please. If it's not full that is. If it is, it doesn't matter, I don't mind.'

'Naw, we're not full, love, but yew're a lady, an't you?'

'I always try to be. Is that a problem?'

'We short of men, see. Never mind, love, you come along, it'll be awright.'

'Are you sure? I don't mind.'

'Naw, naw, wass yewr name?'

I gave him my details. The first class is next Tuesday in the YM. It will be fine. I am only going to learn to dance; I am not expecting to find romance. The man on the phone said he would put a leaflet in the post to me this afternoon.

21st October

The leaflet introducing Franco's Love Lessons (as they call the Tuesday night class) arrived this morning. Franco used to be a national champion. There is a photo of him on the cover. He is tall, slim and very Gallic-looking. It doesn't mention if he's married. I'm surprised to find that I'm suddenly looking forward to this class. And I'm not going to tell Mum and Dad about it yet but will surprise them at Christmas with my dancing skills.

Late evening

I was a little late arriving for class and wasn't sure in which room in the YM it was being held. I stuck my head round one door to enquire. A tall, fat and very Gallic-looking man came rushing up to greet me. 'Yew here for the dance class?'

It was the voice from the phone. 'Er, yes.'

'Cum in, yew must be...' he consulted his sheet of paper, 'Alison.'

I nodded.

'Welcum, Alison, I'm Franco, retired undefeated ballroom champion of Wales and the West Midlands.' He did an elaborate bow. 'Cum and join the others and we'll make a start.'

There were eight of us in the class – five women (Elsie, Gwen, Jane, Rose and me) and three men (Peter, Martin and Nic). Franco, the teacher, expressed his concern at this mismatch but Gwen said there was no need. 'You see, I'm going to be a man.'

'Really?' said Nic. 'How thrilling!'

'And how brave, to come right out and admit it just like that, I do admire you,' said Jane.

'I don't know why,' said Gwen.

It turned out she didn't mean she was planning a sex change but that she and Elsie intended to dance together and they had decided that she would learn the man's role.

'You see,' said Gwen, 'every Saturday we go down the club.'

'With our husbands,' said Elsie.

'And they sit and drink all night.'

'But once a month there's a band there.'

'And they won't dance with us.'

'So we thought we'd do it by ourselves.'

'So, I'm going to be the man.'

'As she's taller.'

'Then we won't have to bother about those idle so-n-sos.'

'We can get on with enjoying ourselves.'

Franco said that really they should have gone to the class on a Wednesday, which is for couples, but they said that was their bingo night. We all said we didn't mind them joining us so it was settled.

Then Franco got us all to sit in a circle and say why we'd joined the class. The reasons people gave were:

Jane – my stars said it was the right time;

Peter - my, er, friend thought it would get me out of the house, stop me brooding;

Rose – I was going to do flower arranging but the class was full;

Martin – I like to set myself the challenge of acquiring a new skill every year;

Nic - as soon as I hear music my feet just want to dance, I can't keep still;

Me – I'm looking for a man (No, I didn't say that really, but said I had reached an age when I felt I should be able to dance).

Franco said that each week he would expect us to change partners and that previous classes had got to know each other by going to the pub afterwards. In fact, they'd had one wedding already and the class had only been going for two years.

We began with waltz. I was partnered by Peter. I would have preferred Martin but there's plenty of time for that. I could feel clamminess of Peter's body through his shirt (buttoned up to collar but no tie). I'll give him the benefit of the doubt and assume it was first night nerves.

I was thrilled to be the youngest woman there. It's been a long time since I have been the youngest woman anywhere. At least, I assume I am the youngest. I'm pretty sure that Jane is older than me in spite of lobe-stretching dangly earrings. She has that look about her: you know she will walk past a baby in a supermarket without smiling at it.

Afterwards Elsie and Gwen decided not to come to pub but the rest of us did as we'd been told and sat round nervously waiting for someone to say something. Peter broke the silence, 'I nearly didn't come tonight, I was very tired.'

'Why, dear? Did you have a late night last night?' Rose asked.

'No, but I was woken several times by a giraffe in my bedroom.'

I started to giggle then realised everyone else was looking serious.

'Oh, you poor thing,' said Rose.

'Has it visited you before?' said Jane.

'Yes, several times.'

'And have you asked it what it wants?'

'I didn't think of that, Jane. Should I have done?'

'Oh, yes, I think so. You might have been able to resolve its problem and it would have gone away.'

'That's a good idea,' said Rose.

'Yes, I always find it best to talk problems through. People say I'm a very good listener. In fact, I'm a bit of an amateur therapist.'

'Really?' said Nic, who'd been wriggling on the edge of his seat. 'I'll have to bring my friend Stefan along to meet you. He's been to three, no, I tell a lie, four therapists in the past year.'

'Poor boy,' said Rose, 'he must have a lot of problems.'

'Problems? Huh, no, he just loves talking about himself! I've never met anyone like him for talking. I tell you, he should be on the stage. In fact,' he leaned forward, rested his elbow on the table and pointed with his fore finger, 'he was in the local panto when I first met him. He was the cat in Puss in Boots two, no, it must have been three years ago. Did you catch it? No? Oh, it suited him no end, he is such a pussy. Ooh, I love to go to the shows, don't you? Have you seen Phantom? I love it, I've seen it eleven, no, make that twelve times. But my favourite is still Les Mis.'

'Les Mis?' Rose asked. 'I've never heard of him. You don't mean Les Dennis, do you?'

'Oah, no! Les Miserables, oh, such drama, such passion, I go all shivery just thinking about it. I weep buckets at the end every time.'

'Personally I much prefer the book,' Martin said.

'A book? Are you telling me that someone has made a book of the musical? How marvellous. Oh, I shall rush round to Waterstones tomorrow lunchtime and order it.'

Martin caught my eye and raised his eyebrow just a fraction. He is obviously a man of culture. Good taste as well. Smart but not overly dressy trousers, a simple shirt, undone at the collar, and a plain jacket. Definite potential. Jane flirted outrageously with him, waiting until Nic had gone to the loo before saying she agreed that Victor Hugo's book was far superior to the musical. She is much older than him, I'm sure and probably of an age when they studied the classics in school. Before my time. I'm not at all familiar with the book, but I've seen the musical. And cried at the end.

28th October, Tuesday

In spite of his shape, Franco is as light as meringue. He chose me to partner him in the rumba (just for the initial demonstration but I'm still rather flattered that he picked up on my natural gift for the South American rhythm). The rumba is a very sexy dance, Franco says. (Another reason why he chose me perhaps? At least I have what could pass in a good i.e. bad, light for a figure.) It is a 'come on' dance, where the women behave very provocatively luring the men in. This is definitely what I need to learn. He said that later he will teach us 'the wiggle' that should accompany it but he thinks that for now we need to concentrate on our feet rather than our bums. I'm inclined to agree with him. Already I seem to have lost the ability to tell right from left.

Nic was my partner this week. He apologised before we started. 'You see, I went to an all boys' school, and I was so tiny, I always had to be the girl, and it's hard to change the habits of a lifetime.'

It wasn't too much of a problem as long as he concentrated. We only crashed badly once when Franco shouted, 'Ladies, two steps forward.'

Afterwards in the pub Nic said, 'I'm a martyr to my feet. I don't like to grumble but, you know, I'm never without pain. Stefan says I deserve a medal.'

Rose leaned forward. 'I never have any problem with my feet because I rely on my granny's secret. It always works for me.'

'No, oh, do tell, Rosie, I will be forever in your debt.'

'Well, what you've got to do is ... no, I don't like to say.'

'Oh, go on, you've got to, you can't keep me in suspenders now.'

'All right then,' Rose lowered her voice even more so that we all had to lean in very close. 'You've got to bathe your feet in — your own wee-wee. There I've said it.' And she sat back against her chair.

''That is so gross, Rosie, it's disgusting. Does it work?'

'Without fail.'

Jane sniffed loudly, 'Personally I am of the opinion that my feet have to work hard all day so they deserve a little pampering. I always use a peppermint and camomile milk footbath from Nature's Blessing. It's rather expensive but I think I'm worth it. And it's all organic.'

'Huh,' Rose said, 'mine's all organic too. And it's free.'

There was a moment's silence while the two protagonists eyed each other up, then Peter, who had been sitting quietly at the end of the table said, 'The giraffe was in my room again last night.'

'The giraffe?' Martin said.

'Yes, just sitting there with a mournful look on his face.'

'How do you know it was a he?' I asked.

Jane tutted, 'Really, Alison, what a stupid thing to say. Now Peter, did you ask him what he wanted as I suggested last week?'

'Yes, Jane, I did.'

'That's excellent, Peter, and what did he say?'

'He told me his name was Benito and he said he wanted a gun.'

'Oooh, and what did you say to that?'

'I said I didn't have one to hand but that if he would come back in a day or two, I would see what I could do.'

'What a splendid answer, Peter,' Jane said.

'But you're not actually going to get one, are you, Peter?' I said.

'I'm not sure how easy that would be but I thought I would try.'

'You can buy anything off the internet these days,' Jane said.

'I really don't think you should though, Peter. Benito sounds like a very depressed giraffe. He might be thinking of trying to kill himself, have you considered that?' I looked pointedly at Jane. 'There aren't many giraffes in this world as it is. One less would be too horrid to contemplate, wouldn't it?'

'Alison's right, Peter. I can't bear to think of a beautiful creature like a giraffe committing suicide. It makes me want to cry,' Rose did, in fact, look close to tears.

'I suppose you're right,' Peter said. 'But what will I tell Benito when he comes back?'

I felt like suggesting that Benito should listen to some of Bev's Leonard Cohen tapes if he wants to know what misery is, but I restrained myself. Instead I said, 'Why not just tell him that you love him? And that you want to be his friend and that you don't like your friends having guns in case they accidentally hurt themselves.'

Peter smiled for the first time that evening. 'What a marvellous idea, Alison, I'll do that. I could be his friend, I am sure. And you're right, the world doesn't need another dead giraffe.'

He nodded serenely then excused himself to go to the loo. The moment he was out of earshot Jane said, 'Really, Alison, I don't think an amateur should interfere in cases like this.'

'So what were you doing when he told him he could get a gun on the internet?'

'People who threaten to commit suicide very rarely carry it through. It is a well-known fact that they are merely attention seekers.'

'And did you get that out of Nanny's Guide to Perfect Little People?'

'I'll have you know that I am doing a course in psychology and I do have some knowledge.' Jane turned away from me to face the others. 'Don't you agree, Martin?'

'What? Oh, I think so, yes, quite probably. Who'd like another drink?

As we left the pub Nic linked his arm through mine. 'I think you were quite right about the gun, Aliss,' he said. 'And it was so sweet of you to get Pete to tell the giraffe that he loved him. Aah, bless. I bet you're a lovely mummy. And as for Jane's poor feet having to work hard all day, well I should say so, shouldn't you, carrying that lot about! I feel sorry for her little tootsies. Now, I tell you what I'll do, I'll get Stefan to meet us in the pub next week. He'll give Jane something to practise on,' he giggled. 'Even if she is only doing an evening class at the Tech in Psychology for Beginners.'

'She's not?'

'She is. I saw her when I went to my Feng Shui class. I waved, "Cooee" to her but she ignored me, silly cow. Oh, I can't wait for Stefan to meet her.'

4th November, Tuesday

I've had a wonderful evening. Martin was my partner for the cha cha cha cha cha oops, I mean cha cha cha. He's not as good as Nic but better than Peter. Most important he is just the right height. That is important in a man. I told Nic and Stefan that when they asked me what sort of man I was after. I said it doesn't matter as long as my head can rest on his shoulder. Nothing else matters. Although a villa in the south of France would be a nice extra. Stefan agreed with me. He said he would never consider a man less than six foot. I am not quite that fussy.

I can tell that Stefan used to be an actor. He is very theatrical. He made us move on from the pub, which he said was far too ~~borjoursie~~ ~~borgoise~~ common, to a vodka bar. Rose decided against coming as she had quilting class the next day and Peter said he wouldn't because of his medication, so it was just Nic, Stefan, Martin, Jane and me who went. Jane only came because Martin was coming and I don't know why Martin came as he didn't drink as he was driving and he was po-faced all evening. I told him so. He said, 'I'm afraid I don't find the spectacle of grown men and women making fools of themselves very attractive.' I don't know who he was talking about; I couldn't see anyone making a fool of themselves.

I have never been to a vodka bar before but Stefan seemed to know most people there and they were all awfully friendly. I had white chocolate vodka. Then I had strawberry vodka. Then I tasted

Nic's bubblegum vodka but I didn't like that very much so I was going to have a cookies and cream vodka but Stefan said it was time to go and he and Nic would share a taxi with me.

Then Martin offered me and Jane a lift home. He obviously hadn't realised that Stefan didn't have a car because he didn't offer him and Nic a lift but it was all right because I did. Jane sat in the front and I squeezed in between Stefan and Nic. Closest body contact I've had with a man — two men — for yonks. I said as much to them. Nic said, 'Ah bless, and it had to be us. Never mind, Aliss, we'll help you find a man, won't we, Stefi?'

But Stefi had fallen asleep.

Chapter 15

5th November, Wednesday

I've spent most of the morning feeling rather sick. I hope I'm not coming down with a tummy bug. Muriel says I am looking peaky. She asked Mr Davies Senior if he agreed with her. He said that I looked my normal lovely self to him and did we know where you could buy Jumping Jacks these days. He is going to his son's house for a bonfire party tonight and he wants to take some Jumping Jacks for his grandchildren. I said I thought they had been banned for being dangerous. He said that was the trouble with today's nanny state. Young Mr D came into the office then and his father scowled at him.

Muriel thinks all fireworks should be banned. 'I will get home tonight and poor Bertie will be under the stairs yowling. He makes so much noise I have the neighbours complaining. Not that I know how they have the nerve to complain with their three sons playing their records at all hours.'

She is going home early to be with Bertie and both Mr Ds are finishing early to prepare for the party. I feel like Cinderella. I've always loved fireworks. I could go to the display in the football ground but it wouldn't be much fun without a hand to grab when I scream.

∞

It's Brian's birthday in three days and I can't decide whether to send him a card or not. He didn't send me one (even though it was my fiftieth) but I won't hold that against him.

Sending him a card would show him that I have moved on, that I harbour no hard feelings against him and that I understand that things have changed and I'm happy with that, but also that I'm still fond of him and would like to maintain a good relationship with the father of my children.

On the other hand, if I send him a card it might look as though I am desperately trying to win him back, or that I am petty and trying to show him up for not sending me a card, or that I am still in love with him.

He'll get cards from the children; he doesn't need a card from me. In fact he probably wouldn't notice either way. I am stressing myself out here for no reason. I won't send him a card.

But I'm still fond of him and don't see why I should let what he, or Gina, might think stop me from doing what I want to do. I've spent too much time over the years caring what other people might think of my actions.

I will get him a card tomorrow.

I called Adam to remind him about his father's birthday but Chloe had already done so. It was good to talk to him. He is well, enjoying himself, eating sensibly, getting enough sleep, working hard and not drinking too much. I was believing him until it got to the last bit. But I'm not going to worry. He is a grown man now and no longer my responsibility.

Which is nonsense of course. He will be my responsibility until the day I die. Do mothers ever stop fussing? Mine hasn't.

6th November, Thursday

I spent my entire lunchtime looking for a card for Brian.

I couldn't decide between funny, manly, modern or retro. The funny weren't and the manly were too grandfatherish unless you're into fishing, cars or golf (Brian isn't), leaving modern or retro. I'm surprised card manufacturers haven't yet designed a card for 'my ex'; I would have thought that would be a big seller.

Eventually I bought a card with a picture of George Best on, saying, 'I spent most of my money on wine, women and song. The rest I wasted.'

Then I decided Brian might read an accusation into that so bought one with two old-fashioned-looking football players on the front and the words, Losing is just the same as winning only the other way around.

Then I feared he might misunderstand that so bought one with a mini on the front. I'd just decided that he might take that as an insult to his manhood when I realised I had already gone over my lunch hour and that if I was going to analyse every card in the shop would never catch the post. So I opted for the mini and tough cookies if he takes it as a slur.

I didn't have time for a dilemma over what to write inside and I simply put, Happy birthday, Brian, Aliss, stuck it in the envelope and posted it before I could change my mind.

Later

Adam phoned to ask me what his dad's address is.

'Haven't you posted his card yet?'

'It's not his birthday until tomorrow!'

'Well it won't get there now!'

'Won't it? He'll get it on Sunday then.'

'Adam, there is no post on Sunday.'

'Oh, Monday then. No sweat, Mum, Dad will be cool about it.'

'Make sure you phone him tomorrow then.'

'Yeah, okay, I'll try and remember.'

'Don't just try: make sure you do!'

8th November, Saturday

I got up to the sound of knocking on the front door. I opened it to find Bev on the doorstep with Charlie and a large suitcase.

'Bev! Are you all right? What's happened? Have you left Simon?'

She barged in. 'What are you talking about, Aliss? Why would I leave Si'

'I just wondered, you being here with a suitcase.'

'It's not my suitcase, it's Charlie's.'

Charlie looked up at me with his big brown eyes and wagged his tail, knocking the vase off the table. 'Whoops,' Bev said. 'You might want to move things that are at that level, he doesn't have a lot of control over his tail.'

She took off Charlie's lead and handed it to me. 'You'll want to put this somewhere safe.'

I wondered if I were still asleep and at any minute Bev would turn into Alan Titchmarsh and Charlie into a floppy-breasted woman.

'All his food is in the suitcase, along with his blanket, dishes, vitamin pills and instructions. There should be enough food but if you need to buy more I'll pay you for it when I get back. He needs walking twice a day but one long one will probably do, and don't forget to poop-scoop. The council are clamping down on that. You don't know how grateful I am that you agreed to look after Charlie while we're away. He hates the kennels so much and wouldn't speak to us for days last time when we got home. I'm sorry I've got to rush but I wanted to leave it to the last minute and Si will be going spare if I don't get back soon. Now be a good boy for your Auntie Alison, won't you, Charlie?'

Bev hugged his hairy face to hers, 'We'll be back soon and we love you lots.' Then she kissed his nose before straightening up and kissing me. 'You're a star. The telephone number of the vet is in the suitcase – not that you'll need it, of course. Gotta go, byeeee.'

I vaguely remember agreeing to consider looking after Charlie while Bev and Simon went on holiday but I thought I'd thought better of it. I obviously didn't mention this fact to Bev. Still, he's here now so I'll have to make the best of it. He will be good company in fact. How hard can it be to look after a dog for a week? Or was it two? I can hear strange slurping noise; I'd better investigate.

Charlie was drinking from the toilet bowl. I thought dogs only did that in cartoons. I spent the rest of the morning unpacking Charlie's suitcase and putting down his blanket. The trouble was, each time I put it down, he picked it up again, looked at me expectantly and wagged his tail.

'It's no good, Charlie, I haven't learned doggy talk yet. You'll have to be patient. Now, what – do – you – want?'

We stood and stared at each other for a little longer but no answer was forthcoming. In the end I let him out to play in the back garden while I did the dishes. He seemed happy so I left him while I went upstairs to get the dirty washing. I was trying to decide if I could squeeze another day's wear out of my favourite jumper when there was a screech of brakes outside. Something clicked in my head.

'Charlie!'

I rushed to the window in time to see a very irate-looking driver shaking his fist at a puzzled-looking waggy-tailed dog. I ducked down below the window sill but could still hear yelling about irresponsible owners. I crept downstairs and peeped through the window to make sure the car had gone before running out to grab Charlie and pull him back into the house.

I had a cup of tea to calm my nerves before erecting a temporary barrier of old bikes, carrier bags and garden tools to stop Charlie getting from the enclosed back garden to no-gate front garden. I am impressed with my own creativity.

Later in bed

With Charlie. No matter where I put his blanket, it seems Charlie likes my bed better. It's not a problem. His weight next to me is reassuring and warm. I'll sleep like a log tonight after having to re-build the garden barrier seven times as well as taking him for a long walk in the woods. Nothing will keep me awake tonight.

Just past midnight

Charlie is lying diagonally across the bed leaving very little room for me. I've tried pushing him but each time I think I've done it, he rolls back again. I'll going to have to adopt the foetal position and snuggle into the remaining space.

1.54 am

I'm convinced Charlie was a foghorn in a previous life. You couldn't call what he does snoring. It is more like the sound of a rocket being launched. After hoovering in vast quantities of air, he goes quiet for a moment — the peace sailors have always known comes before the storm. Then his whole body trembles as he breathes out through his mouth, his jowls flapping in the wind. Plp plp plp plp plp plp plp. I've tried pinching his nose but that just delays exhalation. I'm relieved it's Sunday tomorrow and I'll be able to sleep all day.

5.15 am spare bedroom

I was woken by a hot wet tongue licking my nose. For a brief moment my dream became reality and all of the last eighteen months became a nightmare from which I was finally waking. I was just muttering, 'Go and clean your teeth first, Brian, your breath smells very – doggish!' when I came to. I opened my eyes, sat up abruptly and looked around. Everything looked sort of familiar but there was something not exactly right. The big dog on the bed especially was not right.

8.37 am

It's impossible to stay mad with Charlie for long. He is so affectionate and pleased to see me. It makes a nice change to have a friendly greeting in morning. I'll spend time today encouraging Charlie to sleep in the kitchen on his blanket. His blanket looks very clean. Maybe it is freshly washed and unfamiliar. I think I vaguely recall an old wives' tale about rubbing dogs' blankets in their own pee to stop them wandering. It sounds fairly disgusting and unhygienic but it might have the desired effect. When I let Charlie out I'll wait for him to cock his leg so I can pop his blanket under the stream.

A little later

I followed Charlie around the garden for half an hour before the phone rang. While I was talking to Mum, I had to watch Charlie release the equivalent of the river Thames onto the rose bush. It was probably a stupid idea anyway. Did old wives have nothing better to do with their time than follow dogs? Tonight I'll simply be firm and make him stay in the kitchen.

Charlie is very sociable and much prefers being in my company to being alone. It's been a long time since I've had this effect on a male (unless you count Martin who is showing just a smidgen of interest in my company outside of dance class.) Maybe my effect on Charlie is a good sign.

Later

I can't go to the toilet without having Charlie sitting outside the door crying. I left the door open last time but he rested his head on my lap and started sniffing. I'm not doing that again.

Early evening

I took Charlie to the woods again. I was enjoying watching him rolling on his back until a strange man said, 'You don't want to let him do that.'

'Why not? He's enjoying himself.'

'You've heard the expression, "pig in shit", haven't you?'

'I thought it was clover.'

'Eh?'

'I thought the saying was 'pig in clover'.

'I dunno about that but I know what he's rolling in.'

'What?'

'Shit.'

'Oh no!'

'Badger shit, most like, that's the smelliest.'

'But why would he want to do that?'

'It's what dogs do.'

Much later

I got Charlie into bathroom on the third attempt. The first two ended with me chasing him off the bed and round the bedroom. I had run the bath (using my best bath oil, a present from Chloe for Mother's Day, as Bev hadn't left any doggy shampoo) then attempted to persuade him to jump in by holding chocolate biscuits over water. Mistake. The biscuits crumbled in heat.

Then I tried adopting the weight-lifting pose, feet apart, knees bent, body forward, arms shoved under his armpits. I heaved and I heaved. The only thing that moved was a muscle in my back.

It seemed the shower was the only alternative. I squeezed into my bathing costume and got in with him. I was soaking wet before I realised that the only shampoo in there was Wild Mint and Tea Rose (very expensive and bought when I was feeling low and in need of a pick-up).

Eventually I was satisfied that the smell was gone and let him out only to watch him shake all over the spare bed.

It seemed silly to waste the water and bath oil so I was about to get in the bath when I noticed it was full of biscuit crumbs. I gave up and spent the next hour cleaning the bathroom, clearing doggy hair from the plughole and changing quilt covers on beds.

I fed Charlie, gave him his vitamins, and showered myself again. I was too tired to eat or battle with Charlie so we both went upstairs to bed.

I definitely need to get a man about the house soon. It's impossible to rub Deep Heat in your own back.

10th November, Monday

'Good morning, Tyler and Grimm, veterinary practice.'

'Good morning, I wonder if you can help me. I'm looking after my friend's dog and I've got to go to work but every time I go out of the door, he cries.'

'He'll be missing his owner and seeking constant reassurance that you're not going to go and leave him too.'

'I don't want a psychiatric report; I just want to know how I can stop him crying.'

'There's no need to be like that. I was just trying to explain how he's feeling and his need for attention.'

'Yes, yes, I'd worked all that out for myself. I'm not stupid.'

'Maybe not, but you obviously got out of bed the wrong side this morning.'

'To have got out of bed, my own bed, any side, would have been wonderful. To have slept would have been wonderful. Please, just tell me what I can do to shut him ... to help him deal with his insecurity.'

'That's better. Dogs respond much better to love than to bullying, you know. Now you could try leaving the radio on for him. A nice gentle music channel would be soothing, or a talk channel might make him think you were still there. And you could give him something of yours to cuddle up with. A sweater perhaps. And quite often we find that dogs are like toddlers starting nursery school. They scream while mum's there but as soon as she's out of the way, they settle down and get on with it.'

'So you're saying I should just go and leave him to it?'

'Once you've tried everything you can, yes.'

I left Charlie with Radio 2 and my nightie. I tried to swap it for a duster but Charlie was reluctant to give up his trophy so I stroked him gently, promised I'd be home lunchtime, and kissed him on the nose. (I can't believe I did that.) I closed the front door quietly after shouting over my shoulder, 'See you soon, Charlie, be a good boy,' then crept out of the drive and crouched down behind the low wall. I laddered my tights in the process but couldn't go back to get more as that would have meant disturbing Charlie. I could hear him howling, a howl that turned into a pitiful whimper before fading into a familiar snore. The ratbag. He wasn't missing me at all. I think I'll keep him awake tonight, see how he likes it.

Old Mr Price next door came out when I was hiding behind the wall. He crouched down until he was past the drive. 'It's all right, I don't think they saw me,' he said, as he raised his hat to me.

11th November, Tuesday

'Good morning, Tyler and Grimm, veterinary practice.'

'Good morning, I wonder if you can help me? I'm looking after my friend's dog …'

'Didn't I speak to you yesterday morning?'

'Yes, you did. How clever of you to remember."

'So what can I do for you today?'

'Well, it's a bit embarrassing.'

'Just come straight out with it, I assure you I've heard most things.'

'Well, it's Charlie, he, er, smells.'

'That's quite normal, most dogs smell.'

'No, I know that but this is, um, not just his body odour. It's um, well, he keeps breaking wind.'

'Smelly farts, you mean?'

'Since you mention it, yes.'

'Have you changed his diet? Are you feeding him on something other than his usual food?'

'No, Bev left me with loads of tins of Chum.'

'In that case, I'm afraid you'll just have to put up with it.'

'But it's horrendous. I had to leave the room last night. I missed the end of the film because of it.'

'The George Clooney film? I didn't expect it to end like that.'

'I wouldn't know as I missed it.'

'You could try giving him peppermints.'

'Would that help?'

'No, but it would make his breath smell nice.'

'It's not that end that causes the problem.'

Thank goodness I'm going out to dance class tonight. At least I'll be able to breathe there.

10.35 pm

I have a date! As we were leaving the pub after dancing, Martin sidled up to me and asked me if I'd like to go for a meal and to the cinema on Saturday. I said, 'Oh, yes, the new James Bond is showing, isn't it?' I thought he'd prefer that to a more girly film.

'Quite possibly but I meant *Torres les amores* at the Gallery.'

'Oh.'

'Unless you've already seen it, of course?'

'I don't think it's one I've come across, actually.'

'Really? I thought everyone would know it: it's Fallissimo's masterpiece, in its original language.'

'And that would be, um, Italian?'

'Basque.'

'Oh.'

I know it will be excellent. An experience. Three and a half hours seems a little long but I'm sure time will just fly by. And it'll be good for me. I have been boring and suburban for long enough; I need to broaden my horizons.

And Martin might not be George Clooney – more George and Mildred – but he's a man and it's the best offer I've had recently, or look like having. Not counting Mr Price asking me round to his place to clean the cooker. He would have done it himself but he has 'han hallergy'. I told him, I come out in a rash too when faced with a dirty oven. Which, in retrospect, wasn't a good idea as every time he sees me now he asks how my rash is.

On the plus side, Martin is presentable, male, seemingly unattached and … well, male. He will do to practise on. After the David Davies experience, I need to go gently. And he always smells nice. That has to be a good sign, a man who is fussy about his appearance.

12th November

I've had a long phone chat with Brian. He phoned to thank me for my card. He said he liked it very much and could tell I had put a lot of thought into choosing it. 'I used to like that,' he said, 'the way you always took such care over choosing a card to match the recipient.'

I didn't know what to say so just asked if he had received Adam's card. 'Yes,' he laughed, 'on Monday. I guessed that you'd reminded him.'

'Not just me,' I said, 'Chloe called him too.'

'She's just like her mother. Our children have turned out okay, haven't they?'

I was just about to snap, 'No thanks to you,' when Brian carried on, 'Of course, it's all down to you that they have.'

'Don't be silly, you played your part too. You've always been a good dad.'

'Do you really think so?'

'Yes, of course.'

He went on to ask me about work and then he said he'd seen my photo in the paper. I groaned. 'I know, I couldn't believe it,' he said. 'The reporter must have been a complete airhead. Even with that dreadful photo anyone can see you're nowhere near sixty. You don't even look forty-five these days. I said to Gina, "How on earth can anyone imagine that she's sixty?"'

'And what did Gina say?'

'She agreed it was a dreadful photo.'

'Oh. And, um, how is Gina?'

'She's fine, I think. I hardly seem to see her these days. She's always working late or out with the girls.'

There was a reply on the tip of my tongue but I didn't even have to bite it; I just didn't want to say it.

Conversation carried on in the same vein for another fifteen minutes. Finally I put the phone down feeling ... I'm not sure how I feel. I'll have to think about that.

Later

I wonder if Gina is getting itchy feet now she has discovered that fifty-one-year-old men like to stay in at night and watch sport on television. And I wonder if Brian is finding out that twenty-eight-year-olds are unforgiving about flabby stomach muscles.

I'm sorry if their relationship is falling apart. I'm sorry that our family was broken up for something so flimsy. I can feel no pity for Gina (especially as it's probably her doing and choice), but I'm sorry that Brian will be hurt.

I don't know for sure that there are problems, of course, but I sensed a wistfulness in Brian's voice. A wistfulness, now I come to think of it, that was most definitely absent when we used to go shopping and I would spend ages looking for cards. I don't remember him looking on fondly then!

No, I am sorry if yet another relationship has to fail but, and I am surprising myself here, I don't want Brian back. Assuming he would even want to come back, which he probably wouldn't, I would not have him. I don't need him; I don't want him.

I've moved on. I hadn't realised. I feel as if the blanket that's been over my head for months has been lifted.

I've spent so long wishing things had been different, wishing things had stayed the same, that I hadn't realised that the little light, which Mum has always said is at the end of every tunnel, was getting brighter. Suddenly it's a beacon. I feel as if, any minute now, the Sally Army will come marching in playing their trumpets and shaking their tambourines.

I must phone Bev and Pippa and tell them the good news. No, I can't phone Bev, she's on holiday, I have her dog - who is strangely quiet. I'd better go and see what he's doing.

13th November

8.18 am

'Good morning, Tyler and Grimm, veterinary practice.'

'Hello, it's me again.'

'(sigh) What can I do for you today?'

'I think Charlie may have eaten a sock.'

'What kind is it?'

'Why do you need to know that?'

'Because it will help determine if there might be a problem or not.'

'I see, well, it's white … with pictures of Snoopy on it.'

'(sigh) I meant what kind of dog?'

'Oh, sorry, of course you do. He's black … and he's … he's, um ...'

'You don't know, do you?'

'No.'

'Well, can you give me some idea of his size?'

'I'm sitting down now and he's had to bend down a bit to rest his head on my lap, so he looks like a hunchback.'

'He's quite large then?'

'Yes, you could say that.'

'In that case, I have no doubt the sock will work its own way out, one way or another.'

'One way or another?'

'Yes. He'll either vomit it or pass it in his faeces.'

'Oh.'

'If you're at all concerned, bring him along and we'll look at him. Now, was there anything else?'

'No, thank you.'

Urgh, how disgusting. How could he do anything as stupid as this? What makes people have dogs anyway, when they have the most appalling habits? I hope I'm not there when the sock reappears.

Later

I was there. So were Mr Price and his daughter. I saw them peering over the back garden wall and went out to see what they were looking at. Charlie had half a sock dangling out of his rear end. He was putting up quite a show. You'd have thought he was giving birth. When he saw me, he half hobbled, half dragged his bum, across the grass over to me and whimpered pathetically.

'Is he all right?' Mr Price's daughter asked.

'He's been having that whatdoyoucallit, hasn't he?' Mr Price nodded wisely. 'The stuff they gave me in hospital. I was shitting bricks for days after that.'

'Hush, Dad, Aliss doesn't want to hear about that.'

'Don't worry, and don't worry about Charlie either, he'll be fine. He ate a sock, that's all.'

'A sock? You don't want to give him socks. You want to get some bones from the butcher. That's what my missus used to do.'

'I'm sure Aliss didn't give him the sock deliberately, Dad.'

With that Charlie gave a massive final push. We all held our breath, while he grunted and, at last, the sock dropped out onto the grass. As we all breathed a sigh of relief, Charlie bounded up to me, his eyes sparkling as if to say, 'Look what I've done, Auntie Alison.'

I fetched the spade I've bought specially and scooped up my favourite sock. It appeared to be in one piece. I hesitated for an instant then dumped it in plastic bag.

Some things are worth struggling to save; others aren't.

Chapter 16

15th November, Saturday

Tea time

I took Charlie for a nice long romp in the woods to make up for the fact that I am going out this evening and leaving him. He will miss me; he has got used to us spending our evenings curled up in front of the television with a packet of crisps (cheese and onion for him, smoky bacon for me).

I managed to keep him out of any shit, badger or otherwise, but was happy for him to go for a swim in the lake. He's very fond of water as long as it is not in a bath. I was watching him swimming after the stick I had thrown for him when a voice behind me said, 'I didn't know you had a dog.'

I looked round to find David Davies with an equally big but much neater dog. 'Sit, Lady.' At the word, she sat.

'How did you do that?'

'What?'

'Make her sit?'

'I told her to.'

'That is amazing.'

'Not really, it's not hard to train them.'

'Ha ha ha.' I was so busy laughing I didn't notice Charlie coming out of the water and bounding up to us until it was too late. 'No, Charlie, noooooooo.' If it had been in a film it would have been done in slow motion. Charlie shaking his body, the circular spray of water getting wider and wider until it covered me and David and Lady. Then, when he'd finished, Charlie rolled over on his back in the mud, before taking decidedly interested sniffs at Lady.

'Nooaoh, Charlie, oooahh, nooo,' I groaned and hid my head between my hands. 'I am so sorry.'

A strange noise seemed to be coming from David's direction. I peeked out through my fingers. He was shaking his head.

'Alison, you, I,' he began but he couldn't speak for laughing.

Charlie had lost interest in Lady, who hadn't moved from her position, and had gone to check out the reeds. I dropped my hands to my side and shuffled my feet. I wasn't quite sure what to do. At last David managed to say, 'I have never met anyone like you.'

I was still not sure if this were a good or a bad thing so stayed quiet.

'They do quite a decent cup of tea in the cafe at the beginning of the path. You look as though you could do with one. Do you think Charlie would let us?'

I looked around for Charlie. He was trying to climb a tree after a squirrel.

'A cup of tea would be lovely; I'm sure he'll be fine.'

'I don't think they close until 5.30, and it's only five past, so we should just make it there in time if we hurry.'

'Oh, no, is that the time? I didn't realise it was so late. I'm going out tonight, I have to get ready.'

David shrugged, 'Another time then.'

'No, really, I would have loved to have had tea with you but Martin's picking me up at ...'

'Don't worry, you don't have to explain to me. I realise you have a busy social life. See you around. Come on, Lady.'

And she trotted after him as if she were on an invisible lead.

Bum! Double bum! And triple bum.

Still he was only suggesting a cup of tea, nothing more and I do have a proper date tonight so I shouldn't be overly disappointed.

Now I must hurry to fit in showering, hair-washing and beautifying before Martin gets here.

Later

Martin arrived early. I wasn't quite ready but all the same I didn't think my appearance warranted the look of horror he wore when I opened the door to him. He was holding out his arm towards me.

'Are these yours?' he said. Between the tips of finger and thumb, he held a pair of my knickers.

They weren't even my new lacy ones, but my biggest M&S coveralls. Quick thinking was needed. I took them from him, studied them, said, 'Er, yes. Where did you find them?'

'Your dog just gave them to me.'

'That explains it: he likes to carry something of mine around with him.'

'And you give him your panties?'

'No, of course I don't give them to him; he just takes whatever he happens to find lying around.'

Martin's eyebrows were just shooting up, in disbelief, I assume, that anyone would ever leave knickers lying around, when Charlie came charging in through the back door, along the corridor and out the front door and stuck his nose where dogs stick their noses.

'Charlie, don't do that!'

I grabbed his collar and tried to pull his head away leaving a large blob of slobber on Martin's trousers.

'Oh, dear, here, let me wipe it for you.'

I suddenly realised that wiping a potential suitor's crotch with my knickers was probably not conducive to a future relationship.

'Perhaps you'd better do it. I, er, seem to have made it worse.'

'You never mentioned that you had a dog.'

'That's because I don't. No, Charlie!'

When I looked up from trying to drag Charlie's nose from Martin's crotch, I could see the bemusement in his eyes.

'He's not mine; I'm looking after him for a friend.'

'She must be a very good friend.'

'She is – what do you mean?'

'For you to agree to look after something like that.'

'Did you sneer then?'

'When?'

'When you said, "that"?'

'I wouldn't have called it a sneer, more an expression of distaste. Now, do you think you might shut him in the kitchen before he ruins any more of my clothes?'

'I'll have you know that Charlie is a very friendly, highly intelligent and faithful companion. I am honoured to look after him and I won't be shutting him in anywhere. It's only a bit of slobber, for goodness sake.'

'Well, I'm certainly not prepared to stay here and be covered in, in, dog saliva.' He spat the words out, turned and marched down the path. He stopped when he got to the gate. 'I am very sorry about this, Alison. I had thought, dare I say, hoped, that we could be more than friends. Even after the debacle in the vodka bar I allowed you the benefit of the doubt, believing you were simply foolish and easily led by Nic and his friend. I see now I was the one who was misled. If you choose to put an animal, and not even your own animal, before me, then so be it. Good evening.'

I was so stunned I couldn't even come up with a caustic put-down.

What a prat! I'm better off without him and I'm glad I found out in time, before I wasted any more energy getting to know him. I should have guessed that he would be the kind of man who calls them 'panties'.

However, I'm now dressed up (almost) with nowhere to go. Pippa has her in-laws staying so I can't call her. I could go to the local carvery. I could phone, book a table, enjoy my own company. That would show the Martins of this world. I am woman, I am me. I would appear sophisticated, choose wine to suit me. The waiter would give me some to taste. I'd swill it round my mouth. 'Hm, a nice little chardonnay. That'll do nicely.' I'd enjoy a pleasant meal with just myself for company.

But what would I look at while I was eating? And what would I do while I was waiting for the courses? Pretend to be interesting and mysterious, with an enigmatic smile on my face, as if vastly amused by some inner musings. Or I could take a book. No, it'd be too dark and I'd need my glasses thus spoiling the enigmatic image. Also, the restaurant will be filled with happy families and lovers.

I've bread in the pantry. I'll change into sloppy clothes, make beans on toast (Charlie loves the crusts) and then we'll curl up on the sofa together and watch Bridget Jones's Diary again and I can be grateful that I'm not as bad as her.

In bed

David invited me for tea this afternoon so he must not think I am very dreadful. I am a source of entertainment if nothing else.

But now he thinks I had a date tonight so he will be gentlemanly and back off. How can I tell him that I'm available? It's not the sort of thing one can drop into a conversation easily especially as most of our conversations take place within an office setting. 'Our Young Mr Davies can see you at 10 o'clock and, by the way, I'm free!'

Although now I come to think of it, David seems to appear in the most unlikely places. Almost as if ... he were stalking me.

No, that is a stupid idea. He is a respectable psychiatrist not a weirdo. But perhaps his work has turned his head. Or maybe he is using me as a subject for his research. Like Pavlov's dog.

But actually, things only happen to me when he is around, a fact which would disprove his findings and bring his name into disrepute. If he writes a paper about me, I shall tell everyone that it was all his fault.

Later on in bed

David probably thinks my date was someone I met on Singles Night!!

And what did Martin mean by 'debacle in the vodka bar'? He can't have been referring to anything I did. I was perfectly behaved - as far as I can remember.

18th November, Tuesday

Nic came rushing up to me when I arrived at dance class and made me promise to be his partner tonight. I was happy to agree. Martin nodded curtly at me, 'Good evening, Alison.'

I caught Rose and Jane giving each other a crafty nod. I was puzzled until we were dancing when Nic explained that Martin had told everyone that he had had to cancel our date because of my erratic behaviour.

'My erratic behaviour!'

'Don't worry about it, lovey, you're far too good for him. But do tell, what did you do?'

'I chose a dog over him.'

Nic clapped his hands together, earning himself a dirty look from Franco.

'Sorry, Frankie, sweetie, see, I'm doing it right now. Oh, but I'm on your side, Aliss, what a wise choice. I mean I know you're looking for a man but you're not that desperate surely?'

I am actually.

19th November

I had a postcard from Bev. She is having a wonderful time. 'So good we think we might stay for another week ... or two. Can you keep Charlie for us?'

She is joking. I think.

I'm very fond of Charlie but it's not easy working all day and then coming home and making sure he gets enough exercise. I think I've lost weight though. As well as one glove, two pairs of knickers, a tea-towel, a cushion from the sofa, and four spoons.

It's the possible location of the spoons that is causing me most concern. I don't think he could have eaten them but the uncertainty is causing me sleepless nights. I did wonder if I should ask the vet but then she will think I am a terrible person who shouldn't be left in charge of an animal. She might even report me to the RSPCA. I shall just watch out for any abnormality in Charlie's poohing pattern.

20th November

Mum and Dad called in this evening on their way home from late night shopping at M&S. I made them a cup of tea but insisted they sat in the kitchen to drink it.

'I have to watch Charlie, I think he's about to pooh.'

'Oh, really, Alison, I don't wish to know that,' Mum sniffed into her tea cup.

'Why are you watching him, love? Is there a problem?'

'I think he might have eaten some spoons, and I want to make sure he's not having trouble poohing, that's all.'

'What on earth are you doing giving him spoons?'

'I didn't give them to him, Mum. I was drying the dishes when the phone rang. I remember having some spoons in my hand and I must have put them down and they disappeared. Along with the tea-towel.'

'He wouldn't have eaten them surely, love? Dad said.

'He's eaten things before. Oh, wait, look he's poohing ... he doesn't seem to be having any trouble ... there he's finished. I'll just go out and check.'

'Alison!'

Charlie's pooh was fine and spoonless. Perhaps they will just stay inside him forever. I must casually suggest to Bev that she never considers taking him on a plane: he could set off an international security alert if he went through the metal detector.

Mum wanted to show me the jumper she has bought for Chloe for Christmas. 'Do you think she will like it?'

'I don't know, Mum, I stopped trying to buy clothes for her years ago.'

'Well, she can change it if she doesn't, that's the beauty of Marks. Now that's me finished.'

'What do you mean: me finished?'

'My shopping.'

'What? Your Christmas shopping?'

'Yes. I'll just have to pack the few I bought tonight and I'll be all ready for Christmas. I wrote my cards last weekend. Except for Mrs Harris, you know, Mrs Harris, bad feet and green felt hat. I won't write hers yet, from what Joyce tells me she might not make it to December, let alone Christmas. But apart from her, I've done them all except Brenda and Tom, and I'm not sending them one, not after all that nonsense with the lawn-mower. Bill, have you drunk your tea yet? Hurry up, we can't stay here all night, I've got things to do.'

Mum is very sensible being so organised; I should aim to be more like her. In that respect anyway.

But there is still plenty of time before Christmas; I don't need to panic for ages yet.

21st November

Philip, one of Young Mr D's regulars was in this morning. He was early and he perched on the edge of my desk as he told me about his holiday: he'd just returned from cycling through the Andes. Last year he walked the Great Wall of China. Before his divorce it was Tenerife every year but his wife got their time-share as part of the settlement. He is pleased: it has released him to do the things he has always wanted to do. 'Don't you feel like that, Alison?' he said. 'Now you're free of your husband and the shackles are gone you can be exactly who you want to be, who you were intended to be. The world is your holiday camp!'

'Oh definitely,' I said.

'So have you been on holiday this year?'

'Yes.'

'And where did you go?'

'Um, Tenby.'

'Don't be embarrassed, there's nothing wrong with Tenby. When you're a free spirit like we are, you make of a place what you want to. I'm telling you, Alison, divorce is the best thing that ever happened to me. Not that I would object to finding another soul to share my pleasure with.'

Just then Young Mr D buzzed to ask me to send Philip in, but before I could do so, he leaned across the desk.

'Would you look into my eyes and tell me something, Alison?'

'Um, yes, I suppose so.'

He brought his face even closer to mine.

'Does my right eye look pus-y to you?'

I've checked all of Charlie's poohs and no spoons have appeared. Bev is back tomorrow. I think Charlie has enjoyed his stay here. We have bonded. I will miss him when he goes and would like to think that he will be torn when he realises he has to leave.

22nd November, Saturday

I was sorting out the dirty washing basket when I came across a tea-towel rolled around four spoons. I have no recollection of putting it there.

At least now I do not have to confess to Bev what a neglectful woman she left her dog with.

Later

The house feels very empty without Charlie.

He was very pleased to see Bev and did not even give me a backward glance as he left. He is a typical male: takes what he wants, uses it and then leaves without a 'thank you for having me'. I'm not going to be depressed just because a dog didn't say goodbye. I'll see if there is something on television to cheer me up.

Later again

It was a choice between *Animal Hospital* and *Turner and Hooch*. I decided to watch the film and it wasn't the best decision I've ever made. It should be against the law for animals to die in films. It's one thing human beings getting brutally killed, quite another when it's a poor innocent brave heroic dog.

Pippa called to ask if I have received the books I ordered from the Book Club. She had hers today. I had forgotten that we had both joined. A parcel of free books: that's something to look forward to especially as I've nearly finished my current read.

Very late, in bed

No-one has ever called me Cupcake. Most especially no-one in the form of a 6'2" lean-bodied, Italian-American cop called Joe.

I don't suppose anyone ever will now. I must resign myself to that fact. I should be grateful, instead, that Brian, on occasion, called me his little treacle pudding. I can't recall the occasion now but I'm sure it was well-meant.

I'll be glad when the free books arrive. I can't remember what I ordered but I'm sure they are more worthy than stories about American female bounty hunters. Pippa was delighted with her books: the true story of a rape victim; the latest volume from the Poet Laureate; and an in-depth analysis of the psychological effects of social exclusion.

24th November, Monday

The books arrived today when I was at work. Mr Price brought them round when I was cooking tea. I'm still not used to cooking for one so invited him to join me. I couldn't ask for a more helpful and less interfering neighbour but his style of over-dinner chat takes some getting used to. Tonight's consisted primarily of his recollections of his last hospital visit – after eating stew 'very like this one.'

I waited until he'd gone (after he'd watched *Eastenders* while eating the last of my choccie biccies) before opening my parcel. The books I'd ordered are: the latest Maeve Binchy, one on making the most of your garden by that lovely Irish fella on the telly, and *How to be a Goddess in the Kitchen*. I'm sure that joining a book club can only have an effect for the good on my life. I realise that I am now committed to buying one book a month for the next two years but, by choosing carefully, I can create a library that will serve me well for many years to come.

Later

It seems that, to make the most of my garden, I need half a ton of steel, some chicken wire and several large boulders. I already have most of that in the back garden, although perhaps not arranged quite as Shamus would like it. Still I'm well on the way to garden chic. I'm sure he must get round to mentioning the plants at some point. I'll continue reading from chapter sixteen tomorrow.

It turns out that the full title of the 'cookery' book I ordered is How to be a Goddess in the Kitchen and a Tart in the Dining Room. It promises a 'host of imaginative sexual techniques for every room in the house, using everyday items you'd never have dreamed of'. It's true: I would never have dreamed of using two teaspoons and a balloon whisk in that way. I would have thought tablespoons would have been more appropriate but, then, the only thing I've ever whisked to a peak has been egg white. And that went floppy shortly after. I'm surprised the book doesn't have a brown paper cover and I'm just glad that Mr Price couldn't see what was in the parcel.

At least I can't go wrong with Maeve Binchy. I've never read any of her books but Bev assures me that she tells a good story. The front cover of this one shows a wholesome red-haired girl on a wind-swept promontory. A satisfying yarn, that's what I need to send me to sleep at night.

Later, in bed

I'd expected the book to be set in Ireland but so far it's in New York. Still, there was a lot of Irish emigration to the States so, no doubt, all will become clear as I progress.

25th November

The book is not what I expected from what Bev has told me of Maeve Binchy's writings. I assume the girl on the cover is the woman in the story who is using her supernatural powers for her own evil purposes.

26th November

I told Muriel I am reading new Maeve Binchy and that it isn't what I expected. Muriel hasn't read it but thinks she can recall an article in the Daily Mail in which the author said she had been urged by her publishers to change her style as it was no longer suitable for today's audience. Muriel said she thought Ms Binchy had refused but maybe the pressure on her was too great. I'm not really a good judge as this is my first but I can't help thinking she should have stuck to family saga romances.

27th November

I phoned Bev. She has read this book and thinks it is one of Maeve's best, and, no, her style hasn't changed at all. Well, I certainly won't be reading any more of hers, however Bev does want to borrow *How to be a Goddess.*

Early hours of the morning, in bed

I've woken from a nightmare involving a woman who looked like Brian's bimbo, only with red hair, who was, by the sheer force of her will, making cups and plates fly at me. They were my best cups and plates too. Then Mum appeared, saying, in an Irish accent, 'You should never judge a potato by its onion.'

I'm tempted to stop reading the book but I only have three chapters left to go and I'm determined to discover the Irish connection.

29th November, Saturday

Pippa and Bev came round for the evening. When Bev arrived I plonked the book down on the table in front of her and said, 'Some friend you are recommending this. I've hardly slept since I started it.'

'I told you you wouldn't be able to put it down, didn't I?'

'Not put it down! It was an effort making myself pick it up.'

'What do you mean?'

'It's really scary, I've been having nightmares and I still don't get the Irish connection.'

'What? I know you're a bit of a wimp, Aliss, but I can't see how a story about a woman's search for her roots can be terrifying even to you.'

Pippa had picked up the book and was flicking through it. 'Just a minute,' she said, then she burst out laughing. 'Oh, Alison, you idiot, you've been reading Stephen King!'

'Don't be silly, Pippa, I wouldn't read a Stephen King — he really is much too scary.'

'But you have, look.' She held up the title page of the book for me to see. There in big letters was his name.

'But, what, how?'

'You know what's happened, don't you?' Pippa went on. 'They've put a Maeve Binchy dustjacket on a Stephen King book and you didn't notice. Oh, Alison, you're priceless.' Tears were rolling down her face and Bev, who'd taken a closer look at the book, started laughing too.

When they'd both calmed down, I said, 'I suppose that was why there was nothing obviously Irish about it.'

I don't know why that made them laugh even more.

Before she went, Bev offered to lend me a real Maeve Binchy in exchange for my Goddess book, but I told her she'd have to wait. After Stephen King, kitchen erotica will make a pleasant night-time read.

Later, in bed

I've noticed that I seem to be making people laugh a lot these days. I wonder if I've missed my vocation in life. I could have been a stand-up comedian, a raconteur like Victoria Wood. All she does is tell stories about what people do in real life. I could relate a tale of me reading Stephen King thinking it was Maeve Binchy. But the thing about Victoria Wood comedy is that it is believable: I don't think anyone would believe my SK/MB story.

Chapter 17

1st December, Monday

I've decided I will be organised regarding Christmas this year. I don't want a repeat of last year although I'm still convinced Mum told me that Dad wanted a Barry Male Voice Choir record. I was a little surprised when she mentioned it but assumed it expressed some of Dad's deep-seated yearnings for the fatherland. My intentions were good and I spent two wet Saturday afternoons trudging round music shops in Swansea *and* Cardiff before I could find a CD by the Barry Male Voice choir – in fact there were very few who had even heard of Barry Male Voice Choir. I had tried hard so it was rather unkind of Mum to point out my mistake so loudly (and so often) on Christmas Day. Dad didn't seem too disappointed though not getting the Barry Manilow CD Mum insisted she had told me to get.

But I'm going to double check everything this year and, as a start, shall make list.

Things to do
Buy, write and post cards
Buy, wrap and deliver presents
Stock up on food
Buy extra drinks, just in case
Buy and decorate tree
Order turkey

It's rather worrying that everything on the list involves spending money, but still, it is Christmas. I can't be a scrooge. At least I don't have to put up with Brian moaning.

3rd December, Wednesday

Great Aunt Millie phoned this evening and she was rather more lucid than usual. She asked when I was collecting her for Christmas and said she was glad she was staying with me this year as she has never liked my mother anyway. That came as news to me. As did the fact, rather more importantly, that she is staying with me for Christmas. I told her that I would let her know when to be ready closer to the date. It turned out she has packed already. To distract her, I asked if there are many exciting things happening at the home. She told me that the matron is a man dressed as a woman, and that the doctor drinks meths. I hope both of those details are figments of her mind.

I called Mum to confirm that Auntie Millie was staying with her as usual. 'Oh, Alison, you are getting forgetful. I told you, your father and I are spending Christmas Day with Geoff and, as we're all coming to you on Boxing Day, it seemed more sensible that she should stay with you this year, rather than muddle her about too much. You know how confused she gets.'

I'm beginning to think Auntie Millie is not the only one with that problem. I seem to have lost huge chunks of my life. I can't remember agreeing to have Auntie Millie, or, come to that, everyone for lunch on Boxing Day and I said as much to mum. She said, 'It's the least you can do when poor Trisha is feeding us on Christmas Day.'

'Oh, we're invited too, are we?'

'No, dear, don't be awkward, you know what I mean.'

All I know is that, if I know 'poor Trisha', she'll have everything brought in from M&S, ready prepared. But I'm not upset; I will lay on a truly magnificent spread, all done by my fair hands, that will put Trisha to shame. In fact, I'll start planning now as soon as I've found the magazine from last Christmas somewhere.

Later

According to Delia, my Christmas cake should be nicely maturing by now, having been made in October. I don't suppose two months will make that much difference, in fact, it will probably be better for not having to undergo such a lengthy ageing process. I would be.

4th December

I'm going with Stefan and Nic to see the local amateur dramatic company in *Annie Get Your Gun*. Stefan used to be very big in am dram till he split up with his boyfriend who was enjoying his role as the leading man too much.

I haven't been to an amateur production for years. Not since we saw the Village Players in '*Joseph*' and the pyramid collapsed on the brothers. Brian wouldn't go again after that, said he'd laughed enough to last a lifetime. It wasn't very nice of him really as one of the brothers was in plaster for months. I don't expect things have improved much still it is a night out and I don't get many of those these days.

Later, 11.17 precisely

I have been thrown out of a pub! Me! Thrown out of pub for the first time in my life! I called Chloe to tell her: she was shocked. 'Really, mum! You should know better at your age. Are you drunk?' Most certainly not. Maybe a teensy bit merry but definitely not drunk. I was only drinking cocktails and there's hardly any alcohol in those, they're all fruit juice. Or is that punch? Anyway, I am not drunk. If I was drunk I would not be able to tell the time so accurately.

And what's my age got to do with it? I've raised a prude. I will disown her and will adopt Stefan and Nic instead. They know how to have fun. They love me. We all had sex on the beach.

Annie Get Your Gun was wonderful. Marvellous singing and the scenery didn't fall down. And we only got thrown out of pub because me and Stefan were singing 'Anything you can do, I can do better.' We might have got away with it if Stefan hadn't insisted on singing Annie's part. Although he has a lovely voice and I told him so as they walked me home

'You should go back to am dram, Steffi. You'd be an ass-et. You have such a beautiful voice.'

'I'd love to say the same to you, darling, but I can't. I've heard more tuneful hippopotatuses.'

'Hippopotatuses?'

We all fell about screeching, I bumped into a lamppost, tripped over the kerb and sat in the gutter, still laughing. Nic and Stefan leaned against each other giggling helplessly. I'd probably still be there if a knight in shining mackintosh hadn't stopped to help me.

Sir Galahad, I called him and I kissed him twice. Shame about the hiccup in the middle. But it was only a quiet one. He probably didn't notice. Stefan was jealous, said he wished he'd fallen down so my knight would have helped him too.

The knight looked very familiar, I'm sure I've seen him before but I can't remember where. 'Spect it will come back to me. Sleepy-byes now. Night night, knight. Ha ha, good joke. Must remember that one to tell Stefan and Nic.

5th December

I must be going down with flu. I have a terrible headache and have taken four paracetamol. I don't know or care if this constitutes an overdose. I must stop thinking about death; it's starting to become attractive. Hope these pills take effect soon.

The phone rang at ten past nine.

'Good morning. Davies and Davies, Financial Advisers.'

'Ah, you are in.'

I wasn't expecting this response and I couldn't think of appropriate reply.

'It's David ... David Davies.'

'Yes, I know.'

'You do sound in a bad way.'

'I'm sorry, did you call for a reason? Or was it just to annoy me?'

'I was just wondering how you're feeling today?'

'I'm very well, thank you.' (As long as I don't move too much or try to think.)

'No bruises or a hang ... ah, headache?'

An electrical connection clicked in my brain and a cold shiver trilled its way down to my toes, followed by a hot flush to my face and a galloping pulse.

'Hello, hello, Alison, are you still there?'

I took a deep breath. 'I'm afraid I have to go now. I, er, um, have to answer the phone. Thank you for calling. Goodbye.'

Bugger! Buggerbuggerbuggerbuggerbugger. Look, he's even making me swear now and I never swear. Well, hardly ever and not out loud anyway. My knight. It had to be, of course. Isn't that always the way? I feel like Greta Garbo. Of all the pavements in all the world. Or was that Humphrey Bogart?

Later

It must have been a broken paving stone that tripped me up. I'll go back tomorrow and check. I should sue the Council for irreparable damage to my dignity. I could have been an OAP and broken my hip and died, and all because of their lack of attention to pavements. Yes, I shall definitely sue; it's time people stood up for their rights.

And I will explain to Smartarse, next time I speak to him, that sitting in gutter is not a habit of mine but that, in fact, was the inevitable result of government cutbacks.

8.45 pm

It is a sad reflection on the days in which we are living when OAPs resort to violence over a fruit cake. You would never have caught my Nan behaving in such an unseemly way. I can only assume it is watching too much violence on television that has affected them. Although the question must be asked: what so many OAPs are doing in Sainsburys of an evening anyway. Little old ladies and gents should be doing their shopping during the day and be tucked up with their cocoa and *Eastenders* of an evening. I wonder if the local bus company is running cheap evening excursions.

I do think supermarkets should consider banning zimmer frames or, at least, limiting the hours they can be taken into the store. It should be restricted to, say, between 6 am and 8 am.

If they want justification for what would, no doubt, be seen as disabled-ism, they only have to pose the question: how many zimmer frames does it take to block a supermarket aisle?

Just the one.

I hope the elderly lady who just failed to grab the last remaining hand-decorated just-like-mother's rich fruit Christmas Cake didn't know the meaning of the word she used. I had to look it up in the dictionary myself. And she was surely from the generation of women who stayed at home and baked. That's where she should have been tonight — in her own kitchen, making her own Christmas cake. Or rather, if Delia is to be believed, sitting back smugly waiting for it to mature.

I don't know what the world's coming to. I am a working woman but still I'm making my own cake. It is one of the more pleasurable traditions of Christmas.

A horrid thought has struck me: I am becoming my mother. Except she gets her cake from M&S.

And, as if it wasn't tiring enough having to battle through old ladies with sticks and young men with trolleys full of beer, at the end of it, I still had to pay for all my shopping. I blanched whiter than the almonds in my trolley when the checkout girl told me the total.

Still the pantry is well-stocked now. What a good idea of Sainsburys to have all those special three for the price of two offers on everything that a person might need for Christmas. I'm not sure what I will do with three boxes of Turkish Delight as I can't think of anyone who likes it, but it was such a good deal and will come in useful, for something, I expect. Maybe Delia has a recipe for using it up. Fondued Delight, maybe.

I deserve a drink after that lot. I had to buy brandy for the cake but the recipe only calls for two tablespoons so a little glassful won't be missed.

And I won't need all those chocolate chip shortbread biscuits for Christmas so I might as well open a packet now.

Later

Adam phoned to say his Dad is picking him up and bringing him home on 20th December. It will be lovely to have my baby home again. Adam that is.

I'm not sure what he meant by, 'Getting into the Christmas spirit already, are you, mum?' Was he suggesting I was drunk? I most definitely am not; I have only had a couple of glasses of brandy at the most. I can't judge by the level remaining in the bottle: I don't think it could have been properly full when I bought it. I should have inspected it more carefully. I will take it back tomorrow if it's empty. They can't sell me an empty bottle, that isn't allowed.

Adam is a fine one to talk. I bet he has ~~done some celebrations~~, ~~had some celebrating~~, been out enjoying himself already.

And later

I haven't had any dinner! I went shopping straight from work. That's why I'm feeling slightly light-headed. It's too late to cook now, so I'll have a few more cookies to keep me going.

It's surprising how well chocolate chip shortbread goes with brandy.

The nuts look very decorative the way I have arranged them with bit of holly and tinsel. There's something very Christmassy about nuts although it's a shame Brian took the nutcracker with him.

I'm too worn out to write cards this evening; I'll do them tomorrow after making the cake.

6th December, Saturday

First thing

I have a busy day planned. It's just as well I am feeling on top of life. Brandy must be good for me. I'll do my shopping this morning, then make the cake this afternoon and write cards this evening.

The amount of time I normally spend choosing presents is quite out of proportion to the 'rapture' with which they are received. I've decided that I will no longer be a martyr but will make it easy for myself this year. With this list I should be able to finish the bulk of my shopping by eleven and then spend some time choosing presents for people who will appreciate them.

Mum- Jumper from M&S with receipt so she can change it
Dad - Jumper from M&S with receipt so mum can change it
Chloe
Adam
Auntie Millie - jumper from M&S
Geoff - jumper from M&S

Trisha - jumper from M&S
Pippa
Bev

Late afternoon

I just got back from the shops and I am completely knackered. I'm sure that M&S have put up their prices since last I looked and I refuse to spend that much on my brother and sister-in-law. Last year all I got from them was a rubber plant, which died.

The good thing about book tokens is that the recipient gets the added pleasure of choosing their own gift. Might not be exciting to look at but by the time I have finished with them, they will look a treat. I'll put them in boxes and wrap them attractively. Which reminds me, I must find last year's Christmas cards to cut into gift tags, as advised by the 'green' article in the local paper. I don't want to contribute any more than is necessary to global warming. I have enough hot flushes as it is.

It's too late to start on the cake now. I'll have dinner then write my cards.

Later

I'm so glad they are repeating the first series of *Morse* on television. I've always liked him; he's such a sad character, all alone. A bit like me. Except I am not alone. I have Adam and Chloe. I am very fortunate.

I'll definitely write cards tomorrow after making the cake.

7th December, Sunday

If woman were intended to grate a lemon, she would have been born with metal fingers. I think I picked out most of the flesh and only a bit of blood went in and anyway cooking will kill any germs, I'm sure. The cake is going to be wonderful but I'd forgotten it took so long to cook. I'll have to have beans on toast for dinner. Again.

Later

I wonder what the etiquette is regarding sending Christmas cards to ex-husband and his girlfriend. I don't really want to send one but I don't want to be seen as small-minded. I didn't send one last year as it was still too raw but twelve months have passed now.

It would be very embarrassing if one arrived from them on Christmas Eve. I couldn't rush out and post one then and it's the sort of thing the bimbo would do just to make me look bad. I'll get mine in first just in case.

But what do I write on it? I can't sign it 'with love', but 'from' looks unforgiving. 'Best wishes, Alison' sounds best. Even if she knows I don't mean it.

10th December

I've received a card from 'your milkman, Steve'. I assume this was a subtle reminder about the Christmas tip. I wouldn't want to be a milkman so I'll be generous.

11th December

Had a card from 'your cheery dustbin men'. While I would not want to be a dustbin man, I'm not sure that leaving trail of potato skins, tin cans and mouldy banana peels outside the gate every week warrants reward. However I'm scared of the possible consequence if I do not respond. I'll compromise and write a polite message in a card thanking them but asking them to be a little more careful in future.

On second thoughts will forget the message.

12th December

Had card from 'Amanda, your early morning paper girl'. I'd written a card back and was rummaging in my purse for a suitable monetary gift when I remembered that I don't have a morning paper.

13th December, Saturday

Had card from ex-husband and girlfriend. 'Wishing you a merry Christmas, Brian and Gina.' Card M&S top of the range i.e. v expensive. Quite tasteful, I suppose, if not a trifle large and ostentatious. I much prefer my own, which, though smaller, have a certain something about them - and 10p from the purchase of each pack goes to help, oh, children of impoverished estate agents. Perhaps I should have read the small print before buying. Never mind, I'm sure estate agents can be just as deserving as anyone else.

I'll finish writing my cards tonight ready for posting tomorrow.

15th December, Monday

I'd only been in work for half an hour when the phone rang. It was David Davies.

'Alison, I have some tickets for a dinner dance this coming Friday and I wondered if you might be free to join me?'

'A dinner dance? This Friday? That would be ...' I stopped as a thought sneaked into my head, 'rather short notice.'

'Yes, I realise that. I just thought, if you were free, you might enjoy an evening out.'

'You thought I might enjoy a night out. Ah, yes, of course, I remember those. I don't get many of them, and it's very kind of you to consider me, when I'm such a social outcast, and especially at such a late date. What happened? Did she dump you? Did she realise, just in time, what a tight-arsed turbot she had landed? Well, I'm sorry to disappoint you, Mr Davies, I'm afraid I already have plans for Friday evening — I'm going out with some real friends —people who want to spend time with me not people who see me as a case for do-gooding. Although I must say I am impressed that you managed to put the fire-raising incident behind us. Now was there anything else?'

'Nothing at all, Mrs Turner, I'm sorry to have troubled you. Good morning.'

Honestly, the cheek of the man. His date dumps him and what does he do? Calls up the only woman he can think of that he's confident will be available, and not only that, grateful for being thought of. Well, he thought wrong. I'm not that easy. Or desperate. He might be good-looking and, superficially at least, charming and amusing but I'm not falling for that again. Who does he think I am? Or he is? Huh.

17th December

My attempt at economising – as a single mum – has failed drastically. Cheap and cheerful, 20 sheets for a pound, wrapping paper from the street market is not good value for money. I've thrown away more than I've used. And next year I shall choose Christmas presents purely on shape. I won't consider anything that is other than rectangular.

19th December

I found the unposted cards in the bottom of my bag. I knew there was something else I had to do yesterday. I wonder if the Post Office is serious about last dates for posting? It's probably just a ruse to encourage people to post early. I'll use second class and hope for the best.

Later

I bought first class as I couldn't face the comments from my mother if her card did not get there in time.

Much later, in bed

I've had an excellent night out with girls. We haven't had a good face to face natter for ages. I brought them up to date on the latest happenings at dance class — Martin and Jane have been to the theatre together! Nic saw them and he said they pretended to have bumped into each other by accident — and told them all about my last-minute invite to the ball.

Pippa and Bev have both been to dinner dances this month — Pippa has been to three! — and both pointed out that, if nothing else, it would have been a good opportunity to practise my dancing. Bev also told Pippa that she had seen David at Walco's on

Singles Night. 'He was a bit tasty, you know, Pip. Aliss could do a lot worse than him.'

'Did he explain why he was so late inviting you, Alison?'

'No, he just thought I was desperate for a night out.'

'Did he use those exact words?'

'Well, no, probably not, but it's what he meant.'

'He might have had a perfectly good explanation for leaving it so late. I bet you didn't even give him a chance to explain.'

'What sort of good explanation could he have had?'

'Well, perhaps he was given the tickets at the last moment by someone else who was supposed to go but then couldn't.'

'Yeah, Aliss, or he might have thought he couldn't go because he had a previous engagement but that might have fallen through and he found he could go.'

'Huh, that's a bit far-fetched.'

'You should have asked him, Alison, given him a chance to explain.'

I'm beginning to feel like Cinderella but with two ugly sisters who want me to go to the ball. Still, Franco is organising a special New Year's Eve Dance for all his classes to mingle so that is something to look forward to.

20th December, Saturday

Adam is coming home today. I've made his favourite lasagne for tea. It will be good to have my boy back home with me.

5.45 pm

Brian and Adam arrived with bags of washing. Adam insisted it was all clean, well, almost all, but so screwed up, it was hard to tell. 'You don't need to wash socks anyway, Mum.'

'I think you do, Adam.'

'No, honestly, if you wear them till they're hard, then leave them on the floor for a bit, then bang them against the wall, you can wear them again. No-one washes socks.'

'That's what I used to do,' Brian was grinning.

'So,' I said, 'you're responsible for the epidemic of verrucas spreading through British universities, are you?'

We both laughed and it felt strangely normal. It's been a long time since we laughed together.

I made us all a cup of tea then Adam disappeared to phone his friends.

Brian asked if it would be all right if he invited Chloe and Adam over to his place on Boxing Day.

'Oh. I've got Mum and Dad, and Geoff and Trisha coming over then. I was hoping the children would be here to help lighten the load.'

'Perhaps they could come after lunch? And spend the night. I'll make sure Chloe gets back before Tryboy arrives.'

'Tryboy?'

'Yes, didn't Chloe say he was staying with you from the day after Boxing Day?'

'She hasn't mentioned it but I'm sure you're right. Yes, okay, that'll be fine.'

'I'll pick them up at about...?'

'I expect Chloe will drive them over, she can borrow my car.'

'No, it's all right, I'll pick them up. I'd like to see your parents again, wish them season's greetings.'

I'm not sure whether my parents will feel the same. Although I'm certain Mum has always quietly believed that I drove him to an affair — 'if only you'd paid a bit more attention to your looks, and not let yourself go quite so much.' I don't think Dad is so forgiving though.

Adam re-appeared long enough to say he was off out for a curry with his mates. 'You don't mind, do you, Mum, but it'll be good to catch up with everyone?'

'No, that's fine.'

After he'd gone, Brian sniffed the air. 'His favourite lasagne?'

I nodded.

'You should have told him, he could have joined his mates later.'

'It's okay, he'll have it reheated tomorrow; they always say it's better the next day.'

Brian smiled so sweetly, I almost invited him to join me for dinner but, just in time, he said, 'I'd better make a move. Gina will be wondering what's taking me so long.'

I'm glad he said that then; I wouldn't have enjoyed being rebuffed, however politely he'd done it.

Chapter 18

22nd December, Monday

I collected Auntie Millie from Fairyhill. She was already sitting in the foyer when I arrived, the three woolly pom poms on her hat bobbing up and down, as she tried to keep a birdlike eye on all the comings and goings. When she spotted me, she stood up.

'About time too,' she snapped. 'I've been here for days.'

I got a sympathetic look from an old lady collecting even older relative. 'They're all the same, aren't they?' she said to me.

'Who are?' Auntie Millie asked. 'What's that on your head? Is it a monkey?'

The old lady huffed and marched off. I felt I should go after her and apologise but I could see Auntie Millie's point about the monkey.

I'd intended to wrap the rest of my presents after lunch but Auntie Millie was insistent that she needed to do Christmas shopping. In M&S, we bumped into Mr Davies Senior who asked me what I thought of his choice of gift for his wife. I suggested a lambswool cardigan might be a better alternative to a gents' hair-cutting kit. I was pointing him in the direction of the woollies when I realised that Auntie Millie was no longer at my side. In fact, I couldn't see her anywhere.

The crowd was so dense I decided a woman-hunt was a job that needed more than one. I turned round to enlist Mr D Senior's help but he'd disappeared too. At Customer Services I had to wait ages while a very awkward woman argued with the girl on desk about Marks' sizing policy.

'You used to be able to rely on this shop. If you bought a size 14, you knew a size 14 was what you were getting.'

'Well, it is a size 14, madam.'

'No, it's not; that's what I'm telling you. It doesn't come near me.'

'Perhaps a different size would suit you better.'

'Are you trying to suggest that I don't know what size I am?'

'Oh, for goodness sake,' I butted in, 'anyone with half an eye can see that you're never a size 14, size 18 would be more likely, and while you're arguing, my poor great-aunt could have had a heart attack and be lying in a corner somewhere!'

They didn't have a tannoy they could use but, when I'd explained, the girl said she would call a few of the Christmas temps and get them to hunt for Auntie Millie.

'Okay,' I said, 'I'll go back and search in Ladieswear.' I could hear the size 18 lady muttering as I left, 'If her aunt's anything like as rude as she is, I hope, for their sakes, they never find her.'

I was peering under changing-room doors looking for feet I recognised when an assistant tapped me on the shoulder. 'Have you lost your aunt?' she asked.

I could tell by the look on the girl's face, which reminded me of the matron of her former home, that she had found Auntie Millie. 'Where is she?' I sighed.

'Men's Underwear.'

'Of course, where else?'

I followed her up the stairs to find Auntie Millie looking puzzled. 'What do you do with this?' she asked. I didn't know what to say: I was too shocked to find M&S selling men's thongs.

Before I lost Auntie Millie, I bought a large box of Belgian truffles for Geoff and Trisha. Book tokens on their own might look a little mean, I fear. Now I've spent more than I would have done had I bought jumpers for them as I originally intended.

23rd December

11.25 pm

I've finished wrapping presents! I've just got a few final bits and pieces to do tomorrow. If I buy the bread and veg in the morning, I can stuff the turkey in the … ohmigosh … the turkey. I DON'T HAVE A TURKEY! I HAVE FORGOTTEN TO GET A TURKEY! I don't believe it. How on earth could I do that? What sort of moron forgets a turkey at Christmas? My sort, that's who. I cannot believe I could be so stupid. I've done some stupid things in my life (more than some — lots) but this is taking stupidity to new depths.

I must not panic. Panicking or berating myself will not get a turkey on the table. I must be calm and think. Think. Think. Think ... I am having a heart attack. Take deep breaths. In ... out ... in ... out. That's better. Now, it will be Christmas Eve tomorrow, bound to be turkeys in shops. I'll go to Sainsburys first thing in morning. I'll go to bed now so I can get up early.

Christmas Eve

12.05 am

But what if they are sold out before I get there? I'd better go now to put my mind at rest. Thank heavens for 24 hour shopping.

2.10 am

I've been to: Sainsburys – no turkeys, no more expected; Tesco – no turkeys, no more expected; Asda – no turkeys, might have delivery tomorrow, I mean today, but cannot guarantee it.

I can hear my mother now, 'She's gone to pieces since he left. She needs to pull herself together.' No, I will not allow myself to be the subject of their pity. Wait a minute, the local butcher must order extra turkeys, surely? He wouldn't just order his orders. Would he? No, no, of course he wouldn't, he'd be bound to get a few spare. I'll phone him.

I don't think there was any need for him to speak like that to me. If he doesn't want calls out of hours, he shouldn't have them transferred to his home number. Of course I know it's the middle of the night, stupid man, I'm not an idiot. I'll phone him again first thing in morning.

Or perhaps I'll get Adam to do it.

I don't think I'll be able to sleep for worrying.

9.45 am

I must have been worn out by all that anxiety; I've only just woken up. I called the butcher using a hankie over phone. He thinks he will have some spare but ... he spoken to me before about it? I denied it emphatically. In that case, I am to call back in an hour when he will be able to tell me for sure. I was tempted to say I am unlikely to survive another hour in this suspense but instead said 'thank you' and 'I will'.

11.03 am

I didn't intend to watch *White Christmas* on television but it took my mind off turkey. I love the bit at the end where they open the curtains and it's snowing and you know everything will work out for the best. Wish I lived in a Hollywood movie.

11.30 am

I love the butcher. I will buy all my meat there in future. I had to stop myself kissing him when he handed over a plump 20 lb turkey.

6.05 pm

I hadn't planned to spend Christmas Eve afternoon in the shops but didn't have a dish big enough to cook the turkey in. The only one I could find was made of cast iron and weighs more than the turkey.

According to St Delia, in order to eat lunch at 1.00 pm, I must put the turkey in the oven at 2.30 am. Delia says I am to 'give it a good hot blast for half an hour and then reduce heat'. Stuff that. The turkey should consider itself lucky to be cooked at all especially bearing in mind it was almost the turkey nobody wanted.

I'll watch a bit of television while I'm waiting and at least I won't have to get up too early. Chloe usually manages to control herself until 8 o'clock while Adam would sleep till lunch if Chloe didn't go in and shake him. Long ago I came to the conclusion that Adam's biggest regret in life was ever having got out of his pushchair.

3.20 am

I must have dropped off. I woke with a dry mouth and stiff neck. Then it took five minutes of shoulder-rolling exercises to loosen up enough to lift the turkey towards the oven. Then I found it wouldn't fit: the tin is too big. I took the turkey out of new tin and squeezed it into the old tin. I wrapped foil tightly around it then tied string around the foil to keep it all together. I don't think the green dye from garden string will be harmful. The turkey now has a broken and misshapen breastbone but it serves it right for being so greedy and fat.

Late lunch will be fine. Auntie Millie is a lifelong republican who has never forgiven Winston Churchill for something (she says it was to do with the miners but is unsure exactly what) so she won't mind missing the Queen's speech.

25th December, Christmas Day proper

6.05 am

Auntie Millie brought me a cup of tea (although she does not appear to have used a teabag – or boiled the water) to wish me a happy Christmas. It is a kind gesture. I just wish she hadn't lain down next to me and fallen asleep. Her snoring is keeping me awake and conscious of the cooking smells coming from downstairs. I hope the turkey is all right.

6.35 am

I don't know why I bothered getting up. The turkey is so well trussed I can't see how it's doing. But I'm up now so will start preparing veg.

7.20 am

I have raised a Scrooge. Adam is distinctly lacking in Christmas spirit this morning. I don't think my rendition of *In the Bleak Midwinter* sounded anything like next-door's tom when the tabby down the road is on heat. Adam has gone back to bed, Auntie Millie is still snoring and even Chloe looks to be in deep slumber.

I can't help noticing that my pile of presents appears to be smaller than everyone else's. Even Auntie Millie has more. Still, it is quality not quantity that counts when you reach my age.

10.05 pm

Lovely day. Wonderful dinner, super presents, fabulous children. Only thing missing was man to share it with. I was tempted to call DD to wish him Happy Christmas, to show no hard feelings, but he's probably not at home. He's probably out enjoying himself.

I am very tired and I fell asleep ten minutes into the big film. Now I'll never know what happened to the Titanic.

26th December, Friday

Mum, Dad, Geoff and Trisha arrived at twelve. The kisses and 'happy Christmas' exchange took the best part of fifteen minutes because Auntie Millie kept starting again — she kissed me three times.

Mum was delighted with her jumper, but 'not awfully keen on the colour. Beige is more me, dear. And, now I come think of it, I have plenty of jumpers: a new dressing gown would be more useful. You don't mind if I change it, do you? And while I'm about it, I thought I'd change your father's jumper. The jumpers he's got now will last longer than he will and he does need a new pair of gardening trousers. The ones he wears at the moment are much too scruffy for the garden.'

Auntie Millie heard this discussion and has decided that she does not like the jumper I bought her either. She wants to take it back and change it for 'some of those lacy knickers with no bottom'.

We had just finished lunch when Mum announced, 'Did you know, Trisha, that Alison went out with a psychiatrist?'

Trisha deliberately misunderstood. 'Oh, Alison, I hadn't realised. I knew you'd been finding it tough but I didn't know it was so bad you needed a psychiatrist.'

'No, Trisha, Alison didn't go to see a psychiatrist, although I can understand your mistake. No, no, she went out with one. ON A DATE.' Mum said it in capital letters to make sure Trisha understood, and she continued, 'It was all going wonderfully well until she set fire to Claude's.'

'Claude's?!'

'I didn't set fire to Claude's ...'

'You can understand a man not hanging around when she does things like that, can't you?'

'I did not set fire to Claude's!'

But despite my protestations, I know it will go down in Mum's store of family history as 'do you remember when Alison burned down the poshest restaurant in town?' and will be brought out whenever a 'just like Alison' situation arises.

A little later I was in the kitchen when the phone rang. Mum was passing so she picked it up. 'Hello? ... Yes, I am thank you, a lovely time ... it is me ... yes, a lovely day ... oh, I did, wasn't it beautiful, her Majesty always sets such an example to us ... I couldn't agree more ... no, it's definitely me ... yes, Eunice ... oh, no, Alison's in the kitchen, this is her mother speaking ... oh, do you think so? ... now stop it, you're making me blush ... did you want to speak to Alison? ... No it's no trouble, she's very rudely hovering over my shoulder ... yes, a happy Christmas to you too, byeee ... it's for you, Alison, someone called Nic.'

Nic was with his Dad who had bought the DVD of *Sound of Music* and was insisting that they watch together. 'Bless him, he tries his best to cope with me, so how could I tell him if I had to watch Julie Andrews doh ray me-ing again, I would throw up.'

Brian arrived at 4.30. He brought a bottle of wine with him. He held it out to Dad. 'Happy Christmas, Bill, Eunice.'

Mum jumped up from her chair. 'Thank you, Brian; that is thoughtful of you. Take it from him, Bill, don't just sit there. And are you having a good Christmas, Brian? We went to Geoff's yesterday, had a lovely day. Did you have a good day? I really enjoyed the Queen's speech, did you? She doesn't have an easy life but she puts on a brave face for her people. Oh, here, let me take the wine off you. We'll have this with our tea, shall we, Alison? Why don't you join us, Brian?'

'Brian's just picking up Chloe and Adam, Mum; he's got to go now.'

Brian took the hint, kissed Mum, nodded to Dad and said goodbye to everyone. Auntie Millie caught him by the arm as he was passing and pulled him down to her level. 'Have you brought me any sausages?'

'Not today, Millie.'

'Remember next time, will you, there's a good boy?'

27th December

Brian dropped off Chloe and Adam at four. Auntie Millie was watching from the window and he didn't come in. I asked the children if they'd had a good time. Adam had already flopped in front of the television and just grunted while Chloe said, 'Yeah, fine.'

'Have you had lunch? There's some turkey if you'd like sandwiches.'

'Oh, no,' Adam groaned, 'I'm stuffed; we've just had a curry.'

'Curried turkey already? We don't usually get on to that for a couple of days yet.'

'No, it wasn't turkey. It was lamb roghan josh.'

'Your favourite, that's lucky.'

'Nah, she asked what we liked. And she made bombay potatoes and dahl, and loads of other things.'

'Other things?'

'You know, lots of side dishes, just like in an eat-as-much-as-you-like proper Indian restaurant. And last night we had a Thai dinner.'

'Takeaway?'

'It was Boxing Day, mum, where would you get a takeaway, everything's shut. No, Gina made it all herself. It was cool.'

'Did you enjoy it, Chloe?'

'Yeah,' she shrugged. 'It was fine. Can I borrow your car later to go to the station? The train gets in at six.'

I'd forgotten Tryboy was arriving today. I've relented and am letting him sleep in Chloe's bedroom as Auntie Millie is in the spare room. I wanted to put him in with Adam but neither Adam nor Chloe liked that idea.

I told Chloe he could stay in her room 'as long as I don't hear any, you know, "noises"'.

'Mum!'

I've had to accept that my daughter is grown woman and having sex but I don't have to listen to it as well.

Later, in bed

I decided to go to bed early and read. Not long after I had snuggled down, Chloe stuck her head round the door. 'Can I come in, Mum?'

'Course you can, sweetie. Not watching the film with the boys?'

'No, it's all fighting and time warping and other nonsense. Auntie Millie seems to be enjoying it though.'

She curled up next to me and pulled my dressing gown over her just like she used to when she was a little girl. She began picking at the tufts of cotton.

'Everything all right, Chloe?'

'Yeah.'

'Are you sure? You've been a bit quiet this evening.' I didn't want to add, since you've come back from your Dad's.

'It was all just a bit ... odd at Gina and Dad's.'

'Odd? I suppose it would be. It's the first time you've stayed there and it was bound to be different.' We always used to play board games on Boxing Day evening. 'I don't suppose Gina's got Cluedo.'

'I don't think she's got anything. You should see the flat, Mum, it's all very minimalist.'

'Very trendy. But perhaps not very comfortable?'

'It was okay, but it wasn't that. It was ... I think Gina's getting fed up with Dad.'

'Oh, I see. Did your Dad or Gina say anything in particular to make you think that?'

'No, nothing like that, but it just didn't feel right. And Gina kept getting calls and going off to take them in private.'

'They might have been to do with her work; she's very dedicated to her job.'

'On Boxing Day, Mum? I don't think so. And Dad just looked sad when she disappeared but tried not to let us see.'

'Did Adam notice it too?'

'Adam?! You're joking. He was too busy playing the games Dad's got on his computer.'

'Perhaps they're just going through a bad patch. Once the initial excitement of a new relationship wears off, real life has to resume and it can come as a shock to see your lover in un-loverlike situations. You know what your father looks like in the mornings!' I tried to laugh but Chloe suddenly sat up, looking very serious.

'Would you have him back? If he wanted to come?'

'Oh, Chloe, that is a big question, with a great big "if".'

'Well would you?'

I leaned my head back against the pillow trying to give myself time to work out how to tell my daughter that I didn't want her father back. But I'd misread her question.

'You wouldn't, would you? You wouldn't even seriously consider it, would you? Not now.'

'You don't think I should?'

'No! I know you probably still love him, but you've changed, you've become much more "you" since he's gone.'

'Have I?'

'Gosh, yes. The mum who was married to Dad wouldn't have gone to vodka bars or tried internet dating.'

'I should hope not!' I laughed.

'No, okay, that wasn't a good example, but you have changed. And for the better. And I think you're starting to be happier, aren't you?' She said the last bit hesitantly.

'Yes, I am, much happier. And, no, I wouldn't want your Dad back. I still love him, of course I do — even when I hated him I loved him. It's hard to get someone out of your system when they've been in it for most of your life. But that bit is — not closed exactly — it can't be when we have you and Adam — let's say firmly shuttered.'

'Good.' She snuggled down again then a few moments later said, 'He shouldn't have done it though.'

'Done what?' I asked, even though I knew.

'Gone off with her. If he was going to marry her and be happy then, at least, there would have been a point to all the suffering he's put us through, but now he's going to end up hurt, just like you were, and for nothing. It's so stupid. Men are so stupid.'

Suddenly she seemed close to tears. I stretched out my arms so she could edge up the bed into them. I hugged my confused little girl to me. 'Chloe, you know how complex relationships can be. No, it's true I didn't want to get divorced. I was stunned and broken when your Dad told me about Gina. I know I must have appeared to be a complete wreck. I'm sorry that you and Adam had to go through that. But now I really do believe that it's turned out to be the right thing. You know, I couldn't have said this six months ago, but the pain is over, I'm better. And I'm sorry if your dad is going to have go through the pain he put us all through, but he'll get over that too. And you will. And one day he'll find someone new, I'm sure. Maybe someone who he'll stay with. For more than just a day.' I did my renowned Elvis impersonation as I sang the last sentence.

Chloe smiled, 'You're insane, do you know that?'

'Have you seen my mother? It's hereditary.'

'Oh, no,' she shook her head and hugged me back. Then she said, 'Anyway, I don't think we'll be invited there again for a while: Adam nearly drove Gina round the bend.'

'Your brother? Go on with you, I can't imagine that little angel annoying anyone.'

'He kept leaving plates and glasses all over the place.'

'Adam? Doing that? Never.'

'Gina asked him to take them out to the kitchen when he'd finished but you know Adam. He nods then forgets. And then he'd forget he had a glass and go and get another one. She didn't like it when they started talking football either.'

'Understandable.'

'So she tried to engage me in intellectual conversation. Is shopping the new cocaine? I ask you, on Boxing Day! After a bit I said, "I think there's a Bruce Willis film on now." Then Gina said she'd been planning to watch the arthouse film on channel four, but Dad said, "We can record that, can't we? I think the kids would prefer Brucie-baby." In the end Gina went to bed early and left us watching the film.'

'Probably not the most tactful thing for your Dad to do.'

We looked at each other and burst out laughing.

I hadn't realised Chloe had so many undiscussed issues. I've been so wrapped up in myself and my pain that I've ignored my children's needs. I think Chloe feels better and understands more now, but I must encourage her to talk to me again if she has concerns. And I must do the same with Adam. I can't imagine that he has any deep unresolved issues — about anything — but mustn't assume that just because he's a boy and, well, Adam.

28th December

I was in the middle of gathering all the empty glasses and plates that Adam had left around the house when he wandered through the living room. I thought I should take immediate action regarding 'unresolved issues' and said, 'Morning, Adam, how are you today?' I tried to emphasise 'you' to make him aware that I was interested and had time for him. He looked at me through bleary eyes, said, 'Fine,' and continued on his path to the kitchen.

I followed him. 'You know, Adam, these last couple of years have been difficult for all of us, and I've come to realise that I've been so immersed in my own concerns that I've not been giving you and Chloe the attention that you've needed. But I want you to know that I'm here and I'm willing to listen to you whatever you want to say.'

He was rummaging in the drawer for a clean spoon.

'Do you understand what I'm saying, Adam? Is there anything bothering you?'

'Well,' he yawned.

'It's all right, Adam, anything you want to say is fine by me.'

'Can you get Frosties instead of Rice Krispies?'

31st December, New Year's Eve

Adam is going out with friends, Chloe and Tryboy are dining then clubbing, Mum and Dad are at a 'do' at the Golf Club, Auntie Millie has been promised Buck's Fizz at midnight at Fairyhill — and I'm off to the YM where Franco has arranged a bar. I thought the YM was alcohol-free; I hope it's not an alcohol-free bar Franco has arranged.

I phoned Nic who said not to worry, he and Stefi had already planned on bringing some vodka. 'We'll smuggle it in if we have to, darling. I'll stick it down my trousers. And don't forget you're coming with us to the Am Dram party afterwards. It will be fabulous.'

I'm not sure if a party after the party is a good idea: I always seem to end up in trouble after being with Nic and Stefi. Still, it is New Year's Eve.

I haven't made a New Year's resolution for thirty-five years. I still remember the last one as if it were last week. Sheryl Jones was my best friend, it was New Year's Eve and we were at her house getting ready to go out to our first proper party. I'd told my parents that I was staying with Sheryl but had failed to mention the party. I felt so guilty I resolved to always tell the truth in future. And when Sheryl asked me how she looked I decided the time was right to put my resolution into practice. She didn't speak to me for three weeks *and* told Dick Roberts, who never changed his socks and dribbled when he looked at girls, that I fancied him. Which I most definitely didn't.

I've learned a lot since then and I always think before I speak nowadays. Nearly always anyway.

Franco has promised us a real band, instead of his usual records, and a 'finger food' buffet. He said his wife would prepare it as 'she is very good in the kitchen.' I wonder if Brian ever said that about me. 'Oh, Alison, yes, she's very good in the kitchen. And behind the bike shed.' Don't suppose he did. My cooking keeps stomachs full but bears little resemblance to what Jamie Oliver does. And if I was that good behind the bike shed, he wouldn't have left me for a twenty-eight-year-old.

I wonder if Franco's wife will come to the party tonight. She used to be his partner but she has never come to a class. She is a mystery. I've often thought that mystery is attractive in a woman. I could do with acquiring some enigma myself. I hope she does attend then I can ask her how to bring some mystery into my life. And it'll be interesting to see her: a dancing queen and kitchen goddess wrapped up in a gold-sequinned pinny.

I'm quite excited now. I'm going to wear same dress that I wore to Luke's birthday in May.

I knew I had a good reason for wanting a man about the house: I need someone to help me squeeze into this dress. I'm sure it wasn't this tight last time I wore it. I must have put on weight over Christmas but it'll drop off as soon as I get back to work I'm sure. Although maybe that should be my New Year's resolution: to lose weight, and get fit.

I have a lot of bosom on show but I'm not likely to fall out as I'm wedged in fairly securely. It's rather a sexy effect, even if I say it myself. Especially when I wobble it.

I've managed to reassure Chloe that I don't intend to go leaning over and wobbling my bosom all evening. I told her if I'd known she was still in the house, I'd have been a bit more circumspect in my actions. And song. Although it was a pretty good version of 'Hey, Big Spender, spend a little time with me, bom bom ba bom ba bom!'

1st January

3.25 am

I don't think there was any need for Chloe to shout so loudly.

Of course I know what the time is. I'm not stupid, I can tell the time. How was I supposed to know she would be waiting up? I'm not selfish. I didn't do it deliberately and I won't be sorry in morning.

Chapter 19

1st January, still

New Year resolution 1: I will never go out with Stefi and Nic again.

New Year resolution 2: I will say, 'no,' without hesitation, if anyone asks if I can tango. I must remember to ask Franco when we will move onto the tango. It can't be soon enough for me.

New Year resolution 3: I will give up alcohol in any form but especially cocktails.

I'm going back to bed now and I could be there some time.

11.35 am

Chloe woke me. She said she was checking that I was still breathing but I suspect her motive. She is still mad at me. She didn't say anything but I could tell from the way her mouth pursed when she said, 'Will you be getting up *at all* today?'

5th January

It's hard being back at work after the long Christmas break. Still, I think we all had a good time, some of us especially. I've explained to the matron of Fairyhill that it's not possible for Auntie Millie to come and live with me permanently and that I didn't invite her, no matter what she says. The matron understands; Auntie Millie is not as daft as she sometimes appears. But I'll go and visit her again soon.

I wonder what the matron made of the Ann Summers knickers. I shouldn't have let Chloe take Auntie Millie to town. I don't believe it was Auntie's idea to go in that shop. Although, then again, perhaps I do.

Mr Davies Senior said his wife was very pleased with her lambswool cardie but that she was disappointed that he did not get her the hair-cutting kit she had asked for. 'She's taking lessons, you know.'

'I didn't know.'

‘Oh, yes, becoming quite a little Siegfried Sassoon. I told her I’d get it for her birthday instead but she said she couldn’t wait till May so bought it herself in the sales. See?’ He turned round and patted the back of his head. ‘Not bad, eh? A bit shorter than I normally have but the phone rang when she was doing it. It’ll grow, I told her.’

I can’t start my diet yet while there are Christmas choccies to finish, not to mention three boxes of Turkish Delight, a box of dates, and half a Christmas cake. Also I have to cook for Adam while he’s home so it’s much better to postpone my diet until he’s gone back to uni. This doesn’t mean that I’m trying to wriggle out of dieting; I’m simply choosing the best time to begin. There’s nothing worse than starting and failing straightway.

6th January

The phone rang when I was in Young Mr D’s office trying out a variety of spare keys to see if any fitted the filing cabinet. I rushed to answer it only to find it was David Davies — who else? I might have been panting a little but I don’t think it warranted his, ‘Why, Alison, I never put you down as a heavy breather.’ I could have been having a heart attack for all he knew. Most people breathe a little more heavily than normal when they are rushing. I don’t think this can be put down to excess weight on my part. I’m only slightly podgy round the tum. And on my midriff. I don’t think there’s any cause for concern health wise from my weight. And some men like a bit of flesh.

Yes, men like Internet Barry. They’re the ones who like a bit of flesh. It’s definitely time for my diet to begin.

Later

My scales are obviously suffering from old age; they have lost their accuracy. They can’t possibly be right. I’ll have to go into town in my lunch-hour tomorrow to weigh.

7th January

Lunchtime

It's official: I am overweight. I know because a rude machine in Tesco's told me so.

It used to cost ten pence to weigh; now you have to pay £1 to be insulted by a loud American woman. I'd already put my money in before realising what was about to happen and I would have leapt off if I hadn't resented wasting money.

The machine asked me lots of questions, like sex (there wasn't an option, 'chance would be a fine thing'), age, build (entered medium) and height (think I am about 5'4 and a half but Bev says she is definitely 5'8 and she's not that much taller than me so said 5'6). After digesting this information and repeatedly telling me to stand still, the smug American voice said, 'You weigh 11 stone and 2 pounds. You are ... (careful search for the right adjective?) ... overweight.'

Two teenage boys, an elderly man and a young mum passing by all sniggered.

According to the paper printout, I am 1.3 stone over my ideal weight bearing in mind my height and build. Perhaps I have a large not medium frame.

I still don't think that I need to diet seriously. A little more exercise and giving up Mars bars would probably do the trick. I'll mention to a few people that I am thinking of dieting and see what their reactions are. I'm sure that most will pooh-pooh the idea. I'll start with Muriel.

A little later

Muriel is going to bring in a supplement from the Mail about the greatly increased risk of disease associated with 'being fat'. She said she wouldn't have mentioned it but as I brought it up...

8th January

My 'does Aliss need to slim' survey results:

Pippa said she'd thought of me when she saw an advert in the paper for a new slimming class starting next week in the church hall down the road.

Bev said she might come too as she is feeling as porky as I look.

Mum said it was too late for Brian but it couldn't do anything but help if I ever want to get a new man.

Nic said he loved every bit of me and what was wrong with being cuddly?

Pippa will look for the advert and give it to me at the weekend. It's all right for her; she doesn't know the meaning of the word temptation.

9th January

Brian phoned. He is taking Adam back to uni tomorrow and he wondered if I would like to go along for the ride. 'You can see where he's living and probably meet some of his flatmates. Only if you'd like to, of course; it's up to you.'

I'd like to see Adam's flat and it will be good to have a united front for Adam's sake.

10th January, Saturday

In bed

It's been a long day and I'm ready for bed. It's remarkable how tiring it is sitting in a car for six hours and it's hard not to fall asleep. However it would have been tactful of Brian to ignore my dribbling, or, at least, to not mention it. But, then tact was never his best characteristic.

Tact was also missing when I tried out my 'slimming survey' on him. He is a fine one to talk. Admittedly he had shaped up very well — when he was cheating on me — but I've noticed (and suspect Gina has too) that he has much more middle-aged spread these days. I didn't say that out loud though; I have some consideration for other's feelings.

Adam's flatmates all seemed very pleasant and pleased to see him back. I thought Becky was especially pleased. She looked a nice girl. I asked Brian if he had noticed anything.

'Which one was she?'

'Becky.'

'Becky. Was she the one in the tight ribbed jumper with the navel ring?'

'I didn't notice what she was wearing or a ring in her belly button.'

'It only showed when she stretched up to get the teabags down. I remember because she was struggling and I went to help her, if you recall.'

Ah, yes, I do remember.

We didn't see anything of Sophie over the Christmas period so I assume their relationship is over, which is a shame. I liked Sophie, what I saw of her. It's time Adam found himself a proper girlfriend — he has played the gadabout for long enough. But would a girl distract him from his studies? Although I suspect membership of the Real Ale Society might be doing that already. Indeed a girl-friend might have a more sobering effect.

11th January

Pippa brought the advert for the slimming club. It says, 'Weightwatch World is for life, not just for after Christmas.' The first class is on Wednesday (so won't clash with dancing). Bev is definitely coming with me as Simon inadvertently compared her to a beached whale, although I'm not sure how he could do that inadvertently.

13th January

Tonight was our first night back at dance class. It was lovely to see everyone again but rather disappointing to discover I'd forgotten everything I thought I'd learned. The most exciting news of the night was that Martin and Jane are definitely 'an item'! Franco was thrilled and said that Mrs F had guessed as much at the New Year Eve's party. She is already thinking about hats apparently. Jane giggled girlishly while Martin didn't say much: he didn't have a chance with Jane talking for him, and finishing his sentences. I wish them both well. They are ideally suited.

Stefan didn't join us in the pub after class as he has an audition tomorrow for the Village Players' summer production of *Seven Brides for Seven Brothers*, and he wanted to protect his voice. Rose said her granny used to use a special gargle to look after her voice.

'Oh, Rosie, you never said, was she a singer?' Nic was curious.

'No, she was a teacher.'

'Aaah, bless, so what did she use? Do share so I can tell Stefi, he'll be sooooo grateful because he's such a drama queen about his voice.'

Remembering that Rose used her own wee for bathing her feet, I was dreading hearing her answer but it turned out Granny's secret gargle was only cold tea.

'Oh, is that all? That doesn't sound very good.'

'Give me a chance, that was only the base. Then she added honey ...'

'Oh, yes, Stefi swears by honey.'

'Mustard ...'

'Mustard? Urrgh.'

'And gin.'

'And she gargled with that?' Jane was incredulous.

'Only half of it, she drank the rest.'

I think I'd rather put up with a sore throat. We might grumble but there is a lot to be said for living in today's society.

I asked Franco when we'd be learning the tango. He said, 'When you can tell your left from your right.'

14th January, Wednesday

Bev and I have been to our first slimming class. I was surprised how many overweight women were there. The consultant told us all to sit down, then introduced herself as Lydia and said, 'Welcome to Weightwatch World. First of all let's give each and every one of us a big clap for being brave enough to take this first and enormous step to a new us!' She had worked herself up into a crescendo so the weak applause that followed was a bit of a let-down. 'It's all right, ladies, I now you're all a bit unsure but let me tell you, in just a few weeks' time you'll be cheering just like me.'

Bev nudged me, 'I'll distract her, you make a run for door and I'll follow.' I giggled and Lydia picked on me. 'So let's all introduce ourselves. What's your name, dear?'

'Alison.'

'And, Alison, would you like to tell us all why you decided the time was right for you?'

'Er, um, er, the scales told me.'

'The scales, yes,' Lydia nodded wisely. 'We've all been there, haven't we, ladies, when we've tried everything. When even standing on one leg makes no difference,' she was still nodding, and there was a hum of recognition around the room.

'No, really, I mean the scales in the shop; they told me I was overweight. In front of half of Tesco's.'

'Oh, Alison,' Lydia rushed over and hugged me to her mammoth bosom, 'we all realise how hard it has been for you to share this but we want you to know that we're with you in this every step of the way. Now let's give Alison, a great big clap all of her own.'

The applause this time was much more heartfelt: I had obviously touched some deep nerves. I was quite moved until Lydia singled out Bev who was leaning forward with her hankie over her face. ''Oh, my dear, come here,' Lydia grabbed Bev, who tried to resist, and hugged her. I felt no pity for her: it was just reward, I felt, for taking my discomfort so flippantly.

Then Lydia showed us some photos of herself. 'This is me just eighteen months ago.' She waited for the gasps to die down. 'Shocking, isn't it? I had let myself go completely. You're not going to believe this, I know, but all I lived for was custard slices. I had them for breakfast, lunch, dinner, supper and little snacks in-between. But then a friend introduced me to Weightwatch World and my life changed, as you can see.'

All I could see, standing before me, was a woman who was, at a conservative guess, about size 18. Not that I see this is as a problem, in fact, it's rather encouraging that my consultant needs to lose more weight than I do.

Then Lydia explained the regime. It is quite simple; I can eat anything I like as long as I don't eat anything I like, such as chocolate, bread or cheese.

She said, 'So ladies, remember, members of our club don't diet, we watch our weight. We take control. What do we do?'

There was a confused mumbling, 'We watatk coneight.'

'That's right, we watch our weight!' Then she ended by plugging the week's special offer of three tasty low-fat, low-sugar, low-carb Munchy bars for only £1. 'They're a little past their sell-by date, ladies, but that's the beauty of these bars – age doesn't matter – they taste just the same.'

I was joining the queue to buy them when Bev muttered, 'You can eat a Cornflakes box for free, you know.' I can't help thinking that Bev is not going to take this lifestyle change, as seriously as she should. As seriously as I am. I was initially impressed when I spotted her browsing through the club's directory of Good Points/Bad Points — although I think I have quite enough bad points already — but found she was comparing wine values. For interest, I noted that Chilean white is slightly less bad than Australian white.

I came away feeling much more positive about myself than I have for ages and I didn't go to the pub in spite of Bev's pleading. My new lifestyle starts now.

Later

Trisha just phoned. She said she'd called earlier but I was out. I spoke before thinking and said I'd been at Weightwatch World. She was thrilled and said, 'Oh, Alison, I am so pleased. I haven't liked to say anything but Geoff and I were both getting rather concerned. I know food can sometimes be an escape mechanism but it reaps its own reward and I'm thrilled you've realised that before it's too late. Geoff will be delighted when I tell him.'

'Did you phone for a reason, Trisha?'

'What? Oh, yes, of course, silly me. Now you know it's my birthday in a few weeks' time? Well, I'm having a little dinner party on the Saturday after to celebrate — nothing too grand, just a few friends — and I hoped you'd be free to join us.'

'Me?'

'Of course, now I know you're dieting, I will plan my menu very carefully. The others won't even be aware: it'll be our little secret. And I know my birthday's not for a few weeks but some of my friends lead very busy social lives; they need plenty of notice. Obviously that's not the case with you but I like to get these things sorted out early. So you are free, aren't you?'

I wanted to say no, I'm busy, but I knew that Mum would get to hear of it and would interrogate me until I broke down. I did make a show of having to check my diary, even though I knew only thing in it for February was 'Renew TV licence'. So I am going.

I can't understand it: I've never been invited to one of Trisha's soirees before. Not even with Brian, as a couple. I wonder if she has an ulterior motive. No, that's being unfair. She is just being kind.

Because she feels sorry for me! I don't need her pity; I will call her back and say I can't go after all. I'll say I am very sorry but I've remembered an important engagement; I'll work out later what to say to Mum. I'll phone now before I lose courage.

Later again

Trisha said she could read me like a book and she had anticipated that I would feel nervous but her friends were all perfectly lovely people and that I was not to be silly. They did not judge people on what they did for living. Being an office assistant was perfectly acceptable for a divorced woman. And if I was worrying about what to wear, she would come over and go through my wardrobe if I wanted her to, but she was sure that I must have a little black dress, which would be very suitable. She had written me in now, and that was that.

So — that is that. I am committed now.

15th January

I went to Sainsburys to stock up on diet food. I'd never really noticed before what a wide range is available. I can buy low fat/healthy versions of most of my favourites. I don't have an overly-sensitive palate, so I'm sure I won't be able to taste the difference. This diet, or rather, lifestyle change, will be a doddle. I wasn't even tempted – or rather not overly tempted – to buy a custard slice, in spite of yesterday's reminder about how nice they are. I will lose weight very quickly at this rate.

I bought a Weightwatch World ready-meal 'Saucy Chicken' to keep in the freezer for emergencies but it's rather late now and I've had a long day so I'll eat it tonight. I can replace it tomorrow in my lunch-hour.

Later

Perhaps 'Saucy Chicken' is not one of the better ready-meals. It's not that it was unpleasant exactly but it did leave a slightly bitter after-taste. And it was a rather small portion. I'll buy something different tomorrow: I mustn't judge a whole range on the strength of one meal. And I'll reward myself for sticking to my diet today by having one of the Munchy bars I bought at slimming class.

Even later

I was sure we had some toothpicks in the bathroom. Brian always insisted on keeping a supply there for when he ate steak — or any meat, in fact. He must have taken them with him when he went. I bet picking his teeth goes down well with Gina.

I think I have some sausage sticks downstairs, I'll go and look. I wouldn't have believed it possible for one small Munchy bar to leave so many traces while bringing so little pleasure to one's tastebuds.

16th January

The dentist was very understanding when I phoned. I thought I'd be lucky to get an appointment at all today, but when I called at quarter past eight and explained the circumstances, he said to call in on my way to work. He said his wife has been on a diet for ten years or forever, he wasn't sure which, and in that time her teeth have struggled with more than one so-called healthy bar. He did suggest though that in future I keep a supply of proper toothpicks in the house as they are stronger than sausage sticks and less likely to break and wedge between my teeth.

My visit to the dentist means that my bargain Munchy Bars have cost approximately £5.65 each. Not such a good deal after all.

19th January

Young Mr D went out at coffee time and came back with cream cakes for the three of us — Mr D Senior is in Florida — as he was feeling a bit of the post-Christmas blues and he was sure we were too.

I felt it would be churlish to refuse and I was just trying to decide between an eclair and an apple puff when Muriel said, 'Alison can't eat cream cakes, you know, she's on a diet.'

'Oh, Aliss, I didn't know,' Young Mr D said. 'I'm so sorry, I wouldn't have put temptation in your way if I'd realised.'

He took the box off my desk. 'Muriel and I will go in my office to eat ours,' he whispered, and they both crept away as if I were dead not dieting.

It's true what they say: dieters do it alone.

I've worked here now for about six years and cannot ever remember Young Mr D buying cream cakes for us before.

I've had an apple and a banana for lunch. I am very virtuous and will soon be slim.

21st January, Wednesday

It's my first class weigh-in tonight. I've had a very good week — apart from Saturday when my dreams of custard slices became too vivid to withstand but that was my only real deviation from a strict adherence to rules — and I expect to have lost several pounds. I feel much slimmer and healthier already and I'm confident that this lifestyle will suit me very well.

Later

I can't believe that I only lost half a pound. Perhaps the scales had not been correctly adjusted; I was one of the first to be weighed.

Although Bev was weighed straight after me and she had lost four pounds! Four pounds! How could she do that? She and Simon went out for a meal on Saturday and they went round to her parents' for lunch on Sunday. In alcohol consumption alone she would have used more Bad Points than me.

I can't hide the fact that I am very disappointed. I don't believe that eating slightly more bread than is recommended could have been the sole cause of my poor weight loss, as Lydia suggested. I'm more inclined to think that I have slow metabolism. That is far more likely.

At least my weight went down: one of the ladies had gained a pound.

But, as Lydia was keen to point out, it is only the first week. 'Some people find that it takes a little time for their bodies to get used to the new regime, but just you wait until next week. I bet you'll have a dramatic loss. Just stick at it, Alison. Now let's everyone give Alison a great big clap of encouragement.'

I couldn't help noticing some very smug faces round the room as they cheered me on. I wouldn't be so superior if I had to lose as much weight as they need to.

25th January, Sunday

It's Adam's birthday today. I tried to phone him several times but it was this evening before I finally got a reply. He was sleeping he said. 'What? All day?' I found it hard to believe that someone — even Adam — could sleep right through their birthday.

'I had a late night.'

It must have been very late, I thought. I wished him happy birthday and asked him if he'd received my card. 'Yeah, thanks, Mum. And thanks for the cheque.'

'I'm sorry it wasn't anything more interesting but I didn't know what you'd like.'

'Money's the best, Mum.'

It might be for him but it doesn't offer the same satisfaction for the giver. I've always loved buying presents for my children and watching their faces when they open the parcel to find exactly what they asked for. I like to make them happy and I like to share their happiness too. Ah, well, I'll have to resign myself to having an absent child.

27th January, Tuesday

Martin and Jane refused to dance with each other in class this evening. Martin danced with me and said it was because they felt that, even though they were now a couple, they should not get too accustomed to each other's style as it might spoil them for others. I think he was only talking about dancing.

It was just me, Nic and Stefan who went to the pub afterwards. Rosie and Peter weren't in class and Martin said he was going straight home as 'I have a busy day tomorrow, and, Jane, if you want a lift, would you mind missing the pub? For once?' I could see Jane was torn but too settled in coupleship to risk pushing him further.

I stuck to Diet Cola (=Nil Bad Points) while Nic and Stefi shared a bottle of wine. Nic, who had danced with Jane, told us that she had spent the entire class whispering in his ear how anal Martin could be. Stefi found this hilarious. 'She said that? To you?!!'

Nic roared too, but I didn't see what was so funny. In fact, I found most of their attempts at humour rather puerile. I've noticed this a lot of late and not only with Nic and Stefi. Life in general seems to have lost some of its sparkle. I wonder if there are nasty chemicals in diet drinks that make you miserable. It would explain a lot. And there have been plenty of health scares over the years; I must ask Muriel. As a Daily Mail reader she knows all about the latest scares. It's no use being slim if, in the process of getting there, you've thrown yourself off a tower block.

28th January, Wednesday

I lost two pounds this week! That's more like it — although Bev lost four pounds again. However, Lydia said to me, and I told Bev, that a slow weight loss is much better than a fast one. 'You are less likely to put it straight back on that way.' Bev gave me a dirty look. 'I'm only repeating what Lydia said,' I said.

'You're just jealous because I've got my half-stone badge.'

It's only a bit of sticky paper, for goodness sake. Why would I be jealous of that?

I'm going to start walking to work. I don't know why I didn't think of that before. It will be good exercise and use lots of calories. I'll set my alarm for 20 minutes earlier than usual tomorrow so I can begin straightaway.

Chapter 20

29th January, Thursday

I overslept this morning after sleeping through the alarm. The late start meant that I had to drive to work instead of walking as planned, but I was still slightly late. Young Mr D was not best pleased that there was no-one here to greet his first client. If I'd remembered Muriel's dentist appointment, I would have made an extra effort to get here promptly. Still I'm sure it's not the first time Mr Bevan has had to hang up his own coat, even if he is the closest thing we've got to a millionaire client. He made his fortunes in slot machines according to Young Mr D who was in school with him. He obviously had a lot more luck with slot machines than I ever did.

Later

Young Mr D said that Mr Bevan made his fortune by 'taking advantage of innocent punters'. Judging by his tone, there are issues underlying that comment. He didn't divulge any more in spite of gentle encouragement from me.

I'm surprised that he is willing to deal with someone he apparently considers to be unscrupulous, but money can buy an awful lot of scruples.

While at her dentist's Muriel asked him about Diet drinks. He said that, from a tooth's point of view, water is still by far the best option but he also said that, as far as he knew, there were no recorded cases of suicide linked to Diet drinks.

However Muriel is going to bring in a supplement she kept from The Mail. She said it's called 'Is your food killing you?' It sounds very informative, if not a little scary.

30th January

I can't understand those people who accuse the Mail of being sensationalist: it is nothing of the sort. This is the kind of information that should be made available to — and read by — all clear-thinking adults. It is quite shocking. In fact, I was so appalled by what I read in the first paragraph, I felt unable to read any further for the moment. But I will definitely return to it.

I didn't walk to work this morning as I wasn't sure how long it would take and I didn't want to risk being late again. I need to calculate with care the time it will require. To do that I will need to know the mileage — I can check that when I drive home tonight — and speed at which I will be walking. That is more difficult. I can still remember the excitement when Roger Bannister did the first three minute mile. Or was that four? A minute here or there is not a lot. But obviously he was running so I need to take that into account. Also he was probably a bit fitter than me.

Perhaps I should do a trial walk. I was planning on going into town tomorrow to look for something to wear to Trisha's dinner party, so that will be an ideal opportunity for me to try it out. And it'll be good for me.

31st January, Saturday

I was about to walk to town when I discovered a problem: which shoes do I wear? If I'm trying on clothes I need to be wearing smart shoes, but if I'm walking I need comfy trainers. This won't be a problem when I walk to work as I can keep a pair of shoes there to change into but it was a problem this morning. So I drove instead. But I used the journey to take note of the mileage as I forgot last night.

As it happened I had a wasted journey as I decided against buying a new outfit yet. There's no point as soon I will be at least one size smaller. I made my decision after the assistant suggested a size 16 might be a better fit. 'It would give you a bit of room if you want to move.' She made me sound like a family that had outgrown its home.

I have plenty of time to lose the weight — three weeks — so I don't need to worry. Besides, Trisha will have told her friends I am only a divorced office assistant, so they won't be expecting much.

1st February

I walked round to Mum and Dad's this afternoon. I was going at a steady pace but it still took me half an hour and I think it's slightly further to the office. I'm beginning to think that walking to work is not such a good idea. Apart from anything else, I would need a shower by the time I got there.

Mum is delighted that I have been invited to Trisha's party. Her joy reminded me of the time, in junior school, when I was the only girl in the class not invited to Donna Wilson's birthday party. Mum kept asking me what I had done to upset Donna. I told her nothing but she insisted it must be my fault. When she discovered an invitation stuck between two books in the bottom of my satchel, she picked me up and swung me around. Her daughter was not a social outcast after all.

'Now you will be careful, won't you, Alison?'

'You know I always try to be, Mum.'

'Trisha has some very expensive pieces of porcelain, and some beautiful crystal. She is bound to be using it when her friends come round so do take care. I think I might have mentioned the fire in Claude's to her, so, no doubt, she'll avoid candles, but if she should forget, promise me you'll be careful.'

'Why don't you phone her and remind her?'

'That's a good idea; I'll do that now.'

'Eunice, come back; Aliss was only joking,' Dad spoke firmly. 'Honestly, the way you go on you'd think Aliss was in the habit of setting fire to restaurants.'

'Of course I'm not; I only do it if they don't give me free mints.'

Dad laughed and went on, 'Our daughter knows how to behave; I'm sure she won't let you down in front of Trisha's friends.'

I smiled at Dad. I know Mum doesn't mean half she says the way it comes out, but it can be a trifle wearing sometimes to be spoken of in such a dismissive fashion.

Mum has been talking to Trisha about her party and, apparently, the other guests will be: Trisha's bridge partner and her husband (paediatrician and surgeon respectively); their next-door neighbours (bank manager and teacher); and the managing director of a computer firm.

The way Mum said the final one made something click in my brain. She produced it with a flourish, like a magician. Of course — how thick am I? (I should stop asking myself these questions; I don't like the answers.) I am being set up. Or maybe, and more likely all things considered, he is.

'What do you know about the spare man?'

'He's single and about your age. Bill, didn't Geoff say that he's hoping he'll be able to get a good deal on computers? I'm sure that's what he said. So you will be nice to him, won't you, Alison?'

'You mean my brother and sister-in-law are offering my favours in return for a good deal on computers? Mum, I'm shocked.'

Dad laughed again.

'I don't see what's so funny. They're not asking you to do anything. Just be polite. I'm sure you can manage that. Now I wasn't going to tell you this, but you've only been invited this time because Stephanie, Trisha's accountant friend, will be off on a retreat in Thailand. So if you want to be invited again, you must put on a good show.'

'Yes, Mum.'

She said the same thing before Donna Wilson's party. Sad to recall I ate too much cake and was sick — but I did remember to say 'thank you for having me, Mrs Wilson,' just before throwing up.

4th February, Wednesday

I've put on one pound! I can't believe it. Lydia asked me where I was in my cycle as it could be the wrong time of the month for me. I couldn't remember. My periods these days have a habit of blurring one into another. And anyway, I'm beginning to think every day is the wrong time of the month.

I'll stick to the one diet for one more week and then, if I continue to do so badly, I will give it up. I told Lydia that. She looked downcast and shook her head. 'But have you thought this through, Alison? What is the alternative?'

I don't care! Why should I suffer for nothing?

5th February

Drying my hair this morning I noticed that the skin on my elbow resembles an elephant's bottom. I can say this with authority as I saw a great number of elephants' bottoms on the natural history programme on television last night.

It's Bev's birthday on Saturday. I thought we might have a girls' night out tomorrow but Simon is taking her away for the weekend. 'What about your diet?' I asked.

'That's what I said to Simon,' Bev said. 'But he said, "Stuff the diet, I want to take my slim and sexy wife away for a dirty weekend." I wasn't going to argue with that. Anyway, all the sex he's planning will do me more good than any diet!'

That is the sort of exercise I am missing. I wonder if I should hire a gigolo. Purely for diet purposes, of course. But how do you go about contacting a gigolo? Do they have their own section in Yellow Pages? Or is it all done surreptitiously through the 'Would like to meet' columns of the newspaper? There are so many things I used to rely on Brian for.

Like knowing where to find trades people.

11th February, Wednesday

I'm beginning to feel like Bridget Jones: I am obsessed with my weight. It's a good thing I don't smoke as well; I could only give up one thing at a time. Although I've given up a lot more than one thing. I've given up bread, cheese, chocolate and wine. Lydia keeps telling me it's not compulsory to give these up altogether but she doesn't know me like I do: I am physically unable to eat a little bit of cheese/chocolate/bread. They are substances that only come in big bits (or should only come in big bits).

At least I lost two pounds this week. That makes it — not counting the pound I put on — four and a half pounds I have lost altogether. It's going in the right direction but so slowly. I'll have to try harder this week: it is only nine days to Trisha's party.

That's enough time for a dramatic loss if I try really hard. I should be able to cope with a strict diet for that length of time. I feel a new resolve. Having a specific target to aim for will be a great help. I can't wait to begin tomorrow.

I mean right now, of course. It is a bad habit I have got into of treating myself to a chocolate bar after Weightwatch World. Just because it is a whole week until next weigh-in doesn't mean I should be any less determined. I will put my Crunchie away.

Later

It's very hard to be resolute when there's a chocolate bar in the pantry. It's a good job I have such a strong will.

Later still

It could be considered masochistic, keeping a chocolate bar in the pantry, subjecting one's self to extra temptation. And is it wise? Or necessary? Dieting can play tricks on the mind, make it want to do stupid things. I could end up eating a whole boxful of chocolates just because I have been denied access to one small bar. These things do happen; I have read about them. And I do have a whole week, nine days altogether, before Trisha's party.

I think, bearing these things in mind, that to eat the Crunchie tonight would be the wisest option.

Tomorrow is a brand new day, as somebody once said.

13th February

Young Mr D showed us the card he has bought for his wife for Valentine's Day tomorrow. It is large and very soppy. He has also arranged for a bouquet of pale pink roses to be delivered.

Brian always refused to buy me roses on Valentine's Day. He used to say, 'Have you seen the price of roses at this time of year? It's a rip-off.' He also said, 'And I love you all year round so why do I need a special day to buy you roses?' Which would have been all right if he had ever bought me roses.

I wonder if I will receive a Valentine tomorrow. Or ever again.

Muriel heard me sigh and forced a chocolate biscuit on me. She said just the one wouldn't do me any harm and as they were so small, two would only count as one, anyway.

Valentine 's Day, 14th February, Saturday

The postman came this morning; the thud as the mail hit the floor had a promising ring to it.

But I should have stayed in bed. I don't know why I was full of hope — who on earth did I think would send me a Valentine anyway? I don't have any secret admirers. Not that I thought I did. Not really. But a girl has to dream.

I really am very tired today; I wonder if it's result of extra-strict dieting. Perhaps I should have eaten all of last night's pizza instead of three-quarters. Lettuce might be good for one but it can hardly be expected to maintain a person's body for a day.

18th February, Wednesday

I lost one pound. One measly pound! I have been ultra-good and all I lose is one stinky pound. I grumbled loudly to Lydia. Her answer was that, perhaps, I was not eating enough! 'You mustn't starve yourself,' she said. 'Otherwise your body thinks there is a famine and slows down its metabolic rate to make your food last longer.'

I think it unlikely that my body could seriously believe that we were approaching famine conditions but it is a point to bear in mind.

There's not much I can do now before Saturday. I might as well enjoy my chocolate bar without guilt.

22nd February, the day after the night before

Geoff phoned. He said he will drive my car home later this afternoon.

'Why?' I said. 'Drive it home from where?'

'Here, of course.'

'At your house?'

'Yes.'

'I'm sorry, Geoff, I've only just woken up — what's it doing at your house?'

'You drove it here last night.'

'Oh, yes, of course, I came to Trisha's party, I remember — how did I get home then?'

'We ordered a taxi for you.'

'Yes, of course, it's all coming back to me now. I drove because I wasn't going to drink.'

'That's right.'

'But I did, didn't I?'

'You certainly did.'

He did not sound best pleased. I thought I should have some coffee and wake up some more before probing any further.

I can remember dressing for Trisha's party — I wore my simple black top and trousers aiming for a stylishly-rich under-dressed look — and driving to their house, making sure I was on time: I know Trisha gets very upset at lateness.

Geoff opened the door to me before Trisha took over, introducing me to everyone, with a pointed, 'This is Geoff's sister Alison — I think I've mentioned her to you.' The last person I met was Nigel, the computer man. 'I'll leave you to get to know each other,' Trisha said, pushing us together.

Nigel shook my hand effusively. 'I'm so sorry you've had to come out tonight.'

'That's all right,' I said.

'It's very kind of you. I'm sorry you had to.'

I extracted my hand from his.

'It's not a problem.'

'No, but, oh, I'm sorry, would you like to sit down? I'm sorry, I'm afraid I've been sitting in this seat — let me just plump up the cushion for you.'

'Thank you.'

He sat on the arm of the sofa next to me. We both stared into space for a moment then he said, 'I'm sorry.'

'I didn't say anything.'

'No, I mean I'm sorry I'm not very good at conversation.'

‘Don’t worry, just relax. I’m the same when I meet new people.’

‘I’m sorry to put you through this.’

‘Did Geoff tell me you’re managing director of a computer firm?’

‘Oh, I’m sorry, no, he’s misled you. I’m technical director. Although I suppose I part-own the company so I could be called managing director. I’m sorry, now I’ve misled you.’

Trisha came over then. ‘You two are getting on famously, I can tell. Now, Alison, what will you have to drink? I have some of your ‘special’ in the fridge.’

‘My special?’

‘You know? The drink for people who have special requirements?’

‘Oh, diet cola you mean.’ I glanced at Nigel. ‘No, it’s okay, Trisha, I’ll have a red wine, please. A large one.’

‘Are you sure, Alison?’ Trisha gave me a significant look.

‘Yes, honestly, a glass or two won’t hurt for one night.’

‘Well if you’re sure. And you, Nigel, are you all right? Would you like another or a top up?’

‘I’m sorry I haven’t quite finished this one yet.’

‘It’s all right, Nigel, there’s no need to .... ah, now you’ve finished. Another fizzy water?’

‘I don’t want to put you to any trouble.’

‘It’s no trouble at all, Nigel; let me take your glass.’

‘Oh, yes, I’m sorry, here, thank you.’

When Trisha had gone to get the drinks, we looked at each other and smiled uneasily.

‘Don’t you drink then, Nigel?’ I said.

‘No, I’m sorry, I’m afraid the smallest drop of alcohol sends me to sleep. And that doesn’t make me very popular at parties.’ He laughed. I smiled and took a large swig of the wine Trisha handed to me.

I can remember sitting next to Nigel to eat and him apologising — although not necessarily to me — for: sitting next to me; taking up too much space; not eating his bread roll; slurping his wine; not having seconds; driving a Ford; disliking broccoli; never having been to Croatia; and buying his shirts in Littlewoods.

After that, my memory seems a bit blurry.

Later

When he returned my car Geoff didn't say much only that he thought my plan of phoning Trisha to thank her for a lovely evening probably wasn't a good one. At least not until after the carpet cleaning man has been and removed the red wine stain from their highly expensive Highland Cream carpet.

I have no recollection of any wine-spilling incident but Geoff said it happened just after I'd offered to teach everyone to tango.

23rd February, Monday

Mr Davies Senior came bustling into work this morning; the first thing he said was, 'Has a parcel arrived for me?'

'No, the postman hasn't been yet.'

'I'm expecting an important package. Make sure you tell me as soon as it arrives.'

Every ten minutes he came out of his office and said the same thing.

By 9.50 I was just as excited and couldn't wait for the postman to arrive.

When he did, we were both disappointed: no parcel for Mr Davies.

'Oh, dear, oh, dear, oh dear,' he said.

'Are you sure it was being delivered here?' I asked. 'Not to your home address?'

'Yes, definitely, I told them it had to come here as Barbara is in Cardiff all day and I couldn't take the chance of them leaving it on the doorstep. Dear oh dear.'

'Perhaps it will come by parcel post or special delivery,' Muriel said.

'Yes, that's it,' Mr D beamed. 'Of course, they wouldn't risk sending it by Royal Mail over the weekend; anything could happen in that time.'

'Mr Davies, what is ... '

'Better get some work done. You'll call me as soon as it arrives?'

'Yes, of course, Mr Davies.'

The poor man was on tenterhooks. I found it hard to concentrate myself as I kept watching for a delivery man. I hope his parcel turns up soon or as he said, 'Who knows what will happen?'

Muriel thought it might be a present for his wife and that was the real reason why he was having it delivered to the office. 'A diamond ring, maybe?' she said. 'You can buy them from the television, you know.'

Remembering his choice of Christmas present for his wife — admittedly at her request but all the same — I felt this was unlikely but I did agree that having it sent to the office was suspicious. Neither of us believed his reason for that.

'Perhaps it is med-ic-ation,' Muriel said, nodding, pursing her lips and raising her eyebrows at the same time. I'm not sure what sort of med-ic-ation you would buy by post, but couldn't ask Muriel any more as a client arrived and demanded a cup of coffee. I was tempted to say, 'Me too, if you're making it,' but thought better of it.

I do hope the parcel arrives soon; the anticipation is driving me wild.

Later

The parcel finally arrived at 3.30 pm. I called Mr Davies Senior as soon as I had signed for it and he came rushing out from his office.

'Where is it? Ah, yes, excellent.' He picked the box up and took it into his office. Two minutes later he emerged with his coat on. 'I'll be off now then. See you in the morning.'

'Yes, Mr Davies, but ...'

It was too late; he had gone before I could ask him what was in the box.

Muriel and I looked at each other. 'Did you see what was written on it?' I asked.

She nodded.

'I don't think it's a diamond bracelet,' I said.

'No, I suppose not.'

'Or medication.'

'No, but, you don't know, it could be.'

The only clue we had to the contents of Mr Davies Senior's parcel was the word written on the side: LIVE.

25th February, Wednesday

I'm nothing if not consistent. I lost one pound again this week.

Lydia said that as I am not excessively overweight, it will be harder to lose it. That's moderately flattering but hardly helpful. The rest of class were all very sympathetic but they could afford to be, each of them having lost at least two pounds.

27th February

David Davies has an appointment with Young Mr D on Tuesday morning. He hasn't been in for a while and he didn't speak to me to make the appointment. I only noticed his name by chance when I was looking through the diary. I wonder if he deliberately phoned in during, what he must have worked out is, my lunch-break. It wouldn't surprise me. For a psychiatrist he's not very good at dealing with people.

I've noticed that my hair is looking rather drab. It could do with a cut, and, maybe, a little colour. I wonder if I could have it done tomorrow. Not that there's any rush, it would just be good to have it done while I'm in the mood.

The hairdresser can squeeze me in at 3.30 as they've had a cancellation. A new haircut will suit the new slim(-mer) me

2nd March, Tuesday

10.20 am

David Davies is in with Young Mr D. He arrived on time — which is unusual for him; he is normally here early — and went straight in so there wasn't any time for him to speak to me, other than to nod 'good morning'. I was relieved: he would only have been rude or found something to complain about. He's not the sort of man who would notice a new hair cut or pay a compliment anyway.

10.25 am

They have come out into reception now. I will offer to make some coffee for Young Mr D — he will probably need it — but I'm not offering *him* one. I'll just wait for them to finish talking before I say anything. I've learned it's far better to keep my head down while David Davies is around.

10.30 am

I'm not in the least bit interested in their conversation. I shall continue to enjoy my coffee-break and when they have finished discussing the team for next Saturday's rugby international, I shall wash my cup and get back to work. Some of us have work to do. Like — ah ha, good timing — answering the phone.

Chapter 21

21st March, Sunday

3.15 pm, Ward 9

I haven't felt like writing in my diary for a while. It's nearly three weeks now since I last wrote — and since Dad had his stroke. I'm sitting with him in hospital this afternoon but he's fallen asleep so I'm taking the chance to bring my diary up to date.

It's been a long three weeks.

We none of us, Geoff, Mum or I, left the hospital for the first forty-eight hours after it happened. I don't think we could believe it. Still can't, not really. Not Dad. He's always been so fit.

Today Dad ate — with a little help — most of his lunch and we talked after that. At least I talked; Dad was content to listen. The doctor said it's still early days and that, with physiotherapy, Dad could learn to speak fairly normally again. It's his right side that was damaged by the stroke. Looking at him now sleeping peacefully, it could almost be as if he were taking an after-dinner nap. It's only if you look more closely that you see that his arm is lying limply on the bed beside him, and there is a tiny dribble escaping from the corner of his mouth.

Dad's always been most particular about his mouth, making sure it was wiped clean and that no traces of food remained on his teeth. I remember once he had a tiny piece of cabbage on his front tooth — it was when Geoff and I were about ten and twelve — and we thought it hilarious not to tell him. Instead we kept asking him questions so that we'd be able to see it. At last Dad said, 'you two are full of curiosity this afternoon.'

'It's good to ask questions though, isn't it, Dad?' I said.

When he got up out of his chair and left the room to go to the toilet, we guessed that he'd spot the cabbage in the mirror, so we slunk off before he came back in case he'd work out what we were up to. And then we forgot about it until tea-time. We were already sitting at the table when Dad joined us. He didn't say anything at first, then Geoff asked him to pass the bread and butter. Dad was about to hand him the plate when he said, 'Are you sure you wouldn't prefer ... (here he gave a wide-mouthed grin) cabbage?'

He had stuck bits of cabbage leaf all over his teeth.

I managed to wipe the dribble off without waking him. I didn't want to wake him; he doesn't sleep well at night, the hospital is too noisy, he says. And he misses Mum next to him. 'Get away with you,' she said, when he said that. 'You're always grumbling about me, saying I snore — which I don't.' But I noticed she squeezed his hand extra tightly as she said it.

I was in work when I got the news. David Davies and Young Mr D were in reception; they were finishing off their conversation when the phone rang.

'Good morning, Davies & Davies, Financial Advisers,' I said in my best telephone manner.

There was a snuffling sound at the end of the phone. 'Hello,' I said again, 'is anyone there?'

'Alison...'

'Mum, is that you? Mum, what's happened? Are you all right?'

'Dad ...'

'Something's happened to Dad? Mum, are you all right? What's happened?'

'Hospital, oh, Aliss, I think he's going to die.'

'Mum, just take a deep breath. Tell me where you are?'

'At the hospital.'

'What's happened to Dad?'

'I think he's had a stroke.' She burst into noisy tears again.

'Okay, Mum, don't worry, I'm coming now. Which ward is he in?'

'We're still in Emergency.'

'Okay, Mum, just stay with Dad. I'll come and find you.'

I put the phone down. Young Mr D and David were looking at me.

'It's my Dad; Mum thinks he's had a stroke. I'll have to go, I'm sorry.' The words came out garbled.

'Don't be silly, Aliss, of course you must go, don't worry about anything here.'

'I'll drive you,' David said.

'What?'

'You're in no state to drive, I'll take you there.'

'Are you sure, David?' Young Mr D asked. 'I would take Aliss myself but I have another client in ten minutes. Although I could ask my father to see him — shall I do that? He won't mind, I know.'

'No, it's fine. Get your coat on Alison. I'm free for the rest of the morning. Here, don't forget your bag.'

'There's no need really, I can drive myself.'

'Don't be silly, come on.'

I felt so sick that I couldn't face arguing.

David didn't speak while we were in the car. I was grateful for that. I didn't want to be in pieces when I saw Dad. Mum hadn't said what sort of state he was in: if he was conscious I didn't want him to see me crying. When we pulled up in the hospital car park, I got out. I leaned back in to say thank you, but David was getting out as well. 'There's no need for you to come any further.'

'I'd like to make sure you're okay, that you find your mum and Dad okay. If that's all right with you?'

'Yes, thank you.'

He took my arm and led me into the emergency reception. 'What's your Dad's name?'

'Bill.'

'And his surname?'

'Oh, yes, sorry, um, Jones.'

He asked at the desk and found out which ward Dad had been taken to. He steered me through the maze of hospital corridors until I spotted Mum peering through a window in a door. 'Mum, how is he? What have they said?'

'Oh, Aliss,' she fell on my shoulders. 'He's in there.' She nodded towards the door. The doctor's with him now. They're doing tests.'

'So they haven't said anything yet?'

'No, nothing, oh, Aliss, I thought I'd lost him.' She began sobbing noisily again. I waited until the sobs had eased then asked, 'What happened, Mum?'

'He was just coming down the stairs, he said his head was hurting and did I have any tablets. And you know your Dad, he never takes tablets. Not even for headache, I say to him, why be a martyr, but you know what he's like. So I told him there were some upstairs in the bathroom cabinet and he turned round to go up again and then he fell backwards. At first I thought he'd just tripped and banged his head, and I told him not to be so silly and to get up and ... oooaahh.'

'It's all right, Mum, you didn't know.' I patted her on the shoulder.

'Then when he didn't say anything I went and looked at him and ooooaahh.'

It was hard to get anything more out of Mum, except that the doctor had been in with Dad for about ten minutes and that she hadn't been able to get hold of Geoff or Trisha.

'Would you like me to try and contact them?' David spoke quietly. 'You can't use mobiles in here, but I can go outside while you wait in case the doctor comes out.'

Mum suddenly realised there was someone with me. She looked at me for an explanation; I decided explanations would take too long. 'Thank you, David, that would be really kind. I'll give you their number. It's on my mobile somewhere.' Between us we found it and David left us. Mum watched David go then looked at me. 'Who was that, Alison?'

I was saved from answering by the doctor coming out of Dad's room.

'Doctor, what is it? Is he going to be all right?'

'Mrs Jones, and...' he looked at me.

'I'm her daughter, Alison.'

'Mrs Jones and Alison, perhaps you'd like to sit down.'

We did as we were told. I think we both felt we might fall otherwise.

'Now,' the doctor continued, 'as I think you may have guessed, Bill has had a stroke. A fairly major one, but he's still alive and his body readings are quite strong. But at the moment we can't tell what damage, if any, has been done. We still have a lot of tests to do.'

'Is he conscious? Can we go in and see him?' I asked.

'He's not conscious at the moment,' he began, then seeing my face he hurriedly added, 'not that that is a bad sign. The body needs time to pull itself together. However I must warn you that the first forty-eight hours after a stroke are the most dangerous. The time in which, if another stroke is going to happen, it is most likely to occur. You can go in and see him now for a few minutes then I'll have to ask you to wait outside again, while we do some more tests.'

When David came back, we were outside in the corridor, not saying anything, just holding hands.

'I managed to get hold of Geoff; he's on his way but he was in Cardiff so he'll be an hour or so.'

'Thank you,' I said.

'Have you been able to see your Dad yet?'

I nodded, 'Just for a minute.'

David sat down beside me.

'Why Bill of all people? That's what I don't understand. What's he ever done to deserve this? He doesn't even smoke.' Mum was shaking her head desperately. 'It's not fair, why Bill?'

I just squeezed her hand some more. I knew the answers and so did she: life isn't fair, why not Dad?

'Would you like a cup of tea?' David asked. There's a canteen down the corridor.'

'Thank you but I don't think we should leave here.'

'No, of course not, I meant that I would go and fetch you a cup. You'd like one wouldn't you, Mrs Jones?'

'I think I could manage one, milk, one sugar, please.'

'I'll be right back.'

After he'd gone Mum said, 'Who is that, Alison?'

'His name's David, he's ... just someone I know through work.'

'Is he married?'

I can laugh now but was shocked to hear her ask it when Dad was lying next door, practically dead. I realise now that it was a distraction, something to take her mind off what was happening in Dad's room, or what might happen. That plus the fact that an interfering busybody can never switch off completely.

When David came back with the teas and a choice of chocolate bars, I thanked him then said, 'Shouldn't you be going? Didn't you say you were only free for the morning? Don't you have a patient or someone to see this afternoon?'

'It's all right; I called my secretary and told her to cancel my appointments for the rest of the day. There was nothing vital I had to do.'

'You shouldn't have done that.'

'I wanted to.'

'Oh,' I didn't know what else to say. 'Thank you.'

Mum had been listening. 'A patient did you say, Alison? Are you a doctor, er, David, was it?'

'Yes, Mrs Jones. I'm sorry; there hasn't been a chance for proper introductions. I'm David Davies.' He stood up and shook Mum's hand.

'Delighted to meet you, I'm sure. Have you known Alison long?'

I stepped in, thought I might as well get it over with. 'David is the man I told you about, Mum, the one in Claude's.'

'Oh, no, oh, David, I must apologise for my daughter. I don't know where she gets her clumsiness from, it's not me, she must get it from her...' Mum stopped suddenly as she realised what she was saying, 'Oh, Alison, he's going to be all right, isn't he?'

The three of us sat in a row, our backs to the wall. We didn't talk much, and were barely aware of the low hum of machines, the clattering of trolleys and the beeps and whistles of the life-prolonging equipment. Mum and I were both wrapped up in our thoughts and memories; David was too wise to intrude. He simply sat there with us, a solid presence. I found myself thinking, 'nothing can happen if he's here.' I used to think that about my

Dad. Nothing bad could happen to me when Dad was around. He was my protector, my knight in armour. Now he needed someone to protect him. I closed my eyes and prayed.

When Geoff arrived, David left quietly. He touched my hand as he was going, saying, 'Let me know if I can do anything to help.'

It was about an hour later that Dad regained consciousness. We were all around the bed when he opened his eyes. 'Bill, oh, Bill, you have given us such a fright!' Mum was almost shouting in her anxiety. The doctor asked us to leave while they did yet more tests.

Mum was beside herself. 'He's conscious so that must mean that he's going to be all right, doesn't it?' She kept saying it. I don't think she believed it but she needed that straw. Geoff wasn't saying anything so I tried to calm her down. 'Mum, you remember what the doctor said? The first forty-eight hours are most dangerous. Dad's got a long way to go yet.'

'Yes, but he smiled, he recognised us, that must be a good sign, mustn't it?' She grabbed my arm beseechingly.

I couldn't tell her I had found the half-smile he had given and his poor distorted face more upsetting than his unconscious state.

'Wc'vc just got to wait, Mum.'

Now, two weeks later, there is a definite improvement. But he's still not Dad. I don't suppose he ever will be, not physically anyway. The whole of his right side has been affected in some way. People notice it most in his face, but that's because they don't see him trying to walk or use his hand. The physiotherapist is impressed that he has done so well but he gets very frustrated. He tries not to let any of us see but I could see him, when I was still outside the ward on Thursday, and he wanted to get his cup, and he couldn't and he was crying. I waited until the nurse had spotted him and had helped him compose himself before I went in.

My Dad crying. My Dad never cries. He used to joke that the only time he cried was when England won the World Cup in 1966. Now he needs everything — everything — done for him. Or he needs help, at least. He can't even go to the toilet on his own. My Dad, my big strong, dependable Dad.

People have been so good. Chloe and Adam came home immediately they heard about their Granddad, and stayed until he was out of immediate danger, only leaving after I'd promised to call them the instant — if there were an instant — that they were needed. Trisha has been the typical brick, force-feeding us all. In spite of that I must have lost weight; my clothes are all loose on me. Anxiety must be good for dieting. Perhaps that's why all dieters look worried.

Mum has been staying with Geoff and Trisha, when we could at last persuade her to leave the hospital. Young Mr Davies left a message that I wasn't to worry about anything but to take as much time as I needed. Pippa has cleaned my entire house (think she has been looking for an excuse for years), and Bev has been Bev, making me laugh, making me cry, and being my best friend.

Dad has had so many cards, with such lovely messages. I didn't know he knew so many people. I think even Mum is surprised at the people who have taken the trouble to send a card or letter. Reading some of the notes from people who say how helpful Dad has been to them in all sorts of ways, I've seen a whole new side to him. Of course I've always known that I could depend on him but he's my Dad and you're supposed to be able to depend on fathers, but it seems that any number of others feel the same way.

Brian has phoned a few times, even came into the hospital last Friday. Strangely enough though, Dad fell asleep just after he arrived.

And David's been unobtrusive. He phones most evenings at about 10.30 when he knows I'll be there. I was starting to feel guilty about it, so one evening when he phoned, I said, 'Look, David, it's awfully kind of you to keep calling like this but you don't have to, you know. Just because you happened to be in the office when I had the phone call doesn't make you obligated to call me and I'd...'

'Alison.'

'Yes?'

'Shut up.'

And he's visited the hospital a few times as well. I turned up one day last week and Mum said, 'Oh, you're here, Alison, you could have got the banana.'

'What?'

'If you'd been a minute earlier you could have gone for the banana.'

'What banana?'

'Your Dad was fancying one.'

'Was he? I'll go down and get him one then.'

'No, you don't listen, do you? I've sent David now.'

'You sent David?'

'Well, I was just about to go myself when he appeared so I said, "You wouldn't be a dear and get a banana for Bill, would you?" What are you looking at me like that for? He was delighted to go.'

As if he had much choice when my mother's around.

We went for a walk yesterday. David and I, that is. He suggested it after asking when was the last time I had been anywhere except the hospital. He asked me in front of my parents as well, which was hardly fair. I said, 'Thank you, that's a kind thought, but I really should try and catch up on things about the house.'

My mother snorted.

I said, 'What?'

'Far be it from me to interfere, but since when has housework been a priority with you, Alison? It's very kind of David to offer to take you out for some fresh air — I've been thinking you're looking peaky myself — and it's churlish of you to turn him down. After all he's done for you.'

'I can't argue with that, Mrs Jones,' David said, and I swear he was smirking.

'You go, Aliss, for me.'

How could I refuse then when my Dad said that?

David drove us along the coast a bit and we strolled in companionable silence along the beach. Then on the way back we called into a little cafe for a cream tea. That was David's idea. When he ordered it, I protested, 'Oh, no, just a cup of tea will be fine. I really should try to get back on my diet. It's gone to pieces since Dad has been ill.'

David shook his head. 'Alison, you have absolutely no need to diet, your figure is just perfect as it is.'

It isn't of course but it was nice of him to say so. And they were very nice scones.

Geoff went back to work last Wednesday and I am returning tomorrow. I'm only doing half days at first. Young Mr D told me there was no need to rush back, but I will want to take more time off when Dad comes home so it's better this way. And so many people are asking if they can visit him now, he doesn't need us around all the time. Between making an effort for his other visitors and his physiotherapy, he's worn out and spends most of the time we're here sleeping. As he is now. Still.

I will be going soon: I wonder if I should wake him up before I leave. I could have stayed a bit longer except I'm going to the pub with Bev and Pippa tonight. Bev came in to see Dad with me yesterday evening, and made sure she had him on her side before inviting me. Or rather, telling me we were going.

Later

Honestly, Bev and Pippa have the stupidest ideas. We were hardly settled in the pub before Bev said, 'Well, tell us all about it.'

'Oh,' I sighed. 'Where do I begin? It's been a difficult few weeks. I am just so relieved that Dad is starting to ...'

'No, not that! We know about your Dad; we want to hear all about David.'

'David? There's nothing to tell. No, that's not true. I admit I did misjudge him; he has been very kind and helpful.'

'Yeah, and the rest.'

'What rest? There isn't anything more.'

'Nothing more! You went out with him yesterday! Did you snog?'

'Urrgh, Bev, you know I hate that word.'

'I do beg your ladyship's pardon. Okay, did you kiss?' Bev pursed her lips and made a kissy noise.

'No, of course not. Why on earth would we?'

'You didn't?' Pippa sounded surprised.

'Look, when I say David has been helpful, that's what I mean. Nothing more. He took me out for walk yesterday because he felt I needed some fresh air.'

'He was concerned for you, you mean?'

'Yes. No. Not like that.'

'Has he or has he not been phoning you every evening?'

'Yes, but that's only to see how Dad is progressing.'

'Why should he care about your father?'

'Because he feels involved because he happened to be in the office when I had the news and he very kindly drove me to the hospital. That's all. He just feels ...'

'What?'

'Obliged.'

'Aliss, what does a man have to do?' Bev sighed.

'Honestly, Alison, you are a bit thick sometimes.'

'Thick? Me? Why?'

'It's obviously he fancies the pants off you, isn't that right, Pippa?'

'I might not have phrased it like that, but Bev's right: he is definitely interested. And in you, not your Dad.'

If it had just been Bev, I would have put it down to her fertile imagination but with Pippa ganging up on me as well, I was beginning to waver.

'All right then, if he is as interested as you say, why didn't he kiss me yesterday?'

'He was too much of a gentleman I'm afraid.'

'Yeah, he doesn't want to make any move that might seem to be taking advantage of you when you're in a vulnerable state.'

Pippa gave Bev a look of surprise. 'That's very perceptive of you, Bev.'

'Yeah, well, I'm not completely stupid. The big question is: how is Aliss going to tell him she's ready and available.'

'She can invite him round for a meal.'

'Yeah, a 'thank you for all your help' meal. A bit of subdued lighting, some soft music, and you'll be away. Have you got any condoms?'

'Condoms?' I yelped. 'How did we get to condoms?'

'You've got to be prepared, Aliss. I'll get Si to buy some for you.'

'Don't you dare tell Simon to go and buy condoms for me — what on earth would he think?'

'I expect he'd think, about time too.'

'I should think David would be prepared,' Pippa said thoughtfully, 'but, of course, he might think that you're post-menopausal. No, you'd better not take that chance. It would be dreadful to get so far and then realise that neither of you have got them.'

'I can't believe we're having this discussion. One minute I'm inviting a friend round for a thank-you meal, the next I'm leaping into bed with him.'

'Bit of luck you'll skip the eating!'

'Bev!'

We have agreed that next time he calls — I told him not to call this evening as I was going out with the girls and might be late back — I will invite him for a meal. I will make it quite clear that this is simply to say thank-you for all his help over the past weeks, and that I am not expecting anything more from him.

Later again

David called. He said he wanted to check that I was home safely. And that he had missed our nightly chat.

He said he would be delighted to come round for a meal. We agreed on next Saturday. I thought I'd better leave it until then as I will need a whole day if I am to prepare myself and a meal. But he said he'd call in to the hospital to see Dad tomorrow evening. I said I might see him then.

Even later

I can't go into a chemist and buy condoms. But that's all right as I won't need them. He is just a friend who's coming for a meal.

Later still

But what if things should develop? He hasn't been with another woman for a long time; he might not think to bring condoms. At least I don't think he has been with another woman but I don't know that for sure.

What if he's been with lots? I have only ever been with Brian. What if I don't come up to his standard? I would hate to be tossed aside like a used piece of strumpet. Maybe he has exotic tastes like ... cannot even begin to imagine. I've had very sheltered life. Perhaps I should get a book out of the library. Daphne is a helpful librarian; she might know of a good one. But, no, she would tell Bev.

I could get a video. Urrgh, no. Wait a minute, of course, I have that kitchen tart book downstairs somewhere. I will look at that.

Too late for rational thought

Oh, dear. I think I should cancel the meal: I'm not ready for sex.

But David is very ... sexy. I feel a hot flush coming on. That's all I need: to be menopausal just as I'm dipping my toe in the stream of life.

Chapter 22

23rd March, Tuesday

I called into the chemist's in my lunch-hour. I bought shampoo, paracetamol, flea powder and a pregnancy test kit. I can't go there again tomorrow – or possibly ever. The girl behind the counter gave me a most peculiar look. I'll try a different one tomorrow but I must remember to buy items that will come in useful as opposed to the first things I spot on the counter.

Later

Jane and Martin are engaged! They announced it at the start of dance class this evening. We are all to be invited to the wedding, which is going to happen in September. 'Martin thinks we should wait a bit longer,' Jane said, 'but I said to him, "why?" We're in love so why wait?'

Everyone is delighted especially Franco. He has said he will teach us the tango and we can demonstrate it at the wedding reception. As a present to the happy couple.

I'm delighted for them. And quickly dispelled any feelings of 'it could have been me if I hadn't agreed to look after Charlie for Bev.'

24th March, Wednesday

I phoned Pippa. After making her promise not to tell Bev, I told her about my failed attempt to buy condoms. After laughing hysterically — I expected better of her — she said, 'Oh, Alison, you are an idiot. You don't have to ask for them; they're not kept "under the counter" anymore. You could have picked them up from a shelf.'

It was a bit late to tell me that.

'I'm still not going back to that chemist.'

'That's all right, you can buy them in Sainsburys.'

'Sainsburys?!'

'Yes, you won't have to speak to anyone. Just pick them off the shelf, put them in your trolley, and choose your check-out operator carefully.'

'Why?'

'You don't want a boy who will see you as a mother-figure and be horrified, or a flighty-looking female who will think you're too old for sex and be equally horrified. A sensible middle-aged woman will understand your situation.'

She was being so capable I confided in her my concerns about sex. She was wonderfully reassuring. She is right: if David is as kind as we think he is, then, even if he is very experienced, he will be patient with me. He might even relish the prospect of drawing me out (she said, I'm not sure if I relish prospect of being drawn out).

Later

Maybe I am too old for sex. Or too old to be starting again. It really was most inconsiderate of Brian to run off and leave me at my time of life. It's all very well for men; no-one thinks it odd that men have a sex drive even when they're ninety.

But this is really shutting the stable door before the cow has bolted. All I am doing is inviting a friend round for a pleasant meal. At least I hope it will be pleasant; I haven't planned it yet. HAVEN'T PLANNED IT YET!!! Good grief! What am I thinking of? What am I going to cook for David? I'd better consult my cookbooks.

Later again

I phoned Pippa to ask her opinion of my suggested menu:

Salad of scallops with beurre blanc

Pan fried pheasant with creamed mushrooms

Chocolate and hazelnut cheesecake.

She thinks it's a bit much. She suggested that I do lasagne and salad, with fruit salad for dessert.

'You make a lovely lasagne,' she said.

'But isn't that a bit boring? A bit home-made?'

'That's what he's coming for, a lovely home-cooked meal. What from I've seen of David, I know it'll be just what he'd like. If he wanted pheasant he'd have gone to Claude's. And it means you won't have to be messing around in the kitchen beforehand: you can just dish it up when you're ready.'

Pippa's only met David twice at the hospital. I don't think she can judge from that what he would like.

I phoned Bev for a second opinion. Bev agreed with Pippa. 'Lasagne sounds great. Italian food is always romantic. Anyway, it's not the food he's coming for.'

Bev has a one-track mind. I've noticed this before. Still, they could be right about the lasagne.

25th March

Buying condoms was not the simple task Pippa had led me to believe it would be: I'm now the proud owner of twenty-five of them. I gathered up five packs after the lad stacking the shelves asked me if I needed any help. I never knew they came in so many shapes and styles. I'm just relieved they were all one size.

Later

I was putting the condoms in the bedside cabinet when David phoned. He said I sounded flustered and was I all right?

I hadn't realised I'd bought some strawberry-flavoured condoms; I didn't even know such things existed. Why would ... no, I'm not going there. I'm in enough of a state as it is.

I don't know why I listened to Bev and Pippa. I'm getting myself flustered for nothing I'm sure. David will come round, we will eat, drink, talk a little and then he will leave. Probably he won't even kiss me goodnight.

27th March, Saturday

Lunchtime

Bev just phoned. For the third time today. And that's as well as the twice Pippa has called. Bev said, 'I just thought: have you changed the bed?

'What?'

'Have you changed your sheets? Plumped up the pillows? Got rid of your teddy?'

'I don't keep a teddy on my bed; I keep a baseball bat.'

'That's definitely got to go.'

'But you think I should change my sheets?'

'Yeah, clean crisp sheets are a real turn-on. Not that you'll need it by the time you get there.'

'Isn't it a bit presumptuous changing the sheets?'

'And buying condoms isn't?'

'Who told you I bought condoms?'

'Yeeeess! I knew you would.'

I could hear her jumping up and down. Honestly, Bev can be so immature.

I had only just put down the phone when it rang again. 'Hello.'

'Don't forget to shave your legs — right to the top!'

'Bev!!'

'I know what you're like; you only shave from the knee down.'

'It's all anyone ever sees.'

'Not tonight, Josephine!'

Afternoon

I've prepared the lasagne and fruit salad, and will make a green salad later. I've laid the table and put the bottle of red wine ready with corkscrew and glasses. I've cleaned the living and dining rooms — and just flicked a duster over the bedroom. It was time I put all my dirty clothes in the washing basket anyway. I hadn't noticed that they'd piled up quite so much.

I'm showering when I get back from visiting Dad, then I'll be ready and have everything in perfect control when David gets here.

Later

I mentioned to Mum and Dad that David is coming for a meal tonight. That was a bad mistake. Mum's eyes lit up and she beamed. 'Oh, Alison, that is the best news I have had for years.'

'Better than the doctor saying that he's very pleased with Dad's progress?'

'Don't be silly, you know what I mean. David is such a dear man. And so good-looking. And a psychiatrist to boot. Now you will be careful, won't you, dear?'

For one awful moment I thought she was going to bring up subject of condoms but she said, 'You're not planning on using candles, are you?'

'No, Mum.'

'Good, that's all right then. Wait till I tell Trisha and Geoff; they'll be so pleased too.' She clapped her hands together. 'Isn't it wonderful, Bill? Everything's working out all right at last?'

'Mum, I've only invited David for a thank-you meal. I'm not marrying him.'

'But you wouldn't turn him down if he asked you, would you? I do hope not, Alison; he's the best you're ever likely to find.'

'Eunice?' Dad's voice was firm though still a little slurred.

'Yes, dear?'

'Shut up.'

Dad held out his good arm and signalled me to him. He gave me a great big lopsided hug. 'Have a lovely time tonight. David is a fine man, and he's very fond of you.' He winked at me with his good eye.

I do love them both. Now I must get ready. There's nothing to be nervous about. It's just a meal with a friend. Although my stomach feels rather peculiar; I hope I'm not going down with something.

28th March, Sunday

Mid-morning

Three of my favourite things are:

a sunny Spring morning;
the sound of church bells ringing;
the smell of bacon under the grill.

And I have all of these. Plus a rather divine naked man in my shower. Life doesn't get much better than this.

It is a long time since I have cooked breakfast for a man (excluding Adam and Tryboy). It's a shame I don't have any bread or eggs or mushrooms — I was thinking about other things on my last visit to Sainsburys — but David said a rasher of bacon and half a tomato would be perfect. Just like me. That's what he said. (Like me, he meant, not him.)

It all happened very naturally. I don't know why I got so anxious about it; he is a lovely man. I don't know who was more embarrassed when it came to the condoms. He had brought some but admitted it had been such a long time since he'd needed them it had taken him three attempts to pluck up his courage to ask for them in the chemist.

'You don't have to ask,' I said.

'That's what the girl behind the counter said! "You haven't done this before, have you, love?".' He put on a strong Welsh accent. '"They're just over by there, see, next to the treatments for cystitis and thrush."'

Because we were laughing and at ease, it all seemed perfectly normal and right. And fun. I can't remember it being so much fun with Brian. Even me spilling my glass of water over his shoes didn't spoil the atmosphere. Oh, shavings ...

Lunchtime

David came in just as I was trying to put out the burning bacon. He leaned against the wall, his whole body shaking with laughter.

'Don't just stand there! Open the back door! Quickly!'

He sauntered over and opened the door. I threw out the bacon and the grill pan.

'Did you mean to do that?' David asked as he closed the door.

'What? Burn the bacon?'

'No, throw out the grill pan.'

'Well, it was hot. And I panicked. And stop laughing. You could at least turn off the smoke alarm.'

'I'll do it as we're passing.'

'Passing?'

'On our way back to bed.'

'Back to bed?'

'Well, we don't have anything for breakfast, do we?'

'Nope.'

'So, do you have any better ideas?'
I didn't.

I will shower when he has finished (his second shower in as many hours) and then we are going to go and visit Dad in hospital. I told David he didn't have to come with me, I could go alone if he had things he needed to do, but he said there was nothing else he would rather do. Well, almost nothing!

Time for bed (alone)

David has gone home as he has work in the morning but we have spent the evening cuddling and talking. There's so much we don't know about each other. 'But I think I know the important things about you,' David said.

'And those are?'

'You're gorgeous ...'

'Obviously.'

'And funny ...'

'Is that good?'

'Definitely.'

'Okay, carry on.'

'And kind.' He kissed the end of my nose. 'And loving and sweet...'

'Go on, I'm enjoying this.'

'And a total disaster area...'

'Excuse me?'

'Not to mention a fire hazard, and ...'

He couldn't continue as I was thumping him with the cushion.

I also apologised for my mother.

As David and I walked into the ward together, even from a distance I could see the expression on her face changing as she realised the implications. She leapt to her feet as we approached. 'It's lovely to see you both,' she said. 'Together.' She kissed both of us. 'Isn't it lovely, Bill? To see Alison and David — together?' She was giving Dad significant nods, in case he hadn't noticed. 'Now you sit here, David; Alison, get that chair. No, Mr Thomas won't mind; he never has any visitors. Bring it over here and sit next to David. There, that's right. Now isn't this lovely, all of us here together.'

'Yes, Mum.'

She smiled beatifically at David, then remembered: 'Did Alison cook you a nice meal last night? I do hope she didn't have any accidents; she is so accident-prone. You'll both have to come round to us for a meal as soon as Dad is out of hospital. Do you like trifle, David? I find most men can't say no to trifle. And a roast. A nice bit of roast beef. You're not one of these people who don't eat beef, are you? Can't see the point in it myself. If you're going to get mad cow's disease, you've probably already got it, that's the way I think. In fact, it might be better if you came round before Dad gets out. That way I won't have to be bothering looking after him and I can concentrate on you two.' She beamed as she said it.

'My mother gets a bit carried away sometimes. She doesn't mean any harm; it's just that her mouth speaks without consulting her brain.'

'Probably genetic, I should think.'

'Do you think so?' Then I realised the implication of what he was saying. 'Do you mind? That's my mother you're talking about!'

'Precisely,' he shook his head. 'Not a lot of hope for you I suspect.'

It's hard to argue with a man when he has his lips on yours.

Much later he said, 'Anyway you have yet to meet my mother.'

'Is she anything like mine?'

'There are remarkable similarities.' He nodded. 'I'd like to take you to meet her soon.'

'Are you sure?'

'Yes, she's not that bad.'

'No, I meant, are you sure you want her to meet me?'

'Definitely, although she might be a bit hard on you at first.'

'Why?'

'You remember the Christmas dinner dance I invited you to?'

'The last minute invite you gave me you mean!'

'The reason it was a last minute invitation was that I usually take my mother. She's accompanied me every year since my wife died and she loves all the fuss and attention she gets there, but this year ...'

'I'm starting to get a bad feeling about this story.'

'This year, at the beginning of December, she fell and broke her hip. I said I wouldn't go without her but she told me not to be so silly and wasn't there anyone I could think of that I could invite. I said there was only one person, other than her, that I would even contemplate going with but it was very short notice to ask her. My mother told me not to be so pathetic and that, if I explained, whoever it was would understand and go to the dance with me.'

'Oh. And that was me, was it?'

'Of course it was you.'

'It's not my fault: you didn't explain very well!'

'You didn't give me much of a chance.'

'No, I suppose I didn't.'

'So now my mother knows you as the hussy who had the nerve to turn down her lovely son.'

That's not a good place to be in. I'll have to think of reasons to avoid David's mother.

29th March, Monday

In work Young Mr D asked me if I was feeling all right. Apparently I look different. Muriel agreed. 'There's definitely something about you today,' she said. I told them that I'm fine, absolutely fine.

30th March

I came home early from the pub so I'd be here when David called. He was insistent that I shouldn't give up dance class but less keen to accompany me. He said first I will have to teach him what I have learned.

That won't take long.

Nic was looking at me strangely all through the class. I didn't help myself by standing on his feet at least four times. While we were walking to the pub he snuggled up to me, 'Okay, tell Nic all about him.'

'Who?'

'The man who has brought such a glow to your cheeks and a sparkle to your eyes.'

'Don't be silly.'

'Don't you be silly! You can't fool me, come on, give.'

'Are my eyes really sparkling?'

'Like diamonds in a Queen's crown.'

'And my cheeks glowing?'

'Like a woman's who's had a right rollicking romp in the hay.'

'Nic!'

'It's all right, the others are miles behind us, you can tell me.'

So I did. He was thrilled but I made him promise not to tell Stefan until after the pub. I didn't want everyone else knowing just yet.

31st March

Adam is coming home on Saturday for the Easter hols. I must remember to change his bed; I haven't done so since he went back at Christmas. Although think I recall Pippa saying she'd stripped it when she was cleaning for me. Also I must stock up on food — can't have Adam coming home to an empty pantry: I sometimes suspect the only reason he comes home is to stock up on food.

I wonder how he will feel about David. Perhaps I should phone him and tell him before he gets here. I've mentioned to Chloe that I have been seeing a bit of David — I didn't tell her how much! — but it's different for boys. Adam might feel threatened or excluded if there is another man about the house. Perhaps I should tell David that I won't be able to see him while Adam is home. Or rather, that he shouldn't come to my house during that time. Or perhaps I should ask him what to do; he is a psychiatrist after all.

Later

David and I had very long talk about us and my children. He told me that, as far as he is concerned, our relationship is important. He has not felt like this since his wife died and he feels that we have been through enough together already to enable him to say that he hopes our relationship will be for the rest of our lives. I nearly cried when he said that. No, not nearly: did cry.

He wants to be part of my children's lives as well. 'Obviously I can't or wouldn't want to be their father, but I don't want be kept separate from anything that is part of you. I want the whole package.'

I cried again.

Brian and Adam will get here at about 5 o'clock on Saturday. I will talk to Adam that evening and David will come round on Sunday evening after Adam and I have been to the hospital to see Dad.

I suppose I should mention it to Brian too.

3rd April, Saturday

Adam had hardly come through the door when the phone rang. It was for him and he went off to his room to take it. I offered Brian a coffee as he looked tired. He said, 'A coffee would be nice,' and sat down in the kitchen while I made it.

I was just about to ask how the journey had been when Brian said, 'I've been hearing things, Alison.'

I wasn't sure what he meant: was his mental state deteriorating? I said, 'Oh, really?'

'Yes.'

He gave me an intense look. He obviously wanted to talk about it, so I said, 'What kind of things are you hearing?'

'About you.'

'Me?'

'Yes. And a man.'

'A man? Ah.'

'Are they true?'

'That depends what you're hearing.'

'That you have a new boyfriend.'

Adam chose that moment to walk back into the room. 'Oh, yeah,' he said. 'Chloe texted me about that. Nice one, Mum. It's that guy with the Merc, isn't it? I'm meeting Luke down the pub later so can we eat soon? I'm starving.'

Brian left soon after that.

I managed to pin Adam down long enough to eat dinner and to establish that he was well, working hard, enjoying himself, and seeing quite a lot of Becky. Amazingly Brian and I seemed to have raised a fairly well-adjusted son.

4th April, Sunday

I never thought I would actively encourage Adam to go out drinking. And I only did so as it was obvious that I wasn't going to get a word in edgeways between him and David discussing Manchester United's chances for the treble and the failure of Welsh clubs to get anywhere yet again in any championship.

After he'd gone, David sat back and looked at me. Smugly.

'All right, all right, you were a great success. My son likes you more than he likes me.'

'It's a good job I like you enough to make up for that then, isn't it?'

David suggested that he takes me, Adam, Chloe and Tryboy, if he's here, out for a meal next Saturday. 'An early birthday treat for you,' he said. 'We could go to Claude's.' I threw the cushion at him.

14th April, Thursday

Life has been a whirl for the last two weeks. What with catering for Adam, visiting Dad — the doctor thinks he will be able to go home next week! — having Chloe and Tryboy for Easter, and conducting a love affair (!), not to mention going to work, I've not had time to think. Which is how it should be.

It's my birthday tomorrow. I wonder what David's got for me. He has been leaving health and safety catalogues around, lying open at the fire extinguisher page, but I think that's a joke. I hope it is.

At least I have survived twelve months as a fifty-year old. I didn't think I'd do that at this time last year. It hasn't been as bad as I expected either. Maybe I should write a book: there must be lots of women out there dreading it. It would become an instant best-seller and I would be rich and famous and invited on Richard and Judy. I could call it 'Better than I expected!' No, that's a terrible title; I will have to work on that.

47449645R00179

Printed in Poland
by Amazon Fulfillment
Poland Sp. z o.o., Wrocław